FOUR GENERATIONS OF STRENGTH, FAITH AND PASSION

Shmuel—the educated, cultured father who was forced to draw on startling reserves of strength.

Simon—who learned the law of the jungle in the teeming New York slums.

David—who faced breaking the taboos of his people—and his mother's heart—for a girl of a different faith.

Connie—the outsider who became one of the family's own.

Tracey—the golden child who inherited the legacy of a past so different from the world she knew.

The Kaminskys. Surging onward in a new land, exacting triumph and pleasure from a sometimes ruthless world. *Trumpets of Silver* is a celebration of their love and strength, bringing the passions and beliefs of an ancient people vividly to life.

NORMA HARRIS

TRUMPETS of SILVER

A NOVEL

A SIGNET BOOK

SIGNET
Published by the Penguin Group
Penguin Books USA Inc., 375 Hudson Street,
New York, New York 10014, U.S.A.
Penguin Books Ltd, 27 Wrights Lane,
London W8 5TZ, England
Penguin Books Australia Ltd, Ringwood,
Victoria, Australia
Penguin Books Canada Ltd, 2801 John Street,
Markham, Ontario, Canada L3r 1B4
Penguin Books (N.Z.) Ltd, 182–190 Wairau Road,
Auckland 10, New Zealand

Penguin Books Ltd, Registered Offices:
Harmondsworth, Middlesex, England

Published by Signet, an imprint of New American Library,
a division of Penguin Books USA Inc. This is an authorized reprint of a
hardcover edition published by Dutton.

First Signet printing, July, 1991

10 9 8 7 6 5 4 3 2 1

REGISTERED TRADEMARK—MARCA REGISTARDA

Printed in the United States of America
Original hardcover designed by Steven N. Stathakis

Although the characters in this book are fictitious, the historical and human events are based on fact. Students of history will note, however, that I have taken certain liberties with the sequence of some dates in order to enhance the dramatic circumstances of the story.

BOOK I

1891-1905

PROLOGUE

There was a glance, then a gesture of kindness which ended in blood. The youth was hungry; the soldier promised food. They shared bread and wine and walked together by the church where the youth planned to pray. The youth was grateful for the food and attention. Then the soldier made known his "other" needs. The youth laughed. The soldier was joking. Such a big, strong man. What he sought was in the red-light district on the other side of town. But the soldier was adamant—he wanted him.

The youth protested. The struggle was on. Humiliated, agitated, the soldier raised his knife. On bended knee, the youth begged for mercy, but it was useless. Twenty-four times the enraged soldier's blade slashed the boy's neck, pierced his eyes, plunged through his stomach, his heart and groin. Blood spurted from a severed artery to mingle with the snow. The youth cried pitifully, but no one heard. Then, it was done. Slumped, bloodless near the church, the boy's nightmare was over. But because of it, another would begin.

1

The fading winter had been mild this year, and the icy waters of the Black Sea now held spring and summer promises. Above Alexandrovsky Park, Shmuel Kaminsky and his young son, Joshua, observed the changing panorama of Odessa's noisy seaport below, listened as the whaling ships groaned against their moorings, and watched as hungry sea gulls floated and snatched tasty bits of chum. A thin sheet of ice which had once harnessed the winter waters lay shattered, floating its free-form fragments on a wave-tossed journey to oblivion while the steady chimes of Assumption Church summoned the faithful to Easter services.

In another six weeks the rich would arrive from Moscow and St. Petersburg to bask in the sunshine, to cover their skins with the soft healing mud or stroll along Nikolayevsky Boulevard. Shmuel tousled his son's dark, curly hair. It was good to be alive, to be in Odessa instead of the Pale, where his ancestors had lived in fear and poverty since they had been exiled from Spain. Here, there was a chance to educate his children, for a Jew to make something of his life.

"Come, *yinghele*," he said. "Look how the sun goes.

It's time to leave." He spoke in Russian, sprinkling his words with Yiddish endearments.

"Wait, Papa. Please!" the boy cried. His fancies tumbled from his mouth as fast as his chilled lips could speak them. "Someday I'll be the captain of a great fleet. And I'll sail the whole world and bring presents for everyone: silk dresses for Mama and jeweled combs for Sonia." The music in his voice sounded a sour note. "Though I don't know why. Since her engagement to Sergei, she's been so snooty."

Shmuel laughed. "Forgive your sister, *mein kind*. She's in love. And a woman in love is very fragile. But, after her wedding, you'll want to buy her wonderful things again, you'll see. Now what about me? What wonderful treasures will you buy your papa?"

Joshua thought. Then, discovering the gift, he grinned. "A new violin," he shouted. "And a guitar of rosewood. And I'll grow whiskers, thick and black like yours. And all the people of Odessa will admire me."

Shmuel smiled at the young boy's spoken dreams and recalled his own. "And what of your ambition to become the leader of a great orchestra?"

Joshua's hands flew to his hips and perched there defiantly. "But I can do both!" he said with authority. Then the voice of the child returned. "Can't I, Papa?"

"Of course," Shmuel reassured. "Where in the Good Book is it written no? But come. If we are late for seder your mother will scold us."

In the upstairs music room of the stone house, Sarah placed Shmuel's violin in its royal blue velvet resting place. She would miss his melodies for the next few days. In the hallway, she passed his portrait and paused to admire it. He was handsome and masculine, she thought, with the nose of a hawk, eyebrows like the unfurled wings of a raven, swept back above dark and vigilant eyes. She was very proud of him.

In the bedroom she stoked the fireplace embers and plumped the chaise pillows. There was so little time. The dinner table had to be set with the holiday symbols: some roasted meat to commemorate the burnt offering of paschal lamb, the bitter herbs, the hard-cooked eggs and salty water to remind them of the tears and hardship in their exodus from Egypt.

She hurried to her mirrored table and pinned her chestnut braids with the pearl combs Shmuel had given her for her thirtieth birthday. In her eighth month of pregnancy, she was anxious that the time pass. In a few months, her daughter, Sonia, would become a bride, and she wanted to be slim for the occasion.

As she fastened the bodice of her silk dress, a shade of gray her husband had likened to her eyes, she called her maid, Katya, but there was no answer. How odd, she mused. Where could she be? She heard the grandfather clock and hurried downstairs. She would never be ready, she thought. Never!

In the warmth of her kitchen, she reveled in the aromas of her cooking: matzoh dumplings, clear chicken soup, potatoes smothered in onions and sweet paprika, all brown and braising in the juices of a large roasting chicken.

"Katya! Where are you?" she called again.

Hearing no response, she entered the living room, parted the ecru lace curtains, and peered out. The streets were empty; not a stray dog or cat skulked along the snowy hedges. Not a bird flew in the sky. Then the horrible, dreaded word seized her like a dybbuk. No, she decided, quickly. Not in Odessa. They had permits. Shmuel was a teacher of languages, a respected musician and artist. People here were civilized; there were museums, libraries, schools. What she feared could never happen.

Near the sun room she called Katya again. Now, her voice startled her. There was terror on the fringe of her words. Then her fear grew full blown as the side door burst open and Sonia's screams turned her blood to ice.

"Mama, Mama, come quickly!"

Between gasps, shaking, the tall, slim girl sobbed. "Be . . . Be . . . Benjamin, Sergei, everyone's left the city." Sonia gripped her mother's hand. "Reba's maid said to warn you; they found a Christian child, behind the church." Sarah's heart skipped a beat. "The police say he was murdered, stabbed twenty-four times." Sarah's legs swayed beneath her. "Reba's maid said you'd understand, but I don't, and I'm afraid, Mama. What does it mean? What's happening?"

Sarah stood motionless as reality set in. She fixed her eyes on Sonia's face, and her words, though quietly spoken, had edges of steel. "Quick!" she said. "We must take the carriage and find Papa and Joshua." Then she added, "Before it's too late."

Shmuel led Joshua through the old Jewish sector, where the shops had been closed for the holiday. The empty streets smelled of almond macaroons, homemade wine, gefilte fish, and black horseradish preserves. He could hardly wait for the holiday to begin. He had never been a pious Jew in the religious sense, but one with a keen sense of tradition and respect for his history. He could see himself at Sarah's table, dressed in his dark blue suit, white shirt, and yarmulke, holding a silver goblet of wine, rendering the ancient prayer Jews had recited since the days of Moses: *"This is the bread of our affliction; the bread which our forefathers ate in Egypt. Let all who are hungry, come and share it."*

And it would be that way in every Jewish home tonight. Work would cease. Mothers would light the candles and offer a prayer to God. The story of Exodus would be told with questions asked, and answers given. Then, a door would be opened to welcome the Prophet Elijah. Most of all they would sing, eat, drink wine, and laugh joyfully together.

As they walked, Shmuel buttoned his fur collar while Joshua scuffled his boots in the slush. Suddenly, Shmuel dropped Joshua's hand and squinted ahead. With a quickening heartbeat, he noted a faint orange glow on the darkening horizon.

Joshua craned his neck. "What do you see, Papa?"

Shmuel forced a smile. "Nothing, *mein kind*. A trick of the eye." Dismissing it as illusion, as some long-forgotten memory, he took Joshua's hand and went on. But despite his most valiant efforts, the glow drew nearer, brighter, and more ominous.

"You're hurting me, Papa," Joshua cried. "Let go of my hand!" The child's strident voice brought Shmuel to his senses, and those terrible words flooded his brain: *Pogrom! Cossacks! Oh, God. No!*

In the distance, a thick cloud of dust mushroomed beneath fiery red torches. The rhythm of a hundred horses pounded in Shmuel's brain. Already, he could smell the smoke and fire, hear the cries of the dying and wounded. *Please, God, protect us*, he prayed. Then he strengthened his grip on the boy's arm, and, jerking it, shouted, "Come, Joshua! We must find a place to hide."

Sarah wound the reins of the brass-studded carriage around her wrists and fingers. When the dapple gray was positioned, she lashed the whip against his hide. Minutes later, they were tearing down the narrow cobblestone streets, detouring through the Kalachayevsky Sector. The wind whipped her braids free, and one of Shmuel's combs flew off behind. She felt her wrists and arms nearly snap from their sockets. Always, her eyes searched for Shmuel and Joshua. But they were nowhere in sight. A sharp turn on L'vov Prospekt put Sarah in the red-light district. Then, on Iliyichia Street, Sonia began screaming. "Stop, Mama. Stop! I'm afraid!"

"Get down, Sonia," Sarah yelled. "Shut your eyes!"

The carriage careened downhill through the streets till they hit a bump and flew sideways. When the carriage landed, Sonia fell backward. Sarah's belly tore, and she screamed and fainted.

From their hiding place beneath some steps, Shmuel watched. In boots and long scarlet tunics, their sabers and guns glinting in the torchlight, the Cossacks rode in howling.

Joshua began to whimper. "I'm scared, Papa. Are we going to die?"

"No, my son. God will protect us." While he cradled the fearful boy, he silently recited the Shema.

Across the ghetto, helpless Jews were dragged onto the streets. As they begged for mercy, they were butchered like pigs. Babies were slain in the arms of their mothers, sliced in two like loaves of bread. Within minutes, the Jewish sector was a bloody, flaming inferno.

As Shmuel rocked Joshua, he listened to the boy's heart beating and felt his sweat pour down his temples in an icy rage. He wanted to leap out and kill them. But in the end it was always the same—survival. So, deep in shame, he prayed that the killing would end and the rest of his family, God willing, would be spared.

*   *   *

Sarah lay unconscious on Marishka Ivanovna's filthy, rumpled bed while Sonia cried. The prostitute had found them and given them shelter. A dangerous business, but she had her reasons.

"Wake up, Mrs. Kaminsky," Marishka cried. "You must help, or the child will rot in your womb."

"She's dead!" Sonia shrieked. "She doesn't answer."

"Hush!" Marishka scolded. She crossed herself three times. "She's had a shock, *maya krascievaya*. But don't worry. Her water's broken, and the infant will soon grow impatient. He'll waken her, you'll see. Now help me. The vodka bottle, those towels. Bring them."

Marishka prodded Sarah awake, forced the vodka through her swollen lips. Sarah coughed, moaned, dug her fingernails into the sheets. Before her screams could rise, Marishka stuffed her mouth with rags and bound her limbs to the bedposts.

Sonia watched the birth in fascination and fear. She saw Sarah's hands pull, the body heave, the open thighs quiver. She watched the blood stain the sheets an ugly rust. She wanted to vomit, to run. Absently, she gnawed skin from her fingers, drawing blood of her own. And when the infant emerged, all bloody and wet, she was glad it was over. Then Marishka's voice frightened her again.

"Something's wrong," she said. "Something's wrong with the child."

Fear gripped Sonia as Marishka swung the child by the ankles and struck its rump.

"Breathe, damn you, *breathe*!" Marishka cried. "I have not risked my life for nothing!"

2

*"Hear, O Israel, the Lord thy God, the Lord is One.
And thou shalt love the Lord thy God with all thy heart
and with all thy soul and with all thy might. . . ."*

Shmuel prayed throughout the night, repeating the
old liturgy, which had nourished, sustained, and been
passed from his ancestors to his grandfather to his father
to him. It was long after sunrise before it was over: The
shooting had stopped, the crackling flames had nearly
died, the shrieking had ceased, and his thoughts turned
to home.

Peering outside, his eagle eyes swept the streets till
he was sure it was safe. "Come, Joshua," he coaxed.
"The danger's over. They've gone away."

Shmuel stretched his legs while Joshua slowly
emerged. Faint from hunger and constant vigilance,
Shmuel took Joshua's hand and headed home.

Every turn was paved with horror, smeared with the
bloodied remnants of Jewish life. The once thriving
ghetto lay in smoldering ruins, wrapped in a blanket of
black ash and sucking mud. Smoke enveloped the city.
It covered the streets, which were overpowered by the
stench of death. It could not obliterate the wailing of
dazed survivors who searched for loved ones.

Across Tschinkov Square, a colonnade of old trees,
which had once lined the road like warriors at dress
parade, stood blackened and bare, matchstick soldiers
defeated in fiery battle. The old synagogue was burned
to the ground. Those who had rushed to rescue God's
holy books lay in charred union near the altar, black
pearls in a smoldering shell. In their midst, a woman
sat rocking a dead child. Shmuel was seized with fury.
But it was Joshua who bolted and ran.

For three whole blocks Shmuel chased him through the misery, till he caught him and they fell to the ground. "Why?" Joshua cried. "Why did they do it?"

What was left of Shmuel's breath fell away.

"They do it so the peasants won't know how poor or how cold they are. To show we are no longer the chosen ones. Most of all, they want to show God has deserted us."

Joshua searched the carnage that lay around them. "Has He, Papa? Has He deserted us?"

For a moment, Shmuel hesitated. Then his voice rang with strength and conviction. "No, Joshua. In spite of all this, God's promise is forever. Now come. We must find Mama and Sonia, then help the others."

It was noon as Marishka Ivanovna Poletnikovna sat near the samovar swallowing lemon tea and vodka. She had rescued a family, brought forth healthy, new life, and they had all survived, praise be to God. She refilled her glass and cringed at her reflection in the shiny samovar. At twenty-nine she looked fifty. Her hair, once a brilliant shade of gold, had yellowed like the pages of an old book. Her once bright blue eyes were diluted in sadness. Deep lines plowed through her leathery skin, and her lips, once full of laughter, were two shriveled lines.

She watched them sleep, all cozy, unaware of what was about to happen. Though the pogrom was over, there were things to come. All day long rumors had circulated like wildfire. She'd heard them this morning at the corner newsstand from a policeman, then a friend, and it made her sad. But that was life. The Lord had provided and would now take away.

She dried her tears and tiptoed to the window. Outside was a blur. The silver birch trees were naked and black. Young ebony rooks lay dead on the ground. Then she saw him. Pasha. A boy who'd sell his mother for a ruble. God help her if he found the Jews. She conjured his face in church yesterday at the Easter sermon. She could still hear the priest's voice crying for justice, linking Christ's crucifixion to the Jews, to the pain suffered by the murdered child, droning on and on, till these two incidents, separated by two thousand years, became one, and in seconds the people rose—one virulent organism, screaming, *"Kill the filthy Jews!"* Pasha trampled others to lead the mob. No. She must get rid of them now, and quickly.

"Shmu-el!" Sarah's waking scream was loud.

"Hush, little mother," Marishka comforted. "It's all right."

A neighbor banged menacingly on the wall. *"Silence in there, you miserable whore!"* came the shrill unseen voice. *"Or I'll call the police."*

Marishka banged back. "Silence yourself, old witch, or I'll tell your husband who you've been sleeping with!"

She looked at Sarah and whispered, "Every second you're here is dangerous. I must find your—"

Sarah interrupted. "Forgive me for staring, but I think we've met."

Marishka cultivated the silence. She placed a tattered glove on her own hand and casually declared, "I worked for you, madame, several weeks last spring." Then she told Sarah her name.

Relief shone in Sarah's eyes. "Of course! It was the end of semester. My husband had a graduation party for his English students. Such a wonderful time." She said it as though the words had transported her from the present. "You served blackberry wine and honey cakes in the front parlor." Then, as quickly as it had appeared, her smile vanished, and her next words were an anxious whisper. "But why . . . why have you risked your life?"

Marishka's glove fell to the floor. "Madame Kaminsky, as a Christian, I believe it's the Lord's desire that we love and help one another. Are we not each of us made in His image and likeness?" Her answer gave way to the merest pangs of contrition. "Now rest, while I find your husband."

Marishka prayed at the foot of the Madonna. Then she slipped outside. Alone, she experienced the full weight of all that had happened: the rescue, the birth, her skillful hiding of the horse and carriage in the abandoned barn while the others had gone to loot and pillage. And, though satisfied, she knew she had done it all not for them but for herself. She would miss him, she thought. She would miss her tender nights with Shmuel.

3

"Help me!" an old man begged. His chin and cheeks were raw skin where the Cossacks had ripped his beard. But Shmuel just ran. His mind was on Sarah and Sonia. One by one he chased the death wagons. One by one, he uncovered the bodies, secretly praying they would be someone else's daughter, another man's wife. Everywhere there were chaos and confusion. Shmuel's legs were tired, yet a block from home his pace quickened. When he turned the corner, joy leaped to his throat. Except for a layer of soot, his house had been spared. He took Joshua's hand and began to run. But halfway there, he suddenly stopped.

"What's wrong, Papa?" the boy asked. Shmuel didn't answer. He grabbed Joshua's arm and sneaked behind some bushes. In front of his house stood an armed guard.

As he scanned the area, a thousand thoughts shocked his brain. Was his family dead? Were they hiding inside? Should he approach, or take Joshua and run? With the taste of fear coating his tongue, he took Joshua and inched closer to a confrontation.

"Shmuel Kaminsky!" the guard shouted at sight of them.

Joshua clung to his father's legs like a newborn calf. His son's fear made Shmuel shake with fury. "Yes."

The guard rolled out a scroll and read, "By order of his Majesty Czar Nicholas, all special permits are are hereby revoked, and all Jews ordered immediately from the City of Odessa to the Pale of Settlement. All money and personal possessions belong to the state." He stopped reading and looked up. "You are forbidden to enter this building. Do you understand?"

Shmuel nodded. It was hard to keep from slapping the man's face. "But, Your Honor, I cannot find my wife and daughter. Are they perhaps inside?"

"There's no one inside," the guard snapped.

Shmuel removed his gold watch, given him by his father. "Yours," he said. "For one last look." Because the guard hesitated, Shmuel pressed onward. "In a little while we'll all be gone."

There was dead silence as the guard's cold blue eyes grazed the object. Then the large gloved hand snatched the prize. With his heart in his mouth, Shmuel waited to see if the bargain would be honored. Slowly, the man stepped back and opened the door.

"Two minutes, Professor," the guard snarled. "If

you're not out by then I have orders to shoot you. And I warn you. If you take *anything*, I'll do my duty with great joy."

Shmuel and Joshua rushed through the house. They scoured and ransacked and probed, but there was no one inside. Shmuel didn't know whether to laugh or cry. Even the carriage house was empty and the horse gone.

Downstairs, Shmuel noted Sarah's Passover table set with china, crystal, and silver. The house was alive with the rancid odors of her cooking. Oh God, he thought. They should have been here last night—eating, singing, praising His name. Tears fell. His heart ached with fear and worry. Where were his wife and child? Then his face flushed hot as the guard rapped on the window-pane. His time was over.

Without thinking, he snatched the thin silver candle-sticks from the table and shoved one deep inside each coat pocket. He grabbed the family Bible, a black leather book emblazoned with a tiny Star of David which held the names of four generations of their family. And, taking Joshua's hand, he opened the door.

"What have you there?" the policeman demanded.

Shmuel offered the book. "A Jewish Bible," he said. "Surely the state has no use for such a worthless object."

As the policeman scanned the pages, Shmuel pressed the hidden candlesticks to his body. He felt the silver, cold against his palms. What a fool he'd been to take them. What had possessed him?

The guard handed the Bible back and ordered them to leave. Shmuel took Joshua's hand and slowly walked down the stairs. He was about to run when the police-man's voice suddenly rang out.

"Stop!"

Shmuel's heart fluttered. He waited for a bullet. Instead, he heard a question.

"Tell me, Jew," the guard snarled. "Why do you need the blood of Christian boys to make your Passover bread?"

"Begging your pardon, sir," Shmuel answered. He restrained his anger. He opened the Bible to Exodus and explained how Jews had made matzoh before there were Christians. But the guard pushed him and the Bible fell. When Shmuel bent to fetch it, he faced the barrel of a gun.

On a corner behind a snowy bush, Marishka watched. As the deputy's gun exploded and Shmuel stumbled, she covered her mouth. She was grateful to see him rise again and run with the boy. Thank God, she thought. The guard had meant to frighten, not kill them. She wasn't surprised at the confrontation. Though Shmuel was gentle, he was also headstrong. Some nights they'd make love, then argue about politics or religion and he would be filled with passion. She loved him for that, but now, that passion could bring harm. Relieved that he wasn't hurt, she followed him till their paths crossed and then called him.

Shmuel heard the sound of his name. He turned and saw Marishka. He was terrified to acknowledge her presence, not only because he feared for their lives but because of Joshua. The child would ask questions. So he ignored her. But Marishka's persistent signals drew him to her side.

"Your wife and daughter are safe," she said before he could scold her. "And there's a new baby girl."

Shmuel hugged Joshua, making her repeat the words. Then he asked questions, and within minutes they were hatching a rescue plot. In a few hours the Jews of

Odessa would be making their way to a camp on the hill, and Shmuel had to be with them. All that remained was to take his family safely from Marishka's apartment.

4

The chilled April air mixed with black ash, filling Marishka's mouth with grit. So like the bitterness in her heart, she thought as she headed home. But he was alive, and she was glad. Then again, what did it matter? It would have soon ended. Shmuel's visits had been a temporary joy; she'd always known that. "A man's physical needs in exchange for what you require," he had offered. "Until the baby comes and my wife's good health is restored." Her fault for loving him. So now it was over, snatched in a day by politics, envy, lies, and superstition. Once again she'd be alone.

She crossed the empty streets, climbed the three steps of her building, and left the hall door ajar. That was the easy part of the plan. Upstairs, Sonia and Sarah huddled with the infant in her bed. "It's all right," Marishka whispered as she entered and shut the door. "They're alive. Coming for you when the church bells ring."

Shmuel and Joshua moved slowly. Though the route to the abandoned barn was short, it was dangerous. Havoc lurked everywhere: roving gangs, police, a few drunken Cossacks sprawled like pigs in their own dirt. And though they gestured with bravery, they were both afraid. If anyone discovered that they had a horse and carriage, that Marishka had helped them, they'd all be shot.

Small fires fanned the ghetto. A cloud of white feathers, ripped from bedding—the precious dowries of young Jewish girls—fell like snowflakes to nourish the flames. Fifteen terrifying minutes later, they rounded the final corner and slipped safely inside. Instantly, Shmuel covered his nostrils. Joshua heaved. Strewn with sour straw, dung, and garbage, the barn smelled sickening. But it was holy, too. Because of this place, his family might survive.

After Sonia helped Sarah dress, Sarah took the comb that had remained in her hair, and, with a shy smile, offered it to Marishka, who silently accepted it. Then Marishka took soap, sulfur matches, and her last jar of honey and packed them in a bundle with dried barley, wine, some bits of cooked meat, salt herring, a few potatoes, and black bread. She handed it to Sarah, who refused it all.

"It's not kosher, madame. But I can't believe God expects you to starve. You have children, an infant to suckle, and a long journey. Besides," she continued, "with the generous present of your pearl comb, I can replace it all and more."

Sarah placed the infant in Sonia's charge and kissed Marishka's cheeks. "Bless you," Sarah said. "Whatever God's reason, your courage will inspire me forever." Marishka flushed crimson. She turned quickly and began her work.

She lifted the green chimney of her bedside lantern and placed it on the sink. She removed the kerosene-soaked wick and wrapped it in rags until it was the size of a cabbage. She covered that in newspapers, then snatched matches and an old flour sack from a kitchen bin.

"Here," she said, tossing Sarah some towels. "For you and the children."

"I don't understand," Sarah said.

"There's no time to explain. Just use them when the smoke comes. If all goes well, you'll soon see your husband and son."

Shmuel fixed the carriage wheel. Now, it was time to hitch horse to wagon and wait for the bells. He took the reins, let the gray beast smell him, and spoke with gentleness.

"Come, Kasha. Come."

The animal snorted and backed away. His crazed black eyes floated in a sea of blazing white, and his dark nostrils flared steam.

"Easy, Kasha. Easy."

The frightened horse bellowed. Again and again, he slammed his hooves. As he reared, his blanket fell away, and Shmuel saw the bloodied hide. Poor Kasha, he thought.

With patience and diligence, Shmuel calmed the horse, and he and Joshua climbed into the carriage. As he waited, Shmuel felt the earth settle on his shoulders and the universe hold its breath. If they survived this, what would their lives be like? Old men dream old dreams, but the young must prophesy. What prophesies would there be for his son after this? Suddenly, Joshua broke the silence.

"What are you thinking, Papa?"

Shmuel couldn't speak the whole truth. "Of Mama, Sonia, the new baby. Of my precious violin, which I shall miss with all my heart. And you, my son? What are you thinking?"

"Of getting even," he said. "Of making them pay."

*   *   *

With the package in her hands, Marishka ran down the darkened hallway and thrust open the door. There, she found Grisha the policeman, mounted on a brown stallion beneath the courtyard tree.

"*Kak pazhevayetya*, Marishka Ivanovna?" he called, saluting her with his baton. "Why aren't you with the others? There's Jewish gold in the streets."

The sight of him frightened her. But her resolve was firm. She tossed her incendiary package into a rusty barrel and cried in feigned disgust, "Filthy Jewish lice. I'll be glad when they're *all* gone."

Grisha backed his horse from the tree and laughed. He snapped the reins and slowly rode away. As he rounded the corner and disappeared, she dragged the barrel into the hallway and pushed it on its side. She unraveled the kerosene-soaked package, struck a match, and tossed it inside. A fire soon crackled, and she covered the blaze with the flour sack, watching thick smoke fill the hallway. On to step three, she thought.

"Fire! Fire!" she screamed. The smoky plume trailed her like the veil of Satan's bride. It licked the walls, filling the cracks and crevices of the old building as she prodded the remaining tenants toward the open front door. The diversion worked, and, when the church bells rang, she came for Sarah.

As the bells rang, the horse and carriage charged into the streets. A barking dog ran for Kasha's legs, and the horse went crazy. Shmuel yanked the reins, but the horse kept racing. Stores flew by. A school. They plowed through an old staked fence and passed the church where the bells were ringing. A pack of drunken youths gave chase, screaming ugly curses, tossing sticks and stones. Shmuel's heart thumped with Kasha's hoof-beats.

"Crouch below, Joshua!" Shmuel yelled as they neared an overhead bridge.

Shmuel's body arched forward until they cleared. His arms stretched to the limit as the carriage accelerated. They took a curve on two wheels, speeding into Marishka's courtyard, and headed straight for the tree. Shmuel stood up and yanked the reins until he thought his arms would break. But what frightened him more was the empty courtyard.

Marishka guided them through the smoke. The bells had stopped ringing, and she was terrified as she thought of Grisha. The infant began to cry; Sonia began to choke. Sarah's eyes filled with burning tears.

"I can't go anymore!" Sonia cried.

"No!" Marishka yelled. "We're almost there." An instant later she pushed them into the courtyard.

The carriage missed the tree by inches. When it stopped spinning, Joshua jumped down to steady Kasha. Shmuel reached for Sonia and the child. When he went for Sarah, her legs buckled, and she screamed. With blood dripping between her legs, she faltered backward, but Shmuel and Joshua heaved her on.

There was no time for tears or greetings as Shmuel flogged the horse to go. White foam rose on Kasha's back. Sparks flew from his clanging hooves as his iron shoes struck the cobblestones. With the wind blowing, Joshua glanced behind at his mother's bloodstained dress, at his sister's rigid posture and petrified expression, at the newborn baby, who howled in terror. Beside him, he sensed his father's shame. No more tears, he thought. Not for him.

His breathing grew shallow, his legs restless as he felt an uncontrollable anger building. The events of yesterday and today had solidified in him a coldness, a hardness of heart. His freedom had been stolen. His family had been deprived of life, of liberty, of all they loved, treasured, and possessed. It wasn't right. It wasn't fair!

Near the top of a hill, almost out of the city limits, this growing anger enveloped his body and erupted in a flash. He leaped suddenly onto Kasha's wet back and pulled the reins. When the carriage slowed, he jumped to the ground.

"No!" Sarah screamed as she stretched out her arms. "Come back!"

"I will!" Joshua yelled. He slapped Kasha's buttocks. "Wait for me on the hill."

5

The carriage flew, and Sarah continued weeping.

"Hush!" Shmuel scolded. "You're scaring the child."

"Oh, Shmuel. My son, my son!"

"Do as I say," he ordered. "You've been given new life to protect. I forbid you to think of anything else."

The buildings flew by, and the streets of the city narrowed to a single dirt road. An hour before the sun cast long shadows, they found the caravan. The community had gathered to bury their dead in a small forest near the stream which led to the Pale and an uncertain future.

The procession was endless: Pregnant mothers in tattered coats and babushkas. Wild-eyed, bewildered children hiding behind their mothers' skirts. Strong sons pulling their aged parents in filthy wheelbarrows or donkey carts. Strapped to their backs were broken treasures snatched in haste—pots, pans, a blacksmith's hammer, a sewing machine, cherished photographs, holy books.

The brave tended the wounded while the strong dug the graves. No time to prepare or cleanse the bodies, to comb the hair, to pare the fingernails, no time for anything but grief and duty. They wrapped the men in sacred tallises, the women and children in cloth shrouds. They laid them side by side in simple graves. Then the wailing began. Prayer upon prayer, layer upon layer, song upon song. Those who did not believe sang of revenge. Those who believed sang of confusion. All who'd survived sang of guilt. Not only had death and destruction visited, abandonment had come too. Once again they were strangers in a strange land.

> For out of the ground wast thou taken;
> for dust thou art and unto dust shalt
> thou return. And though He slay me,
> yet will I trust Him.

As the cold earth was sprinkled upon the dead, weeping widows ripped their clothes. Babies wailed and whimpered. A grief-stricken mother dashed headlong toward her daughter's grave. Three women restrained her as she sobbed on her knees. The men joined the wind in a mournful kaddish song.

Once again they were united by tyranny. The rich were now poor. The poor were still poor. But those things in which all were rich remained. The state had taken their possessions, murdered their children, and raped their wives. It had violated their rights. But their beliefs could never be shaken. And those beliefs— which passed from father to son, from mother to daughter, and which were taught in the sanctity of the home and in the synagogues and in the way they lived and in the food they ate and in the holidays and traditions they loved and celebrated—would not only survive but triumph. For them, God's promise remained the same. You cannot kill the spirit, nor destroy the seed of Abraham. And so the heat of the ghetto fires did not separate them but forged them closer.

An old man jumped on a rock when the ceremony was over. "Listen," he cried. "The dead on this hill will not be forsaken. They rest in the earth until the sound of Messiah's silver trumpets awakens them. Never forget that! We have not lasted three thousand years because we are lucky."

The sky was gray as Joshua's weary legs stumbled down a rocky slope not far from his home. He was close to his objective, and he cursed the hand of daylight, which revealed him. He wanted the darkness of night to swallow and shield him. He wanted the sun to set, the lamplighter to light the night with deceitful shadows. He wanted that, and so much more. He wanted revenge.

As he reached his father's house, he peered over the stone wall surrounding it. Quickly, he sprang back and crouched low. The guard was sitting on the back steps, cradling his rifle and munching an apple. The sight of the food made Joshua's stomach churn with hunger, but all he could do was wait for dark.

In the woods, tall timbers reached for the sun's last rays in a lover's embrace. When they parted, it grew cold and dark. The men lit fires and built shelters. The women shared a watery soup. Now there were decisions to be made.

Inside her tent, Sarah slipped in and out of fever. She was terrified. For years she had hidden an awful secret from Shmuel, and in a few unconscious minutes it could all come tumbling out. The fever made her vulnerable as never before. May you never know the pain I've suffered, she thought, looking at her sleeping infant. May you always remain as peaceful as you are this day.

It was a peculiar irony, Sarah thought. Born into such turmoil, the child was so calm and serene. A clean slate, she mused. So God will etch the sorrows and the joys, later.

A shadow fell across Sarah's face. It was the midwife's wrinkled hand on her forehead. "A little rest, some chicken soup is all you need," the midwife said. Skinny and small, she had eyes like hard black coal on white snow. She touched the baby's head. "Such a beauty," she murmured. Then she left.

Sarah's fever continued, and with it her fears. Every time she dozed, she wondered. Had she said it? Had she even come close? She heard herself sobbing, felt Sonia place a compress on her forehead.

"What did I say?" she demanded.

"You keep calling for Joshua," Sonia answered. "That's all."

When Sarah fell asleep, Sonia left the tent. She was glad to be away from her mother. She knew if she opened her mouth even once, her anger would spill out. Joshua! Joshua! Now the baby. No one cared about her. Today she had tasted fear, had lost a future, had seen birth and death in all their ugliness. In a few months she would have been married with a family of her own. Now it was over, and she didn't know why.

This morning a child had been murdered, and she was sorry for that. But what did it have to do with her? *Oh, Mama, Papa. Help me. I don't understand.* And though Sarah and Shmuel loved her, in their silence and ignorance, neither had consoled or explained. And in that unintentional neglect, a terrible misunderstanding was born, a feeling of isolation that would haunt Sonia the rest of her days. She built an invisible cocoon and placed herself inside it, promising that whoever entered, she would prey upon with great satisfaction. Throughout the night she nursed and strengthened that web but shared none of her misery. And ultimately she came to her own conclusions: There was no God. No Covenant. There was no Redeemer, no resurrection. No Paradise. Only lies and isolation.

Joshua had fallen asleep. When he opened his eyes, it was dark and the policeman was gone. He took a deep breath and sprinted past the bushes to a row of hedges that ringed the fruit orchard. He rushed for the house in a burst of speed, then dropped to the ground, prone beside the raised cellar door. With his chest heaving, he unlocked the latch and, with the quickness of youth, vanished inside.

As he made a sudden move toward the staircase, a book fell. Heavy footsteps above sent him behind an old cupboard. The cellar door creaked open, and a shaft of light swayed from a lantern hovering above. Joshua crammed himself closer to the wall, where a hairy black spider sat inches from his face.

"What's going on down there?" a male voice boomed.

The spider's web gleamed white then dark in the light, and the hairy legs crawled toward Joshua's nose. Adrenaline shot through his body as the boots traveled halfway down the stairs. Then the boots retreated, and the light went with them. With the slam of the front door, urine soaked Joshua's trousers, and its odor trailed upward. Angered further, he lifted the fallen book to kill the spider, then changed his mind. The spider had done nothing, and the book was a Bible.

Sarah placed the child at her breast.

"So," Shmuel said. "What will you call her?"

"Anya," Sarah said. "For my grandmother."

His joy was in observing them, in watching the mother nourish the child. But he was worried about Sarah too. Overnight she had grown old. Fear curled the corners of her mouth, nestled in the droop of her shoulders and in her eyes. Her face was streaked with dirt; her hair was a mass of leaves and snarls. Blood painted the sleeves of her gown, crusted the red welts, the black and blue bruises where the horse's reins had cut her. Oh, *Shuraleh*, he thought. Please forgive me.

The cellar was filled with memories. Toys, books, his father's music, Sonia's hope chest, which would have gone upstairs next week. None of it would ever be seen by them again. Suddenly, something shimmered in the cupboard. A silver spoon he and Sonia had chewed on as children. He thought of the new baby girl and slipped the spoon inside his pocket.

He tiptoed upstairs, turned the doorknob, and entered the kitchen. It was bright with moonlight. The stove where his mother had cooked, the table where they had eaten. No! He mustn't look. He felt his way blindly to the dark wooden staircase. He took two hasty steps at a time until he stood in front of his father's portrait. The sight of it upset him so he ran to get what he'd come for. Satisfaction overwhelmed him as he snatched it. But now, he wanted more.

He scooped his mother's pearls from a dish. He thrust Sonia's diary inside his shirt. Then a quick, careless turn dashed a crystal kerosene lamp to the floor, where it shattered like crushed ice. He felt sad at first, then smiled at its significance. He knew now what he had to do.

Shmuel went deeper into the forest to gather firewood. As he walked, creatures of the night watched. Owls, wolves, bats. And his thoughts were bedlam. If only he could shut them out as a child shuts the door to a cluttered room. Oh, Joshua, he thought. Please come home. Though I don't fuss like your mother, I am choking inside. Every moment you're gone, a little of me dies wondering if you're warm, hungry, tortured . . . dead. He shuddered with his last thought, and slumped to the ground in a heap.

"Help me, Lord," he cried. "I don't understand. Every bird has a nest. Every squirrel, a tree. Beneath these rocks, the lowliest worms have a place. You confuse me. You command that the cut of a chicken's jugular be swift and humane, that the *shochet*'s blade be sharp so the animal does not suffer. Are we not as good as they? We are Your children, God. Yet here we sit, alone, friendless, and without a home."

He wiped his eyes with his sleeve and buried his head in his arms. When it was over, he walked to the stream and scooped handfuls of cold water to his face. Then he straightened his spine and returned to the tent.

Joshua smashed every crystal lamp until the house reeked of kerosene. He opened a window near a sloping section of roof and struck a match. His fingers trembled as the flame died. He lit another as a door slammed and a voice boomed, *"Who's up there?"*

Crouched near the open window, Joshua struck another match, but the breeze blew it out. He dumped the matches into a pyramid on the floor and lit another. The pyramid ignited. Fiery fingers pointed the way. He was fascinated as the flaming snake devoured everything. Before the guard could reach him, he gathered his possessions and leaped onto the sloping roof. All the way down, he was joyful, with his pride burning close to arrogance. But his joy was short-lived as he jumped the stone fence and found a Cossack on a white stallion.

"So, little brother," the drunken Cossack said with a grin. "What mischief have you done?"

Joshua stiffened with terror.

"Speak!" the Cossack ordered. "Show me what you have!" His spirited white horse reared as he cracked his whip around Joshua's waist. But Joshua had had enough. He snatched the lash and yanked at the Cossack. The startled soldier fell and cracked his skull on a rock. Blood gushed from his ears and mouth, but his open eyes stared accusingly. Joshua reached to shut the lids, but five cold fingers curled around his ankle. He yanked his foot, but the Cossack held strong. Fear chilled Joshua's bones as he lifted his other boot and smashed the Cossack's wrist. The soldier finally gasped and died. With the house burning like a torch, Joshua mounted the stallion and galloped away.

"Someone's coming!" the lookout called. Everyone took clubs and crouched in position. This time they would fight. The noise followed Shmuel as he skirted the stream, and he gripped his wooden staff tighter. From behind a tree, a figure darted toward him. He felt his brain explode, blood invade every organ of his body. He screamed, raised his club above his head; then a voice cried out . . .

"No, Papa! Don't! I rescued your violin."

Shmuel's first instinct was to hug Joshua. Instead he shook him like a rag doll. He slapped his cheeks until Joshua fell to the ground. Schneider the tailor tackled Shmuel to keep him from beating the boy senseless. With Schneider between them, Shmuel stared into his frightened son's eyes and saw his own reflected shame. What he was beating was not Joshua but the very thing he hadn't the courage to be.

With joy and relief, Shmuel wiped the blood from the corner of Joshua's mouth. In the shimmering firelight, they clung together, drowning in each other's tears, sweat, love, and understanding. On this night, and by these acts, a bonding had taken place. A young boy had become a man, and a father had become a son. Neither knew what the future held, but a cord had been severed, and they were now aware of deeper ties. In the city below, a small fire raged. On this hill a smaller one warmed the hearts of a boy and his father.

6

During the night a light snow covered the land like the lace of an old woman's shawl. It quickly melted when the sun rose. Sarah wakened feeling better. The fever had gone and with it her fear of discovery. She peered from the tent and saw Joshua curled inside Shmuel's arm. She gave a joyful yell and, clutching Anya, ran to her son.

Joshua told them what had happened in great detail. He gave Sarah her pearls, handed Sonia her diary, and twirled the silver spoon above little Anya's head. "Two Kaminskys have chewed on this prize, little one," he said. "You shall be the third."

After a meager breakfast, they hitched Kasha to the carriage.

"So, Schneider," Shmuel said as his hand clasped his friend's. "We go to the Pale and wait for Messiah."

Schneider's laughter was a mockery. "Sure, Kaminsky. Messiah is coming. On the next train, maybe." He had just reduced the hope of every Jew to a sarcastic joke. But the fear he'd exposed was real. When Shmuel didn't laugh, Schneider fell helplessly onto his shoulder and sobbed.

"I understand," Shmuel comforted. "You've lost a loved one. But don't lose your faith, too. We are still the family of Abraham. Take comfort in that."

The caravan made ready, and, though no one spoke of it, Shmuel dreaded what lay ahead. The journey would be difficult. In the Pale there would be hardships—poverty, hunger. No education for his son. No dowries for his girls. His cousin Abram could help when they arrived, but who would give him steady work? He was a violin player, a teacher of music and languages. To poor people, music and languages were luxuries. But he would endure.

One behind the other, the caravan followed Shmuel's carriage down the narrow dirt road, which sloped gently to the right where tall pines bordered both sides. Suddenly, the hill was bare, and Shmuel's eyes caressed the landscape that had been his home for nearly sixteen years.

Odessa.

Long gray ribbons of smoke rose from black chimneys and waved good-bye. Odessa: his greatest joy and now his worst pain. It spread below him in a misty blur, and he thought of the things he would miss. The opera house on Lastochkina Street. The archaeological museum. The university, the conservatory. His students, his classes, his morning walks on the promenade. And the places of relaxation. The teahouses where he'd played chess and argued politics, the library, the ballet and theater. The sweet, sweet winds of the Black Sea. Most of all he'd miss his home. The pogrom had ended a happy life, but, as he listened to little Anya coo and gurgle, he knew it was also a beginning. God may taketh away, but He also giveth, he thought. And he turned his head from the past and snapped the reins toward the future.

"Giddap, Kasha!" he shouted. "Giddap."

For a long time no one spoke. They listened to the birds chirp, to the stream rushing by. But it wasn't long before Joshua began a litany of questions.

"Papa," Joshua said. "Who are the Cossacks? Why did they come?"

How to condense so much history, Shmuel wondered. "Today they are the czar's way of keeping us in line. But long ago they came together to free the Ukraine from Tartars. Some were peasants, serfs, criminals, an adventurous nobleman or two."

"But why are they after us?"

"It began when the Polish princes were afraid to collect land taxes, so they hired Jews to do it for them. Jews took the work because they had nothing else. But it created problems. When the poor were taxed to death, they rebelled, and a man named Chmielnicki formed a band of Cossacks to fight for justice. But instead of the princes, he blamed the Jews. He and his men organized pogroms. *Pogrom* means 'riot.' Together, they murdered and raped, maimed and looted. They put Jewish men in chains and sold them as slaves. With the help of some priests they forced conversions, destroyed Jewish holy books, and preached that we killed their God."

"How can a man kill God?" Joshua asked.

The impudence of youth, Shmuel thought. And the ignorance of old men. He had no answer and shrugged.

"Why didn't the Jews fight back?"

"With what, Joshua? Their bare hands? They were out-numbered. Guns were forbidden. When some fought back, they suffered more. They weren't allowed citizenship."

"So what do we do now, Papa?"

"We go to the Pale, where the czar has ordered."

"What's the Pale?"

Again the wry smile. What indeed is the Pale? Shmuel thought. "It's where I come from; Mama too. The home of our ancestors." He corrected himself. "Well, not like Palestine. But our home for hundreds of years."

"Where is it?" Joshua asked. "Will we be safe?"

Shmuel chuckled. "It depends on who owns it. Today it belongs to Russia, but who knows what tomorrow brings."

"But *what* exactly is it?"

"Ach! Joshua. Must you know everything?"

"Yes," the boy replied.

The intelligent brown eyes were trained on Shmuel. The crop of black hair, singed by fire, curled over his forehead. So he needs to know, Shmuel thought. So I'll tell him.

"Before Russia," Shmuel said, "the Pale belonged to Poland. Thousands of Jews who fled the Crusades and Inquisitions lived there. When the Russians conquered it, Catherine the Great didn't know what to do with these 'exotic people.' When she changed her religion, she thought they should change too. But they refused to become Christians, so she punished them. She drew a line around their land and called it The Pale of Settlement. *Pale* means . . . 'boundary.'

"She forbade them to leave, to travel or enter Russia. Because of that they couldn't join unions or guilds to work. They grew poor, and the Pale became a no-man's-land without any laws. So the Jews were left to govern themselves. For guidance they used the Bible and the Talmud, and it worked, until Czar Nicholas."

"What did he do?" Joshua asked.

"What didn't he do would be easier. He forbade the Jews to practice their religion. But by this time religion had become their way of life. He forbade them to wear their garments. He ordered their beards and hair cut; he burned their holy books. He skinned men alive and hung their carcasses on trees. He passed hundreds of laws to make them convert. Then he set brother against brother, offering money to any Jew who would secretly point out a bar mitzvah boy for conversion, to serve twenty-five years in his army . . . *khappers* these men were called. And he spread old rumors that Jews used Christian children's blood to make matzoh for Passover. Which brings us to today."

"The murdered boy at the church!" Joshua cried. "Passover! Is that why all this happened?" Shmuel nodded. "But the Bible forbids eating blood."

"You know and I know. *They* don't."

"Then how did you get an education?" Joshua asked. "How did you come to Odessa?"

"A new czar, Alexander II, opened the schools to Jews. He offered jobs in the cities. I could play the violin. I spoke many languages. So Grandmother Anya signed the marriage contract, and Mama and I left."

"Then why is it happening again?"

"Because, Joshua. People are starving, and the Russian government is afraid of revolution. Much easier to bring the peasants together against the Jews, than fix the problem."

"Will the Cossacks return, Papa?"

"Let's not think about it now," Shmuel said. "Let's have good thoughts and pray we make it. With God's help."

"I don't know," Joshua said. "Maybe it's time for man's help."

7

Sarah stretched her legs. They had been traveling for almost two days, but she didn't complain. They had been lucky. Unlike other families, hers had been spared. She glanced at Sonia, who was slumped in back. Since the pogrom, Sarah worried about her. Joshua had faced the danger and conquered it. Little Anya was a baby. She and Shmuel had been through pogroms before. She had even experienced one alone on a visit to her mother. But Sonia was delicate. She'd never been this dirty or frightened. Never experienced such humiliation. Sarah watched her: Her dark, almond-shaped eyes, all crusty from tears. Her long dark hair a tangled mess. Her pretty mouth with its two perfect points, pulled in a sneer. Sarah's love and compassion brought many silent promises. She'd help Sonia trust again, create a home of beauty, gather a good dowry if she had to steal it. She'd scrub floors and take in washing, but her Sonia would wear pretty clothes again.

Sarah watched the countryside unfold. They passed small villages, a strip of land where a farmer and his swaybacked horses plowed an unyielding earth. In the hills, tips of swaying pines painted white clouds on a canvas of bright blue sky. The sun bounced stars across the rippling surface of a windblown lake where a few white geese swam. The caravan frightened them, and they headed for safer haven. Do not trust that which is different! their wings kept saying.

Before sunset, the caravan made camp. Shmuel fed Kasha, then opened a newspaper Schneider had purchased. There was news of the pogrom. It spoke of the murdered youth. Then something else caught Shmuel's eyes. A silent anger coated his mouth as he read on. Marishka Ivanovna had been found dead, nailed to a tree with her tongue cut out, suspected of aiding the "enemy." He crumpled the paper, deciding not to tell Sarah. Inside, he cried like a baby.

For the next week Joshua's questions ceased. As if an answer he had been seeking had finally been found. Then Shmuel decided the family would leave the caravan and go on alone. The following morning they said good-bye.

The next days were almost pleasant. They rested, ate soup with vegetables and some fish Joshua had caught with his bare hands. They watched rabbits, squirrels, and birds. They lay on soft beds of leaves. Still, nature and her soothing harmonies couldn't erase the memories. That was when Sarah had a brilliant idea. Divine inspiration, she thought. It came to her in a flash as they passed a town on market day. As people passed, they had smiles on their faces. Smiles. She hadn't seen them in a week. With each new moment the idea grew until she knew it was the answer. When they were close to the next town, she asked Shmuel to camp.

"Make me a deep hot fire here, and another one there."

"Listen to her," Shmuel told his children. "She has no money and wants not one fire but two." He turned to Sarah. "So what will you cook, *Shuraleh*? A branch? A tree? A little froggy?"

"Just do as I ask," she replied.

Sarah carried Anya while Sonia followed behind. In a while they were in the center of a bustling market-place. There were stalls filled with vegetables, sour pickles, kosher meats, fish, everything she could hope to find.

Sarah reached inside her pocket and unstrung the

pearls Joshua had rescued. Pearl after pearl left her hands as she bought flour, a rolling pin, candles, kosher wine, bricks. She was excited. She would make matzoh as they had in the days of Exodus. She would light candles and bless God. They would eat soup and chicken, drink wine, and make the day a turning point. The czar of Russia could take their house but not their Passover. They were not animals, defined by a government. They were people with a history, a long tradition of laws. And *those* laws and *that* history would again restore order to their lives.

Sonia walked behind Sarah, who carried little Anya in the crowded marketplace. She was angry, terrified of strangers. She shied away at the brush of an arm or a garment and hovered close to Sarah. As each pearl vanished, her anger grew. A beautiful pearl for flour and vegetables. A pure white pearl for an old pot. Magnificent pearls for a kosher chicken, for some bricks, for a rolling pin and board. They were her legacy, the pearls Sarah had promised for her wedding day, cast now before swine in a cheap bazaar. And for what? Passover? Matzoh?

God! Was all of this true? Her father and Joshua. Her mother. Their faith in God, continuing as if nothing had happened? Did no one feel as she did?

She hated being a Jew for the first time in her life, despised this bazaar where women wore wigs and babushkas, smelled of chicken fat and garlic and onions. She'd grown accustomed to perfume, oils, bath powder, and silk dresses. It was all so disgusting. And this trip. Squatting in the bushes like a filthy cow. Wiping her bottom with a worm-infested leaf. This would not be her life!

She felt Sarah's nudge and followed her from the

bazaar. At her mother's urging she carried little Anya. The child's soiled diaper sickened her.

"Come," Sarah said. "We'll go home and put our lives together."

Your life, Sonia thought. Not mine!

At camp, the fires were going. As the flames roared, Shmuel added the bricks Sarah had purchased. He used the small fire to boil water pumped from a farmer's well. Then Sarah cleaned and *kashered* her chicken, removing all traces of blood with water and salt. She let it simmer in the water, then added vegetables. While the men bathed in the stream, Sonia washed their underwear and hung it on branches. Half an hour later everything was dry. Then Sarah and Sonia bathed, and Sarah was ready to bake matzoh.

She placed the flour in a pot and added warm water. After mixing and kneading, she patted the dough into round, flat cakes, always aware of the timing. She could not permit them to rise. She placed the cakes on the hot bricks, and within minutes they were ready. Before sundown, Sarah spread a blanket. She lit the candles and recited the blessing. That night, they had a feast for their stomachs, but, more important, nourishment for their souls. Then Shmuel read from Exodus and Isaiah. He explained that what had happened to them in Odessa had happened also to the children of Israel in Egypt. Then Shmuel uttered the single wish Jews had always made since their dispersion. "Next year in Jerusalem."

"Not next year," Joshua corrected. "This year!"

8

The Passover dinner had restored their dignity. The next morning Shmuel's words reflected a new outlook as he loaded the carriage and announced, "We face an unknown future, but with God's help we'll make it. So from now on, no looking back. No talking about Odessa. No talking about what used to be. There is only *now*, the future and our lives in Kashkoi." He took little Anya from Sarah's arms and raised her above his head. "This is what we affirm," he said triumphantly. "*L'chaim*. Life!"

Shmuel's words had granted them permission to stop grieving. From that moment on, they sang as they drove, told stories and anecdotes. At night they camped near a fire.

"Who's Cousin Abram?" Joshua asked.

"He's Papa's brother's oldest son," Sarah said. "They grew up together in a town called Kashkoi. Abram and his wife, Golde, came to visit when you and Sonia were small. Don't you remember, Sonia? He had this potbelly, and Joshua tried climbing on his lap but kept sliding down."

Everyone laughed but Sonia.

"What kind of work does he do?" Joshua asked.

"He owns a big fruit orchard," Sarah said. She looked to Shmuel, who confirmed her memory with a nod. "Golde had this lovely fur stole and gorgeous long pearls around her neck. Remember her hat, Shmuel? With all the fruit on it?" She giggled. "It must have cost a fortune. It looked so real our horse tried to eat it."

Again, everyone but Sonia laughed.

Then Joshua changed the subject. "What do we believe in, Papa? I mean, as Jews?"

"We're not religious," he said. "But Mama keeps the Sabbath and the holidays and we both believe in God."

Sonia's outburst cut Shmuel like a knife.

"So where was this great God of yours when the pogrom started? When women and children were being raped and murdered? Why did He create such a miserable, evil world?"

Stunned, Shmuel pretended otherwise. "God didn't murder or rape, Sonia," he said. "That was man. And the world isn't evil or good, it's just the world." He reached to hug her, but she pushed him away.

"Well, you can believe such garbage, but I don't."

"Don't talk to your father like that!" Sarah shouted.

"Leave her," Shmuel said to Sarah. "She has a right." He turned to Sonia and lowered his voice. "To believe in God is easy, Sonia. Not to believe, even easier. It's the truth you must never stop searching for. But until someone shows better, I'll believe in Him, in Torah, in Abraham, Isaac, and Jacob. Something of great value has been preserved for thousands of years, and there must be a reason for it."

Spring: a time of hope and resurrection stole the chill from winter. It taught the trees to reach for the sky. And on the morning of the third week, they found the land alive with wildflowers. Over and over the earth kept repeating: *There is hope and harmony in nature, a rhythm to the seasons and to life*. A few days later the road curved downward, the trees vanished, and the wildflower carpet turned to many shades of brown. Where there had been valleys and mountains, the land became a barren plateau. Except for one small meadow and a patch of pine forests, brown land merged with blue sky in a flat horizon. Shmuel felt pangs of fear. He had forgotten what the Pale was like, forgotten why he had left it, and the memories came rushing back like a hurricane.

"How far is Kashkoi?" Shmuel called to a man passing in the opposite direction.

The raggedy man cupped his palm to his lips and yelled, "Two more versts." He pointed over his shoulder.

Shmuel thanked him and snapped the reins. "Soon, angels," he said to his family. "We'll be with Abram."

They crossed a wooden bridge and drove through town. Chickens fluttered and squawked in the roadway. Cows and horses grazed in the fields. New spring shoots of corn and beets covered the flat ground. There were houses and people, a synagogue with its windows gleaming in the last rays of sunset. In the distance, a small meadow, a blue pine wood above a gentle ridge of hills. Half a dozen stores ringed an outdoor marketplace brimming with people. They passed a police station and beyond that some beautiful homes.

"There it is, Sarah," Shmuel said with excitement. "Abram's house. Look, everyone! Look!" His smile gleamed, and his voice resonated. "Fix your hair, Sonia. Button your dress, Sarah, and clean the baby's chin. Joshua, close your collar and scrape the mud from your boots." Shmuel fixed his own clothes and ran a hand through his unkempt hair. In front of the walkway, he stopped the carriage and hopped into the gutter. They had been traveling this day without any rest, and his arms and legs were sore. "I'll go first," he said.

Sonia scanned the large white house with its red roof. "They look rich, Papa."

Shmuel glanced at his daughter. "Be a good girl, Sonia. And please, for tonight, keep your feelings about God to yourself."

At the front door, Shmuel knocked lightly. He twirled the brim of his hat in his hand as he waited, turned toward his family when no one answered, shrugged, and smiled feebly. He was frightened no one was there when the door suddenly opened, and his portly cousin locked him in a warm embrace.

"Shmuel!" Abram said warmly, in Yiddish. "Golde! Come quick." Soon the whole family was inside.

Without a single breath Shmuel told all that had happened. He spoke of the ghetto and the Cossacks, of the plans for the wedding and bar mitzvah, all their dreams dashed by the czar's new laws. Abram commiserated while Golde, and Lena, the housekeeper, set the table.

"Here, eat this," Golde said at dinner. "Try this. Taste this. How the children have grown. Quick, Lena. Light the samovar for tea, and bring lots of sugar." She was charming—three chins with pouches beneath twinkling brown eyes, and a thin crown of faded yellow braids around her head.

After dinner, Shmuel asked Cousin Abram if they could talk. The short man with his gold fob spread across his large stomach brought Shmuel into a small parlor, where they drank schnapps and smoked expensive cigars. Shmuel finally found the courage to ask Abram for help.

"You are *mishpocha*, family," Abram said. "Of course I'll help. Tonight, you'll stay here. Tomorrow, there's a small house across the road. I lease the land from the Gentiles, and you can stay there. It's not fancy, not like you and Sarah are used to, but a little cleaning, a few curtains, and it will be fine."

For the first time in three weeks Shmuel breathed easy. He sat back admiring all the lovely things in his cousin's house: green velvet curtains, cream silk sofas with lace trim. "So, Abram. It's been good for you? I mean, the czar's new laws haven't changed things?"

"It's the same," Abram said. "What can you do? You pay a little here, a little there, and they leave you alone." Abram set his cigar on a crystal ashtray. His small eyes were nearly swallowed in a broad smile. "Anyway, don't worry. I'll watch for you."

Golde sent Lena home so she and Sarah could be alone. "Sometimes it's dangerous when they're here. They go to church on Sunday and tell the priest if we say anything bad about the czar."

Sarah rinsed a shiny pan, which mirrored her reflection. It was the first time she had seen herself since the pogrom. Her beautiful chestnut hair was dirty and streaked with white. There were dark circles beneath her eyes. She was skin and bones in dirty rags.

Unaware, Golde clattered pots down into the cupboard. Three chins became one as she lowered her head. "You'll like it in Kashkoi. Nice people. Just stay away from the Bierkoff family. Six little girls, and the woman has time to be a busybody. Abram says there are terrible rumors about her husband. As for the goyim? Don't go near. We get along; but on Easter, they drink and go crazy. So cross the street when they pass, and don't look them in the eye."

Sarah wasn't listening.

"We have two market days," Golde went on. She squeezed her ample hips between two cupboards. "Tuesdays and Fridays. The Friday one starts at four in the morning, so we can shop and be ready before sundown. Wednesdays, the women wash clothes at the stream. We laugh, we gossip, and the clothes clean themselves." Golde must have realized Sarah wasn't listening. She waddled behind and swung Sarah around. "So, what's going on here?"

Sarah fell into Golde's strong arms and wept.

"Shah! Shah!" Golde said, rubbing the space between Sarah's shoulder blades. "It's all right! Just tell Golde."

"Oh, Golde," Sarah said, pushing away. "Look at me. Like my children's grandmother."

Golde tilted Sarah's chin. "You've had a shock, *mamaleh*. It's a terrible thing, a pogrom. But tonight you'll take a hot bath and wash your hair. Upstairs," she whispered, "I have a few silk dresses from when I was thin, a hundred years ago. A little rest, some food, you'll be like new." She hugged Sarah. "Now dry your eyes."

That night Sarah and her family slept peacefully, unafraid for the first time in weeks.

The following day they wakened to a breakfast of oven-baked rolls and coffee with real cream from Abram's milk cows. There were fresh eggs, homemade strawberry jam, and chunks of newly churned butter that melted over hot cereal. When it was time to see the new house, they scrambled outside with joyful anticipation, which soon turned to disappointment. Their new home was a one-story wooden hut with three small rooms, an old stove, and a bare earthen floor. The porch was crumbling, the roof old, and the windows were broken. Outside, some barren birch trees stood near a small barn and an outhouse.

"It's not like Odessa," Cousin Abram said, pressing money into Shmuel's hand. "I'm sorry."

"It's beautiful," Shmuel said. "And we thank you from the bottom of our hearts."

Each day they made the house more livable. Sarah and Sonia scrubbed the inside; Shmuel and Joshua fixed the roof, windows, and porch. Golde gave them tables and chairs, some straw mattresses, pots, pans, dishes, old bedding she had stored in her attic. At night, while the children slept, Sarah sewed curtains, and in a few days they were laughing again. There was food on the table, a roof over their heads, fire in the hearth, and a sacred mezuzah on every door.

By the end of the week the house was a home, and early Friday an excited Sarah headed in the darkness to the market. Like a child she ran from cart to cart buying flour and yeast for *challeh*. Apples for baking. A plump chicken to roast. Matzoh meal, onions, sweet paprika, salt, saffron, soup greens, and a little wine. Tonight would be special. Tonight Abram and Golde would share their first real Sabbath in Kashkoi.

At home, Sarah set a reluctant Sonia on a barrel in the backyard, where the girl pulled feathers from a plump hen. It was her first time at the chore, and a choking Sonia was soon covered with snowy feathers. She placed the feathers in a sack, to be cleaned and used for bedding, and gave the plucked chicken to her mother.

When the chicken was clean and soaking in water, Sarah made a *kishke* by stuffing the skin of the chicken's neck with bread crumbs, salt, flour, minced onion, bits of shredded carrot, and *schmaltz*. She sewed both ends, plunged it in boiling water, and roasted it on a bed of onions and paprika. Then she made her *challeh*.

After the last rise, she divided the dough into two loaves. Before baking, she pinched a tiny ball from each loaf, and, saying a blessing, tossed each ball in the oven to symbolize the offerings of the olden days. As the bread baked, she cooked her chicken. And an hour before sundown the food was ready, with the kitchen clean as a pin.

While Shmuel and Joshua went to synagogue, she nursed Anya, washed her face, and combed her hair. Then she put on one of Golde's silk dresses. She was excited as she prepared, aware that with the sinking sun came the Sabbath, came joy and solemnity, came twenty-four hours to contemplate totally and be in the Lord's presence. From the moment the Sabbath began, no money could be carried, no business spoken of, no cooking or cleaning done, no light kindled. Even the paper in the outhouse had to be torn in advance, and every servant and animal given rest. It was a time for God and family.

When the moment came, Sarah covered her head with a piece of lace. She blessed her family, then sparked the match to light the candles resting in her mother's silver candlesticks. She closed her eyes and, with her delicate tapered fingers, spun a magical web across the flames, bringing both fists to cover her eyes. Doing this, she sang an ancient Hebrew prayer that blessed her Maker, feeling a special warmth tonight. Though as Jews they had once again been dispersed, they had lost nothing of real value. Home was being together, honoring God on a Sabbath night. And she smiled, knowing that all over the village of Kashkoi, and everywhere the sun was setting, across the Pale and around the world, displaced Jews were in shul reading the same Torah page, blessing the Lord and celebrating the Sabbath. And in these ancient acts and traditions they were connected, bound together, historically woven in an intricate and endless tapestry of God's beautiful design.

THE PALE

Consider a place so barren that sand and dust blow to grit in a man's mouth, forever etching their marks on his throat and lungs like bits of jagged glass. Consider the bleakest landscape, where few young trees can survive the summer heat, where the spring mud is one foot deep, where the everlasting winter ground freezes over to sharp ice and the bitter, cold air numbs the breath on a man's lips. Consider also that whatever grows in such a brutal place as this will be strong, hardy, and perennial.

9

The Pale was meant to contain and isolate the Jews, to keep them from the guilds and unions. In addition it was a buffer to discourage invading armies. But the Pale was also a people, who, cut off from everything else, turned inward, a people who could have perished but chose instead a life of spiritual beauty, which gave them their only security. Day and night they prayed that Messiah would come to end their misery and reward their devotion.

Without man's law, God's 613 commandments guided their lives and gave them meaning. Every task, no matter how menial, had a prayer. Prayers for sleeping, eating, waking, washing. Prayers for hope. Prayers kept their minds off trouble and centered them on God and on the fulfillment of His Covenant.

As the Kaminskys settled into the routine of small village life, Yiddish became their main language again. Sarah covered her head respectfully, Joshua studied more seriously for his bar mitzvah, and Shmuel spent more time in the synagogue. Only Sonia remained the same. She hated God's laws, hated the village, hated the way they lived, and refused to speak Yiddish.

Sarah noticed Sonia's distress and prayed for God's guidance. Later, she spoke to Shmuel about finding a matchmaker. Love would soften her daughter's hard heart, she thought. Love, and the joy of children.

* * *

Four weeks after they'd settled in, Sarah's neighbor came with a cinnamon ring. She knocked on the front door as four of her six children hid behind her skirts.

"For you, Mrs. Kaminsky," she offered. "I'm Bierkoff; next door. It's nice to have a new neighbor."

Sarah was wary. This tall, slender woman with her dark hair piled on her head was the one Golde had warned her about. Yet there was a sweetness to her, and Sarah invited her for tea. She declined, pointing to a wagon near the road.

"My husband's taking us to Kishinev, where we buy and sell things. Maybe next time."

Sarah glanced at the woman's husband. A large cap covered his head, and his owlish profile curved downward toward a receding chin that had no beard. He seemed uncomfortable and nervous.

"We'll talk sometime," the woman called, walking away.

"I don't know your first name," Sarah shouted after.

"Rachel," she replied. "That's my husband, Maurice."

Before Sarah closed the door, something in the woman's hair caught her eye. "Rachel!" Sarah shouted. "That comb. Where did you get it?"

Rachel put her hand to the back of her head. "A present from my husband," she said, smiling. "He bought it near Odessa. You can borrow it, if you like."

When Shmuel returned that night, Sarah was angry. "It's my comb, I tell you. The one I gave Marishka."

"A mistake," Shmuel said. "It just looked like it."

"No, Shmuel." Sarah's skirt rustled as she paced. "Abram and Golde warned us. No one really knows how they make their living. Bierkoff could be a *khapper* for the czar's army."

Shmuel tried to calm her. "I've met him, Sarah. He's a simple peddler who goes from town to town. It's possible he bought the comb like Rachel said. If you want, I can ask."

"No!" Sarah shouted.

"Then please don't worry. Not even the czar will take a mother's only son."

That night Shmuel lay with his chest against Sarah's back and his face buried in her long hair. "*Shuraleh*," he whispered. "Soon, I'll make money to buy you a new comb."

Sarah turned to face him. His features in the moonlight were like a little boy's. "It's not the comb," she said. "It's important to separate friends from enemies."

They fell asleep. Sometime later, Shmuel wakened with a start. Loud voices sounded outside the window, and he parted the curtain. When his eyes grew accustomed to the dark, he saw two men standing near the birch trees. He recognized the constable astride his horse. But the other man, though he looked familiar, was a blur. As the two men parted, Shmuel wondered. Was it the *khapper*? Were they planning a pogrom? Frustrated, with no answers, he returned to bed.

The following days led to the warmth of summer and a settling in of their lives. To earn money, Shmuel offered violin and language lessons. But few families could afford him. He supplemented his meager income with odd jobs, while Joshua worked in Abram's orchard and Sonia and Sarah took in washing. It upset Shmuel to see Sarah toil. She had been raised in wealth, with servants, good clothes, the best foods. Yet she was also rooted in reality. When her father had died of a heart attack, Sarah had returned to care for her sick mother, staying until the woman had passed on. Then she'd sold the family business at a good profit, settled her mother's affairs, and come back to Odessa. She would manage, Shmuel told himself. They all would.

On days of rest, they'd picnic behind their home in the wide meadows near the edge of a blue pine forest. The train would whistle by, and they'd eat black bread and pickled herring and laugh at Anya crawling everywhere. They made new friends, went to synagogue. And as the days and nights passed, their sad memories of Odessa faded. Color returned to Sarah's cheeks. Joshua grew stronger as his bar mitzvah day approached. Little Anya grew too big for the drawer she slept in, and Shmuel and Joshua built her a crib. Only Sonia brooded. She watched the neighborhood mule go round and round, strapped to a mill wheel. He looked miserable, with his large brown eyes downcast, ears forward, and nose drooped to the ground. She would not spend her life like that, she swore, on a treadmill, on a journey going nowhere. That would never happen. Then at the marketplace Sarah purchased a book which kindled a spark. It was by a writer named Leo Tolstoy, and its title was *Anna Karenina*. At night, Sonia would read of courtship, of romantic love which brought back memories of her fiancé, Sergei, and she placed her hopes back on course. One day she'd meet him. Someone tall and handsome and very rich who would take her away from the misery and bondage of Kashkoi. He would be the one to free her, not God's stupid laws. And as though providence had heard, she found some little creatures which became in their innocence a symbol of that promise, and Sonia began to smile again.

Sonia wakened one morning to screeching and the sight of Cousin Abram's yellow cat hunched and stalking. She put on a housecoat and ran, reaching the place moments before he pounced.

"Shoo!" she hollered.

The cat ran off, and Sonia scooped two little birds into her hands. The tiny black fledglings had fallen from a nest and were the size of teaspoons. Sonia carried them into the house and made a nest of rags in a soup bowl. For food, she soaked bread in warm milk, forcing it down their throats with a thin wooden stick. No one believed they'd live, but to everyone's surprise they thrived. Sonia was thrilled.

It was the first time since the pogrom she was absorbed in something other than her own misery. Sarah saw this as the healing of Sonia's wounds and the answer to her prayers.

"Look," Sarah said to Shmuel. "Look at her smile." But Sarah's joy was premature.

Sonia's smile was there. But it was not just because of the birds, it was rather a secret smile of waiting, a smile of knowing she would eventually leave this place just as surely as her birds would learn how to fly.

Life for Shmuel was more difficult. Though he spoke valiantly and put on a joyful public array, deep inside he suffered. After enjoying the freedom of Odessa, of being a man of stature with a teaching position in an honored conservatory, he was now reduced to the company of disinterested children who had neither talent nor appreciation for their parents' sacrifices. Yet wherever he found it, he did his work graciously. Occasionally he'd play his violin at weddings or at the homes of rich Gentiles where the price was a ruble—a king's ransom. In reality, the money they lived on was earned by Sarah, Sonia, and Joshua. When there was no work, Shmuel would walk to the meadow behind the Russian Orthodox church and play his violin. Where others prayed to God with their voices, Shmuel played music.

*   *   *

As the melody flowed, he wallowed in the endless and delicate whispers, the hearty bellows, the myriad voices that sang to him and crept through the emptiness of his soul. The notes flowed through his bloodstream and beat with the rhythm of his heart. They were the voices of purity, love—a religious experience.

Around and around, an endless ribbon of melody left his strings and floated through the trees, scaling the pond, caressing the flowers, humming with bees, and riding the breeze to a window of the Orthodox church, where the black-garbed village patriarch stood listening. Shmuel released his sorrows, his needs, letting the music voice his hopes. With the last chord he fell to the ground exhausted and stayed there till Joshua came running to find him.

10

It was Wednesay night, long after Shmuel had returned from the synagogue, when Sarah heard him close the door. Later, he came to bed and curled his leg acoss her thigh. Though she welcomed his affection, she had just ceased her menstruation and held her desires in check. With the flat of her palm she reached lovingly behind and patted his knee saying, "Tomorrow. I will go to the *mikvah*."

Because a woman is the giver of life, she is taught to cleanse herself in a ritual bath. As a bride, she goes; after giving birth, she goes. After her menstrual flow, she goes. And Sarah fled at first starlight the following night to immerse herself and prepare for Shmuel's bed.

In the steamy underground cavern, she undressed and scrubbed herself in a tub, paying special attention to her teeth, nails, feet, and hair. According to law, she combed the snarls from her wet hair and removed her wedding ring. It was necessary for her whole body to be open to the water. Then she wrapped herself in a towel and waited for the keeper.

Inside the small room which contained the bathing well, she unwrapped and let the keeper inspect her. Pronounced free of all dirt and loose hair, she was given permission to enter. She dropped her towel, and stepped down into swirling waters which flowed in from the nearby stream. She parted her legs and arms, allowing the clean water to seep into every pore of her body. Then she slipped below until all of her was immersed. Coming up, she recited a blessing.

Others did this because of religion; she, as a matter of tradition. It bound her to her past and to her people in a special way. But the *mikvah* spoke to her of other things as well. It made her remember sex was not just the function of two animals grappling with the flesh but rather something holy and sanctified by God.

When she was dry, she dressed and covered herself completely, hurrying through the darkened streets, allowing herself the luxury of arousal and desire, of imagining Shmuel beside her on a fresh bed of sweet-smelling sheets. Gradually desire grew to a powerful need. They would make love tonight for the first time since the last months of her pregnancy, since Anya's birth, since the pogrom, since leaving Odessa. They had come through catastrophe. And the words *that which does not kill me makes me stronger* came to mind. And though she couldn't recall who had said it, she felt it deeply. She was going home to her husband's bed. They would embrace, and express their deepest feelings.

Shmuel smiled knowingly as she opened the door. They had a secret together. He was fixing something with a hammer as she entered, and she glanced shyly at him, then turned away. She fussed with the children, knowing all the while what both she and Shmuel were thinking. The anticipation was magic, as if they were newlyweds again. She'd brush by him and feel a powerful urge to touch his arm. He'd pass by her and chills would run down her spine. She'd watch his eyes change from vigilant to flirtatious to coy, notice his strong muscles tighten and relax, his sensitive fingers move as he worked. Soon, his hands would caress her.

And then it was time.

"Come, Shuraleh," he whispered, when the children were asleep. He headed for the bedroom. "Keep me warm."

In the small bedroom the moon glanced through the open window. She caught the faint scent of lilacs, which grew outside. She let him slowly undress her, feeling excitement and heat flow through her body like the spring waters she had just visited.

"Sarah," he sang.

The sound of her name echoed through her ears, traveled the length of her neck and spine, tightened her thighs and calves till her toes curled. When he sang it again, it raised the nipples of her breasts. Tender, loving words spilled from his lips like honey from the comb, all sweet and rich.

"Hold me, Sarah. I've missed you so much."

He kissed her tenderly, then deeply. He drew her long hair from her neck and inhaled her skin. One by one he loosened the buttons of her gown until it fell away and she stood naked in the light. For a long time his eyes kissed the curves of her hips, her milky breasts, her long neck. Then the song spilled from his lips again as he drew her to him. "God help me; how I love you."

She clung to him. It was exciting, as though they had been together for the first time. So many times she had heard women in the marketplace complain of their husbands' lack of affection, of their brutishness in bed, which she never understood. Her Shmuel was loving, patient, sensitive, so giving in every way. Together they were like bow and violin, neither making sense without the other.

And tonight, the music was sweet.

His mouth brushed hers in gentle kisses. The soft hairs on his lips and chin tickled like butterfly's wings. She leaned into the kiss, drew her palms around his strong, muscular shoulders to pull him closer.

His chest was against her bosom, his strong arms curling around her back as his fingers traced the bones of her spine one by one until they reached the cleft of her buttocks. He dipped his lips and tongue to her breasts, gently lapping and sucking the pointed nipples, and she felt her milk flow into his mouth. She loved nurturing him this way. Drink, darling, drink, she thought. I will love you this way forever.

He took her hand and led her to their bed. She lay on the clean sheets and soft pillow which he contoured with his hand. He lay beside her, curling the ends of her hair around her pink nipples and staring into her eyes.

"You're so beautiful, Sarah!"

Her heart fluttered like a young girl's. Did he know how special he was? How much joy he had given her?

"And I love you," she answered.

She closed her eyes as his lips and tongue sought hers in a passionate kiss. It had been a long time, and she had almost forgotten his taste. When he pulled away, she caught her breath. Her hands roamed his hips, his back, his muscular thighs till their fingers wound together in a tight clasp. He squeezed her so hard she thought her hand would break. His thighs quivered beside her as one arm drew her toward him. Her own moisture grew from a secret well deep within her body. He rolled her on her back as his long, sensitive fingers caressed the insides of her thighs, stroked her mound, and prodded open the soft, moist lips, slipping into the creamy darkness. She thrust her hips and spread her knees to let him know she was ready. The first time she had received him in pain. Now, there was only pleasure.

He was soon over her, inside her, and the small fire which had simmered before the *mikvah* burned as hot as a fever. His buttocks rose and fell, and she joined his rhythm. His first thrusts were slow, carefully sketched as an artist would draw a canvas. Then he went faster. A thousand colors flooded her brain: blues, whites, yellows, oranges, finally a searing red.

"I'm exciting you," he demanded. "Say it! Say I make you happy!"

"Yes, yes," she answered. "Oh, yes."

Her head rolled. "Kiss me!" she cried.

He raised up again and plunged deeper as sweat from his neck and shoulders dripped onto her chest. Then he grasped her waist, and, arching his back, let his wet heat fly. And in that moment they became lovers again, two, dissolved into one.

11

It was the perfect time for Joshua's bar mitzvah. Chicks became roosters. Ducklings became drakes. Wheat grew as tall as a man and was ready to be harvested for the High Holy Days. And as that life force around him matured, Joshua prepared for the ceremony that would symbolize his coming of age.

Sarah noticed the line of down growing above her son's lip. She saw it in the candlelight the night he and Shmuel sat at the table discussing the bar mitzvah ceremony and Joshua's voice cracked. She looked down at her son's face, which was at once that of both boy and man, and she wanted to kiss him.

"How will I remember everything, Papa? How do I keep from wetting the Torah when I kiss it?"

"You'll remember." Shmuel laughed. "But you don't exactly kiss the Torah. You kiss the fringes of the tallis and place them on the prayer you recite."

"Right. Right. Oh, God. Why am I so nervous?"

And the words from the Bible came to Sarah in a rush:

> *"And there shall come forth a shoot out of the stock*
> *of Jesse,*
> *And a twig shall grow forth out of his roots.*
> *And the spirit of the Lord shall rest upon him, . . .*
> *And with the breath of his lips shall he slay the wicked.*
> *And righteousness shall be the girdle of his loins."*

The ceremony was beautiful. Joshua recited Pinchas from the Book of Numbers where Moses was told to go up to Mt. Abarim to view the Promised Land. As Joshua spoke, Sarah's eyes misted over. Her son was handsome and strong. And though he would always be her baby, now she would have to let go. Yet, as he stood near the candles in his ivory tallis and silk skullcap, long-ago moments rambled through her mind: Though I am your mother, she thought, one of many who has watched her son become a man before God and the Jewish community, I will always recall your babyhood: the way your fists would ball and open, the way your legs would kick the covers and your rump would point in the air while you sucked your thumb and slept on your elbows and knees. I will always remember your first tooth, your nakedness, your constant curiosity, your willing ways and winning smile, the bouquets of wilted flowers you used to bring me. And though tonight you cut the strings of dependence, the strings of my heart can never be severed. I love you, Joshua—face and hands smeared with red beets and orange carrots, a noodle stuck to your dimpled chin—and no matter what you do or become, I will remember these things and love you till the day I die.

Shmuel could feel Sarah's eyes warming his back, lighting Joshua's face like a spotlight. But he kept the smile that was glowing inside him from traveling to his own lips. This ceremony, though a happy occasion, was also solemn and reverential. Tonight Joshua not only passed from boy to man but accepted responsibility and obligation as well. Now, he would fast on holidays, take part in a minyan. Now he was ready for marriage.

Ach, Joshua. Where has the time gone? Shmuel thought. Thirteen years ago, you were an infant, a squalling mass of arms, legs, black curls, and, even then, a strong will. Who would have known how severely you would be tested? Yes, tonight you recite prayers and blessings. But how many in this synagogue know of your daring exploits? Of the test of manhood you passed superbly only months ago? And that is the irony. Tonight they test you as a Son of The Commandments. But when the day was cold and bloody and the lives of your family were at stake, you passed another test. So, my son, what future awaits you? How will you fit into the scheme of things? What is God's plan, and where will life lead you? or you, it? Who will be by your side? Most of all, when will you grow restless and leave us?

* * *

"May God grant you the patience of Job, the wisdom of Solomon. And may you be a blessing to your parents, your family, your community, and especially to God," the rabbi concluded.

The ceremony ended with celebration, with sweet *challeh* and wine and the company and good wishes of friends. And in the days that followed, Joshua stood taller and spoke with more authority.

God gave the Jews 613 commandments. A year after Joshua's bar mitzvah, the czar passed 650 laws directed only against the Jewish people: Among them were taxes on Sabbath candles, which were already scarce, on ritually slaughtered animals, on kosher food, yarmulkes, and books, on synagogues and the garments Jews wore. The laws attacked the heart of their religion and government.

To avoid trouble, they paid bribes to constables and magistrates, and they found clever ways of doing things. Six boys would sit at a single table where one Torah lay open. They learned to read upside down and sideways. The community pooled resources, sharing food and holidays. Thus, they drew closer to one another and closer to God. What the state sought to accomplish backfired. Those who were marginal in their devotion turned more fervently to God. Those who had forsaken their heritage came back again out of spite. The czar's divisionary laws made Jews more aware than ever of who they were. Then came a rumor that among their neighbors lived a *khapper*. The rumor grew until it reached Sarah's ears, and she flew home to tell Shmuel. "A boy Joshua's age was taken four miles from here." Sarah looked into Shmuel's eyes. "What can we do?"

"I don't know," he said.

"Maybe we can send him to America, to Cousin

Chaim in Chicago?" Sarah produced their meager savings from a sugar bowl. "Perhaps Abram can help." When Shmuel said nothing, Sarah yelled.

"Shah!" Shmuel said. "Look how you made the baby."

Sarah put the crying child in a chair Shmuel had made. She tied her with a towel and placed a dry cracker in her hand. Lowering her voice, she began again. "This is no laughing matter, Shmuel. We must do something, now."

The following year, rumors of the *khapper* escalated and the men in the village met illegally in the cellar of the synagogue. A single candle flickered as Joshua sat near the rabbi's son, listening to the group, whose members ranged from Orthodox Jew to agnostic.

"There is an enemy in our midst," the blacksmith said. "We must find out who the *khapper* is and expose him."

"Then what?" the rabbi asked. "Another will take his place. If the czar wants men for his army, he'll find a way."

"To hell with the czar!" the tailor shouted.

"Shah!" the rabbi said. He spit three times to ward off evil spirits.

"School will now be forbidden. There are new quotas."

"There are always quotas for Jews," the blacksmith said. "Unless it's for the czar's army. Then there are no quotas."

Nobody laughed.

Joshua leaned forward, absorbing every word.

"So what is new, gentlemen?" the rabbi asked. "Once again they want to destroy us. But still we endure. Why? Because of Torah and God's promise. Let them do their dirty work. God will be the final judge. Let us look only to Messiah."

"Why do they want to destroy us?" the rabbi's son asked.

"To remove the evidence," the rabbi said.

"What evidence?" Joshua heard himself saying.

"That God gave us Torah. That they could be wrong." The rabbi laughed. "They should know that what they do works two ways."

"What do you mean, Papa?" his son asked.

"The Pale may keep us in, but it also keeps *them* out. This way we know the bloodline."

"What the devil are you talking about?" the tailor demanded.

"How else will we know the seed of David? How else will we know Messiah when he comes?"

"So, you think they do us a favor," the tailor ranted. "You think God uses them to play games? Ridiculous!"

"Well, I don't care," the baker's voice boomed. "Our families aren't safe. We must do something!"

"Do what? With what?" Shmuel cried.

The rabbi opened his Bible, but the baker's fist hit the table.

"Put it down, Rabbi! The answer isn't there." He removed a booklet from his pocket and fanned the pages. "It's here, in the pages of this book." The men were shocked, the rabbi speechless.

"And this answer, what is it?" Shmuel asked.

"A homeland," the baker replied.

"A what?" everyone asked.

"A homeland," the baker repeated. "A place where Jews will be safe, where no one will come in the night and drag us away. A place to practice our beliefs. A land where we are free to defend ourselves."

"Blasphemy!" the rabbi shouted in a rage. He pounded the table with his fist. "Such a land only God can give!"

"No!" the baker shouted. "It's for free men to seek

and find." He passed around several books he had hidden in his coat pocket. "Read for yourselves, my friends," he said. "It's an idea whose time has come."

"And what do you call this idea?" Shmuel asked.

"Zionism," the speaker said. And the meeting ended.

Night after night Shmuel pored over the seditious booklet. He found that the idea intrigued him. Having lived in Odessa, he knew how precious freedom was. The booklet was called "Auto-Emancipation" and was written by a doctor named Leon Pinsker, a man who had created the piece out of the realization that Europe's long hatred of the Jews would never die. In it he attacked those Jews whose belief systems were centered on waiting for a messianic answer to Jewish suffering. He attacked equally those who thought the answer was in assimilation into the country of their birth, when over and over true citizenship of all countries was denied to Jews. Since Jews had been dispersed, they'd been ghettoized everywhere, and Pinsker knew acceptance would never happen. Jews were doomed to a life of endless persecutions if left to the mercy of other governments. They needed a home of their own. When Shmuel realized Joshua had been reading the book also, they began to talk.

"It's terrible not to have a home, Joshua. When our ancestors lived in Spain, they soon discovered they were not Spanish. In Italy, not Italians. In Poland and in Russia, neither Poles nor Russians."

"Then Doctor Pinsker is right," Joshua said.

As time passed, Joshua realized the world was truly divided into two parts. Jews and Gentiles. That awareness had burst uninvited into his consciousness in Odessa, but now, in the Pale, it was a poisonous and deadly liquid that trickled drop by drop into his veins. *Don't do this, it will make the czar angry. Don't do that, the policemen will lock you up. Be careful of the* khapper. *Don't insult a Gentile. Always, always, be on your guard.*

Day after day, fear became his playmate, an invisible teacher that soon fitted his arms and legs like shackles. He could not think of anything else. Jew. Jew. Jew. Who is my enemy? Who is my friend? When a Gentile smashed his nose, Shmuel forbade him to fight back. When one threw dirt on Sonia or teased little Anya, he was told to ignore it. He obliged, but day by day it became harder. A day would come when he would fight back, do what any normal man would do, and he would probably pay dearly. Day by day a new religion was being formed in Joshua, and that religion, called Zionism, lay in the pages of Dr. Pinsker's book.

12

It was harvesttime 1894, when Sarah realized she was pregnant. Everyone was happy but Sonia. There was barely enough food for five, she thought. Six would reduce them to starvation. Rosh Hashanah and Yom Kippur had passed, and Sukkos and Simchas Torah were coming. They had feasted and celebrated the new year in peace and harmony, fasted and atoned for past sins on Yom Kippur. Now, according to tradition, they would build a Sukkos tent to celebrate deliverance and thanksgiving.

Shmuel and Joshua created a simple hut with strong walls to keep the chill out. They covered the top with living branches so the stars could shine through to show God's constant presence. They decorated the inside with the names of Abraham, Isaac, and Jacob and with the symbolic bouquet of a perfect yellow citron and the branches of palm, myrtle, and willow trees. They ate every meal inside the hut; they drank wine and prayed. Finally, Simchas Torah, the last day of Sukkos, had them dancing in the streets.

A week later the village matchmaker found a fine young man for Sonia. At first, Sonia wouldn't hear of it. Then she saw him one day and changed her mind. He wasn't handsome, but his clothes and stature spoke of money. It wasn't long before their parents were introduced.

Theodore Raskind was the only son of Yetta and Anschul Raskind, a rich tobacco merchant who had special permission to leave the Pale and travel to Turkey on matters of commerce. Theo's parents didn't care about Sonia's meager dowry, which consisted of one feather quilt, two down pillows, and a secret something Sarah had been saving. Anschul, once a poor peasant, had made a fortune growing tobaccco and courting the wealthiest Gentiles in the largest cities of Russia. He provided the finest merchandise, and they trusted his judgment. To him, Sonia's dowry was insignificant. That she was the daughter of a scholar, a young woman who spoke Russian and some English, made her an asset to his son's future. Besides her education, Sonia was pretty, healthy, able to give him grandchildren not only to inherit but to expand his business. The world was changing. A new century was around the corner. His son and his son's future children needed a modern woman.

Theo's mother adored Sonia. Not only could she read and write, but she had manners, knew how to set a table with china and silver, how to plan a French menu and arrange flowers. She had good taste and could deal with servants. Unlike most village girls, who feared the Gentiles, Sonia was at ease ordering them about.

Two weeks later, a *shiddach* was made, and after the marriage contract was agreed upon, the families planned a celebration. In keeping with tradition, to show his respect for Sonia's parents, Theodore installed a new wooden floor in Sarah's kitchen.

At the engagement celebration, there were wines imported from France, caviar from Iran, and pâtés, things Shmuel and Sarah hadn't tasted since leaving Odessa. Sarah made honey cake and brought hard-boiled eggs to symbolize the new life the two would share. After the celebration, a plate was shattered to seal the arrangement. Theo presented Sonia with a ring, a perfect white pearl surrounded by tiny diamonds, which his mother had selected, and a Bible, covered in white silk, in which they would write the names of their children. Sonia gave Theo a new tallis, which Shmuel had selected.

Yetta took Sonia on shopping trips. They bought handmade lace, silk, and velvet for her trousseau. Jewelers were summoned for diamond earrings, proper for the wife of a rich man. She was fitted for dresses, hats, and handmade leather boots. Sonia's dream was coming true.

"We'll have a good life together, Theo," she'd tell him. "We'll have a beautiful home, and I'll make you proud."

"And we'll have lots of children," he'd say.

And she'd answer, "Of course," but quickly change the subject.

He'd take her hand, gaze deep into those dark and curiously Oriental eyes which became slits whenever she laughed, and sometimes she'd let him kiss her cheek.

Two weeks after their engagement, Theo and his father went to Turkey. The day he left, Sonia decided to set her birds free. She held them above her bed and tossed them into the air. They went up and came fluttering down, wildly flapping their black wings. It wasn't long before they were gliding around her room. Day after day, she moved their crumbs closer to the curtained window. Their little bodies had grown fat from bread and milk, and worms Joshua had dug from the ground. Their legs were strong and warm as they perched on her finger, and finally she knew the time had come.

"Will they be all right?" Sonia asked Sarah.

"Of course."

"But look. They seem so little and helpless."

Sarah watched them fly around the room. "No, Sonia. You made them strong, ready for winter. God will give whatever else they need."

The next morning Sonia rose early. The sun was shining, and the sky was a deep blue. She let the birds out of the cage and placed bread crumbs on her windowsill. This time she opened the window, and her birds were instantly drawn to others tittering in the trees. The fattest of the two cocked his head toward the chirping and flew around the room. He landed on her finger, perched there, peering at her in a strange way, and she wondered what he could be thinking. She felt a sense of satisfaction as his little heart beat against her finger. When she closed her eyes for an instant, the other bird flew away. A second later, the one on her finger followed. The warm place where it had perched grew cold as ice, and her hand fell to her side. She swallowed a sob, knowing she would miss them. Loving was a deadly business, she decided.

When Theo and his father returned from Turkey, Sarah invited the Raskinds to dinner. She set her table with fall flowers and silver that Golde had loaned her.

Her soup was liquid gold. Her homemade noodles were as fine and sweet as angel's hair, and the plump roasting chicken was crisp and brown. *Kasha varnitchkes* were spiced with salt, fresh black pepper, and *gribbiners*— cracklings she'd made with onions and chicken fat. Her thin silver candlesticks shone on the table.

Everyone noticed Theo mooning over Sonia like a calf.

"So, Theo, how was the soup?" Sarah asked.

"Wonderful!" he replied. He hadn't even tasted it.

"And how is the cake?" Shmuel asked.

"So sweet," he replied. He hadn't even touched it.

There were also baked apples topped with Sarah's cherry preserves, and a twist of lemon.

Joshua studied Theo with arched eyebrows and a silly smirk. He'd never seen a man act this way before.

The following day, to show his appreciation, Theo's father sent a milk cow and half a dozen egg-laying hens. That same morning, Shmuel went to synagogue to thank God for Sonia's good fortune.

The chill of fall had finally passed, and a thick white snow blanketed Kashkoi. The pond froze over. Roofs sprouted long, glittering icicles. Day and night, plumes of thick gray smoke floated skyward from chimneys, and the harsh crack of falling timber echoed through the land. The wind bit its sharp teeth through the house, and, to keep her family warm, Sarah sewed each of them a set of winter underwear.

For the children, life was filled with sliding down ice hills, throwing snowballs, building snowmen. Outside, their noses ran, their cheeks became frostbitten, all rosy red and purple. Their boots were stuffed with rags to keep their feet dry, and every morning Shmuel shoveled snow from house to barn. Inside, they passed the time near the fire making feather quilts, telling stories, drinking hot lemon tea with schnapps. After the dinner dishes were cleared, Sarah knit Chanukah presents.

Sitting in her rocking chair by the firelight, shoulders covered with a crocheted shawl, Sarah's fingers would fly, and the needles would click a string of warm mittens, colorful hats, long scarves, bulky sweaters, tight leggings, and thick socks.

At night, Shmuel and Joshua played chess or checkers while Sarah rocked Anya in a rocking chair and Sonia played jackstones with the dried knucklebones of sheep. When Sarah nursed Anya, she sang of Ruth and Esther, of the ancient lands from which her people had sprung, and of the legends which had sustained them through their sorrows. Sometimes Shmuel saw a bright light glowing around his wife and child which made him believe the next boy-child born in the village might be Messiah. He'd sit by the fire reading Torah, Talmud, history books, and he would glance at his family and feel a pull so strong he'd sense God's design not on the pages of his book but alive and flourishing in that very room. As Sarah rocked, as the child suckled, as the tiny, contented fingers twisted the ends of Sarah's long braid, it was a vision which gave him peace and strength, and a powerful knowledge that though the past had been a trial, the future was always being born.

In late March, dark gray clouds merged into a blinding mist. Joshua had been fishing with his basket when the drops began to fall. He ran home as fast as he could to stand at his window as a hungry wind snapped the weakest trees, swallowed the brittle branches and spit them out. For three days water beat against the house, surged from the hills in a deluge of rocks and thick mud. The sky grew black as coal while thunder rumbled. Veins of lightning flashed in the sky, hurling electric daggers at the earth. Then the heavens cracked open, and drops as large as eggs pounded the roof. The whole house shook as water overflowed the eaves and dripped into pots in the kitchen, closets, and bedrooms.

In the barn, the chickens cackled in their wet roosts. The cow pulled against her tether, mooing in distress. When Shmuel and Joshua ran to milk her, she was stuck in mud. Shmuel made a bed of planks and straw for her to stand on, and the two pulled her to safety. Shmuel milked away her pain while Joshua gathered chicken eggs.

Then the rain abated, but not for long. The hills rushed down again in a cascade of mud so powerful it dug a trench through the center of the town which swelled to a wild river. Outside, a chair floated by, and with it, a child's toy. Four days later the bridge fell.

Then it stopped. The sun rose. The mud dried to clay. They repaired the bridge and began replanting: corn, wheat, beets. The season would not be a good one, but they would survive. Then Passover came without incident, praise God, and, as talk of the *khapper* died, life seemed peaceful again.

In May, Sarah's first labor pains came. She was a little apprehensive because of a strange dream—she'd walked through the forest with a butterfly. She wakened that night to the glowing apparition of her mother. She was startled but not afraid.

"Mama, what's the matter?" she heard herself saying.

"You'll have a son," the vision replied.

"Will he be healthy?"

"Yes, and no," the ghost answered; then it began to fade.

"No. Wait!" Sarah screamed. "Tell me what you mean!" But the figure vanished and Shmuel wakened to calm her.

13

This time Sonia watched without fear. There were no ropes, no rags. Just the child's head, then shoulders emerging naturally. But there was pain. For ten hours Sonia sat holding Sarah's hand, encouraging her till it was over.

"You have a healthy son," the old midwife said.

An exhausted Sarah didn't look up. "I know," she said. She wasn't sure about the rest of the dream, only that, with a brother, Joshua was now in danger.

The midwife entered the kitchen. "*Mazel tov*," she said to Shmuel, who was pacing. She was a hunched bundle of rags with a black babushka on her head and streaks of Sarah's blood on her wrinkled hands. "You have another kaddish."

"A son?" he said.

"So what else is a kaddish?" She washed her hands.

"And my wife?" Shmuel asked.

She gummed a piece of *challeh* snatched from the bread bin. "A good long rest is what she needs."

Relieved, Shmuel fell into the rocker.

"To tell the truth," the crone whispered, stuffing *challeh* into her pockets, "she's not so strong. It would be better not to have more children." She took as much food as her pockets would hold, then left.

For a long time Shmuel sat wondering about what the old woman had told him. He was wild with worry. What did she mean? Then Sarah called, and he went to her room and took the baby. The child had no hair, just a nub of nose on a red face, and a wide open mouth screaming in discontent. The continuing cries brought Sarah's outstretched arms to comfort again.

"What's wrong?" Sarah sang, taking the baby back.

"Don't you like your papa?" She put the child to her breast, where it found her nipple. "Look at him," Sarah said, smiling. "Isn't he beautiful?"

Shmuel gave a halfhearted smile. He was upset at the way Sarah looked. Wet hair clung to her forehead. Her lips were parched. There were bloodstains on her nightdress. He made up his mind then and there he would never touch her again.

The calendar of shtetl life is not measured by time but moves from birth and *bris* and *shiddach* and marriage to Shabbos, Passover, Rosh Hashanah, Yom Kippur, to memorial *yahrzeit* candle, and ever on. It is not measured by days but in human events, in keeping alive the memories, in telling the history, in celebrating the holidays, and in naming the newborn child after those who have passed on, completing the cycle of life and death. Thus, eight days after his birth, Sarah's new baby was circumcised and named for his maternal grandfather, Saul, and in that ritual ceremony he became another witness to the Covenant.

The morning of Saul's *bris*, Shmuel was given a seat of honor in the synagogue and called to Torah. At home, where the ritual would take place, the minyan arrived. Each of the ten men was dressed in a suit, a tallis, and yarmulke. The sleepy infant was taken from Sarah's arms and the door to her room tightly shut. Like other women, she would choose not to see the *mohel* bring a knife to her child's naked body or to hear her baby cry. She would sit like a queen in a pretty gown while the women of the village fussed over her. As the time drew near, the drowsy infant was wrapped in thin white linen, placed on a white silk pillow, and carried high above everyone's head to the *mohel*, who would perform the ceremony. The *mohel* rubbed the baby's gums with cherry wine and placed him on the lap of the *sandek*—a man honored to hold the child. As the baby slept, the *mohel* said a blessing and quickly cut the foreskin. For a few moments the baby cried, but the taste of some sugar soon distracted him. He was cleaned and bandaged, while, out of respect for the human body, one of the minyan buried the foreskin outside. Wine was poured, glasses were raised, and Saul's Hebrew name was pronounced.

"Shlomo, son of Shmuel, you have just tasted pain," the rabbi said. "May you taste also of joy and salvation." He placed his hands on Saul's tiny head. "And may God bless you and keep you faithful unto eternity."

14

A riot of spring flowers filled the fields: orange poppies, red roses, yellow sunflowers, lavender lilacs. Once again there were birds and bees buzzing through Abram's fruit orchards. It was time to prepare for Sonia's wedding. But the czar's newest laws brought problems.

"After our wedding, Theo wants to go to America, Mama." Sarah's heartbeat quickened. "His father says that's where the future is, and his mother's afraid of the new laws."

"Cousin Abram said not to worry. They'll pay bribes like the rest," Sarah said.

"Some say bribes won't work now, because the czar has a railroad to finish."

That evening, Shmuel sat near the fireplace reading Talmud. A worried Sarah had waited all day to talk to him. "Shmuel," she began. He raised a finger to silence her until he'd finished the passage. When he looked up, her voice had a twinge of dread. "Can you imagine? They talked about going to America."

"Who talked?"

"Sonia and Theo."

He glanced back at his book. "Children!" he said. "What do you expect? They're young. They have dreams."

"From dreams like this can come reality." She realized that Shmuel wasn't listening, that he had returned to the pages of his book. "Shmuel!" she insisted. "Please listen!"

This time he closed the book. "Shuraleh," he said, "you worry too much. About things that will never happen."

But tears filled Sarah's eyes as she explained. "Sonia hates Kashkoi. And the Raskinds want to build an empire. They'll all go away, and we'll never see them again."

Shmuel placed his arm around her shoulder. "Shall I talk to them?" he asked, kissing her forehead.

"I don't know." She leaned against his arm. "If they go, I'll miss her. They'll have grandchildren I'll never see."

Shmuel's arm tightened around her. "Of course. It's only natural. But they must build a life together like we did. You have to let go."

She looked in his eyes, and her words came quickly. "If she goes to America, we go too." She clutched her heart. "I'm afraid, Shmuel. Afraid for Joshua, too. I know Cousin Abram's paying bribes, but the laws keep changing. The czar could take him. Sonia could leave. Our family could fall apart if we don't do something."

"Sh, sh," he comforted. "So, we'll go too, if that's what you want. Now dry your eyes and stop crying."

A few nights later, Shmuel decided to see Abram about borrowing money. Perhaps Sarah was right. Besides her fears, every day brought a new ache, and the thought of growing old in Kashkoi upset him. Some days his arms and fingers were so painful and stiff he couldn't use them. If it continued, he wouldn't be able to play the violin. If he couldn't play, he couldn't earn a living. In America he could support his family at other trades.

He opened the front door and followed the path. Suddenly he noticed Maurice Bierkoff hiding behind some trees. As Shmuel crossed the street, Bierkoff said nothing. Shmuel couldn't understand what Bierkoff was doing. He decided then not to go to Abram's house but to the cherry orchard instead.

Before he entered the orchard, he turned and glanced back. Maurice was gone. In his puzzlement, he sat in the orchard to figure it out. It was then he heard two spirited voices in the dark. They spoke in Russian, which frightened him. In the Pale, Jews spoke Yiddish to one another; a man who could not speak Yiddish was an enemy. He parted the leaves, but the men's faces were hidden. He cupped his ears and within seconds knew it was the constable and another man, the same two he'd seen from his bedroom window.

"What is it this time?" a man's voice asked.

"My share has gone up again," the constable said.

"It's always going up," the man said. "But the risks I take go up too."

"That's *your* problem," the constable said. "Your safety is not my concern."

"You don't really care, do you?"

The constable laughed. "Why should I? You make twenty rubles a boy."

"But you'll take half now, which leaves me nothing."

"Business is business."

Shmuel realized he was thirty feet from the *khapper*. He was jubilant and terrified.

As the men bantered, Shmuel tried tracing Bierkoff's familiar owllike profile, tried attaching it to the faceless man hidden by the trees. But the two figures turned and disappeared. Suddenly a twig snapped behind him, and a strong hand clamped Shmuel's mouth. He struggled, but the strength of the aggressor was too much. Shmuel's painful left arm fell useless, and he went limp to the ground.

"Don't speak," a voice whispered. "When I let go don't breathe."

The hand slid from Shmuel's mouth. Staring upward, Shmuel looked into Maurice Bierkoff's eyes. "They're coming back," Bierkoff whispered. "Get down before they see us."

"What are you doing here?" Shmuel asked softly.

"I must find the *khapper*."

"Why? You have girls."

"I have two sons who are dressed like girls. One of them will soon be ten. Sh! Here they come."

The men returned, and those alien voices began again.

"I have two boys for you this month," the familiar voice said. "Theodore Raskind, the son of a rich merchant."

"They've taken him already," the constable said. "They found a book by Dr. Leon Pinsker in his possession. The whole family will be arrested tonight."

Shmuel's body became numb flesh.

"And the other?" the constable asked.

There was silence.

"Tell me, Jew! I haven't got all night."

The voice was low, but Shmuel could still hear the answer. "Joshua Kaminsky."

Bierkoff's glove covered Shmuel's stillborn scream.

"Excellent!" the constable said. "If I get him tonight, your district will have no pogroms."

Suddenly, the constable shifted, and Shmuel thought he would die. There in the moonlight stood his cousin Abram.

He sat in raging anger as the constable and Abram parted. Then he leaped to follow, to rip Abram's throat with his bare hands. But Bierkoff grabbed and held him.

"Go home first," Bierkoff said. "Get your boy out of here. We can deal with Abram later."

Stumbling through the streets, Shmuel raced home. He flung open the door, hit the stove, and toppled some dishes. The crash brought Sarah running from the bedroom. "What's wrong?" she begged. Before she could light a candle, Shmuel told her Joshua's fate. Like Shmuel, she was dumbstruck. But together they acted quickly. They wakened Joshua, explaining as he dressed, and Sarah packed his things. Shmuel took money from the sugar bowl and gave it to him.

"Hide it!" he commanded. "Be careful, but not afraid. There are good and bad wherever you go. To survive, you must know and risk the difference."

The noise wakened the children, and the house was in turmoil.

As Joshua reached for the doorknob, someone pounded outside. Everyone stood frozen as Shmuel's, Sarah's, and Joshua's eyes collided.

"Out the back window," Shmuel whispered. "The midnight train will take you to safety."

With one foot on the window ledge, Joshua kissed his parents. "Write," Sarah cried. "And trust in God."

Joshua was gone, but the pounding outside continued.

A few moments later, Sarah lit a candle and Shmuel

opened the door. Standing on the porch was the angry constable. Behind him were four mounted policemen and a pack of hounds. His eyes bore through them as he made his pronouncement. "By order of the czar, Joshua Kaminsky will report to the army for work on His Imperial Highness's Trans-Siberian Railroad."

"Such an honor," Shmuel said. "How proud he'd be. But he left a few days ago for Kishinev."

"I don't believe you!" the constable yelled. He motioned to his men, pushed Shmuel aside, and entered. "Search!" he ordered. The soldiers opened doors and closets, slashed pillows and mattresses. In a few minutes the house was a shambles. "We'll get him," he said. His eyes narrowed. Sarah trembled. "My soldiers and dogs will track him down."

Joshua scrambled up a hill, praying to God for guidance. The cold night air made his lungs ache. He was frightened, disoriented, unsure in the darkness. Brambles snagged his clothes. His boots kept slipping in mud and slime. Out of breath, he paused to look below. Five swaying lights and a host of howling dogs were heading toward him. There was no time to rest; he gripped his things and ran for the pond. If he waded through water, he might throw the dogs from his scent. He listened for the train whistle, but there was only silence. His legs ached, and he kept coming back to the beginning. Why was this happening? He had committed no crime. Yet he was being hunted like an animal. If they caught him, he'd be sent to the czar's army for twenty-five years, isolated from his family, and converted to Christianity. Why? Because he was a Jew? Again, he looked below. Five swaying lanterns drew larger, nearer, and more ominous. He swallowed the bitterness that sprang from his belly, then ran for the pond.

* * *

Sarah's thoughts were a jumble. Joshua. Hunted by the czar's soldiers. A child whose fate was now in God's hands. And what about Sonia? When she would learn in the morning of Theo's abduction, how her heart would harden. Then there was Abram, may God strike him dead. And her babies, crying and terrified at the commotion. She rocked Saul while Shmuel soothed Anya. Both prayed the night would pass and Joshua would find safety.

Joshua's eyes played tricks on him. Two lanterns went left, three went right, and he knew instantly the soldiers had split up. His heart pounded as he turned and ran for the pond. His chest heaved; pain lodged in his legs, crept up his buttocks, and bored through the small of his back, where his spine worked to keep him together. He was terrified, conjuring comforting images: his father's eagle eyes, the smell of his mother's long hair, the sound of Anya giggling in the morning as he tickled her toes, Saul, his room, the night when the book on Zionism had given his life new meaning. And Sonia and Theo. The sound of Mama's voice and Papa's violin. Papa's violin. God.

With the dogs howling, the constable and two of his soldiers continued up the steep slope. "He's here," the constable shouted. "Listen to the dogs." He cracked his whip against his horse's hide and pushed the others onward. Near the hill's crest, the horses were panting, white with sweat; the dogs howled their confusion. The constable stopped suddenly, cracked his rifle, and motioned the others upward. As two soldiers reached the hilltop, one horse stumbled and fell downhill with its rider.

*   *   *

Crouching low, Joshua felt the night leering at him. There were primitive forces, the darkest, weakest parts of his nature emerging. The frightened child saw death, heard a wolf cry. Trees with long, ominous arms and giant claws leaped to rip out his throat. This meadow, once a constant companion and source of joy, now talked only of fear. Suddenly, a gun glinted. Voices carried on the wind, and his eyes gathered the darkness. With his muscles on fire, with deep pain biting holes in his legs, he felt something grip his shoulder. A single cold hand, with the strength of an ox.

Two shots rang out across the valley. They ricocheted from rock to hill, from earth to sky, from house to house, piercing the membranes of Sarah's skull. She felt her ears burst as her screams filled the house. Shmuel thought she would go crazy.

"They've killed him!" she screamed. "They've killed my son!"

15

In the haunting hours before dawn, Shmuel comforted Sarah. Since the gunshots, she had not stopped weeping and trembling in his arms. He was so lost in easing her pain, in murderous visions of Abram, he couldn't feel his own agony or hear a tapping at his door. But the noise grew persistently louder until it claimed his ears, and he finally answered. Sarah trailed behind, clinging to him in the darkness.

Passing the hearth, Shmuel grabbed the poker and with a deep breath tightened his fingers around it. Cautiously, he lifted the latch, hearing his heartbeat as it came undone. Suddenly the door burst open, and a figure rushed in. With the poker poised to strike, Shmuel stood face-to-face with the village priest.

"I can only stay a moment," the priest said, closing the door. The poker came down, and Shmuel was lost in the black robe, the headpiece and flowing black veil, the frightening cross that gleamed from the prelate's neck. "Your son is safe."

Shmuel grabbed Sarah as her knees gave way and helped her to a chair. "But the gunshots . . ."

"A soldier's horse fell and had to be destroyed. I hid your boy in the rectory until the next train."

Sarah and Shmuel stared at each other.

"So you must wonder," he said. "But not all of us accept the government's ideas. Besides, I consider you a personal friend, Mr. Kaminsky. Many times you played your violin in the meadow and your boy came to fetch you. It gave me great joy." His hand touched his heart. "I did what I had to."

Shmuel had no words. A sworn enemy stood before him. A hatred learned at his father's knee now mingled with gratitude and shame. "You've given us back our lives, sir. Is there a favor I can grant in return?"

The two men stared into each other's eyes, and a thousand years of hatred melted like rock in the heat of a volcano. "There is something," the priest said. "Play your music again, in the meadow. And send word when you hear from your son." Then he opened the door and left.

Joshua heard the whistle, the rumble of steel. He saw the glowing headlight bear down. He stood where the priest had said the tracks would switch and waited for the train to slow. As the steam cleared, he leaped on the last car and hid in an empty compartment.

At the border, his hands stopped shaking, and he left his hiding place. In the third car, he sat beside an elegant gentleman. The man, in his thirties, was slim with a black mustache, a full-grown beard as black as coal, and dark eyes that reached deep into Joshua's soul. Dressed in a white silk shirt and a suit of dark blue broadcloth, he wore a fur-lined Tyrolean cape across his shoulders and a black Persian lamb hat. He smiled as Joshua sat down. "Traveling alone?" he asked in Russian.

"Yes," Joshua said, avoiding his gaze.

"And where are you coming from?"

"Odessa," Joshua said.

"And where are you going?"

Joshua couldn't answer. Where indeed was he going? "To Vienna," he said arrogantly.

The man smiled. "And so am I. We'll travel together."

When the sun rose in Kashkoi the next morning, there were horror stories everywhere. Besides Theodore, several sons had been *khapped* and the Raskind family jailed and denounced. Shmuel and Bierkoff met that afternoon to make plans for Abram. First they burned his fruit orchard. Then they took turns spying at his window. When they knew whose sons would be taken, they sent anonymous messages so the boys could flee. The constable grew suspicious of Abram. On an anonymous tip, the constable searched Abram's house and arrested him. Shmuel and Bierkoff had planted Dr. Pinsker's book in the house. Though Abram swore innocence, he was taken away in chains. It was left for

Golde to sell their possessions and move to her family in Warsaw.

With Theo gone, Sonia ranted and raved for months. Sarah could do nothing to comfort her. Then a letter came from her cousin Chaim which led to a discussion with Shmuel. "When Sonia recovers, we'll send her to Chaim in America."

"What are you talking?" Shmuel shouted. "Sonia needs us. Can't you see how miserable she is?"

Sarah took his shoulders. "We can't continue this way, Shmuel. We starve, we live in terror. We work like pack animals with no future. I'm crazy with fear for Saul. How long before he becomes fodder for the czar? In America, Sonia can work. She'll send money, and we'll follow."

It was difficult for Shmuel to admit Sarah was right. He was depressed, agonizing over what he couldn't correct. Finally he told Sarah he'd think about it.

A month later there was a letter from Joshua.

September 10, 1896

Dearest Family,

Arrived safely in Vienna and the city is beautiful. So many different people—Germans, Italians, Hungarians, all living in harmony. On the train I met a gentleman named Theodore Herzl. He helped me find work as a dishwasher and a place to live. I believe he's going to change Jewish history. I'll be traveling to meet him next August in Basel, Switzerland, where he's organizing a congress of Jews who are seeking solutions to our suffering. Kiss everyone and please don't worry.

All my love, Joshua

For the next six months Sarah prodded Sonia. "Papa and I think you should sell your ring and go . . . to America."

"Mama!" Sonia cried. "What are you saying?"

"I'm saying that as the eldest, you have responsibilities."

Sonia flung herself on the bed, hit the mattress with her fist in a fit of pique. "Stop it, Mama! You're not making sense."

Sarah sat beside her and stroked her hair. "Every day the czar makes new laws, Sonia. The people are frightened. How long before another pogrom? You're a grown woman. You can go to America, to Chicago. My cousin Chaim will help you find work. Whatever you save from your pay you can send us. Oh, Sonia, I beg you. Only God knows what will happen if we stay. They'll take Saul," she said, spitting three times to ward off the evil eye. "I couldn't take it again."

For days Sonia thought. Maybe her mother was right. Maybe America *was* the answer. All the letters from Chaim said the streets were paved with gold. If that was true, she might find a rich husband. Someone to give her a good life. The security of money was all that counted. And one night, after ironing all day, after Sarah had served a thin, meatless borscht for supper and her stomach screamed with hunger and the children cried and her father's shoulders drooped with terrible burdens, she made the decision to go.

16

The new czar, Nicholas II, began his reign denying all constitutional rights. At his winter palace, he said, ". . . I shall guard the principle of autocracy as firmly and uncompromisingly as it was guarded by my never-to-be-forgotten deceased parent." All Russia shook. Shmuel knew terrible times were at hand. Whenever a czar stifled dissent, the Gentiles turned their anger toward the Jews.

From Bierkoff, who frequently traveled to Moscow and Kiev, the village learned that synagogues and schools would be boarded up and sold to the highest bidder unless they were converted into charitable institutions. Prominent Jews tried to save their most holy shrines by turning them into hospitals and orphan asylums. But the czar's ministers found them unacceptable, and the shrines were destroyed. Then one day Bierkoff was arrested in Moscow and beaten for looking "Semitic." Fortunately, he had the proper papers and, after a month at hard labor, he was released. But other Jews were not so lucky. Signs were posted everywhere, announcing that anyone who captured a Jew without papers would be rewarded. New laws of residence prohibited travel from shtetl to shtetl. Thus a man doing business in Kishinev returned to Kashkoi to find himself taxed as a new arrival. Sometimes he was forced from his home, leaving his family destitute.

During the time Bierkoff was jailed, Shmuel and Sarah helped Rachel with the children. Sarah invited them for Sabbath dinner, and it was Sonia who noticed Rachel's comb.

"It looks just like yours, Mama."

After dinner, when Shmuel walked her home, Rachel said, "Sarah likes this comb I'm wearing. Maurice bought it in a little town near Odessa. I could ask him to buy her one." It was then Shmuel told her of Anya's birth, and of Marishka's sacrifice. From that moment on, Rachel never wore the comb again. A week later, she and her husband were reunited.

In May 1897, Sonia stood at the railway station in the town of Drosk, ready to leave for America. Speaking fluent Russian, she passed as a Gentile. When she arrived in Hamburg, Germany, she sold her pearl and diamond ring and, using half the money, purchased a second-class steamship ticket, which allowed a more privileged trip and easy entry into the United States.

The morning she left, Shmuel hitched Kasha to the carriage and tossed her small suitcase in the rear. Sarah looked determined as they said good-bye. "You'll settle in, Sonia. You'll find work, save, and, in a little while, we can join you." Sarah felt awful. Her firstborn child was leaving, and all she could do was urge and inspire when she wanted to hug her. "Think of how happy we'll be when we're together. Always remember. What happened to Joshua must never happen to Saul." Sarah tried not to look in her daughter's eyes. She knew if she did she'd break in a thousand pieces. "Now here's a present."

Sonia took the box Sarah had given her and opened it. In the palm of her hand were the last two pearls from Sarah's elegant necklace, made into earrings. Sonia closed her fist around them and began to cry. She knew Sarah had kept them through meager meals, through the coldest of winters, and she was deeply touched. She put them on her ears, hugged her mother, and climbed into the carriage.

17

Sonia was relieved to find Cousin Chaim waiting at the train station. The trip had been exhausting, and, though accommodations had been decent, the sea had been unfriendly. Her short stay in New York City had been equally unfriendly, and she was glad to see a sign that said, HELLO, SONIA KAMINSKY.

Though she was not inclined to affection, she welcomed her cousin's light hug and followed his clicking heels through the noisy crowd.

"So, Sonia, you had a good trip?"

"Very nice, Cousin," she said, in her best Yiddish. He was small, with bushy eyebrows and boundless energy. His thin mouth smelled of licorice.

"You didn't get seasick?" he asked.

"Just a little," she replied.

"How're your papa and mama?"

"Very well, thank you."

Chaim claimed her tapestry bag from the porter, and they entered the street. A blinding sun made her eyes water, and the moment she saw the city it repelled her. She hated the heat, the tall, ugly buildings, the crowds, the stink, the noise. She felt as though a million people were pushing against her, men in their derby hats, high starched white collars tightly binding their necks, smoking smelly cigars which made her cough, and the haughty women, in their straw hats and colored ribbons, with the hems of their long skirts sweeping the filthy streets.

They waited on a corner before taking the yellow-and-red streetcar which Chaim called the "Jit," and after a jostling fifteen-minute ride they took another streetcar. Half an hour later they were in front of a four-story, ivy-covered, red-brick mansion standing on a tree-lined street, one mile from Lake Michigan.

"Here is where you'll work," Chaim told her.

Sonia looked at the mansion. "I don't understand," she said. "Papa said it would be a factory."

He took her luggage to the front door. "A maid's job, Sonia. All I could find. It's not fancy, but you'll eat well and make a few pennies to send home."

Chaim removed his hat and rang the bell. Sonia's heart leaped to her throat. She'd never had a job before, and she was frightened. Who were these people? What would she be asked to do? Then the front door opened, and a white-haired lady in a high-necked long blue dress and starched white apron invited them in. Chaim coaxed Sonia inside, dropped her bag on the floor, and hugged her. "See you in a week," he said, and left.

Sonia followed the white-haired lady up one side of a double staircase, past a library and an art gallery with hand-carved woodwork and black-and-white marble floors, to the fourth-floor attic, where she found a cubbyhole with a bed, a dresser, and a sunny window.

"This is your room," the woman said. Her voice was squeaky, chalk on a blackboard. "I'm the housekeeper, and you'll call me Fitz, which is short for Fitzsimmons. Mrs. Cohen and her son are your employers. Now, sit over here so I can check for lice." Sonia sat by the window as Fitz checked her hair. "Six and a half days you'll do as you're told," Fitz said. "On your half day off you'll act like a lady or go out on your ear. Any questions?"

"What kind of work will I be doing?"

Fitz laughed. "Why you'll be the queen of Chicago, darlin'."

Fitz closed the door, and Sonia lay down and cried. Though Chaim had been sweet, she felt alone. So many sacrifices made, and for what? To work as a servant? She missed her family. Then Sarah's last words rang in her ears. She thought of Kashkoi, of straw mattresses and spring mud, of Cossacks on horseback, of the work just to keep dust off the table, of the constant hunger and fight to stay alive. At least in Chicago she would be safe, she would be paid for her work, and maybe she could rescue her family.

In a few days, she settled in and found the work easy. On her days off there was theater on Wabash Avenue or concerts at the Chicago Opera House. Foreigners arrived daily, all looking for jobs and a new beginning. Some went west for farmland, while others like her found work as servants or in factories and stockyards. Austrians, Poles, Croats, Slavs, Italians, Hungarians, Africans, an enclave of Russian Jews, which she avoided.

She tasted new and forbidden foods: Greek, Italian, French, spicy sausages that would have made her parents die. She even worked on the Sabbath, and God didn't strike her dead. She went to Lincoln Park on Sundays, read newspapers which reported that Italians didn't bother to learn English because they were lazy and should all go to Florida or California, where they'd be more comfortable picking oranges. That Germans beat their children and used their wives as they did farm animals, and that their music was an abomination. That the Irish drank too much and the Jews were stealing jobs and working on Sundays, when everyone knew Sunday was the Sabbath. That Negroes were coming North to seek freedom from southern lynchings and slavery and were all filled with voodoo religion and it was too bad if they couldn't hack it in the big windy city. Whose fault was it that they were ignorant and often turned to vice? All these new ideas filled her ears as the crowds of immigrants grew bigger and bigger: "coons," the rich called them. "Hunkies, dagos, kikes, Polacks"—all of them mindless, worthless, all looking for the elusive American dream, which everyone knew immigrants were too dumb to find.

It was Sonia's second month at the mansion when she met her employer's son, Charles Cohen. On that day, Mrs. Cohen entered the kitchen in a huff. She explained that Charles had returned from a trip and was sick in bed with a cold. She wanted a breakfast tray arranged and sent to his room.

Mrs. Cohen was a tiny woman, generously endowed of bosom, with a small waist and slim ankles. She had poufy brown hair, a powder-dusted face, and red Kewpie-doll lips. But her black eyes were piercing and alive. Against the whiteness of her skin, her nostrils flared into tiny dark holes. At one glance Sonia knew her black wool skirt and silk blouse had come from Paris. As she spoke, she flourished a platinum and diamond-studded lorgnette, studying Sonia as if she was seeing her for the first time.

"A soft-boiled egg, dear. Some dry toast and weak tea for Charles." Then she muttered something and left.

When the food was ready, Fitz arranged the tray with flowers and told a nervous Sonia to take it to Mr. Charles's room.

Dressed in a long, light gray cotton dress with a starched white apron and cap, Sonia carried the tray to the first floor. She set the tray on a belter table outside the room and knocked on Charles's door. When she entered, he was sitting in a huge Victorian bed, dressed in a silk nightshirt and reading a newspaper.

"Put it over here," he said, indicating a place across his thighs. He never looked up from his newspaper.

"Another pillow," he ordered, gesturing behind his back.

As Sonia placed the tray on his lap and fixed a pillow behind him, she noted his flabby face, a small double chin, and a mustache of thick black hair above well-defined lips. But his brown eyes were filled with energy and were as piercing as his mother's. Suddenly, he looked up, and his features softened.

"You're new," he said, setting his paper down.

She nodded, wondered if she should curtsy.

"What's your name?"

"Sonia. Sonia Kaminsky."

His stare made her self-conscious. "Turn," he said, circling with his finger. She did as she was told. "Now pour the tea."

That's when everything went wrong. She was so nervous, the tea spilled everywhere, and Sonia began to cry.

"There, there," he comforted. He got out of bed and put on a robe. "It's all right."

"I'm so sorry," Sonia said. "Fitz will kill me."

"Don't worry about Fitz," he told her. "Just change the sheets and forget it."

Sonia's workdays were generally the same. She polished fruitwoods, black-and-white marble floors, gilt chairs. She swept cashmere carpets, dusted famous paintings. Then one day she was summoned to the basement, where she discovered another world.

"Come in," Mrs. Cohen said. "And close the door."

Sonia entered an aviary. She was enthralled and delighted. In all her life she'd never seen anything like it. A heat-controlled indoor garden filled with splendid canaries and tiny finches, most of which flew free. She was nearly speechless.

"I must leave for a few days," Mrs. Cohen said, without looking at her. "And I need some help. If this canary doesn't eat, it's going to die. Do you think you can feed it while I'm gone? I'll show you how."

Sonia peered into a wooden box and saw a tiny ball of moist yellow feathers, sadly wasting away in a nest of white cotton. She shared her own experiences, her own remedy of bread-soaked milk.

Mrs. Cohen lifted her lorgnette and paused to examine Sonia's face. Then she headed for the door. "Don't stand there, young lady," she said. "If you know how to help him, do it!"

Sonia took over, and in a few days the bird was breathing easier. Two weeks later it was singing.

Because of this success, Mrs. Cohen frequently called on Sonia. But Fitz became jealous. When Mrs. Cohen was away, Fitz would find fault with Sonia's work. Then Charles would come to her aid and make Fitz angrier. He'd place his hand over Sonia's when she'd spill or drop things. Fitz, noticing this, told Sonia that Charles was a womanizer, but Sonia wouldn't listen. Charles's affection for her soon began to blossom. That made Fitz enraged. Charles would excuse Sonia from certain duties. She'd find small gifts of perfume or lace hankies beneath her pillow. And it soon became clear. Though she didn't care for him romantically, one day she could be the mistress of this house.

18

Joshua took his seat in the great Basel Casino. He was dressed like the rest, in formal attire, loaned to him by a friend. This was Herzl's idea. He was a journalist and knew the international press would be there in droves. He wanted the first Jewish congress to look like a distinguished parliament to the rest of the world.

Above Joshua's head, a great balcony ringed the hall. One hundred ninety-seven delegates, mostly scholars, rabbis, intellectuals—the cream of world Jewry—gathering for the first time since the dispersion. The Orthodox Jews thought that Herzl was crazy, that by searching for a homeland he was trying to do God's work. Those who believed they had safely assimilated into European societies openly criticized and condemned him. But still they came, and Joshua swelled with pride. Someone banged the gavel on the podium, and the noisy hall came to order. Then a rabbi recited a prayer.

Black-bearded Herzl took the stand. He looked striking, mysterious, authoritative, Joshua thought, just as he had the day they'd met on the train. His voice was mesmerizing as he addressed the vast array of people, thanking them for coming. Then he acknowledged the presence of some non-Jews, diplomats whose governments had sent them to "see what those damn Jews were up to."

He shared his plans and ideas. He told of his experience in Paris and how the Dreyfus affair had shocked and hardened him. A single Jew, accused and convicted of an act of treason, for which he was later exonerated, and a whole country cried, "Death to *all* Jews." In such an enlightened country, he had not thought it possible. It proved to him, he explained, that no matter how modern a society was, no matter how educated, Jewish hatred in Europe was like a coiled snake ready to sink poisonous fangs. Then he unfurled a flag, and the screaming began. Even Joshua was shocked at his boldness, but it showed how deeply Herzl was committed to his idea. The flag was white, edged with blue stripes, like a tallis. Inside was a Star of David. Speeches began. Fighting. Debates. They disagreed on everything but the need for a homeland.

"Assimilation is not an answer!" a delegate shouted. "Anti-Semitism has reached new heights in Russia."

"Temporary," a small voice cried. "As the czar fixes things, the problems will go away."

"It is said there is a time for silence," someone shouted. "And a time to speak."

"It is also said," another man shouted out, "that the tallest sunflower is cut before the rest."

An angry man leaped to his feet. "Wake up, everyone. That kind of thinking has kept us in chains for centuries."

On and on they argued for nearly three days, and Joshua was exhilarated. From then on his destiny was clear.

KASHKOI

The second letter they received from Joshua was read when the dinner table was cleared. Sarah had been carrying it all day long in her pocket, where it had stayed warm, splattered by a bit of chicken fat, which seeped through her apron. Its postmark was Switzerland. And it was thick with news.

"Open already!" Shmuel cried. "It'll grow cobwebs."

Anya sat by the hearth near Shmuel. Saul sat in Papa's lap while Sarah read.

Dear Family,

I am in good health and hope you are too. Of course I miss you. Only a son torn from his family's bosom can know how I feel. Sometimes I think I'll never see you again, but I still see your faces above the Sabbath candles.

The world I'm in is intriguing, filled with exciting people and ideas. Across Europe, Doctor Pinsker's book has created a furor, and everyone agrees: we'll never be safe without a homeland. As long as we live under someone else's rule we dance to the tune of slavery and death. Gentiles don't want us in their countries and we Jews will not disappear. So I'm going to Palestine.

Then he explained what had happened.

Several months after Joshua's letter, one came from Sonia. A letter from America was like gold, and Sarah called the neighbors to join them when they read it.

December 20, 1897

Dear Mama and Papa,

I miss you very much and hope you are well. Life in America is interesting, and I'm safe, living in a beautiful house. I work as a maid for people who own a clothing factory. At night I go to school to learn better English. The mistress of the house

*seems to like me because she raises birds and I help
her with them. They bring back memories of home
and how much I miss you. Here's a dollar I've
saved. I'll send more when I'm able.*

Love, Sonia

Every month Sonia and Joshua would write letters.
Each would enclose money, which Sarah hid in the
sugar bowl. Every week Sarah would count it to see
what she'd saved, but too many times she used the
money to feed her family. After a while she despaired
they'd ever have enough to leave.

Still, they went to synagogue, celebrated holidays,
and clung together in hope.

Little Anya grew by leaps and bounds. She loved
bathing in the streams where the women washed their
clothes or waiting for the sun to rise. She'd wrap herself
in a blanket and sit on the porch finding comfort as the
light cracked the horizon. Then she'd dress, march to
the chicken coop to scoop fresh eggs for her mother,
talk to Kasha, and reassure the cow that Papa would
milk her. Sarah had invented a romantic tale about the
day Anya was born and about the woman, Marishka,
who had been kind enough to help them. Anya loved
to hear the story. And she learned easily, everything
that came her way: cooking and sewing from Sarah,
Russian and English from Shmuel.

Anya had mischievous little ways, which included the
audacity to test God. She'd commit little sins, like
touching money on the Sabbath or fashioning squares
out of the soft melted wax of the Sabbath candles. God
never punished her, and this made her love Him more.
On Sundays she'd put on Sarah's long dresses, tinting
her cheeks and lips with beet juice, and sing and dance.
During the week she'd stand outside the window where

Shmuel was teaching violin or language and howl like a ghost. It would frighten the male students and make Shmuel angry. He'd shoot her a reproving glance, make a stern gesture, and she'd run like a colt. Then at dinnertime a smile would slip across his lips, and he'd suddenly burst out laughing.

Of all Sarah's children, Anya loved the holidays most. She was curious; she asked questions and questioned answers and questioned the answers again. Some Sunday mornings she'd hide in a tree and stare at the white church on the hill, fascinated by the priest in his flowing black robe, his black hat, and long veil, and the people inside, and she'd wonder why the God they worshiped hung on a cross. Most of all she wondered why their God had a face and a body when her God had none.

19

PALESTINE   MAY 18, 1900

Joshua, Herzl, and a contingent of men traveled to see the fruits of their labor. They visited the first sponsored immigrants who had gone to settle the land since the congress had assembled. Their journey had been long and difficult, and the sun was scorching. But what they found when they arrived made it worthwhile. Men, women, children dressed in shorts and hats, with kerchiefs wound around their sweating necks, all working the soil with their bare hands, pulling rocks and boulders from the ground and planting tree seedlings.

It was just as Herzl had envisioned: small houses, vegetation, and green grass were replacing useless sand dunes.

Though they had no equipment, little water, and no supplies, though mosquitoes sucked their blood and malaria lurked everywhere, there was hope and spirit, possibilities for a future. Industry, agriculture, freedom from want, fear, worry, a chance for their children to experience a real life. And Joshua knew he would fight and die for it.

KASHKOI

It had rained for ten days, and Anya and Saul sat near the window, where Saul handed Anya the Book of Masada, indicating she should read it to him for the thousandth time. Happy to please the slowly developing child, she began.

"Once upon a time," she said, "there was. a place called Masada. It was built by a wicked king named Herod and stood deserted on a mountain in the hills of Judea. After Jerusalem had been conquered by the terrible Roman soldiers, a brave man name Eleazar gathered a group of Jews who loved God so much they would not give up their belief in Him or in their freedom either.

"They went to Masada, where they lived and fought the Roman soldiers for three years. At the end of the third year, the soldiers were close to the top, and Eleazar called his people together. He told them he'd rather die than be a Roman slave or give up his love for God. Then he asked each man to decide. Did he want to be captured and live under Roman rule? or die with him at Masada? They all agreed with Eleazar and made plans to commit suicide." Anya explained what suicide was, then went on with the story. "Now, Eleazar and *all* the people of Masada are in Heaven with God."

"Tell me 'bout 'No and the Ork,' " Saul said to Anya, and she hugged him for those words.

"Listen, Mama," Anya called to Sarah. "Saul's talking."

The boy took Anya's hand and led her to his bedroom, where he gave her another book of Bible stories. As the rain beat on the house, they sat on the rag fireplace rug where it was warm, reading and turning the pages. The firelight made Anya's hair shine like marmalade on dark toast, and the glow from the coals darkened the pupils of her blue-gray eyes.

"Once upon a time," she began, "God looked down from Heaven and said to Noah"—she deepened her voice—" *'Man is very wicked. He doesn't listen to Me. Only you know or hear My voice. So I'm going to flood the whole earth with rain and only you and your family will not drown.'* "

Saul lay with his blanket, on his left side, sucking his right thumb and twirling a piece of his black hair between two fingers of his left hand. He listened with devotion, occasionally blinking his brown eyes until he was fast asleep.

Anya went to school for a few hours each day, but the rest of the time she spent in Sarah's kitchen, learning how to bake and cook and sew. She had a knack for handling dough, for baking, for cooking, for stitching a fine seam, and Sarah knew she'd make a wonderful mother some day. Besides all this, Anya was blessed with an intelligence born not of books but of common sense and instinct. She understood people, could commiserate with and help them. Sarah especially loved Anya's attention to Saul, whom she now realized would never be as bright as the other boys his age.

20

In the spring of 1902 there was great unrest. Rain. Crop failure. Talk of revolution. Fear spread like wildfire. Poverty increased, and Jews yearned to leave but couldn't get the papers or money to do so. Fifty percent were unable by law to ply their trade. Even leasing land to grow food was now prohibited. Sales of liquor were forbidden, and grain merchants could no longer travel. If a Jewish parent was lucky enough to find a school to accept his child, he had to pay tuition for a Christian child as well. Jewish consumptives were barred from all hospitals and put into jails. In Kiev, Jews were hunted by police dogs. To pay for this special service, the Russian government double-taxed all kosher meat.

At a drunken festival, Jewish homes and small stores in Nicholayev were destroyed. A thousand Christians waited in wagons to carry off Jewish property. When they found none, they destroyed the Jewish cemetery. In Vilna, a servant girl accused a Jewish barber of trying to take her blood to bake his matzoh. They threw him in prison for four months. With virulent support from Russian newspapers whose caricatures and stories portrayed Jews as human garbage, with help from local governments who wished to divert attention from Russia's real problems, with the churches preaching and the public schools teaching anti-Semitism, the czar achieved his purpose. Afraid of a revolution, he had shifted the spotlight from his inability to govern and paved the way for the worst wave of pogroms ever to hit Russia.

It was Passover, and the sun was setting. Shmuel left the synagogue wondering if he should consult the midwife about Sarah's failing health or maybe take her to a doctor. Though the children's letters cheered her, she was depressed. She'd lost a great deal of weight in the last year, and after Saul's birth she'd accused Shmuel of not loving her anymore, of not wanting her in the way a husband should want his wife. He'd explained things, but his explaining didn't satisfy her.

As he walked beside Maurice and Rachel Bierkoff, he grew silent, listening to every rock that crunched beneath his boots. What could he do? Joshua was gone. Sonia was gone. Something was wrong with his beloved wife, and he was unable to help her. He felt guilty, a failure. Perhaps if he'd been able to earn money, they could have left this place and their family would still be together.

Lost in his thoughts, he did not see the danger until it was upon him: In the near distance, the familiar mushroom cloud appeared beneath the glow of flaming torches. Bierkoff screamed first. *"Run! Run! Pogrom!"* He pulled Rachel's arm as people streamed from the synagogue and ran for cover. From the corner of his eye, Shmuel saw Anya and Saul skipping to meet him. His heart stood still.

"Good *Shabbos*, Papa."

Shmuel knew he could never reach them in time. Behind him, a Cossack and his sword were fast approaching. So he stopped and screamed. *"No! Anya.*

Go back! Take your brother and hide!" Instantly
Anya snatched Saul's arm and ran toward a covered
barrel. She lifted the top and pushed Saul inside.
Crouched behind, she watched the Cossacks plow
through the screaming crowd. They sliced Bierkoff's
finger with its gold wedding ring, ripped Rachel's earrings from her earlobes. One chased an old woman
creeping beneath a cart and drove his sword through
her neck. The force was so great he could not remove the saber from the ground. Rocks shattered glass.
Then the fires began. All along Anya kept trying to
calm Saul.

"Please, Anya. Out! Out!" he cried.

She slapped the barrel and warned him to be quiet.

Then Anya saw her father. He was lying on the
ground beneath a burly lieutenant astride a black stallion. Shmuel was cowering, begging for mercy. The
Cossack's horse reared, and a saber sliced the skin of
Shmuel's arm.

Anya watched in horror, praying to God for a miracle. As the Cossack's sword raised again, a young
Christian lad covered Shmuel with his own body.

"Aside, Sasha!" the Cossack ordered. "Move away!"

"Enough! Andre Andreivitch," the youth said. "The
man's done nothing."

The Cossack laughed. "I have orders, Sasha. In the
name of Czar Nicholas—I demand you—"

Someone shouted the Cossack's name. He looked
from Shmuel to Sasha, who was still protecting him,
then to the summoning voice. Deciding, he burrowed
his spurs into the horse's sides and galloped away. Before Shmuel could thank him, the blond youth was
gone, but Anya never forgot his face.

Because of the pogrom, Anya was plagued with nightmares. Death lurked everywhere. It floated in the

streams. It stalked her in the tall grass. It hid behind every door. She smelled burning flesh, saw blood, heard Saul's cries coming from the barrel. And even though Papa had said "out of pain always comes good," she was confused. She could not understand the Christians. She could not understand why some Jews had been spared and others not. What was death? she wondered. Who was chosen? And where was God?

21

For days after the pogrom, an already troubled Sarah couldn't think straight. She stayed indoors, kept candles burning, and kept Saul close to her side. She was obsessed with Saul's safety and swore the czar would never lay a hand on him. She cursed the world, stopping short of cursing God. She thought of Anya, Joshua, and Sonia. Then she took to bed. She didn't eat, couldn't sleep, and spoke to no one until the Sabbath came and she had to shop. She met Rachel Bierkoff in the marketplace and learned that her son's foot had been slashed by a Cossack's saber. Rachel seemed strangely happy. "Don't worry," she said. "The czar, may he rot in Hell, did me a favor."

"What do you mean?" Sarah asked.

"With such an injury, he'll be excused from the czar's army. Thank God it happened now, while he's young and can mend easy."

As Sarah left the marketplace, a strange peace came over her. In the madness of Rachel's words lay the answer to Sarah's own nightmares. When she realized the power of her decision, she smiled. All she needed was courage and the right setting. It would happen, she knew. Very soon.

"Come, Saul. We'll go on a picnic, just you and me."

Saul clapped his hands. It had rained for two days, and he'd had to stay inside the dreary house. Since the pogrom he hated closed places. Sarah sang as she packed a lunch of Saul's favorite foods: a blintze with jam, a roll with butter, candy. But she took other things as well.

"Come, *yinghele*," she called, running toward the meadow. "We'll pick flowers and catch butterflies." Saul's innocent laughter caught on a breeze.

The boy ran through the field, scattering birds, happy in the open spaces, as Sarah's thoughts were growing darker and darker.

"Here's a place," she said, stopping at a rock where a gathering of trees wept their leaves to the ground.

Saul scampered after a butterfly. His shiny black hair flew behind; his outstretched hand sought the butterfly but snatched at air. Disgusted, he stomped his foot on the ground.

"You'll find another one," Sarah called.

With every beat of her heart Sarah hardened like stone.

It was now or never. No turning back. A shudder of revulsion ran through her as Saul hugged her. Courage, she thought. It's for his own good. He'll understand. He'll be happier when it's over. She stuffed Saul with preserves. With sweets. Then a butterfly flew past, and as Saul reached and caught it, she called his name.

"I got it, Mama. It's twinkling in my hand," he said.

"Bring it, *yinghele*," Sarah called. "Lay your hand on the rock and let me see."

Saul ran to share his prize. But as he stretched out his fingers on the rock, Sarah raised a hatchet and brought it swiftly down. Blood spurted everywhere, and their horrible screams made a hideous melody. When she looked at Saul's right hand, three fingers were gone.

In the meadow, Sarah rocked her sobbing, bloody son, feeling glad, thinking how lucky Rachel Bierkoff had been. The Cossacks had done it for her. But to keep her son from the army, Sarah had been forced to maim Saul herself.

"What have you done?" Shmuel cried when Sarah carried Saul home.

"I had to," Sarah said, smiling oddly. "Don't you see? Now they can't take him in the army."

"I see that you're crazy!" Shmuel screamed. He flung his hand against Sarah's cheek, threw her to the ground, and kicked her. Welts raised on her hip; black and blue marked her thigh. But Sarah never flinched.

After the incident the children avoided her, and Sarah stayed in her room. Anya did the cooking, baked the *challeh*, and lit the Sabbath candles, while Shmuel sat holding Saul. When Shmuel grew tired, Anya took his place. Soon, the days turned to weeks, and Saul's hand healed. But by doing what she had done, the half-crazed Sarah lost her son, not to the army but to herself. As for Anya, there was another lesson. She had not just the Cossacks to fear but her mother as well.

22

At the Sixth Zionist Congress, Herzl presented a new plan. Joshua, now a tall, handsome youth with black curls and a short black beard, sat listening as new Zionist federations from America, England, and the Pale mounted the platform. The Russian Jews came in droves, and the stories they told were chilling. Joshua knew it was time for his family to leave.

Then new talk centered on settling territories besides Palestine. But few liked the idea. Clarifying his aims, Herzl explained how he'd sought help from the kaiser, a friend of the sultan of Turkey. But William II wavered from one day to the next, and the sultan opposed Herzl's plan. Then Herzl offered the Turkish sultan, ruler of the Ottoman Empire, a good deal of money, and the sultan's opposition faltered. With this encouragement, Herzl went begging money from wealthy Jews, but most refused to help. Then the English government proposed a homeland in British East Africa, a place called Uganda, and Herzl placed the question for discussion.

"Traitor!" they screamed.

Joshua was disgusted. No one appreciated how hard Herzl worked, or how physically ill he was.

"How can there be Zionism without Zion?" they screamed.

The English offered Cyprus.

"They only want us there to protect the Suez Canal."

Herzl tried to make the delegates understand that any home, no matter how temporary, was better than no home at all, but the youth of Russia had had a bellyful. They were sick of pogroms. They wanted a home. They wanted *Eretz Yisroel*, the land God had given.

CHICAGO, ILLINOIS

When Sonia received the letter from Shmuel, she was upset for weeks. Many had died in the Kashkoi pogrom, many had been injured. All the money Sonia had worked for and sent to her family had been stolen. Sonia feared she'd never see her mother again. And what Sarah had done to Saul made her ill. Her mother was going mad, and she had to do something. She sent a note of deep regret and enclosed all her money.

Three weeks later, Mrs. Cohen died of heart failure. The entire household was in chaos. Charles sat paralyzed in his room, which gave Fitz more control. That made Sonia crazy. After sitting *shivah* for seven days of mourning, Charles went to Sonia's room and talked for hours. Then it became a habit. When Sonia finished work, she'd find him sitting on her bed clutching his mother's belongings: a book, a scarf, her lorgnette. And it soon became clear. Charles trusted Sonia, leaned on her. He was vulnerable, and she could easily manipulate him. Money. It was all that mattered.

Then Fitz threatened to fire her for someone else's mistake. And the next time Charles came to Sonia's room, she welcomed him with a smile. One year to the date of his mother's death, their wedding took place, and a month later she was pregnant.

Shmuel received Sonia's latest letter and gave it to Sarah, who put on her spectacles and began to read.

> *September 7, 1904*
>
> *Dear Mama and Papa,*
>
> *Charles Cohen and I were married a week ago in a small ceremony here at home and I am now the mistress of a beautiful house. We are going on a honeymoon just as soon as the Christmas season is over; a train to San Francisco, then a boat to a tropical island called Hawaii, which is in the Pacific Ocean on the other side of the United States. When I return I'll write you everything. Meanwhile, here is our wedding photograph which I hope you like and steamship tickets for passage to America. Come quickly, Mama and Papa, and kiss Saul for me. I miss you all very much.*
>
> *Love, Mrs. Charles Cohen*

Shmuel and Sarah passed the wedding photo from one to the other and thought Sonia looked beautiful in her white suit and veiled hat. They would have been even happier, but their thoughts were elsewhere. Though Sarah was mending, Anya was gravely ill.

Since the pogrom, since Saul's fingers had been severed, thirteen-year-old Anya lay with her once rosy face as ashen as dust. She didn't talk. She didn't laugh. She hardly breathed. When Anya's fever finally caused delirium, Shmuel took her to the only doctor in Dreshevsky, half a day away.

Dr. Bender, an old, wrinkled man with thinning gray hair, large elephantine ears, and thick glasses which magnified his eyes, examined Anya carefully. But he couldn't find a thing wrong. The child was thin and pale, her eyes were listless, and her symptoms were an endless mass of contradictions. He listened to her heart, her pulse, examined her glands, her eyes and ears. He saw her tongue, pushed and prodded everywhere. But when he was through he shook his head and sent Shmuel home. "Give her whatever she wants."

His conclusions were no conclusions, which baffled Shmuel. "How can a person just die from seeing a pogrom?" he asked. He never mentioned what had happened to Saul.

"People die from loneliness, mister. They die from a broken heart." Dr. Bender spoke with his hand cupped over Shmuel's ear so Anya couldn't hear. "By me, mister, she has very little time," he said, patting Shmuel's back. "Be good to her. *Nu*? I'm sorry."

Shmuel cried all the way home. He was angry and hurt; he blamed the czar. Even more, he blamed himself for being weak. He asked God to make her well again, and give him strength. By the time he reached home he'd decided to lie.

"She's going to be fine," he told Sarah. "Dr. Bender says she just needs time."

But Anya continued to linger. And six months later a letter came from Sonia. She had suffered a miscarriage and begged them to all come to America. Sarah sat down and wrote a note to Sonia explaining the reason for their delay.

CHICAGO, ILLINOIS
MAY 1905

Sonia was angry when Sarah's letter came. First it was Joshua. Now, Anya. When would they fill *her* need? She had sacrificed everything, and for what? Her family was still in Kashkoi, trapped because of that miserable little wretch. It was Odessa all over again. And whenever she thought of Anya, it made her blood boil.

"You've spilled the tea again!" Sonia yelled, scolding her new maid. "How many times do I have to tell you?"

The small girl, fresh from Russia, with yellow bangs and newly bobbed hair, was shaking. Tears glittered in her round blue eyes as she tried to wipe up the mess. "I'm sorry, madame," she said. "I'll do better next time."

KASHKOI
JULY 1905

In the dead of night the Kaminskys' front door rattled. Shmuel lit a candle while the others hid in their rooms. When he opened the door, he found a tall young man standing on his porch.

"Joshua?" Shmuel whispered.

"Papa!"

"Quick! Inside. There's a price on your head."

The door locked, and they quickly embraced. They soon parted, and Shmuel's teary eyes caressed his son's body from head to toe. Joshua was tall, nearly six feet one, with broad shoulders and thick, black, curly hair. His brown eyes sparkled with life and danger, and his even white teeth lit up the room. His skin was dark, bronzed by the heat and sun of the Holy Land, and his arms rippled with strength. When Shmuel found his voice, he summoned the family.

Sarah knew him instantly. She ran to Joshua and

wound her arms around his strong back. Her tears fell as her head rested against his chest. It was a long time before she pulled away or said anything. Behind Papa's trousers, Saul hovered. Joshua stooped down.

"Come, Saul, kiss your big brother."

The shy child backed away.

"And where's my Anya?" Joshua asked, standing again. He headed for her bedroom, but Shmuel stopped him.

"She's been sick, Joshua. We don't know what's wrong."

Joshua moved his father's arm and went to the room. He stared at Anya, and couldn't believe his eyes. The last time he'd seen her, she'd been a happy bundle of mischief. Now she was a drenched rag on wet pillow. He leaned to kiss her forehead, lifted her from the bed, and carried her in his arms. "*Katzella*. It's me. Your big brother."

For the first time in ages, Anya actually spoke. "Joshu-a? I missed . . . you."

"What's wrong with her?" Joshua asked. He set Anya near the hearth.

"They don't know," Shmuel said. "She's been like this since the pogrom."

Joshua's fist slammed the table. "You've seen a doctor?"

"Yes," Shmuel said. "We've done everything."

"Then get her out of here."

"We will, son. When she's better."

"No! Do it now!" Joshua said. "That's why I'm here. In a few weeks there'll be a terrible pogrom in Kishinev. The Cossacks will try to wipe it off the face of the earth. Next, is Kashkoi. You must leave, Papa, or they'll kill you all."

After Shmuel promised they would go, the two

talked, endlessly: about Sonia, the Bierkoffs, Abram and Golde, Herzl's funeral, Anya. Finally, the incident with Saul.

"I understand," Joshua said, taking his mother's hands. "It must have been hell for you to make the decision. But you're not the only one to do it. I see it all the time: chopped toes, punctured eardrums, a blinded eye." He kissed his mother's hand. "May God forgive you."

Joshua took Saul's injured hand. He kissed it and looked into the boy's eyes. "Don't hate your mother, Saul. One day you'll understand, and with God's help you'll forgive her."

For the first time since the incident Shmuel grasped the meaning of Sarah's desperate act. Finally, he understood her intentions. She was a mother whose only sin was trying to protect her child. He was so overcome he had to change the subject. "Tell us about the Holy Land."

Joshua's brown eyes caught and reflected the room's light. "It's beautiful beyond belief, Papa. Hard work. But we are determined." He made a fist, then laughed. "Most people don't agree with me, but in a strange way the others have done for us what nature does for animals. With all their hatred over the centuries, they've weeded the weak and left us strong. What we have in Palestine are those who are not so easily intimidated. Believe me, we are shaping our destiny for the first time."

At 4:00 A.M. there was a noise outside the front door and, without a single good-bye, Joshua escaped through the window. Once again he headed in the dark for the rectory, where the priest waited to help him. Once again the soldiers and dogs gave chase. Twenty minutes later gunshots rang out, and Sarah clutched her heart. Then, like a miracle, Anya rose from her place and ran into the streets calling Joshua's name. It was as if she had never been sick a day in her life. But no answer came. Not a word. For hours the family clung together in hope, waiting to hear. At daybreak they found the blood-soaked body in a gutter near the house.

BOOK II

1905~1929

23

It was midnight. They camped in the woods with fifty others, waiting for the smugglers' signal. Shmuel crouched on a carpet of autumn leaves recalling the night of Joshua's visit, remembering the shots, the awful waiting, then the bloody body. Even now it wrenched his heart thinking of what the soldiers had done to the gentle priest, what a price he'd paid for not giving Joshua away. His tongue had been split, his body riddled with bullets. Shmuel could not attend the funeral. A Jew in a Christian cemetery—and a priest's burial at that—would be suspect. Witchcraft, they'd call it. So he paid his respects at nightfall. Then he made the decision to leave.

When Anya's strength returned, Shmuel made inquiries. Proper passports would cost one hundred kopecks each. To gain them, the trip to Drösk meant two silver rubles and bribes to police with the chance of refusal. So Shmuel chose the only way. For half that amount he acquired papers illegally, then all were smuggled by underground railway to the border town of Brody.

Now, at the border, carrying only what they could and with money and tickets sewn into the lining of his coat, Shmuel and the others waited. Bullfrogs croaked to a cricket symphony. In the moonlight, an owl's yellow eyes glared down. For a long time they had been walking, hiding, running, tested to the limits of their endurance. Now they were minutes from freedom. Though Joshua had begged them to go to Palestine, Shmuel had refused. He wanted the end of his days with Sarah and the children to be in a peaceful place.

America.

Suddenly, a distant light. A gust of wind. Gunshots echoing. A planned diversion sixty yards away. That was the signal. Shmuel hoisted Saul on his shoulders and sloshed through the icy stream.

"Run, Sarah, run! Hurry, Anya. Quick!"

The current was strong. Anya helped Sarah as they pushed onward. Then one quick burst of speed into the arms of safety.

Freedom! Freedom! Out of the Pale. No more boundaries, no more restrictions, no more separation from the rest of mankind. Put on your Judaism. Put on the Lord's cloak. Gather the laws in your arm and kiss them. Feel the sweetness of the prayers on your tongue. Hear God's psalms in your ears.

24

The train to Königsberg screamed in the night. Inside, they were packed like sardines, all roasting in a mixture of foul body odor and rancid food. Shmuel's head spun with bells, whistles, voices, the screeching of metal against metal.

At Königsberg, they were separated; men, women,

children herded like cows, as German doctors and nurses screamed, *"Shnell! Schnell!"* pushing them to showers of ice cold water and smelly soap. They were disinfected, for which they paid a fee, then taken to *Diergemacht*, a prisonlike structure. They slept on cold tin floors until two weeks of quarantine had passed, then boarded a train for Hamburg, where members of the German Jewish Society hustled these nineteenth-century embarrassments from their civilized twentieth-century midst.

At the pier the family waited in line, listening to a poor man plead with a ticket taker. He had purchased his steamship tickets on the installment plan, but they were forgeries.

"What is he saying?" the man asked Shmuel in Yiddish. "Every month for two years, I paid."

"Nish git! Not real," Shmuel interpreted.

"Tell him he has to go back," the ticket taker added.

"Dafts aheym gayen," Shmuel interpreted.

The man went crazy. *"Nein! Nein!* I can't go back," he cried. "I have two sons. Please, mister. Pity."

The ticket taker called a guard.

Shmuel bent to Sarah. "I can't stand it," he said. "Look at the first-class people, Sarah. We don't belong. I could change Sonia's fancy tickets, and we could all go steerage. The man's family and us. *Nu*, Shuraleh. One last mitzvah before we leave?"

Sarah didn't think. "Go!" she said, without looking at him. "If you don't, you'll regret it."

Shmuel quickly made the exchange.

The man fell to his knees. "God bless you," he cried.

With their tickets stamped, Shmuel and his family walked toward the busy pier.

As Shmuel searched for their ship, Anya followed behind. The air was clear and windy, and she covered her dark blond curls with a babushka. She took deep breaths of Hamburg air and smiled at the sea gulls, at a family of pigeons strutting across the pier. She looked far out to sea at the tugboats, at small ferries and huge steamers. She listened to the sounds of horns and whistles.

"There it is!" Shmuel suddenly shouted. "Look!"

Anya followed the direction of his finger until she saw it. *Die Kastendam.* A great black whale with a white stripe and three black smokestacks that percolated white smoke. They hurried down the noisy platform with their few possessions.

"So, Sarah, we made it," Shmuel said. "Liberation!"

Sarah was exhausted. "Or a watery grave," she mumbled.

They waited in a long line until the first-class passengers were aboard. Then they walked down a wooden plank into a smelly, windowless room that had a cold metal floor and six-by-two-foot beds, one above the other in tiers of three.

"Here," a steward said, as they passed. He carried a stick and often used it. He handed each a tin cup, a fork, a spoon, a hard pillow, a thin straw and seaweed mattress, and a pail for both washing and eating. Three hundred people filled one compartment with a single bathroom.

"Go left!"

"Go right!"

"Don't you hear good?"

Smack!

Suddenly they heard the departing whistle, and the ship began to move. On the pier, people looked upward, waving hankies and shedding tears. On board, happy faces, crying faces, frightened faces, faces without expression, all wondering about an unknown future.

* * *

From the moment the journey began, Saul came alive. He ran everywhere, talking to strangers, something he'd never done before. He tied a stick to his tunic with a small length of rope, calling himself Eleazar, leader of Masada, exploring places on his own. Long before the pogrom and the incident with Sarah, it had been obvious that Saul was slow. He couldn't speak clearly until he was six. He tripped and often dropped things. He hid from everyone, losing himself in the world of Bible stories. He had no friends and stayed close to home. But on the ship, something had given him confidence.

"You love it here, don't you?" Anya asked, the second day.

"Yes," Saul said. "It's like 'No' and the Ork.' "

When he said that, she understood. The ship had brought his fantasies alive. Noah and the Ark. Eleazar and Masada. The stories he loved to hear.

Anya's top bunk lay beside that of a spirited young woman with wild, black hair and round, brown eyes that slanted downward. She smoked, talked incessantly, and wore lip rouge.

"Sheyna Levy," the girl said in English. She pumped Anya's hand furiously. "How you do?"

Anya replied in Yiddish, and Sheyna corrected her.

"No more Yiddish, Anya. We go to America." And the friendship began.

For days, Sarah had been sick to her stomach with pains in her chest. A tonic Shmuel had purchased for nausea proved nothing more than a worthless concoction sold by a con man. He stayed close to her, hoping the pains were just from excitement.

* * *

Though the smell of vomit, urine, and feces and the sound of human misery filled the steerage compartment, there was joy, too. On deck, a handsome Irishman who had gotten his sea legs played a concertina while his family danced. Others gathered to listen, and in music they were united. Some made friends and talked of a rich life in the New World. High above them, they saw glimpses of that life, as wealthy men and beautiful ladies danced the night away.

On the fourth night Anya couldn't sleep. She walked from the lower deck toward a lifeboat, where she leaned on the ship's rail. The night was cool, and the bulky coat and dark green scarf Sarah had crocheted kept her comfortable. She had never seen such a sight. A shimmering sea with no horizon. A glorious moon. So peaceful. Then a sudden commotion, a shuffle of feet down some stairs, followed by a pleading face staring at hers, a glimpse of the past that brought instant recognition. She felt confusion, then a kind of knowing as the pleading face and figure vanished beneath the tarp of a lifeboat.

A lieutenant and two sailors ran toward her. Their eyes darted everywhere.

"Did you see him, miss?" they asked in German.

"See who?" Anya replied. She understood.

The lieutenant was shaking with anger. "The stowaway."

As the wind blew, Anya moved to the lifeboat and closed the flapping tarp. "No," she said. "I saw no one."

The officer bowed, clicked his heels, and left.

When it was safe, Anya lifted the tarp, peering at two of the brightest blue eyes she had ever seen. Jewels, she recalled later. "You can come out now," she said in Russian. "They've gone."

25

Anya smiled as the blue eyes hesitated. Soon, two bruised masculine hands emerged, and the body followed. Hair, a fringe of damp straw in disarray. Big bones and a strong chin. Broad shoulders, small waist, and narrow hips. Long, lanky legs in brown boots. "Thanks," he said.

"No. It's I who must thank you."

The youth registered confusion. "I don't understand," he said. "Have we met before?"

"You saved my father's life," she said.

"You must be mistaken," he said. "I'm a born coward."

"No," she insisted. "A Cossack nearly killed him but you covered him with your body. It was very brave, and I've never forgotten."

His face lit up. "I remember," he said. "In Kashkoi. Your name is Kaminsky."

Now *she* was confused. "How did you know?"

"I'm a musician, a poet. I knew your father's work. What a terrible waste his death would have been."

"And you were willing to die for him?"

"Funny," he mused. "I never thought of dying."

The following night Anya shared her miserable food with him. Moldy white bread and boiled potatoes. She took it to the lifeboat, where he ate it and they talked. Sasha, they called him, but his real name was Vladimir Constantinovich Constantine. He'd been a student at Moscow University.

"The day after the pogrom," he said, "I began to see the injustice. Later, I wrote poems which the officials called propaganda. They summoned me and burned them. Can you imagine? How dangerous can a poem be? Then I formed a resistance committee and was arrested. When war with Japan came, they let me out." He stopped. "I must be boring you to tears."

"No! Please go on. It's fascinating."

He waited, as if to see whether she meant it, then continued. "The czar predicted a quick victory, but the Japanese executed a surprise attack on Port Arthur and destroyed our navy. Students everywhere ran to save Mother Russia. None of them knew what the war was really about. It was just a diversion. There they were, dying for no other reason than the czar's fear of revolution at home. God rest their souls."

He paused as he savored the last bit of potato.

"You should stay and fight too," he said putting his cup down. "It's your country too."

Anya smiled. "No, Sasha. It's not. It never has been."

"Then it *will* be, after the revolution."

"I doubt that," Anya said. "My father says if it succeeds they'll outlaw religion. No real Jew would fight for that. For hundreds of years we've been begging for the right to practice our religion. No, Sasha. This war belongs to you. We have a different battle."

With her back to the moon, Anya's hair claimed a silver halo. "But I still don't understand why you left Russia," she said. "Why you're a stowaway."

He stared at her, as if wondering whether he could trust her. He must have decided he could. "I was part of the march on Petersburg. The czar's palace. Father Gapon, thousands of us went to protest the terrible conditions. People were poor, hungry, and cold. We went peacefully, with flags, pictures of the czar and czarina. We sang songs and prayed. Hungry men, women, children, begging to be heard, begging for food. We only wanted him to listen."

"And then?"

"At Narva Arch they ordered us to stop. When we didn't, the Horse Grenadiers plowed through like we were garbage. Father Gapon reorganized the group, and we continued. Now we were angry, more determined. We went to the square, knelt and prayed. Then a volley of shots rang out." His eyes glistened as he lowered his lashes. "It was an execution."

She knew how difficult it was for him and waited.

"Because of that, workers struck in Moscow, Minsk, and Riga. Lawyers, doctors, teachers. Bloody Sunday they called it. I left because . . . because I beat a soldier who murdered a hungry child. Now there's a price on my head."

Anya thought instantly of Moses and the Egyptian he'd killed. "I understand," she said.

"Why am I telling you this? Why are you listening?"

"Because I want to hear." She paused. "Until now, I've never even spoken with a—"

He filled in the word for her. "Goy?"

She laughed. Teeth even and white flashed against her creamy skin. "Where on earth did you learn that?"

"You'd be surprised," he said.

"Actually, I was going to say Gentile, but goy will do."

"It's not derogatory?"

"Not unless you mean it to be. It's in the *way* you say it. In the context of the sentence."

His hand grazed hers. Chills ran down her spine. "Your mouth, Anya. It's so pretty." She blushed. "Forgive me, please. I'm just a silly poet who says what he feels."

They were both silent, as if a spell had been cast. Then Anya spoke nervously. "So, you want to destroy Russia."

"No!" he insisted. "I want to save it. I want to bring it out of chains and into . . . Your eyes, Anya. They're magnificent. The color. Blue? Gray? Green? What color are they?"

Her face grew warm as she turned toward the sea. "You were speaking of Russia."

He leaned to her cheek and whispered. "Something's wrong with your ears, Anya. I was speaking of your eyes."

When he said her name it was music, violins and cymbals crashing in a great symphony. *Anya. Anya. Anya.* They were so close their breath mingled in a single mist. There, in the naked reality of their lives— she fleeing persecution and heading for uncertainty; he a stowaway, hunted and running from his homeland— they were discovering a great power. Love. First love. *Forbidden love.*

Anya went to bed that night with all her senses alive. She concentrated on his form, his eyes, his long back, on his hands, which were so like her father's. An artist's hands, she thought. A poet's hands. The hands of a caring man.

Sasha. Sasha. Sasha.

She saw his face as she tried to sleep. Hair of silken straw, eyes so blue and startling, changing instantly from soft to fierce, a man's broad nose, which began at his forehead and stopped above a gaily swirling mustache that framed a full upper lip. But more than his looks attracted her. His passion for justice, his sense of fair play. It made her feel that she could count on him, that he was solid as a rock.

As she tried sleeping, her hands rode her naked thighs to her hips, to her breasts, where they rested at her nipples. When the image of his face flashed again, she was so embarrassed she pulled her hands away. Yet the more she tried to suppress it, the more he haunted her. What would it be like? she wondered. What would it be like to hold, to kiss . . . to kiss a Gentile?

*   *   *

The following night there was a pale moon and a gentle breeze in the air. "Sasha," Anya called.

The tarp rose, and those flashing eyes made her heart stand still. No, God, no, she thought. Don't let this happen to me. "I brought you some food."

His head peeked out. The hands, arms, chest, and long torso followed.

"Here," she said. "I'm afraid it's not very good."

He sipped the cold soup. "Food is meant to nourish the body, not please the palate."

"Ah, yes; I forgot. You're a Bolshevik or something."

"Or something," he said, smiling.

When he finished they walked to the railing, where they shared more thoughts. She, her life in Kashkoi. He, a desire to free Russia and bring its people from the dark ages.

"What will you do in America, Sasha?"

"Wait for the army to stop searching, then go back to fight the czar and write a new constitution."

"But you'll get caught. They'll kill you."

"I'm not afraid to die, Anya. For the right reasons." He leaned on the railing. "And what will you do?"

His answer had shaken her. She wanted to hold him, to tell him to leave the wars for others to fight, to leave history for someone else to change. "Maybe I'll go to school," she said. "Or get married."

He cupped her face. His eyes pierced her heart and kindled her soul. It made her dizzy and confused. "Marriage," he said. "I've always wanted that too. A real home, and lots of children. But I have many things to do before that." He stopped. "Why do I sense your fear, Anya, your doubt in me?"

"It isn't you I doubt," she said. "It's the czars. They've ruled for so long, and you want to change things

overnight. It's not realistic." She feared for him, for
what he didn't know about the world's meanness.

He kissed her fingers, searching her eyes in a way no
one had before. Then he held her. Knees weak, unsure,
all the fire inside her suddenly flaring. She fit perfectly;
head on his chest, nestled between his chin and shoulder. He smelled of damp wool, but mostly of danger.
"I must go," she said, pushing him away.

"No. Don't. Please!"

But she was gone.

26

The following day Anya walked with Sheyna. Each carried a pencil and paper, writing down new English
words. Suddenly, Sheyna stopped near Sasha's hiding
place, and Anya's jaw went slack. Sheyna leaned her
back against the lifeboat, bracing her plump little elbows across the rim.

"I tell you my dream, Anya," Sheyna said. "I go to
America and become a big millionaire. Millionaire must
know good English." Sheyna lit a cigarette. "And you,
Anya. What do you dream?"

"I dream of a husband. And a family."

Sheyna made a face. "Feh! You make like goy. In
America pretty girl like you can be rich."

Sheyna flipped the cigarette butt overboard. "So,
where will you go?"

"To Chicago. To my married sister."

Sheyna tickled Anya's chin. "Too bad. When you
tired, come to New York. Hester Street. Four five one."
And she wrote it down.

The setting sun that night was a circle of white heat, an empty space where a hole had been burned through the sky. There were no stars, and dark clouds rumbled a warning.

Anya brought Sasha's dinner and tapped on the dinghy. "Here," she said as he came out and stretched his legs.

Sasha was hungry, and it pleased her. What didn't please her were her obsessive thoughts. She wondered what his parents were like. If he favored his father or mother. If he had sisters or brothers. A girlfriend.

"How are your parents feeling?" he asked, dipping his bread in the lumpy gravy and eagerly chewing.

"Father's fine, thank you. But Mother's a bit weary."

"I'm sorry to hear that. And your friend?"

Anya blushed. "So you understand English, too."

"Little bits," he said in English. "Like you." Then he returned to their familiar Russian.

Music filtered down from first class, and he reached for her hand. "Come, Anya. Dance with me."

They waltzed with her cheek resting on his shoulder, with his chin nestled in her curls. As her breasts pressed against him, her hand found his neck; his muscles stiffened and his breath rushed through her hair. Then lightning crackled, and a hard rain began to fall. He pulled her into the lifeboat and covered them with the tarp. Beneath that covering, hands and shoulders touched. They were face to face, nose to nose, lips inching closer until they brushed. It was like kissing the wind.

"I want to write a sonnet for you," he whispered. "Something so beautiful it would wound people to hear."

She stared at him in the shadows. The kiss had been everything she'd ever dreamed. She felt dizzy, like she'd finished a glass of wine. But fear hovered, too.

"Dearest Anya, forgive me," he pleaded. "You're young, and I'm going too fast."

There was nothing she could say. She was drawn to him like a magnet, charged with the same power that now shook the sky. She wiped some raindrops that clung to his eyelashes, drew the wet hair from his forehead. Slowly, their hands wound finger by finger in a slow tango. An instant fire invaded every organ of her body, and before the rain stopped she threw back the tarp.

"I must leave, Sasha," she said, and he let her go.

Below, Shmuel cradled Sarah. Her spirits and energy were drained. She had spent the first week vomiting bile, and her skin was green. He tried to coax her into the fresh air, but she refused. "No, Shmuel. I can't."

He cleaned her, wiped sweat from her forehead. Then he remembered the present Rachel Bierkoff had given him, and he pulled it from his pocket. "For you, Shuraleh," he said. "From Rachel." He'd hoped the sight of the comb would make her feel better, but it didn't.

A week before they reached port, a terrible storm rose. Sharp winds cut like knives, and rain poured down in buckets. Anya stayed below as the ship rose with the mountainous waves, then dropped again. Outside, the crew donned yellow slickers and stretched ropes across the rails to keep those who were retching from falling overboard. For three hours the ship hurled the weak, sick, strong onto the floor. And then it stopped, and the sea grew calm. The sun came out, order was restored, and Saul begged Anya to tell him the story of Masada again so he could feel Eleazar's strength in his body.

"Say about America," he said when she finished.

Anya kissed him. "America will be like candy. A Sabbath without end."

"I be bar mitzvah?"

"Of course! With honey cake and wine."

Saul stood up, his "sword" dangling at his side. "Find me, Anya," he cried. Then he ran away, giggling.

That night, Anya headed for Sasha's hiding place. Dinner was moldy stew with very little meat. He ate hungrily, ripping the bread with a man's appetite, asking where the food had come from.

"My family, others," she replied. "No one can eat it."

"What do they eat instead?"

"Water, tea. Sugar, when they can find it."

"They'll starve," he said. He pointed to the top deck, where people in long gowns and furs were dancing. "That's what has to change, Anya. No human being should ever go hungry."

After eating he tried to hold her. "No, Sasha, please," she protested. She didn't mean a word of it. He caressed her shoulders, pulled the kerchief from her hair so her braids flew free. For a long time his eyes warmed her face; then he reached beneath his sweater and took a chain, a simple gold-link chain that hung from his neck, and, kissing it, placed it around her neck.

The chain warmed her skin, and this time it was she who kissed him. With fire and hunger, with a need she did not understand. Her hands trembled as they parted. It was all confusing, all happening so quickly.

"Anya," he said. "It's time to stop fighting. Something special is happening between us."

"God help me, Sasha. I feel it, too."

He kissed her again. "Then it's settled. We'll be married in America. Love is the most important thing in the world."

The faces of her parents came instantly to mind. "No, Sasha. No! There are all kinds of love. Love of country, parents. You and I—it can never be."

"I know what you're saying. But I don't care. I can love my country as well as you. You can love your parents as well as me."

"No, Sasha. It's more than that. I'm Jewish. It's a way of life I could never desert or deny."

"I'd never ask you to deny it."

"Then you'll convert?"

"I wouldn't ask you to become a Christian. Why make me a Jew?"

"If you want me, Sasha, it's the way it has to be."

He took her shoulders. "What are you saying? This can't be the end. We must find a way."

Their heads became two shadows against the moon as a star zoomed across the sky. They closed their eyes and made a wish.

"What did you ask for?" he said, when her eyes opened.

She laughed. "I can't tell. It wouldn't come true."

"Well, I'm not superstitious, so I'll tell you mine." Before she could cover her ears he had spoken it. "I wished we could always be together."

Tears filled her eyes. Because he had told her, she knew it would never happen.

27

Several days before they reached port, Sarah felt almost human. Shmuel encouraged her to come out and see the ocean so they could recall it in their old age. And one night, dressed in a skirt and blouse, she walked onto the deck where the Irishman played music. A crowd was there. People clapped. Children whirled. Faces were everywhere, laughing and smiling. It was a time to celebrate hope.

Shmuel jumped to the center of the ring and clapped his hands. "Come, Sarah!" Sarah's hand rose in protest. Then Anya coaxed too. She took Sarah's hands and pulled her into the circle, where they swayed to the tempo. Anya's braids flew loose and bounced on her shoulders, and Sarah laughed as they circled one another.

"Da, ditty, dum, dum," Shmuel sang. Shmuel's arms folded across his chest, his knees bent, and his feet kicked outward in a Russian folk dance. Everyone cheered as Sarah twirled. Her cheeks were pink again. Her face was alive, and she grew bolder and wilder, dipping her shoulders left and right. Then her smile suddenly vanished, and her eyes were wild with fear. She clutched her bosom and staggered backward.

With Anya screaming, Shmuel caught Sarah before she fell to the floor. A crowd gathered, staring down at her as Shmuel fanned her face.

"Air," he shouted. "Give her air!"

Anya began to push them away. "Get back!" she cried.

Sarah's head fell on Shmuel's shoulder as he carried her through the crowd down to her bed.

While Anya searched for a doctor, Shmuel rocked Sarah back and forth. "We'll go to the opera, the theater, to a beautiful synagogue." He promised her a dozen silk dresses, jewels and a fur coat. "But you have to get well, fat, with a double chin. In a few days we'll be in America. You don't want Sonia to see you like this."

Sarah's eyelids drifted closed, and Shmuel felt the flesh rip from his body. "No!" he shouted. "I forbid you to die! Remember the dream, Sarah. America. We must share or it's nothing!"

Sarah motioned for Shmuel to come close. He bent to her mouth and at first heard nothing. Then she murmured, "Marishka . . . you. I forgive."

He wept on her bosom. His beautiful Sarah was dying, and all she could think about was him. "Oh, God," he prayed. "Help her, please."

Anya returned. She had been unable to find the ship's doctor and wanted to be at Sarah's side.

"She's been calling you," Shmuel said when Anya came in. "Go to her."

Anya sat at Sarah's side. She took her hand. It was cold as ice. As Sarah struggled to speak, Anya brought her ear to the dying woman's lips.

"Before I go . . . I must tell you . . ."

Anya listened as Sarah's deathbed confession flowed into her ear. The girl was bewildered and shocked. Surely, Sarah couldn't mean it. Her mother was delirious, confused. Yet, somehow, it made sense. Anya looked at Shmuel and shrugged. She could never tell him. She could never tell anyone what her mother had just said.

Suddenly Sarah gasped. Her eyes opened and closed. "Saul," Sarah whispered as Shmuel ran to her. "He must . . . forgive me. And, Anya," she gasped. "Always remember who you are." Then she slumped backward, and life went with her.

They buried Sarah at sea. Shmuel removed his shoes and tore the cloth across his heart in mourning. For the rest of the journey, he lay in her bed with Saul clinging to his side.

The last day at sea everyone was vaccinated. Anya stole away to the lifeboat to see Sasha. She had continued to bring food and water, even after Sarah's death, but had spent little time with him. Now she wanted to say good-bye. The moment she saw him, she knew she would really miss him.

"When will I see you?" he asked. He tried to touch her, but she pulled away.

"You don't understand, do you?" she said.

"Oh, Anya. I care. And I want you."

"Want. Care. That's not reality!"

"I'm a man and you're a woman. What could be more real?"

"Please, Sasha. I've just lost my mother."

She began to cry. "Tonight's the last time I see you," she said. "Tomorrow we go separate ways."

For a long time she didn't move. Then Sarah's death-bed words echoed in her ears, and she found the strength to run.

"Anya!" he called. "I love you! *Never forget that.*"

28

CHICAGO, ILLINOIS

"Caroline? Where are you?" Sonia hiked the skirts of her blue silk dress and raced up the staircase.

"In here, madame," Caroline called back.

Sonia found the blond-haired maid in the library, polishing the black marble fireplace. Angrily, Sonia rushed to the windows where the sun blazed through and quickly drew the curtains. "What's the matter with you, damnit? These are cashmere carpets. How many times do I have to tell you to close the drapes at noon!"

"Sorry," Caroline said. She continued polishing.

"Is the large room ready for my parents?"

"Yes."

"And the two smaller ones?"

"Yes."

"Good! When you're done, finish the kitchen. I want things perfect when my husband arrives with my family."

NEW YORK CITY PIER

Charles Gordon Cohen was born in Chicago in 1870, the only son of a rich German textile merchant and his Viennese wife. Spoiled and pampered, he was sent to the finest schools, where he mingled with the best families, developing only two real interests in life: ladies and birds. He knew a good deal about the naughty pleasures of the former and kept the latter because wild things fascinated him and linked him to his mother. When he married Sonia, he thought she'd make the perfect wife. She kept a firm hand on his house and servants, presented a fine table for his business associates, and cared for his birds. In short, Sonia was just like his mother.

Because his father had been a genius, his various business enterprises ran themselves, and except for six yearly visits to New York's Seventh Avenue, where he ordered new fabrics, Charles spent his time in sexual encounters. Through his father, he'd made connections with men in high places, men who conveniently helped him remove himself from those "tight" spots he sometimes found himself in. In exchange for extravagant campaign contributions, he could call on almost anyone, at almost any time, and ask for almost anything.

He could not know he'd need one of those favors when he met his wife's family, on Ellis Island.

The day they arrived the air was crisp. As they headed for Ellis Island, everyone rushed to the rails. The voyage was over. They were in the land of the free. People cried, hugged, kissed. They held their children above their heads and waved at the famous statue.

Sweet Liberty Statue. Sister to women. Lover to men. Mother to children. Savior of them all. There she stood in her pale green gown with her crown of points, the vigilant look in her eyes, a book of knowledge in one hand and the flaming torch of hope in the other.

A renewed hope was alive for everyone except Shmuel. Hope had died in his arms six days before. It had not been just the end of Sarah's life, but the end of his. A link in a long and loving chain, snapped forever. Life would never be the same.

The captain guided the ship as a flock of screeching sea gulls soared to greet them. The whistle blew. Smoke billowed from the stacks and rose to the blue sky. Then the engines wound down like an old clock, and the ship glided into its berth. The anchor gears creaked, and the great iron crosses splashed into the water. Wooden planks were set, and they lined up to leave. Italians, Poles, Hungarians, Russians, Armenians, Irish, all crying, laughing, shouting, waiting to kiss the ground. Down the planks they went, human cargo with rag-bundled dreams.

The building that housed them was huge, with a skylit cathedral ceiling and an enormous American flag on the wall. They were tagged like sides of beef and sent to wait. They sat on bundles, perched on wicker baskets, stood in endless lines, leaned against walls or on one another, and waited. They were examined for sca-

bies, lice, trachoma, ringworm, tuberculosis, and ve-
nereal disease.

Then came the interviews and endless questions. "Do
you have a job?" "Do you have family here?" "Are
you healthy?"

When suspicions rose, they were marked like Cain
and sent upstairs for more careful examinations. Some
jumped and swam ashore. Some were sent back to Europe. Some died of fright. A few committed suicide.

The doctor who spoke in Russian took his stethoscope
from Shmuel's chest. "You and your daughter can stay.
The boy returns."

"What do you mean?" Shmuel asked.

The doctor lifted Saul's battered hand. "With this,
he's a liability."

"How can a child be a liability?"

The doctor didn't look up. "If you die, who cares for
him?"

"I do!" Anya shouted.

While Shmuel pleaded, Anya and Saul were left to
sit on a bench outside the doctor's office. Anya could
hear her father through the transom, begging for pity.
Most of the immigrants cleared for release were now
heading in launches for the pier. It was terrifying to see
the sunlight fade.

Saul put his arms around Anya and lay his head in
her lap. *"Shah, tateleh,"* she said in Yiddish. "Papa will
fix it."

Then he began to cry out for Sarah. It was the first
time he'd acknowleged her death in words.

Anya comforted him. She rubbed his skinny shoulder
blades, telling him not to worry, that Sarah had gone
to Heaven, to be with Noah and Eleazar, that one day
soon he'd see her again.

An hour later the door opened, and Shmuel stood

tired and defeated. He sat down, lifted Saul's chin, and kissed the boy's forehead. "You have to stay here," Shmuel told him. "Just for tonight."

"No!" Anya shouted.

Saul's frightened eyes darted from Anya to Shmuel. Once again he cried for his mother.

"Please, Anya," Shmuel shouted back. "Be calm. You'll only make him worse." His words softened as he spoke to Saul again. "You'll stay here, and the nice people will look after you. You'll sleep with other boys your own age in a big room, and tomorrow morning we'll come and get you."

Anya ran to the doctor's office, pushed open the door. "I'm Saul's sister," she begged. "Let me stay with him. He's little, afraid of the dark and closed rooms. He was trapped in a barrel and—"

The doctor glared at her. Steely eyes above frameless glasses. "This is not a hotel, miss," he interrupted. His Russian was impeccable. "And your brother will do just fine. Now I don't know how they behave where you come from, but in America we knock before we enter."

Anya wanted to throw something at him, but she offered apologies and closed the door instead. Shmuel's hand fell on her shoulder when she returned. Together, they watched Saul walk away with a nurse.

"Smile, Anya," Shmuel whispered. "Wave as he goes."

Her hand rose in a gesture of good-bye as Saul left. Before he disappeared, his tiny fingers curled around the doorframe. "Be brave," Anya called. "Think of Noah and Eleazar."

It was almost dusk when the last launch landed on the pier. They found Charles holding a sign with their names written on it. They shook hands and told him everything. Charles's Yiddish was rusty as he expressed sadness about Sarah and promised action for Saul. He took them to a hotel where they rested, and he placed a few phone calls. By the time they'd finished dinner, Charles had secured a hearing for Saul's release. In the morning, Charles pleaded their case before a "friendly" magistrate, and a kindness was repaid. This truly was a great land, Anya thought. She ran from courtroom to taxi, to pier, thinking of Saul as she boarded the launch.

As a light rain fell and the waves tossed, Anya buttoned her coat. She recalled the terror in Saul's eyes when they'd left him yesterday. Now it would change. She'd take him home and protect him. He'd go to school and be tutored for his bar mitzvah. Saul. Her body trembled with joy at the prospect of seeing him again.

The instant the launch landed, Anya ran ahead. She raced into the great building, waving Saul's release papers. She spotted the doctor's office and smiled.

"There it is!" she called to Charles and Shmuel. This time she knocked before she entered.

"Here," Anya said, breathlessly. She handed him Saul's release papers.

The doctor glanced at them, then at her satisfied expression. It seemed to anger him. With a sneer he rose and pulled Saul's file. "Follow me," he said.

Anya headed straight for the dormitory where they had left Saul the day before, but the doctor turned right. Confused, she caught up and tugged his sleeve. "I don't understand," she said. "Where are you going?"

The physician glared at her. "He cried all night," he snapped. "It disturbed the others, so he was isolated. Don't worry. We gave him pencil and paper to play with."

"Are you crazy?" she shouted. "I told you he was afraid." She ran to Shmuel. "Papa, did you hear? Saul was alone."

The doctor ignored her and stopped at a room. He thrust a key in the lock and pushed, but the door wouldn't open. Again and again he repeated his efforts without success. Finally, the door gave way.

Anya rushed into the empty room and looked around. "He isn't here," she cried.

"Nonsense!" the doctor snapped.

Then a strange shadow swayed across the floor.

It took a while for them to follow it upward, to realize it was Saul's body hanging by the rope he'd used for his sword. Pinned to his coat were some simple words written in a child's scrawl. GO TO HEVEN. BE WITH MAMA END ELEZAR IN MASADA.

29

CHICAGO, ILLINOIS

Sonia waited on the steps of the mansion. Members of her staff, Chaim, and the rabbi stood behind her. Charles had telephoned from New York City after they'd buried Saul in a Brooklyn cemetery and explained what had happened. For three whole days she could not believe it. She had sacrificed so much, had married Charles to give her parents a new life, and now it would never be. Her young brother had taken his own life, and her mother lay at the bottom of the Atlantic Ocean.

The shiny black car inched toward the house. The crunch of gravel beneath the wheels sounded like bones breaking. Her bones. Her mother's. Her brother's, too. She waited in her black silk blouse and long black wool skirt as the limousine stopped. When the car door opened, she was shocked at the shadow that was her father. His back was bent like an old tree; his arms and legs were limbs that had weathered a great storm. His hair was gray and unruly. His speckled beard, usually tailored and trimmed, was matted. And those eagle eyes were dull beneath chaotic eyebrows. Gone was his aura of strength. He was reluctance, inertia in a dirty black suit. Beside him, Anya. Almost fourteen now. Slim, beautiful, with strawberry blond curls peaking through a babushka, an ample bosom, and huge eyes. Sonia felt the old jealousy coil around her throat.

Sonia hugged her father, kissed Anya politely, and took Shmuel to his room, where Chaim and the rabbi helped him settle in. Anya joined Sonia for hot tea in the kitchen, and they spoke in Russian.

"If only we had gone first-class," Anya cried. "Mama and Saul might still be alive." Sonia was enraged.

"What do you mean? I sent first-class tickets."

"But they were ashamed, Sonia. All those people in fancy hats and furs, and we came from the forest like ragpickers." Then she explained what Shmuel had done.

Sonia's teapot slammed down. "Damn him!" she said.

"Don't, Sonia. It's a wonderful mitzvah to share."

"Some mitzvah!" Sonia said. "Papa gets good marks in God's Book and Mama and Saul are dead."

"That's not fair!"

Sonia's almond-shaped eyes flashed. "Was it fair what happened to Mama and Saul?"

"Please, Sonia. Not so loud. Papa has enough guilt for an army. It would kill him to hear you."

"I hope he does, goddamnit!"

"Sonia! Don't curse God. What will be, will be."

"God!" She laughed bitterly. "So, you still believe."

Anya looked skyward. "Forgive her. She's upset. She doesn't know what she's saying."

"Don't apologize for *me*, Anya!" Sonia cried. "I haven't kept kosher since the day I left Kashkoi. I haven't kindled a Sabbath light either, and your God hasn't struck me dead. If He's there, He's too busy finding people like Mama and Saul and feeding them gall."

"Excuse me, Sonia." Anya stood up. "I've had a long journey and my heart is breaking. I've lost Mama and Saul. I will not hear reasons to also lose God."

It was midnight. Charles found Sonia at her pink marble dressing table in a white lace negligee with tiny pearls scattered across the bosom. He entered her room in his blue velvet smoking jacket and paisley print ascot.

"I'm glad you came," she said. They spoke in English. "I wanted to thank you for being so good to my family."

Charles nodded, watched her brush her hair. Long and sensuous, it was. Black as night and lustrous. "Glad to help," he said. He stood behind her, watching her pretty face in the mirror. "Your father's an intelligent man," he said.

"Long ago, maybe. *Now*, I don't know."

"And your sister."

Sonia's brush strokes grew shorter.

"Very pretty," he said.

At this moment, Charles was moved by Sonia's exotic beauty, by her strength, by the controlled tones of her voice, and he wanted to hold her not out of lust but with empathy, because she had lost a mother and a brother and he understood that pain.

He placed his hand on her shoulder and rubbed gently. After his mother's death, Sonia's closeness had soothed him, and he thought perhaps his closeness would help her now too. He was mistaken. He felt her disgust as she rose and walked away. A long time ago they'd spoken of children. Two miscarriages later, he'd given her room. Now, he wanted a son, and she damn well knew it. He walked to the door of her bedroom. "I'm here if you need me," he said. A second later he was gone.

When the door closed, Sonia was relieved. How could he? Especially now? Sex under any circumstance was revolting. Just the sight of that dark hairy line that descended like an arrow from his navel to that grotesque lump of flesh that swelled between his thighs disgusted her.

Sex.

Thrashing like dogs and cats in the streets. Then, the soiled linen in the morning when the maid came to clean. To think the servants knew she did—*that*. And *that* was what men and women sought from each other. And *that* was what Papa had shared with Mama. And *that* she detested with all her heart.

Sonia joined Anya and Shmuel in the ritual of *shivah*. Seven days of mourning the death of her mother and brother. They covered the mirrors to avoid the face of pain. They turned the calendars to the wall so time would stand still. They kindled memorial lights to symbolize and recall the light that had gone from their lives and sat on hard boxes to stay in perpetual discomfort. But the meals they ate symbolized new life: hard-boiled eggs, foods that were round in shape to remind them that death is part of an ongoing cycle. And Sonia hated it. Her beautiful house was filled with horrid little men, gum-snapping Chaim and his minyan of ten in their black suits, and beards, and black hats, and silly white shawls. Thrice daily they entered her house without a greeting, because greetings were considered too joyful. And when it was over, she was glad.

*   *   *

Shmuel watched Anya fluff his pillow.

"Remember when the pogrom happened?" she asked. "How you said, 'Out of pain always comes good'? It's the same for you, Papa. You must get out of bed and eat."

She shook him. A lump of flesh in a large bed that emphasized his frailty. A shell with no mind or being.

"Breakfast, Papa," Sonia called from outside. She opened the door to his room and seemed surprised at Anya's presence. "Is everything all right?"

"He misses them," Anya said when Shmuel did not respond. Anya fussed with the buttons on his nightshirt. Sonia placed a tray across his thighs.

"Of course he misses them," Sonia said, tucking a napkin inside his nightshirt. "He just needs to—"

"Stop it!" Shmuel shouted. "You're treating me like an idiot. I've lost half of myself and neither of you understands. Go, please. Leave me be."

Alone, Shmuel prayed harder. He thought if he'd been a better Jew, God would have spared his family. In his confusion he summoned the rabbi.

"It's okay to be angry," the young rabbi said. He had a black beard and warm brown eyes. "God understands." He put a comforting arm around Shmuel's shoulder, and Shmuel felt the heat of that hand warm his bones. "It's terrible to lose a wife and a son. Tell me about them."

As Shmuel spoke, he rocked back and forth. "My Sarah was beautiful," he said. "No matter what it was, she found good. Not once in all the years we were married did she complain, and she had plenty."

"And your boy?" the rabbi asked.

"What can I tell you? My son was special." Then he explained what Sarah had done to Saul's hand.

"I understand," the rabbi said.

Shmuel was racked with pain. "*You* do! But will God?"

"Shmuel," the rabbi said. "The Bible tells us God is loving and merciful. A loving and merciful God forgives."

Shmuel rose in a fury. His fist pounded the table. "And what if there is no God?"

The rabbi took Shmuel's hand, and one by one unclenched the fingers. He looked deep in Shmuel's eyes. "If there is no God," he said, "then at whom are you angry?"

30

Two weeks after they arrived, a letter came from Joshua. He was safe in Palestine, working in a new settlement. He had no idea that both Sarah and Saul were dead, and Anya cabled him the news.

Over the weeks Anya found her older sister an enigma. With monetary things Sonia was generous to a fault. She had had a kosher kitchen built for Anya to prepare foods for her father and provided the necessary utensils, but she added a bite to the giving. She'd tease Anya about the dietary laws, teasing which turned sometimes to disagreeable banter, or outright scorn and contempt. Anya avoided confrontations and kept the peace. She never told Shmuel what was happening. Some things were best left unsaid. But it wasn't easy. Sonia was difficult to understand. Her strength lay in an uncanny ability to cull other people's weaknesses, to sense them, identify them, then file them away for future confrontations. When angered, she'd whip them out. That tendency kept Anya from getting too close. Then Sonia would do one mitzvah after the other. Crazy. Like she had demons fighting inside her. One day she took Papa's measurements from his old clothes and had six outfits made for him. She did the same for Anya. Dresses, skirts and sweaters, pretty lingerie. But then she'd push Anya around as if the gifts had somehow entitled her to do so.

The rabbi had promised Shmuel the pain would abate. But it choked him when he looked at Sarah's things. It strangled him when he walked to the lake. His life became a series of dark nights and blinding mornings sandwiched between endless days of gray, a meaningless repetition which magnified his shame. He'd had a bellyful. Guilt about Marishka. The tickets. And what was it Cousin Chaim had said? Some silly remark meant to comfort.

"God sends us only what we can bear."

And he had answered, "What are you saying? That if I were weaker, my wife and son would still be alive?"

But he read Job and Lamentations, and he said kaddish. And as the rabbi had promised, he lost himself in the soothing prayers, in the rhythms and rocking, in the endless motion of ritual. Sometimes he could feel Sarah's hand or sense her presence, a fleeting image in a doorway, a gray dream, some gauzy apparition obscured by his tears. He knew then she would always have mystical contours in his mind. Courage, she was. Limitless love, she was. A sovereign heart filled with goodness. But gone, now. Gone forever.

Three months later, Shmuel finally began to notice life around him. He explored his daughter's beautiful gardens and house, heard the endless ticking of her many clocks, her singing birds, her constant creation and nurturing of sounds as if she was terrified of silence.

Her mouth was a fountain of words, her hands always filled with things. Then he realized how life in America had changed her. She had embraced the New World and relinquished the old ways. With no parents to remind her, with no Cossacks, no accusations of Christian children's blood in her matzoh, there was no reason to keep the faith. Except for love. And that was what it was. Sonia didn't love Judaism. And as her father it was his duty to bring her back. He could not know that task would bring great pain.

It was Sonia's usual nightmare. The pogrom. The runaway carriage. Anya's birth and Sarah's screams. Then she wakened at 7:00 A.M. in the safety of her Victorian bed with her heart racing. But this morning there was a racket beneath her bedroom window. She rose and peered below to see her father hammering at her front door. She was glad finally to see him out of his room but couldn't imagine what he was up to.

With prayers said, and the oblong silver object's head slanted toward the inside of the house, Shmuel drove the last nail home. Finished, he polished the filigree silver and cleaned up his tools. Then the front door swung open, and there stood Sonia, in a royal blue velvet robe, with her long black braid draped across her right shoulder. When she saw the silver object fastened to her door, her eyes turned to ice.

"Papa! What have you done?"

"Something *you* should have done long ago," he said.

She checked her anger as they entered the house and went to the kitchen. "I know how you feel," she said. "But this is *my* home, and I don't want a silly good-luck charm on my door."

Shmuel glared at her. "A mezuzah's not a charm. It's a commandment. It reminds you you're a Jew."

They entered the kitchen. "To tell the truth, Papa, I'd rather forget."

"Like forgetting to breathe, maybe."

She placed his coat over a chair. "No. I just don't accept the old ways anymore. This is America. When you came, you left the czar in Russia."

"The czar maybe. God, I brought with me."

Sonia whipped around. "Can't you get it through your head, Papa? I'm finished with religion. I no longer need to worship."

"No, daughter. You still worship. But his name is money." He held up a silver spoon. "It's very nice, but as a God it will always fail you."

She smiled as she said it. "Perhaps. But it brought you to America. That's more than your God ever did."

31

At the end of May, another letter came from Joshua. He had received their cable.

Palestine   *March 1906*
Dearest Family,

Your news makes me grieve. I will sit shivah *and say kaddish, but I cannot come to America. Besides the money and danger of reentry (the Turks have imposed immigration restrictions), there is much to do. I will not burden you with details, but just say I miss you and that life without Mama and Saul will never be the same. I will work harder than ever so others will not suffer their fate.*

My deepest love, Joshua

Anya clutched Joshua's letter and went to Shmuel's bedroom. Her father was asleep on his bed with his glasses on his forehead and a book rising and falling on his chest. She removed his glasses and placed the book on his nightstand. Planting a kiss on his forehead, she shut off the light and scurried to her room. She did not notice the gentle steps behind her until she opened her bedroom door. Startled, she turned. "Charles! I didn't hear."

He whisked by her and swung the door shut. But the meager force he used left it slightly ajar. "Forgive me, Anya. I didn't want to wake the others, but I need to talk."

She followed him in, wondering what couldn't wait until morning, and sat beside him on her bed.

"It's Sonia and me," he said, beginning. "It's no secret we haven't an ideal marriage, but I want a child. Since her last miscarriage, she refuses to . . ." He turned his shame to the floor, finishing in a single breath. "She refuses to see me."

Anya now understood why Charles went to Caroline's room at night, understood Sonia's continuing bitterness.

"What I can do?" she asked.

"Maybe talk to her. Woman to woman."

Although he had many faults, Anya liked Charles. She remembered his kindness to Saul and her father. His kindness to her. She couldn't turn him away without at least trying. But what could she say to a sister who seemed to hate her?

As she agreed to help him, he leaned to thank her with a kiss, and the slightly open door moved a fraction of an inch. Neither Charles nor Anya saw it, and when Charles made his way out a second later, the hallway was empty.

A few weeks later Charles went to Anya's room

again. But Anya had nothing to offer him. Though she wanted to help, she had so far found Sonia unapproachable. Alone, she'd rehearse little speeches, but in Sonia's intimidating presence she said nothing. Her formidable sister could keep her at arm's length with a look. Some evenings she'd gather her strength and walk into Sonia's sitting room. Then Sonia's icy glare would force idle chatter instead. And though she grieved for Charles, the task eluded her. Realizing that, she wrote Charles a note and asked Caroline to deliver it.

When his wife summoned him to her room that evening, Charles was ecstatic. Aroused, he showered and shaved and put on black silk pajamas and matching robe. He walked the hallway feeling the seeds he'd sown with Anya beginning to sprout. But when he entered Sonia's room, he reaped the whirlwind. She stood near her vanity in a green velvet gown, holding a piece of paper and hurling ugly accusations.

"I don't know what you're talking about," he insisted.

Sonia crumpled the paper and tossed it at his feet. The moment he finished reading, he understood.

Dear Charles,
   Please come to my room tonight at nine.

                                              Anya

"Where did you get this?" he demanded.

"One of my little birdies."

Charles tried to explain, but every word dug a deeper hole. Frustrated, he tossed the paper aside. "What you're thinking isn't true, Sonia."

"Oh, stop protecting her!" Sonia insisted. "I've seen the two of you kissing in her bedroom."

He recalled the innocent exchange and felt disgusted. "Only *you* could turn such sweetness into filth."

*   *   *

Anya stood listening outside their door. She had gone to tell Sonia that Shmuel wasn't well. After a few moments she ran to her room, where she spent the next hours pacing. How could her sister say such horrible things? And Papa. What if Sonia showed him the note she'd sent to Charles? What would he think? She slumped into a chair, sobbing, wondering why Sonia hated her. Though there were problems between them, she'd always cared for and respected her sister. Deep down, she'd thought Sonia cared too. She'd been wrong. And the awful part came when Anya realized that Sonia had been waiting for this moment.

Well, she was grown up now. She didn't have to tolerate it. And though leaving Papa would be painful, that was what she had to do. She'd find a place to live, support herself, send for Papa when she could. Who needed this big house, these fancy clothes anyway? The idea of being alone was scary. But better to face her worst fears than live with Sonia's hate.

She packed her things, dressed, took paper and pencil, and wrote a brief note to Sonia and a long, loving one to her father. Then, with bag in hand, she crept down the long staircase to the front door.

"Anya! It's two in the morning. Where are you going?"

Anya turned. Charles was leaning against the doorway of his study with a snifter of brandy in his hand. Anya could tell from the way he spoke it had not been his first. "I heard you fight, Charles. It's better this way."

"But, Anya! You're barely sixteen."

They both turned as Sonia's voice boomed down the landing. "About the same age I left Kashkoi to work as a maid."

"Please, Sonia!" Charles shouted. "You've said enough."

Anya trembled as more of Sonia's coldness drove through her. There was something she could have said to hurt back, something terrible, but she held her tongue. "You're my sister, Sonia. I've always looked up to you. Now? I just feel pity."

"Save your pity, Anya. You'll need it yourself. It's cruel out there. Time to learn God doesn't exist."

Anya ran into the darkened street, still hearing Sonia's cruel words. The wind from Lake Michigan tore through her coat as abandonment and isolation carved her bones. She finally dropped on a lighted curb and sobbed her heart out. Once they had been a family. Now, they were scattered to the four corners of the earth. Worst of all, her own sister hated her, and she didn't know why.

"Oh, God!" she cried. *"What is wrong?"*

She heard the chug of a motor, then a horn. It was Charles searching for her in his automobile. She watched him park, then come to her. He hugged her and gave her his handkerchief. As she dried her eyes, he apologized for Sonia and offered her money, which she refused.

"Then let me drive you somewhere."

She didn't know where she was going. "Thanks. With God's help, I'll manage."

"Where will you stay?"

"Friends," she said. She hadn't any.

She handed his handkerchief back, but he stuffed it inside her purse.

"It's all my fault," he said. "If only I hadn't asked you."

"No, Charles. You did us a favor. Sonia's wanted this for a long time. Go back. For Papa's sake. Maybe things will change."

He looked at her in the strangest way. "You're something special, Anya Kaminsky. Very special."

She felt her cheeks warm. The moment was awkward, each feeling emotions neither had asked for, understood, or could express.

"Take care," he said finally. "Call collect if you need me. The New York office. It'll be our secret." Then he hugged her, stood up, and left.

Waving, a teary-eyed Anya watched the auto disappear into darkness. When she opened her purse, money floated from his handkerchief. Dear Charles, she thought, gathering it. She was so grateful. She put the money back and noticed a strange slip of frayed paper. Upside down, the writing made no sense. Right side up, it made her smile. Now, she had a place to go.

32

NEW YORK CITY

Anya crossed the gutter. The heart of Hester Street had not yet begun to beat. Though the street throbbed from sunup to sundown, now it was only 5:00 A.M. and circulation was still sluggish. Before long, though, the street would be a teeming mass, with pushcarts lined against the sidewalks and peddlers screaming in a life-and-death struggle to survive.

In front of a six-story brown apartment building, she checked the address. She trudged up four dark flights smelling fish and onions, hearing the whirring of sewing machines behind closed doors. On the fourth landing, a naked bulb dangling by a frayed cord flickered on and off near a smelly toilet. She dropped her bag near Apartment 4B and knocked. A grumbling voice soon called, "Stop, already. You're giving me headache."

The door opened, and one sleepy eye peered out. There was an awkward moment as the eye studied Anya, then happy recognition brought a wide open door and a welcoming hug. "Oy, Anya! From the boat."

Anya followed a disheveled Sheyna Levy inside.

"Sit. Sit. I'll make a glass tea," Sheyna said.

While Anya apologized for waking her at such an early hour, Sheyna reassured her. "Don't worry," she said. "I go to work soon. Just speak in English, Anya. English!"

Sheyna set a samovar on the stove and pulled pumpernickel from a covered bin, slapping the counter. "Lousy cockerroaches," she complained, cutting bread and spreading some jam. "Every day a battle." She coaxed the reluctant Anya. "Eat. Eat. I got plenty more."

Anya knew Sheyna did not keep kosher, but she had not eaten for days and was starved. She asked God's forgiveness and hungrily devoured the offered food.

After breakfast, Sheyna showed Anya the apartment. A kitchen and a tiny bedroom with double bed and dresser, surrounded by soiled green wallpaper and peeling paint.

"It's nice," Anya lied.

"Feh!" Sheyna said, holding her nose. "But it's mine. And nobody tells *me* what's doing."

As Sheyna dressed, Anya explained why she'd left home, how difficult it had been to leave her father.

"It happens. So what will you do?"

"Find a room, take care of myself."

"Hmmmmm," Sheyna said. "You could stay by me."

"Oh, no," Anya protested.

"Why not? We share rent. You can sew?"

"Yes."

"Good! Sleep now. Tomorrow I take you to Triangle Shirt Waist." She winked. "My gentleman is a foreman."

The following day Anya was hired. Then she and Sheyna discussed living conditions. If Anya was to live with Sheyna, the house had to be kept kosher. With Sheyna's promise not to break the dietary laws, Anya scoured the kitchen and consulted a rabbi. Certain utensils had to be discarded, others purchased new. Old ones that could be made kosher were done so according to rabbinical instructions.

Then the routine began.

Every morning, below the six-story tenement buildings, row upon row of glass-windowed stores squeaked their awnings out to announce the day. As the wives swept the sidewalks, the husbands set out their goods. Pushcarts huddled side by side in the filthy gutters like a long wooden train going nowhere. Then the knife grinders and junk dealers on their rickety wagons, pulled by swaybacked nags with swollen bellies, would begin yelling their wares. And people, children, dogs, and cats spilled into the streets.

Anya's work seemed easy. In a dimly lit corner of a crowded factory, she'd stitch a ruffle on a blouse. Ten hours every day for eighty cents a day, she and a hundred immigrant women crammed into small working spaces sewing. Sheyna complained about a frayed electric light cord. "There'll be a fire here," she'd tell the foreman. "One day will be a burning."

"So bring a bottle seltzer," he'd reply to laughter.

At night Anya came home with her foot aching from pushing the treadle. Her eyes burned, and she coughed lint. She'd change, scrub the rusty tub down the hall until her skin peeled, then take a bath—if there was hot water. After dinner, she and Sheyna would read the Bintel Brief, an advice column in the *Jewish Daily Forward* where immigrants asked help on matters of love, family, or work. Sometimes the letters were funny or silly and made them laugh; sometimes, they were sad. Always, they were interesting.

One day ran into another. Sheyna taught Anya to use lip rouge, to style her hair. At first Anya refused. But when she saw how she looked, she loved it. When there was free time, they went to museums or Yiddish theaters on Knish Alley. On Thursdays, they'd go to *Khazermark* or Pig Market, a name derived from old Ethiopian bazaars, where anything could be found. Even a doctor, a dentist, some educated man who needed a day's work. One Thursday Anya hid her head in embarrassment as Sheyna pulled a hat from a pushcart.

"So, Anya," she said winking. "Look on this garbage. How much?" she asked the peddler. She jammed the royal blue velvet on her head and picked up another.

"Hoo-hah! From that hat, you'll get a husband," the peddler said.

"A horse, maybe," Sheyna laughed. "A husband? No. How much?"

"Forty!" the peddler called out.

"Twenty, and not a penny more."

The peddler pleaded in Yiddish. "Please! lady, I have a family. Thirty cents even." Sheyna walked away. "All right, already!" the peddler screamed, and the hat was hers.

Sunday mornings, they'd share bagels, lox, cream cheese, and coffee. They'd go for walks and listen to soapbox speakers preach socialism, unionism, communism, Zionism, and anarchy. They'd listen to *klezmer* music—Yiddish blues—on street corners, and drink tea in a kosher deli. Then, a letter arrived from Shmuel. He was upset. Sixteen-year-old girls needed to

be chaperoned. Besides, he missed her. Anya wrote
back that she missed him too but could not return.

On a Sunday morning in May, Anya sat on a ledge
cleaning windows. She had a feeling she was being
watched. Turning, she saw the usual pushcarts and people below her. It was nothing, she decided. Nothing at
all.

The next day Anya went to work with Sheyna. That
night, she came home alone. She had dinner and was
ironing when someone pounded on the door. Startled
at first, she relaxed when Sheyna called, "Open, Anya.
I forgot my keys."

The next night Sheyna was gone again, and Anya had
that same strange feeling. She pulled the shade, slipped
on an apron, and set some soup and chicken on the
stove. As she waited for the food to warm, someone
knocked at the door. Remembering Sheyna's forget-
fulness, she ran. When she opened the door, her heart
stopped beating. When it started again, she could hardly
speak.

33

A nosy neighbor cracked the door open as Anya hugged
Sasha and pulled him inside. It seemed a hundred years
since she had seen him, and she was hungry for the
details of his face. The soup boiled over and hissed,
and she invited him to share her food.

"Like the boat," he said. "You're feeding me again."

Seated at the table, they chatted in Russian. She
couldn't stop staring. He was handsome in the way poets
are described: dreamy, passionate, tense. The tall frame

was the same. The hair, long. The blue of his eyes even clearer, and the mustache, gone.

"I've been across the street, watching," he said.

"How did you know where to find me?"

"Your friend was near the lifeboat when she gave her address. I memorized it and prayed you'd come."

He shared the story of his swim from Ellis Island, the friends who'd helped him acquire a job as a house-painter for a man who owned tenement buildings. "He crowds the poor into firetraps and makes a fortune. And the paint I use? Made to last only three months."

Still the revolutionary, she thought.

"So. What do you think of America?" he asked.

"I love it." She breathed deeply. "I feel safe for the first time in my life. When my English improves, I'll be a citizen."

After dinner they went for a walk near the river. They sat on some rocks listening to the waves pound the shore.

"What are your plans?" she asked.

"To stay; return when I can. My friends are in Paris, organizing. There'll come a time when all of Russia will quake, and I'll be there when it happens."

"You scare me, Sasha. The Bolsheviks are screaming for blood."

"I'm not a Bolshevik, Anya. Just a simple poet who is angry that people are starving, that twelve-year-old children are dying in a senseless war. Russia is falling apart, but the czar doesn't care. He claims God put him on the throne to govern. Sometimes I think that's why revolutionaries become atheists."

"But I've read about the czar's *new* government. One that's helping the people."

"With the czar at the head?" He laughed. "When he doesn't like the reforms, he dissolves it and forms an-other. Two dumas already, and the second is about to fail. Like you, I'd hoped it was the answer, but the czar gives with one hand and takes back with the other. Now, it's hopeless. The people are sick of broken promises. When the time comes, it will be a bloodbath."

"Oh, Sasha. Be patient. Change takes time."

He pulled a curl that sprang back to her brow. "Turn, Anyushka. Toward the light." She did. "It's just as I remembered," he sighed. "Apricots and gold. Promise you'll never cut it. Promise!"

His fingers lifted and separated the long strands of hair that fell like a waterfall down her back. She didn't have the heart to tell him that after marriage it would be covered, seen only by her husband.

"I haven't forgiven you, you know," he said. "For when your mother . . ." He turned away. "It hurt not to comfort you."

She explained how she'd needed to be alone, how the only medicine that helped was a healing solitude. After a while, she realized he wasn't listening, just staring at her neck. "It's there," she said, smiling. "I've never taken it off."

He reached across and lifted the chain. "One day I'll buy you a charm, something special to wear on it."

They held each other for a while, until the silence unnerved her. "What are you thinking, Sasha?"

"What does a poet think when he sees what he loves? A bowl of sunlight on a cold day. A field of daisies. Sugar, in a child's mouth. The pale heart of a perfect yellow daffodil." He held her even tighter. "You're rooted in the deepest part of me, Anya. Grafted like a rose since the day I first saw you. Thorns and all."

Desire radiated from her body. Time stood still. Nothing had prepared her for such a perfect moment as this, but she was frightened too. "It's late, Sasha. I must work tomorrow."

Walking, she was aware of his profile, of his strength.

It was all a beautiful dream. She encouraged him to talk. She loved his fire when he spoke of change and correcting injustices.

"One day, Russia will have a constitution like America," he said. "Everyone will have the right to speak without fear. They'll have food, education, doctors, lawyers. Freedom, Anya. The possibility to do as they wish."

Near a corner, he held her so hard she couldn't breathe. There were kisses on her face and throat. "I love you, Anyushka," he murmured. "Marry me, please."

She covered his lips with her fingers. "Please, Sasha, don't spoil it."

They saw each other during that summer. At night they'd sit together on a small hill in the park. It satisfied her to be near, to touch him, but it frightened her too. She tried never to think of her promise to Sarah, of Papa, Judaism, tradition, but the truth was a cloud above her head. At work, the needle that pierced the blouse she sewed pierced her heart as well. Their love went against everything she believed in. But the forces that pulled them together were equally strong. When she wakened, she saw his face. Sleeping, he was her dream. She was filled with sexual desires she did not understand.

Sometimes she imagined herself as his wife, the mother of his children. She'd see him standing at the head of her Sabbath table with a skullcap on his head, a raised glass of wine, reciting the blessings. They'd have sons and daughters who would change the world. They'd live in a house with beautiful gardens and share a long, happy life. But those thoughts always ended in nightmares.

One night he told her of his brother's death. He

explained how he'd mistaken his brother's books for his own. How he'd accidentally placed a revolutionary tract he'd written inside one of Mikhail's books. "When Mikhail returned the book, the librarian reported him, and he was arrested. A week later he was hanged." His head fell into her lap. "They took my brother's life as an example to the others, and I will never forgive myself or them for that."

She held him as he cried and pledged revenge. When he'd calmed, she spoke of little Saul and her own feelings of guilt.

All along, she looked for things to dislike so she could send him away. But she only found things that made her love him more. And the closer they grew, the more her guilt overwhelmed her.

She went to synagogue one Friday eve, thinking the prayers, the rabbi's talk would strengthen her commitment. It nourished her soul, yet late that same night she returned to Sasha's arms like a moth to a flame.

Their walks continued. He brought her flowers and wrote poems. They sat together, and sometimes their kisses were passionate and sometimes they were sweet. At night they'd sit on her rooftop and watch the moon rise. And never once did he ask for what he needed as a man. But she thought about it, and one day she cornered Sheyna at lunch.

"The first time, it hurts," Sheyna said. "But just a little. But when you love, and if he takes his time—it's Heaven. But you're a good girl, Anya. Don't do something to regret. From such Heaven can also come Hell."

All day long, Sheyna's words haunted Anya. *When you love—it's Heaven.* It made her wonder why Sasha had never tried to touch her that way. When they came together that night she found the courage to ask.

"We've been together for weeks," she began. "Not once have you tried . . ." She couldn't finish.

He sank beside her and took her hand. "Anyushka," he responded. "A man who truly loves a woman would never soil her. Of course I want you. But the time must be right."

She leaned against him, secure. There was nothing more she needed to know.

The following night, he seemed lost in thought. Finally, she asked, and he answered.

"Have you ever wondered what brought me to hear your father play? What brought me to his side when the Cossacks came? To the boat where you saved my life? Each time, I think, the answers are the same. God does not play games."

That's when he gave her a present. A small gold Jewish *chai*, a charm to be worn on his chain, the symbolic linking of their love. "They told me it means 'life,' " he said.

"Oh, Sasha. It's so beautiful, I could cry. Help me put it on. I want to wear it."

Sasha pushed the link through the chain and placed it around her neck. It lay gleaming in the hollow of her throat, near a pulse which had given it a life of its own.

On a stifling afternoon in July, Anya put on a cool yellow dress and ran to the park. They had not been together for two whole days, and she could hardly wait to see him. She struggled with desire as they walked the wooded trails, and to keep herself from caressing him she chattered about her work at Triangle. Then, a sudden sun-shower made them run for cover beneath a huge oak tree, where they watched the downpour. She was glad for the excuse to huddle beside him, but he dropped her hand and suddenly darted out.

"Sasha, don't! You'll catch cold."

"No, Anya, come! It's delicious."

He was drenched in minutes, laughing as he spun in the pouring rain, with his head drawn back, his arms outstretched, and his mouth wide open as if the sky were a hive dripping honey. Delight showed on his face as tendrils of wet hair spun down his head and neck, as the rain soaked through his clothes and shoes. It wasn't long before his contagious laughter and persistent coaxing made her join him. Free, happy, they held hands and whirled, splashing each other playfully, cleansed by the forces of nature. Then, just as it had begun, the shower stopped, and the sun came hotter than ever to dry them.

The day glazed to butterscotch. The sky turned orange, purple, then midnight blue. Exhausted, wrapped in each other's arms, they fell asleep on a bench, and it was morning when Anya wakened to the sound of crested blue jays screeching in the trees. She didn't move or disturb Sasha, just listened to the morning come alive, feeling happy, and wondering where this all would lead.

34

Sheyna cornered Anya the following day. "I think we should talk about your boyfriend."

Anya looked away. "What boyfriend?"

"You think I'm still a greenhorn, Anya? You ask me questions from sex, you don't come home last night. What am I? A dummy? Besides, it's no secret. I saw you already, clinging on him like lint on my blouse. So ask him to supper."

"I can't," Anya replied.

"Why? He's so bad?"

Anya's continued silence and avoidance met Sheyna's persistence, then Sheyna blurted out, "Oy! God forbid! He's a goy."

"Sheyna, please. You make him sound like garbage."

Sheyna was shaking. "Garbage, I have use for. His people killed my parents. Me? They raped and left for dead."

It was the first time Sheyna had told her, and Anya comforted her friend.

"Please, Anya. Don't go," Sheyna begged. "Inside you is a trusting young girl who will only get trouble."

"Sasha's not like that. You'll meet him." Then she told Sheyna about him.

"So, it's your life, Anya. In America, you're free. Sure I'll go," she said. "But like the old Yiddish saying goes, 'With one rear end you don't dance at two weddings.' "

They made dinner plans. Anya put on the green dress she'd arrived in. Sheyna wore a black skirt and white shirtwaist. To make an impression, Sasha borrowed a three-piece suit with a shirt and tie. Then they met at a kosher restaurant and chatted politely.

Sitting between them in a booth, Anya felt torn. Love and faith. Forces of equal strength were splitting her in half.

"The food is lovely," Sasha said when they'd finished dinner.

"What you were expecting?" Sheyna said bitterly. "Christian children's blood?"

Anya kicked Sheyna's foot and glared.

"Sorry," Sheyna said. "I didn't intend it."

They had dessert in silence.

At 10:00 P.M., the door to their apartment slammed shut. "You *wanted* to spoil it," Anya shouted in Yiddish.

"I'm sorry, Anya. I didn't mean it to sound that way."

"I don't believe you. How could you say such an ugly thing?"

"It was a slip. Oh, Anya. You're so young, so innocent. You don't know. In the heat of anger, he'll turn on you like a dog and call you a kike."

"We're not married yet, Sheyna. Just friends. But what you said was unforgivable. We Jews have suffered terribly. But, I've known wonderful Christians. The woman who brought me into the world. A priest who gave his life for my brother. And dear Sasha, who put his body between my father and a Cossack's sword."

"Sure. A few good ones here and there. But when they spit on you for two thousand years, a few doesn't matter."

Rosh Hashanah and Yom Kippur came, and Anya went to shul feeling unclean. Listening to services, she knew that her relationship with Sasha was wrong, that it could never be more than it was; still, her feelings were strong. Her hands moved to the *chai* Sasha had given her. She felt it choking and wanted to rip it from her throat. How silly, she thought, getting hold of herself. Then she turned her attention back to the prayers. A week later, a letter came from Papa.

> *My dearest Anya,*
> *The holidays were difficult without you but my faith sustains me. Yet, the truth is I'm afraid that when I die it will all go with me. I don't understand Sonia's hatred of Judaism or even Joshua's mission in Palestine. I'm only grateful for you. Without you, who would light candles for Mama or Saul when I'm gone? So, I thank God and pray every*

day that the new year brings you health, a good
Jewish husband, and sons to say kaddish.

Love, Papa

Anya crumpled the letter and cried. That night, she
told Sasha they would have to part.

"No, Anya. Don't throw away our magic."

"Sasha, please. I have obligations."

"To yourself, to me. This is a new century, darling.
People are thinking differently. They bathe together at
beaches with their arms and legs exposed. Kings will
be deposed and land returned to those who own it.
Women are marching to vote. Revolution is everywhere. And we are only simple people who love each
other. To throw that away would be a sin."

She hid in his arms. For tonight, his will would pre-
vail.

The next nights passed slowly. She couldn't think of
Sasha without weeping. In the morning she ate silently,
then went to work. At night she ironed, finding comfort
in the hiss and heat of the heavy iron and the order it
brought to the wrinkles. In the mirror, she saw confusion. Sasha was decent, good, loving. Everything a
husband should be. But he wasn't Jewish. She recalled
a friend at work who had changed the color of her hair.
Two weeks ago it had been mousy brown. Now it was
red. She looked pretty, but the roots were growing
back. And that was when it was final. It didn't matter
that she'd changed her hair, the dark roots would always
be the same.

The night she intended to tell Sasha, he came late.
His face looked sad, as if he knew what she was going
to say. He was upset about something and placed his
head on her lap. She brushed his hair. It was filled with
crisp leaves, dropped from trees that would sleep for

the winter like their love. She wondered how the leaves got in his hair, why his breathing was uneven.

"I have something to tell you," he finally said. "I've been lying near our hill for hours, and what I have to say is killing me." He looked away. "I'm going back. To Finland, then Russia. Things are happening I must be a part of."

She sighed with sadness and relief. At least they could part without hurtful words. "When will you leave?"

"Tomorrow."

Said simply, while she'd been dying. "So soon?"

He pulled her to him. "Wherever I am, you'll be there."

They walked the streets which had been their playground. And in the back of her mind, she wondered, that just as God had played a role in their meeting, so He'd dealt them a parting hand. Would this be their last time together? Would he get hurt, take sick, or . . . die? *Oh, Sasha. What do you know of revolution, except in poetry? What do you know of starvation, suffering? Your convictions are only words.* She had lived the czar's terror. Her mother had died from it. Her brother had been a suicide. Her family, Jews everywhere, scattered across the earth in search of a home. Was Sasha's strength real? Could he survive?

They rode in a carriage through the park. The horse's clip-clop brought a remembrance of olden days. When the carriage left, he held her. "Whatever happens, I'll always love you, Anyushka. It's the only thing that will never change." Then he walked her back home.

"It will be good," he said at her door. "You'll have time to miss me." He tilted her chin. "No. Please. I can't bear to see you cry." He walked down the steps and looked back. He blew a kiss. Then, with hunched shoulders and hands in his pockets, he turned and left.

"Keep warm, Sasha!" she called. But he was gone.

Alone in the kitchen, she thought her heart would burst. It was like a death she could not even mourn. In bed she lay in a fetal position, hands across her mouth to still her cries. And as the days passed, the pain continued. Circles grew under her eyes; her thoughts spun in a centrifuge with no end or beginning. One day ran into the next, and her life had no meaning.

35

PALESTINE

The land is sweet, pink and gold, and the wailing desert winds sing a history of the world. In Deuteronomy, God gave the Land to the Israelites, and they lived there rejoicing, suffering, producing great kings, queens, rabbis, wise men, prophets, and madmen. But the same wailing winds brought conquerors as well.

For years the Jews fought to keep the Land, but like others before him, the Emperor Hadrian drenched the rivers with their blood. He burned their sacred scrolls, set up graven images. He passed laws forbidding the teaching of Torah. Even the name Jerusalem was obliterated and a new city built upon its ruins. What Hadrian intended was clear. The God of the Jews and all Palestinian Jewry were to be struck from the earth.

Executions began: rabbis, the high priests, scholars, judges, interpreters, scribes, those who could spread the teachings. And though he wrought great havoc, in the end, Hadrian didn't succeed. Though many Jews were killed or sold into slavery, others escaped to Acre, Tiberias, Hebron, and Safed, where they continued to live and practice their religion. Most scattered to the four corners of the earth, taking with them God's 613 commandments, Torah, and the knowledge of God's promise in Amos.

> *Behold, the days come, saith the Lord,*
> *That the plowman shall overtake the reaper,*
> *And, the treader of grapes him that soweth seed;*
> *And the mountains shall drop sweet wine,*
> *And all the hills shall melt.*
> *And I will turn the captivity of My people, Israel,*
> *And they shall build the waste cities, and inhabit them;*
> *And they shall plant vineyards, and drink the wine,*
>   *thereof;*
> *They shall also make gardens, and eat the fruit of*
>   *them.*
> *And I will plant them upon their land,*
> *And they shall no more be plucked up*
> *Out of their land which I have given them, saith the*
>   *Lord thy God.*

With more invaders and conquerors, the shape of the Land called Palestine continued to change. In 634 the Muslim armies battled for possession. In 639 Caliph Omar ibn al-Khattab took Jerusalem. Fifty years later, Caliph abd-ul Malik built the Dome of the Rock, and in time the city which held the sites of three great religions declined. It fell into the hands of Seljuk Turks, which outraged European Christians, who swore to seize it back. So began the Crusades.

The Crusaders took Jerusalem in 1099, ruling for one century. Then the Egyptians came, and the Mongols. The thirteenth century brought Osman, son of Ertugrul, who founded the Ottoman Empire. Under Suleiman the Magnificent, it reached like an octopus from Hungary to Mesopotamia, to Egypt, to Tunis, to Tripoli and Algiers. By the seventeenth century the empire began to crumble. Greece broke away. Then Serbia, Albania, Romania, Tunisia, Cyprus, and Bulgaria. Untended, the Land turned to dust. Ottoman rule had created anarchy. With unenforceable laws, with a thousand-years' war, the Land dried to a sea of shifting sands. And while it lay dying in the cruel sun, three forces came together for the rights to its bones: Arab nationalism, Jewish Zionism, and English imperialism.

SAFED, NEAR THE
SEA OF GALILEE 1908

When Joshua Kaminsky arrived, a powerful few landlords owned most of the territory. They rented tracts to sharecroppers, who tilled the soil for food and a little money. Some of the land owned by Greeks, Arabs, and Turks was available for purchase, and homeless Jews were eager to buy. The landlords laughed as they sold barren, worthless, malaria-infested wastelands, covered with flies and jackals, or alkaline grounds with boulders as large as trucks.

But the Jews drained the swamps, fought the malaria, and treated the earth. They dug it by hand, removing boulders with pickaxs and leverage. They had other tools as well: strength, conviction, devotion, determination, and desperation.

The place Joshua and his group settled was flat and scorched from the sun. The hot, dry air was alive with dust, wind, flies, and the smell of decay. A small river trickled by, and when it rained the whole valley flooded, leaving a muddy breeding ground for mosquitoes. Still, the Jews loved the land. Something finally belonged to them.

Eventually, they found a communal way of living.

The collective, or kibbutz, as it came to be called, brought safety. Members could support one another financially and emotionally as well. Tilling the soil together, each played a part in the creation of new life. In their own way they were imitating God's work. Taking bare earth and breathing life into it.

At Joshua's kibbutz they built sleeping quarters, kitchens, schools. With the swamps drained, they dug irrigation ditches to collect and distribute rainwater. They cut canals, plowed, planted, sowed, threshed, and reaped. Where nothing had grown for a thousand years there were now tomatoes, fig trees, orange groves, and grape arbors. But as the kibbutz grew, so grew the struggles: drought and plagues of locusts.

Then came a different plague, one of hatred.

The rich men who'd sold them the land watched it bloom. They grew jealous and fearful that their old way of life would die. The rich liked the low wages they paid poor Arab laborers. They enjoyed the privilege of absolute power. And when their fear reached a saturation point, they printed anti-Jewish tracts, doctoring photographs to show Jews desecrating Islamic holy places.

Unaccustomed to acknowledging borders, Bedouins brought their goats to graze on newly planted grounds. At first there were arguments as the Jews explained the concept of ownership. But each had a different history on his side. Then the arguments ceased and stealing began. But it was the ambush of two men by unknown marauders and the murder of a young Jewish girl that brought the kibbutzim to a meeting.

"I'm going back to Russia," a man shouted in Yiddish. "At least in the Pale there are no locusts."

"Milk and honey were promised," a woman cried. "My children have eaten only dust."

On and on they went, and when he'd had a bellyful

Joshua pounded the table. "Listen to you," he shouted. "Like the children of Israel when Moses took them from Egypt. Are you forgetting why we came? Jewish blood once fertilized this land. Now, it's our last hope. If we don't make a place here, we'll always be at someone's mercy. Jews from the four corners of the world must be united again. To live without fear, czars, pogroms, or Dreyfus affairs. How long must we cower in basements hoping they'll let our children live? Wake up! Unless we stay and fight, our people will disappear from the earth."

As Joshua took his seat, a voice came from the back. It was deep and sultry, the sound of a confident cat with manicured claws.

"You're right," the female voice said, addressing Joshua. "But people must be allowed to speak."

Joshua craned his neck. In a few moments his eyes claimed the speaker's face, and his heart raced like a pony. It was a young woman with short, dark copper curls against caramel skin, bare arms and legs that were small boned but well muscled, with a leanness that comes only from hard work. She had flashing green eyes above a small nose that was sprinkled with freckles. As his stomach dropped to his toes, he realized he'd missed her remarks.

". . . and a printing press. But more important, we need training in weapons; men, women, and children to carry guns and guard the settlements at night."

"Children!" several voices shouted. "You're crazy!"

"Why not? At twelve and thirteen, Jewish children die fighting for Russia. In Palestine, the cause is their future," she said.

"And where will we get weapons and training?"

"From me," a man's voice said.

There was a hush as a striking man in a knee-length black cape rose in the darkest, farthest corner of the room. His wide-brimmed hat shadowed piercing black eyes and covered long black hair. Beneath a wide nose sat a black mustache, a full bottom lip, and a pointed beard.

"This is Avigdor Levi," the woman said. "A member of Ha-Shomer, a group who believe in self-defense." The man removed his cape, and people gasped. A bandolier of bullets covered his chest; a gun sat in a leather holster at his right hip. At his side stood a rifle. "This is the language we must learn to speak if we are to survive."

"That will only cause problems with our Arab neighbors."

"We already have problems," someone said. "Weapons will earn us respect. Unless our neighbors respect us, we will always be in jeopardy."

"Have we forgotten how to reason?" a man asked.

"How do you reason with a gun at your head?"

"But there are laws against this."

"When have Jews enjoyed the right of law?"

After more heated debate, they took a break. There was much to discuss, including a rescue the coming week of two dozen Russian refugees arriving illegally. But when Joshua noticed the beautiful young girl wander outside, he followed.

He learned her name was Yael. "It means 'mountain deer,' " she explained.

"And I am Joshua," he told her.

"Warrior of the Hebrews. But a prophet of Islam, too."

They sat in an orange grove, talked about the meeting and the problems. He told her how he'd come to Palestine, of Herzl, and of his youthful dreams of being a symphony conductor. She shared her past, a life different from his own.

"I was born north of Safed, above the Sea of Galilee," she said. "My ancestors were weavers for the Turkish sultans. Then the Druse came, and my people had to leave. They lived in Jerusalem until taxes forced them out. In the olden days, if you couldn't pay, the government took hostages. My great-great uncle was taken for a debt, and they could never ransom him back. To this day, no one knows what happened to him."

Watching her, Joshua realized how shy and inexperienced he was with women. Talking to men, giving orders was easy. He was Joshua, a leader, looked up to in the kibbutz. In Yael's presence, he was a puppy dog with its tail between its legs.

As she talked and laughed, her eyelashes struck her round cheeks, freckles scrunched across her nose. But it was her mouth that intrigued him, moist, with a single star-shaped freckle on a full lower lip. A crumb, he thought at first, and reached impulsively to brush it away. When his fingers touched the mistake, he apologized.

"It's okay," she said, laughing. "Everyone does it."

She explained about the Land, and the similar sufferings of the Arabs under the Ottoman yoke. "We have much in common with them. They call Abraham Father of the Faithful. And the Koran, their holy book, reveres the very same prophets we do. We're cousins, in a way."

"You know so much about the history of these people."

"I've lived here all my life. I know Torah and I speak Arabic, too. I'm as close to some Arabs as I am to Jews. We're alike in many ways. Good. Bad. Shaped by history and events. While Europe drowned in the Dark Ages, the Arabs shaped art, architecture, even medicine."

"Then how can you support weapons against them?"

"I'm not against them, Joshua. My people have lived here since Abraham. I'm for me. This is my home, too."

Though Joshua tried not to, he thought of Yael often. He dreamed of her, too. She'd come to him in a diaphanous gown in a tent of candlelight, where they'd drink champagne and eat sweet baklava. He'd toast her beauty and say amusing things while she'd play with his hair. They'd whisper in each other's ears, and their bodies would draw close. He'd bring her gifts: a poem, a perfect flower, a woven shawl purchased from the old city. They'd recline on silken pillows amid the scent of citron, watching candles flicker. And when the last flame would die, he'd make love to her. He saw the color of her hair, her eyes, her skin, in the landscape. She was a blossom of the Holy Land, and he prayed one day the flower would be his.

While Joshua fought the elements in Palestine, the bloodiest pogroms in Russia's history were taking place. City after city was subjected to organized mayhem carried out by the Black Hundreds, a czarist police force who hounded the Jews in an orgy of death and destruction. The victims fled for their lives to America and Palestine. But in Palestine it was now against the law for Jews to enter. So they found ways to circumvent the law. Baksheesh, or bribes, were paid by some, while those without means claimed to come to the Wailing Wall as pilgrims, then later disappeared into the vast desert and a network of Jewish communal life. Those who could not get papers took other risks. Passage was booked on old, leaky cargo vessels that arrived at night. By prearranged signal, those on board would jump several miles before port, to be rescued by other Jews in small rowboats. The danger lay not only with the Turkish government but with robbers who combed the beaches waiting to kill the refugees and steal their valuables.

It was nearly midnight as Joshua and his small group of men searched for signs of danger on a deserted strip of calm beach along the Mediterranean. They were six, hidden beside three rowboats behind a bank of rocks, listening, searching with binoculars for the signal—three flashes of light.

At 2400 hours, their rear guard arrived, five members of a second kibbutz. Among the contingent, Joshua was stunned to see Yael. With one eye on the rolling sea, he whispered, "Why are you here?"

"To guard you," she whispered back.

"Yael! Be serious."

"I'm the best shot in the kibbutz, Joshua!"

Because he feared for her life, he turned to the man beside her and said, "Who's in charge of this unit?"

The man looked at Yael, then at him. "She is," he told Joshua and walked away.

Before he could say anything, the signal came from the darkness. Within minutes they were rowing to meet the refugees. Half an hour later they were back without incident.

Riding home on the donkey carts, an embarrassed Joshua thought of Yael. He pictured her in mortal combat and was deeply troubled. Women were mothers, sisters, wives, daughters, to be protected and cared for. They were to keep the Sabbath, to bake *challeh*, to raise a family and keep a home. Yet, this was a new land, with new problems, requiring new solutions and, above all, new thinking. Was he wrong? Was he right?

Days before Avigdor Levi had come to his kibbutz, some men had been beaten and a young Jewish girl had been raped and her throat slit. Perhaps, if she'd carried a gun, she would still be alive. But that was different. It was one thing for a woman to carry a gun for protection. Another for her to be part of an army.

An army? Of men? *And* women?

New lands were purchased, and the kibbutz grew larger. They continued working the soil and planting crops: fig trees, orange groves, olives, tomatoes. They raised chickens and farm animals; they slept on mats made of hollow reeds, ate flatbread and chick-pea paste with lemon and garlic. There were secret whistles to announce their comings and goings, and in their spare time they debated what their society would be. They played chess, checkers, and cards, read and formed music groups. At night, they told stories around campfires, danced and sang. Some fell in love, got married, had children. It was the dawning of a new age. Most of all, it was their first taste of freedom.

As carefully planned canals and ditches claimed the excess rain, the water worked for, not against them. There was now an abundance of food, which they sold at market bazaars. With the earned money, they bought equipment and farm animals, and, as their yield and the goodness of their lives increased, the marauders did too. There was jealousy and fear, and those in power continued to make trouble. Finally, pistols and a few rifles were purchased from Turkish arms dealers, and each man, woman, and child was instructed in their use.

In the following weeks Joshua and Yael saw each other frequently. He was consumed by his love for this girl, whose intelligence and beauty always took him by surprise. He'd attended the First World Zionist Congress, had been in the presence of men like Theodore Herzl, had met brilliant, influential people. He'd discussed world affairs, fled the Cossacks as a boy, but no one had affected him like this ninety-eight-pound female.

They met every Sunday, alternating rides to each other's settlement. They'd dine, sing, then share wine at a huge campfire. Finally, he asked her to walk with him one night. She was in sandals and khaki shorts and shirt, with that copper-colored hair more fiery than ever in the campfire light. Away from the others, he took her hand to help her over a hill where her curls tickled his nose and the scent of honey and almonds from her skin flooded his nostrils. Sitting against a sand dune, they shared more wine, and after a few long swigs his tongue began to loosen.

"I suppose you know how pretty you are."

"You've had too much to drink, Joshua."

"No, I haven't."

"If you really mean it, then say it in Hebrew."

He tried to say the words, but the language had always eluded him. "You . . . pretty," he said in Hebrew.

"Good!" she said smiling.

Encouraged, he continued. "Me . . . think . . . nice . . . you."

"Excellent!"

"Me . . . you . . . more . . . than . . . friends?"

"A question or a statement?"

"This is ridiculous, Yael," he said, throwing out his hands. "I'm a man, a leader, for God's sake. Don't treat me like a child."

She held his bearded chin and looked in his eyes.

"In Hebrew, Joshua," she said. "Say it in Hebrew."

He moved toward her. She made his mouth water. "Yael."

"Good beginning."

"*Ani ohev otach*," he said sheepishly.

Yael burst out laughing.

"What? What did I say?"

She clutched her stomach, doubled over from laughter. "You said—" She laughed again. "You said, 'Your goat is on fire and I want to kiss it.' "

The following Sunday she apologized. "I teased you last week, but I couldn't resist. Your Hebrew was beautiful."

"You mean I said it right? That you fooled me?"

She nodded, backing away as he came toward her. Suddenly, a chase was on. Across the sands they ran, laughing. The night was warm and soft and fitted them like a glove. The only light came from a distant campfire and a few torches along the road. She was fast, swallowed by the night, and Joshua searched everywhere. But the desert revealed nothing. Then a giggling sound gave away her hiding place. Pinpointing it, he crept on all fours, pouncing over a sand dune and landing with one leg on top of her. She lay on her back with him astride her. With his weight on his knees, he drew his fingers around her throat in a choking gesture.

"Give me one good reason not to do this," he said.

Gazing at each other, their bodies touching, they shared a moment of extraordinary stillness; it was as if the earth had forgotten to spin. Then it began to whirl, and he lowered his body to hers, feeling the rise and fall of her bosom against his chest. Slowly, his hands drifted from the exquisite softness of her neck to her shoulders. Slowly, his lips reached toward hers. His arms scooped behind her back, and as he lifted her gently from the sand, her head inclined backward and her eyes drifted closed. He was so near her parted lips, he felt the melding of their souls. He kissed her, and, from the deepest part of her throat, drew the breath from her lips. He savored the honey bouquet, drawing slowly away, gazing into the dreamy green of her eyes as the contours of her mouth turned upward and her face relaxed in an expression of contentment that mirrored his own feelings.

"Forgive me, Yael. Forgive my stupidity that night on the beach. Forgive my boldness now. I'm not used to this. I can fire a gun, or live for days without food and water. But you—you've made me a hopeless mass of jelly."

He watched her smiling lips part, the white teeth gleaming at him. Her fingers spread and coiled around his neck, threaded through the dark curls of his hair with an extraordinary strength. Answering him, she pulled him to her mouth. The pit of his stomach was a mass of knots as he realized he was falling deeply in love. All his life he had dreamed of a girl like her. All his life he had prayed to find her, envied the easy way other men had of just taking what they wanted. He had never been able to do that. Women were his sisters, like Sonia and Anya, or mothers, like Sarah—may she rest in peace.

He rolled on his stomach against his excitement. "I've loved you, Yael," he said. He felt crazy as he said it, as if his tongue no longer belonged to him. "From the first moment I saw you. Please don't break my heart."

She turned on her side, resting on a sand-planted elbow. Her mouth was against his ear. "I love you too, Joshua."

His spine rippled like the tinkling of piano keys.

"That day you spoke at the meeting," she said. "I thought my heart would burst with pride."

"Tell me what I said and I'll shout it again." He repeated her name, "*Yael. Yael.*" Then he grew still. "I have a secret to share." There was a tear in his eye. "Something I haven't told another soul." He paused. "I heard a bird today."

"A bird? Oh, Joshua. Where?"

"Singing over there in the orange grove."

She sat up and looked in the direction he pointed. "A bird," she said softly. "There hasn't been a bird here in a hundred years. Oh, Joshua, do you know what that means?"

"Yes," he said. "New life. It begins again."

They were married on a sandy hill beneath a starry sky, and everyone was invited. Yael, in a white peasant skirt and blouse, and Joshua, in his clean, pressed khakis, with an embroidered yarmulke on his head. They joined hands beneath a *chuppah*, a handmade blanket tied to four dowels used for planting. Their rabbi, carted in by donkey from a nearby village, helped them make their vows as they promised to love and honor, forever. The celebration lasted all night long: singing, dancing, food from their own gardens.

At midnight, Joshua carried his bride to a tent far away from the compound. Inside, he placed her on a mound of pillows and made love to her until the sun rose. When he left the tent that morning, he knew that by marrying her, he had finally made the Holy Land belong to him.

36

Anya pushed through the glass doors of Cohen & Son. She gave her name and sat in the reception room waiting for Charles.

"Anya! How did you know I'd be here?"

"Papa wrote me. Isn't it wonderful about Joshua?"

"Yes." He ushered her from the reception room into his office. "Papa and Sonia are happy about it. Here. Sit down." He pulled a chair alongside his large wooden desk.

"How are you, Charles? How is everyone?"

"We're all well. Naturally your father misses you." Her heart ached suddenly. "And I miss him."

"Do you need anything?" He reached in his pocket.

"No. Thank God. I'm fine."

She looked at the racks of beautiful tailored clothing in the corner. "What's Papa doing?"

"He and Chaim go to temple. Otherwise it's Maxwell Street and Lyons's Delicatessen. They see Yiddish theater a lot. Two weeks ago Glickman's Palace had a Jewish *King Lear*. The two of them wouldn't shut up for days."

"And you, Charles?"

"Me? I work. I fight with the unions. The new immigrants coming in are a handful. Things are changing so fast I can't keep up. They're calling for a major strike."

"Don't be angry. I must picket too."

He smiled, touched her hand, then quickly pulled away.

"So. How's Sonia?" she asked.

"She manages," he said. "She does lots of charity. Hospitals. Veterans. Museums." His face suddenly lit up. "We won a prize at the bird show. A blue ribbon."

"Oh, Charles. I'm so glad for you."

His eyes strayed to the wall. "Listen to me talk about a bird. I love them, but after I die they can't run my business. Cohen & Canary. Doesn't sound as good as Cohen & Son." Silence. "We think of you, Anya," he went on. "Papa and I. And in a strange way I think Sonia does too. She never really meant what she said. She's just bitter and took it out on you. You understand." Anya nodded.

"Can I buy you lunch?" he asked.

She hesitated. She wanted desperately to connect with someone in her family, but it couldn't be him. "I can't, Charles. A million things to do. Another time, perhaps."

"Sure," he said, disappointed. "So what's new?"

"Citizenship classes. Struggling with English. Working at Triangle."

"Triangle! That firetrap? Come work for me, Anya."

She said it quickly. "No, Charles. I'm happy there."

"And what do you do for fun?"

She thought. There hadn't been much fun in her life lately. "There's a Purim dance tonight. A contest to crown Queen Esther. My friend Sheyna wants me to enter."

Anya finally accepted Sheyna's apologies. It was difficult staying angry at someone who had rescued her when she'd come to New York alone and friendless, and who had suffered so terribly in her own life. So Sheyna had acted badly with Sasha. A mistake. But it was time to put the anger away. Now, they stood near the bedroom mirror preparing for the Purim contest.

"Pass the flowers," Sheyna said.

Anya handed Sheyna the make-believe lilacs. She felt silly as Sheyna pinned the purple flowers over her Gibson girl hairdo. But then she felt silly a lot these days. Nothing made sense. She went to work six days a week including the Sabbath, God should forgive her; she'd lose her job if she didn't. She was separated from her loving father. She had not been with Joshua on his wedding day. And in spite of what Charles had said, she knew Sonia hated her. And, Sasha. The one thing in her life that made sense was not only forbidden but gone.

The months without him had passed like a drudge, the ache, the emptiness in her stomach diminishing slowly. She'd forget sometimes, lose herself in the moment. Then she'd see couples walking hand in hand, or the rain would fall, and she'd burst into tears. She'd wonder where he was and find a thousand reasons for why he hadn't written.

"Look. It's finished," Sheyna said. "Stand up and turn around." Anya rose obediently and spun. Her long lilac gown, emblazoned with silver Stars of David, whirled at her slim ankles. "Gorgeous!" Sheyna went on. "Now walk. No! Not like a *shlump*! Straight. And smile. It's Purim, Anya. God commands this night you should be happy."

By 1909, there were some thirty-four dancing academies in the area between Houston and Grand streets, all of them respectable places for young Jewish men and women to meet. It was necessary to reach out in new ways. Most young people had come to America without parents, without the benefits of family-arranged marriages. Most could not afford marriage brokers, with

their detailed reports of job and health histories. So the
academies became a substitute, with their weekly and
holiday dances. For twenty cents, they provided respectable atmospheres for friendship, companionship,
and, if one was lucky, marriage.

Sheyna pushed open the door to the Grand Academy
of Dancing and held it for Anya. She wrote Anya's
name on the contest list and went inside. The room was
decorated for the holiday, softly lit, with a bar for soft
drinks, tea, or coffee and a tray of *hamantashen*, three-
cornered pastries named for Haman, the villain of the
Purim tale. The entertainment began promptly at nine,
with a reenactment of the story of Haman, prime min-
ister to the Persian King Ahashueres, who issued orders
for the execution of all Jews because of his obsessive
hatred for a single Jew named Mordechai. Unknown
to Haman, however, Mordechai was the uncle of the
king's wife, Queen Esther, and, with her help, Haman's
plan backfired.

A handsome young actor named Morris Barber read
all the parts, using different hats and voices for each
character. Each time he read Esther's part, he put on
a crown and veil and spoke in a high voice. Each time
he read the villain Haman's part, he wore the three-
cornered hat while everyone stomped their feet, whis-
tled, and booed. When he was finished, the queen's
contest began.

Pretty Queen Esthers came from every corner of the
room to claim the crown, until three finalists were left,
Anya among them. When the ballots were tallied, Morris placed the silver crown on Anya's head. Then the
queen's dance began, and Morris waltzed Anya around
the room.

"You're the prettiest girl here," he whispered in Yiddish. She smiled but said nothing. "I mean it!" he went

on. "Remember the girl who was second? Her dress was so tight, even I couldn't breathe."

Before long, Anya was laughing, and before the waltz was over, other young men were cutting in. At the close of the evening, Morris drove Anya and Sheyna home in a borrowed car. When they arrived, Sheyna went upstairs so Morris and Anya could talk. She told him about Kashkoi, her father's career as a violinist and teacher. He spoke of his family, all dead, a father who had been a peddler, a mother to whom he had been devoted, and a brother. Most of all he spoke passionately of the theater and recalled his first performance.

"I was in Lublin," he began. "A full house, people standing in the aisles. I was only sixteen, but when the lights went down it was magic."

His voice was extraordinary, deep and soft, like liquid velvet, doing things to simple human speech she'd never heard before.

"What's it like to be an actor?" she asked.

The corners of his mouth lifted in a smile. "We're all actors, Anya. Every morning we get up and dress in costumes we call clothes. Men shave. Ladies paint their faces. When we go outside, we make-believe we're rich if we're poor. Or nice, if we're mean. We even smile when we're angry. Shakespeare once wrote, 'All the world's a stage, and all the people players.' Could be, he was Jewish?"

Anya giggled. She loved his face, his animated, handsome, aquiline profile, the wavy black hair covering his ears. Brown eyes that were large and sleepy, as if he had just awakened. Strong jaw, square, with a deep cleft in a chin that lay beneath a full mouth. Once she'd seen a picture of Michelangelo's David—it looked like Morris Barber.

When she said good night, he asked if she would come

to hear him sing. "Friday night. At the Reform temple on Henry Street."

At Sheyna's urging, Anya went. Later, she met Morris outside, and they walked home together. She couldn't put her finger on why, but he seemed disappointed. Then, a block from her home, he broke the silence.

"You didn't like it."

She stopped. "Oh, no, Morris. I did!"

His face brightened. "Really?"

"Oh, yes. The candles, the people, everything."

"And?"

"And your voice, Morris. It's so beautiful."

"Naw! I was a little off-key tonight."

"No," she assured. "You were perfect."

"Perfect? Really? So, what especially was perfect?"

She was beginning to understand and brought enthusiasm to her comments. "Well, it was rich, like, like velvet."

"Maybe you're right, Anya," he said, smiling. "Sometimes it's hard to take a compliment."

When Anya came home, Sheyna was waiting up. "What did he say? Did he get fresh?" She smiled. "Wait. You'll get married. I can feel it in my bones."

"Don't be silly, Sheyna. I hardly know him."

Sheyna sat up. "Did your parents know each other when they got married?"

Soon, Anya invited Morris to a dinner of roast chicken, soup, potato *kugel*, freshly stewed fruit with just the right amount of lemon and sugar. Later, Morris sat in an easy chair and talked about his beginnings as an actor.

"There was a pogrom in Vilna, where I was born," he said. "Cossacks, horses, people screaming. I was five, but I had to watch. Then a circus came to town. Animals, dwarfs, a real giant. That's when I knew."

He told her all that. But he couldn't say the rest. How he hid in the cellar and watched three Cossacks hang a man. Or the funerals he loved: seeing the bodies, hearing the wailing of the women in their black clothes. Or the time his mother gave birth to a dead child, pulled from her thighs. All of it fascinating, all of it theater. Most of all, he couldn't tell her about his love for gambling.

"After my parents died, I had no reason to stay in Vilna, so I left with a troupe of traveling actors, and I've been acting ever since." He looked at the chain around her neck. "It's pretty," he said. "Gold?"

"Yes," she answered and changed the subject.

The second week in May, Morris rowed her across Central Park Lake. They picnicked and listened to an outdoor concert. His head bobbed with the music; his hands conducted and his feet tapped.

Before long Morris proposed marriage, and Anya had to decide. She liked him. He was fun to be with. What was more, he needed her, almost the way Saul had. Somewhere inside him lived a little boy, and the mother in her responded to that. He wasn't Sasha. Her heart didn't beat fast. But Morris made her laugh and forget she was alone and lonely. Then a letter came from Sasha telling her they would marry when he returned from Finland. That's when she knew what to do. It was the letter that helped her make up her mind.

37

Anya knew marriage to Sasha would be a disaster. Where would they marry? A church? A synagogue?

Fair to neither and unfair to both. Where would they live? Here on Hester Street? The neighbors would laugh. And how could she deny her father and her people? Or ask Sasha to deny his? Who would be their friends? And their children's friends? What holidays would they celebrate? It was an endless war of questions without answers. That was when she took Sasha's chain from her throat and placed it at the bottom of her drawer.

When she gave Morris her answer, he kissed her and pledged his devotion. She gazed into his soft, childlike eyes, at the yearning to become something better, and knew she would stand behind him. When she wrote her father of her decision and he replied with happiness, she knew she had done the right thing. Soon, they began planning a small wedding.

Sheyna helped Anya make a gown of white organdy with leg-o'-mutton sleeves and a lace veil. She bought white satin slippers, hose, and satin ribbons for trimming. They rented a furnished place on Hester Street, an exact duplicate of the one Anya shared with Sheyna, with a tub down the hallway and a big front window.

The *Shabbos* before their marriage, Morris went to temple, where he was called to Torah and given a special blessing. The night before the wedding Anya went to the *mikvah*. On their wedding day, Shmuel arrived by train, and, while Charles checked into the hotel, Shmuel took a taxi to Anya's old apartment. When her father entered, she could hardly believe her eyes. He was out of breath from the stairs, as thin as a rail, with half a head of snowy white hair. He used a cane, and his once vigilant eyes were cloudy, the irises nearly petrified.

"Oh, Papa. I missed you," she said, hugging him.

Shmuel scrutinized her from head to toe. "God bless you," he said in Yiddish. "Except for the coloring, you look like Mama, may she rest in peace." He faltered, and she went to help him. "I'm all right. Don't worry," he said. "I feel good." He took off his jacket and alternately flexed his muscles with his fingers locked behind his head. She watched the small biceps jump. "Like an ox," he said. "And still your papa."

Anya sat beside him in the easy chair. "Was your trip nice?"

"Very nice. I've always liked trains."

"And how is Sonia?"

He didn't look at her. "Believe you me, she wanted to come. Lately—her stomach's not well."

"Oh, I'm sorry. Is it serious?"

He shrugged. "Who knows? Sonia doesn't say much."

Anya talked about the new apartment they had rented, about Morris's acting career, and Shmuel seemed excited.

"Does he know about my violin?" Before she could answer he said, "Ach! Who cares? That was a hundred years ago." He held out his hands. Anya saw the gnarled fingers trembling. "I don't play anymore."

She kissed his palms. "It must be hard for you, Papa."

She put her head on his knees and became a child again. His frail hands caressed her long hair, over and over. They stayed that way until he lifted her chin. "I brought Mama's comb. Wear it for the ceremony. She'd like that."

At the synagogue, Morris and Anya stayed in separate rooms until the service. Two of Morris's friends witnessed as the rabbi and Morris signed the marriage contract, or *ketubah*. The responsibilities of the bride and groom were part of the standard text. Morris was to provide food, clothing, shelter, and sexual satisfaction. Anya was to love, honor, and obey.

In her room, Anya was a mixture of solemnity and

joy. She had given a white handkerchief to Morris to signify her acceptance of the contract.

"Something old," Sheyna said, placing Sarah's comb in Anya's hair. "Something new." She pointed to Anya's new dress. "Something borrowed." She gave Anya her own pearl earrings. "And something blue." She removed the small bridal bouquet from a white box. A pretty blue ribbon was woven into the stem. "It's an American custom."

"Oh why am I so nervous?" Anya cried.

"Here," Sheyna replied. She gave Anya some spirits. "That's why God made schnapps."

Then the ceremony began.

Morris walked down the aisle to the maroon velvet *chuppah*, where the rabbi waited. Anya followed with Shmuel, who carried a candle in memory of Sarah. Reaching the *chuppah*, Shmuel remained at Anya's side, symbolizing the union of families and not just individuals. Blessings were spoken by the rabbi, wine shared between bride and groom, then a simple gold ring, a solid circle to show that life has no end or beginning, was placed on Anya's finger.

Shmuel stood with his hand in a fist over his heart, his body rocking back and forth through time, through the joys and sorrows, listening to the rhythm of the service, shedding tears of remembrance. May it be with you, dearest daughter, he thought, as it was for me and your beloved mother, may she rest in peace.

The rabbi read the *ketubah* out loud and gave it to Morris, who gave it to Anya. He reminded them that God's first commandment was to be fruitful and multiply. Then he pronounced them married. As Morris smashed a cloth-wrapped glass beneath his foot, a symbol of the fragility of life and marriage in the midst of joy, there were shouts of *Mazel tov*, and a celebration followed.

Sheyna listened to the music and watched them dance. She was happy for Anya but feeling envious too. Morris Barber would be a great husband if Anya could tame his wildness. Not that it should *all* be tamed. Every man needed a little wildness. Like her father, for example, a gambling man of many schemes, a man with a dozen faces, a hundred ideas, none of which had borne fruit. Creditors and landlords had hounded them. But she loved him and blamed her mother for his failures. Mama had never understood him. She'd berated him when he needed acceptance and encouragement. If he'd had them, maybe one crazy idea would have succeeded and their lives changed. They'd have left the miserable town she grew up in, and her parents would still be alive. She'd have had pretty clothes, an education, a dowry. Most of all, she would not have become "damaged goods," from whom mothers kept their sons away. But that was the past. And she had her eye on the future.

At 10:00 P.M. Anya kissed her father good-bye, then headed with Morris for the new apartment. Morris was drunk, laughing as his friends helped him to bed. While Morris slept, Anya opened presents. Towels from Sheyna. A set of sheets and pillowcases from the workers at Triangle. A samovar from Morris's friend Abe. From Charles and Sonia, a hundred dollars. But Shmuel's were the most precious gifts of all: Sarah's candlesticks, the family Bible, and a baby's silver spoon. She opened the Bible to where the family history lay and wrote, *Morris Barber and Anya Kaminsky, Married June 21, 1909*, then went back to the bedroom. Morris was snoring. Disappointed, she put on her new white nightgown and lay beside him.

38

In the middle of the night, Anya wakened to Morris tugging at her nightgown. She lay quietly as he climbed on top and thrust himself inside her. The pain and pressure were so intense she bit her hand to keep from screaming. Minutes later, he shuddered and rolled away. As he slept, Anya cried. Sheyna had said it would hurt, but she had not expected the absence of tenderness and affection. Maybe next time, she thought. But the next time, and even after that, was the same. He'd come to bed and lunge inside her. Three short thrusts later it was over. Then he'd roll over and go to sleep. She hated it. She would never get used to being treated that way. Oh, Morris, she thought. How different it is from what I imagined. Then she thought of Sasha.

The day Anya returned to work after her honeymoon, Sheyna chided her at lunch for covering her hair. She thought the custom old-fashioned, but worse, hypocritical, because Anya worked on the Sabbath. Anya told her it didn't matter. Better to keep some laws than none at all. Then Sheyna asked questions about the wedding night, which Anya answered because she had a question of her own.

"He does things that confuse me," Anya said.

Sheyna slid closer. "What things?"

Before she lost her nerve, she said it quickly. "He wears these *things* . . . on himself. Fancy balloons."

Sheyna seemed bewildered. "They're called raincoats, Anya. But a man only wears them so he won't have children." Then she explained.

All day long, Anya thought about their conversation. By the time she came home she was furious.

"We have to talk, Morris," she said.

He tried to be funny, got down on his knees. "Oh great princess, I'm listening, you're talking."

"Stop acting, Morris. Be serious!"

She reminded him of the rabbi's words. "God's first commandment is 'Be fruitful and multiply.' "

"Two times two is six," he joked.

"Please, Morris!" She took his arm. "I want children. As many as God will give."

"So, who says no?"

She breathed in courage. "You. And your raincoats."

Morris's face turned the color of red wine. "Who told you such a word?" he demanded.

Anya didn't answer.

He banged the table with his fist. "Sheyna!" he said. He pointed an ominous finger at her. "I forbid you to see her anymore. I won't have my wife listening to *coorves*."

"Shah, Morris. Sheyna's not a prostitute. She's just experienced. Besides, I have no one else to ask."

Morris took Anya's hands and sat her down. "Do you love me, Anya?" She nodded. "Did you promise when we got married you'd help my acting?" She nodded again. "If you get pregnant, you can't work. If you can't work, I'll need two jobs. So, when do I audition? I'm too young to forget my dreams."

She put her arms around him. His body was stone. "I'd never ask that, Morris. Never! But I'm strong, and if God grants a child, I'll work at Triangle until the end, then take in piecework."

"And from where will you get a sewing machine?"

"I'll buy it. With the money Charles gave us."

Morris stood up and walked away. "You can't," he said. "I made an investment that failed."

*   *   *

In the end, Morris's raincoats failed, too. Within three
months Anya was pregnant. When Morris found out
he was angry and didn't talk to her for days. Sometimes
he stayed out all night, then came home and criticized
the way she looked. Anya knew her marriage to him
was a mistake, but she resigned herself. She was going
to have a baby.

During the pregnancy, Morris took a part-time job
at Triangle, and Anya continued working, saving every
penny she could. Then a letter came from Shmuel. He
wanted to be there when the baby came, and Morris
agreed. They bought a cot and put it near the stove,
where Shmuel could be warm. They hung a curtain
across a string so he could have privacy. And when he
arrived, two weeks before the baby's due date, Anya
couldn't have been happier.

The birth of olive-skinned, blue-eyed little Sharon made
everyone happy. Shmuel's visit stretched to weeks,
months. Finally, it was clear he did not wish to return
to Chicago. He liked living with Anya and Morris. Morris and Shmuel had things in common. They went to
Yiddish theater, where for a few pennies they saw the
reenactment of their old lives in czarist Russia. They
could watch a pogrom onstage, but this time walk away.
They went to Yiddish *Romeo and Juliet*, where Friar
Lawrence became a learned rabbi and the feuding families were Orthodox and Reform Jews. Or to Yiddish
Hamlet, in which a newly ordained rabbi returned home
to his father's funeral and his mother's marriage to an
uncle.

Yiddish theater was growing rapidly. Actors cla-
mored for a union, picketed, or lay their bodies across
streetcar tracks. After a few weeks of mayhem, the

Hebrew Actors Union of New York was formed. It was good for those who were already working. For Morris, it was a headache. To get a job now, he had to be a union member. To become a union member, he had to get a job.

Still, Morris studied every day. He made faces in the mirror, applied makeup, and practiced accents. He'd follow old people, lame people, people with hunchbacks. He tried imitating and understanding what they were feeling. Anya admired him, though it sometimes drove her crazy. She never knew who she was living with. One week he was an Indian, another, an Oriental. He covered his eyes to be blind, turning the house into a shambles, or stuffed cotton in his ears to be deaf.

Then an opportunity came for Morris to audition and join the union. Anya begged him to sing or do comedy, but he did *King Lear*.

"Come back next year, Mr. Barber," they said when he finished. "Get a little more experience."

As they headed home, Morris was inconsolable. "It will happen in time," Anya reassured him. "Be patient." Then she patted her belly and told him Sharon would soon have a brother.

In the midst of Canal Street, Morris screamed. "Are you crazy? I can't feed another mouth."

The following day a solemn Anya went to Charles for a loan. Without question, he gave her money for a sewing machine. A week later Morris was hired as a cantor in a nonunion drama. He was thrilled as he practiced morning and night. But on the eve of the opening performance, he missed his cue and was found shooting dice with the janitor. Promptly fired, he was sent home without pay. More unfortunate, a member of the union had been in the audience, and when Morris's review came up, he was rejected again.

The following week Sheyna visited Anya and the baby. As they shared tea, they got to the subject of Morris.

"So. You're not happy with him?"

"Could be better, Sheyna."

"He's sensitive, Anya. An artist."

"Maybe. Maybe not."

"What are you, a maven? What do you know from acting?"

"I know Morris is no King Lear."

Sheyna sipped her tea. "Reminds me of my father—he should rest in peace. I believed, but my mother laughed behind his back. Support Morris, Anya. Don't laugh behind his back. Who knows what will happen."

Anya thought of Sheyna's words for days. She had never once laughed behind Morris's back. Yet, there was truth there too. Another baby due. Sharon. Shmuel's failing health. Those were her concerns. So maybe Sheyna was right. So maybe she'd try a little harder.

39

One Wednesday evening a man looked up at a familiar tenement. Cold, he shifted from one foot to the other as a light in the upper window went on and a woman's silhouette moved against the shade. After a while he entered the building and knocked at the door. A familiar voice soon called out, and the door opened.

"Oh, it's you."

Sasha peered beyond Sheyna to see Anya's face.

"She's not here," Sheyna said.

"Where is she?"

"Happily married, if you must know."

"I don't believe you," Sasha said.

Sheyna wrote the address on a piece of paper. "See for yourself."

On Friday, March 25, a letter arrived from Joshua.

January 12, 1911

Dearest Family,

Yael, the baby, and I are well and there's another child on the way. How I wish you could be here. We've enlarged the compound and bought new land for refugees that pour in daily. The stories they tell are so horrible we must provide shelter. We've built two hospitals, schools in Jaffa and Jerusalem and circulate two Hebrew daily newspapers. Little by little, we make progress. Don't be alarmed if there are rumors of war. We'll be fine.

Love, Joshua

At 5:30 P.M. the following day, Anya heard a commotion. She opened the window and saw an ominous black cloud hovering above Washington Place. Below, crowds scurried toward it like mice.

"Papa!" she cried. "Stay with Sharon!"

She ran into the street, where word spread that the Triangle factory was on fire. She tried not to think the unthinkable and rushed through the human chaos, past the fire trucks, through the crowds jamming the streets. As she turned the corner, bright orange flames licked a smoky, black sky. She craned her neck upward, gasping as men and women hurled themselves from eight-story windows like flaming rag dolls. The smell of death was everywhere. With all her strength she pushed through the mob, searching the dead and wounded for Morris and Sheyna, but she couldn't find them.

"You all right, miss?" a policeman asked.

Anya couldn't answer.

Dazed and frightened, she stumbled through the milling crowd and headed home. She didn't know what seized her, but as she passed Sheyna's apartment building, something made her climb the stairs. As if by rote, she reached the door and banged on it with both her fists. She was taken by surprise as Sheyna's voice vaulted from inside.

"Sheyna! You're safe!" Anya cried. "Thank God!"

The door opened and Anya fell into her friend's arms.

"Triangle's on fire," Anya sobbed. "I can't find Morris."

On and on, she pleaded for Sheyna's help.

"I'll get dressed," Sheyna said. Anya tried entering the apartment, but Sheyna barred the way.

"Wait downstairs," Sheyna whispered. "I got a friend inside."

Sheyna closed the door and returned to her bedroom.

"What's wrong?" a man's voice asked. "Was that Anya?"

"Yes," Sheyna said as she dressed.

The man quickly grabbed his trousers.

"Stay. She's downstairs. Triangle's on fire, and she's very upset."

"That filthy firetrap. God! What if she sees me?"

"Don't worry. Just wait ten minutes, then lock the door when you leave."

There was no Morris at the hospital, no Morris at the morgue. Anya was frantic, and by eight o'clock Sheyna took her home. In the apartment, Shmuel was sick and the baby crying. Ten minutes later, Morris walked in, and a weeping, happy Anya ran to his arms. He had gone to an audition, he explained, near Broadway, and got a small part.

The months of pregnancy passed quickly. Spring turned to summer as Anya's time drew near. Her legs and back hurt, but she kept on working. Things were looking up. Morris was getting closer to joining the union. What was more, he was taking Anya's advice, preparing a comedy sketch. Then, on September 2, Simon, named for Saul, was born.

The following winter Shmuel caught cold and found it hard to climb the stairs. "It's the last stages of a bad chest cold," the doctor said, reassuring Anya. "A little chicken soup, and he'll be fine." Anya took Shmuel home, but his condition didn't change. Two weeks later Anya wakened to find Sharon at her bedside.

"Mommy. Get up. *Zeyde* won't gimme breakfast."

An alarm rang in Anya's head. She leaped out of bed and ran to Shmuel, pushing his curtain aside. She found him stiff as a board, unable to breathe. She dropped to her knees and massaged his icy hands.

"Oh, Papa. Papa. What's wrong?"

Shmuel's lips moved but no words came out.

"*Morris*," Anya screamed. "*Come quick!*"

Morris ran and carried Shmuel from the bed. He rushed to the open window yelling, "Breathe, Papa. *Breathe!*" He cradled Shmuel and told Anya to run next door and call the doctor. Five minutes later, Anya returned, but it was too late. Shmuel's vigilant eyes slowly closed, no longer to observe or look lovingly upon his family. The shaking hands relaxed and fell limp. The mouth that had always spoken wisdom was now without expression. Only a single tear remained in the corner of his eye. Anya put her arms around Morris, leaned against his back, and wept.

Tradition says to bury quickly, simply, and they did. Though Sonia and Charles tried, they did not arrive for the funeral. Instead they visited the graveside on the fourth day, then went to see Anya, who sat *shivah* at home. It was the first time they'd been together since Chicago, and the two sisters embraced. But without warmth. Not even the death of their beloved father would bring forgiveness. Sonia entered on Charles's arm, dressed in black fox furs, a black, ankle-length wool suit, and handmade boots. A black veiled hat covered her dark hair, with its tiny strands of gray peeking through. It enhanced her alabaster skin and dark, slanted eyes, which now had tiny crow's-feet.

Anya's life was exactly as Sonia had expected. A common husband, common friends, a hovel for a home, though it was clean as a pin. She refused the offered food and couldn't wait to leave. She hated the East Side odors of chicken fat, despised the women in their silly wigs alongside their black-frocked, bearded husbands. These Jews had not escaped the Pale, they'd brought it with them to Hester Street.

Sharon touched Sonia's fur. The child was clearly fascinated. "Pretty," Sharon said.

Sonia tickled Sharon's nose with a fox tail, which made the child giggle. The little girl put her head on Sonia's lap and, sucking her thumb, lay there contentedly.

"Don't bother Tante Sonia," Anya said to her daughter.

"It's all right," Sonia said. She lifted Sharon onto her lap, observed the child's smooth olive skin, black curly hair, and bright blue eyes. In a few minutes Sharon curled her chubby arms around Sonia's neck and hugged her. The feel of the baby-soft skin gave Sonia chills, and she recalled instantly the two miscarriages she'd suffered. It was more than she could bear, and she said her good-byes.

"I love you, Tante Sonia," Sharon said at the door.

"And I love you," Sonia replied.

Inside the limousine, Sonia loosened the fur, untied and lifted her veil. "Thank God it's over," she said. She took a cigarette from her purse and waited for Charles to light it.

"Since when do you smoke?" he said, accommodating her.

She laughed. "For a year, Charles. If you were home more often, you'd know that." She exhaled a cloud and waved it from her face.

The car moved slowly through the crowded streets, past the pushcarts, the filthy children roaming the gutter, rusty, flaming barrels where the peddlers slapped their cold hands together. The sight of it sickened her, and she made a face, tapped the driver's glass partition, and said, "Faster, please."

"Will you sit *shivah* in Chicago?" Charles asked, when she sat back. Sonia looked at her husband as if he were a stranger.

"I thought perhaps, out of respect . . ."

"I loved my father," Sonia interrupted. "But I'm no hypocrite. The minute I get home that 'thing' on the door will be removed, and I'll mourn him in my own way. I don't need a rabbi. I've never accepted the nonsense they preach. And I don't intend to start now."

40

A cloud of cigar smoke filled Anya's kitchen.

"Two cents," Morris's friend Abe said.

"Raise to five," Morris countered.

"Five?" Abe shouted. "The rules are two and four."

"You don't like five? Quit!"

Abe grumbled and put a nickel in the poker pot. Two rounds later the cards fell and Morris squealed, "Aces. Back to back." He was pulling in the money when Abe stopped him.

"Not so fast," Abe laughed. "Three fours."

Morris threw his cards down in disgust. "Since when did you get the other four?" he asked.

"My hole card, that's where."

By the end of the evening Morris had lost five dollars. The following day the landlord came to collect the rent, and Anya had to stall him once more. Again she went to Charles, and he wrote her a check.

A week later Sheyna came to Morris with a business proposition. The design of a child's smock. Made for a few pennies, it could be manufactured to sell at a huge profit. Sheyna had her share of the seed money and Morris needed his. He begged Anya to go to Charles again, but this time she refused.

That night, Morris lay awake thinking of ways to get the money. Sheyna's plan was good as gold, and he knew it. If he didn't buy in, he'd never forgive himself. He could have tons of money. Then he could study with the greatest actors in the world. Besides, what did Anya know? She was just another dumb greenhorn like the rest. By 5:00 A.M. he'd had enough. Quietly, he got out of bed and dressed. He ate a piece of bread and butter, made a decision, and left.

At 2:30 the same day, Anya knocked on Mrs. Silverstein's door. She asked the old woman to stay with the children so she could pick up and deliver her piece-work. By four o'clock she returned to make dinner.

Friday morning, Anya went to polish her silver candlesticks for the Sabbath. She opened the cupboard door, but the space was empty. Hysterical, she opened and slammed every drawer until Sharon and Simon were crying. She consoled the children with cookies until Morris came home.

"Thank God you're home," Anya said. She put on her hat and coat. "I'm going to the police. Mrs. Silverstein took my silver candlesticks."

As she headed for the door, Morris blocked her way.

"Don't go," he said. His eyes scoured the floor. "I pawned them. Your gold necklace too. I needed the money for Sheyna's business." He threw the pawn tickets on the table. "Don't look on me that way. I did it for you."

For a full minute Anya didn't speak. She just stared at the table, feeling tears and anger choke her throat. She wanted to smack him, to hurt him as he'd hurt her, but the children were watching. So she stared at him with contempt, opened the door, and left.

Outside, she stopped to button her coat, but didn't notice the man standing in the doorway across the street. She just walked with her head down, thinking of how Morris had pawned two hundred years of tradition without a second thought. And Sasha's necklace. All she had left of a great joy in her life. How could he be so callous? Then again, she shouldn't be surprised. Morris was Morris, a charming clown in public, a selfish man in the privacy of their lives. Someone who would never understand her or grow up. Then it hit her hard. She had married him for all the wrong reasons, and she was unable to fix it. But she thought of her babies as well. Two little ones who loved their father dearly. And she was a mother first. Whatever their problems, whatever Morris had done, her children were all that mattered. That was when she turned around and walked home.

As he'd done many times before, Sasha held his breath as Anya passed. And though every pore in his being urged him to scream her name, he pressed deeper into the shadows and stayed silent. She was married; she had children. He wouldn't spoil her life for the world.

As he watched the door close behind her, his dreams of taking her with him dissolved like the snow in the gutter. He had come here to see her, to take her away. Now, it could never be. So, he'd return to the apartment in Greenwich Village and wait for word from the committee. He'd put his mind back on the revolution and never think of her again. It was finally over, he decided. Everything but the memories and heartache.

Anya forgave Morris for taking her things. A few weeks later she went to pick up more piecework. She walked home through the snow, keeping her head down, with her gloved hands wrapped tightly around her bundle. Though Morris's investment with Sheyna was in the early stages, it did look promising. As she headed down Grand, she passed a kosher deli and thought some hot tea would taste good. She pushed open the door and sat at the counter with her bundle at her feet. "Tea, please," she said, loosening her scarf.

As she waited, she looked around. In a far booth, a familiar face caught her eye. She waited a moment to let it register, then realized it was really him. She lifted her bundle and ran to the booth, waiting until the man looked up.

"Anya?"

"Oh, Sasha!"

They sat opposite each other, looking, smiling, sharing the years they had been apart. While she spoke of her children, he talked of his work with the revolutionary committee. He said he was glad she was happy and joked about his broken heart.

As time passed, she realized the magic was still there. He made her heart stand still, do flip-flops. He made her head spin and her stomach knot. Married or not, the mother of two, Sasha would always be her first love.

He told her where he was living, then asked if she still had the necklace.

"I took it off the day I got married."

"I understand," he said.

As they shared more missed years, the deli door opened, and Anya heard Sheyna's broad laughter. She scooted down behind a plant, praying she wouldn't be seen. But Sheyna was talking so loudly, Anya's curiosity was aroused, and she peeked. She saw Sheyna and a male companion through the leaves and felt suddenly sick.

"It's all right," Sasha said when Sheyna and her friend had gone. "They didn't see us."

Anya stared blankly at him. "It doesn't matter," she said. "I saw them."

Morris came home late that night and told Anya about his day. He'd been busy looking for buyers. When the children had gone to sleep, Anya asked many questions.

"What is this? The Inquisition? I already told you."

"Don't lie, Morris. I saw you with Sheyna in the deli today. You were kissing her cheek."

Morris didn't flinch. "There you go, Anya. Jumping to conclusions. This is America, for God's sake. Not the old country. We sold an order, so I kissed her." He threw a handful of money on the table. "Here," he said. "For your candlesticks and necklace. I see they mean more to you than I do."

The following day Anya felt ashamed. Morris and Sheyna. Behind her back. How silly. Just like her and Charles. Or as innocent as she and Sasha sitting in the same deli. She would apologize to Morris the next day, she decided.

She called the baby-sitter and took the pawn tickets to redeem her things. She walked down the street feeling better, thinking of Sasha, just a little smug that after all these years he still cared. It was nearly noon, early, when she finished shopping and decided to visit Sheyna.

She climbed the stairs clutching her candlesticks, holding the necklace in her pocket. She had complained so much about Morris these last months, it was time to praise him for a change. Always, an understanding Sheyna had wise things to say, and Anya enjoyed their frequent talks. Thank God for such a good friend, she thought.

She knocked. When the door opened a crack, Anya shouted, "Boo!" and barged in. Inside, she stood frozen. Morris was at Sheyna's kitchen table dressed in his underwear.

"What is this?" Anya demanded. "What's going on?"

Morris scrambled for his trousers. Sheyna grabbed a cigarette. When neither answered, Anya's rage bore down like a speeding locomotive.

"It's nothing," Morris said, buttoning his trousers. "My pants got dirty and Sheyna cleaned them."

Morris's stupid remark made Anya's blood boil. She went to him and slapped his face. "Stop it!" she shouted. "We're not in a theater. Stop acting for once in your life."

As she spoke, it added up. The incident at the delicatessen. Her private talks with Sheyna. *Sheyna*. Always defending Morris. Maybe they were together during the damn Triangle fire, too. How could they be so cruel? "Will one of you have the decency to tell the truth?"

When no one answered, Anya turned and left.

She raced nonstop into the cold street. She stumbled, the betrayal digging so deep she thought she was bleeding. Every part of her ached, and it didn't take long to realize she was running to *him*.

She hammered the door with her bare fists, ranting and raving till he opened it. She went limp in his open arms, and he carried her inside. Sobbing and shuddering in their familiar Russian, she told him everything.

"Oh, Sasha. How could they humiliate me so?"

"Perhaps you expect too much, Anya. No human being is perfect."

She pushed away. "Is it naive to believe in marriage and fidelity? In friendship? The whole world's changing, and I don't fit in."

After a while, she grew tired of hearing herself and became more aware of his strength. She felt protected again and held his hand as her fingers traced the lines of his palm.

"Your lifeline is long, but broken in two places."

"The first break belongs to you," he said, smiling.

"And the other?"

He shrugged. "Only time will tell."

She gazed into his eyes. The sweet, familiar love of her young innocence stared back at her. She felt healed, as if his soothing energy had made her stronger. The power of that thought frightened her, and she moved away.

"I feel better now," she said. "I should go."

"No, Anya. Don't. I'll make some tea."

She hesitated, then agreed to stay.

While he fussed in the kitchen, she looked around. The place was small, its only light a roaring fire in the fireplace. There were books scattered everywhere, modern paintings, and a Spanish guitar leaning against a wall. A Chinese screen of red-and-black lacquer separated the kitchen from the bedroom and stood near a chess table on which a game was half played. She helped Sasha when he returned with a tray holding two china cups of steaming tea and asked him to talk about Russia, anything but her problems.

He told her how long he'd been in America, that all along he'd been watching her, believing she was happily married and not wanting to disturb her. Then he talked about the work he was doing.

"As I predicted," he began, "another duma failed. The czarina has this crazy priest at court, Rasputin. *He* advises *her* while *she* advises the *czar*. If it weren't so sad, I'd be laughing. Now there's talk of war in Europe."

She mentioned Joshua's letter from Palestine.

"Yes. He would have heard about war there, too. Germany is banking a railway through Turkey, and new trade routes will open. They'd rather kill each other than share the riches."

"Is the Holy Land in danger?"

"I'm not sure. I only know we must change what is wrong in Russia. Too many good men have already been jailed or exiled. There are forty-five thousand political prisoners in Siberia alone. We send them messages with invisible ink to keep their morale up."

"How can you see ink if it's invisible?" she asked.

He took a seemingly empty page from an envelope and placed it near the fire. The heat of the flames revealed the words. It amazed her.

Their eyes met and lingered as they sipped their tea. Feelings of love, hunger, denial welled to the surface and reached across an eternity of wasted years. As the tension between them mounted, her spoon clattered to the floor, and Sasha knelt to retrieve it. Suddenly, his arms wound around her ankles, his head lay against her thighs. He looked at her from the floor, pleading, with tears in his eyes.

"I can't help myself, Anya," he said, choking on his words. "If you stay, I'll only make love to you."

She trembled with fear at the power of his warm breath on her body. God! How she wanted him. Images of her children, Morris, her marriage vows flashed in her brain. Over and over they collided until she put the cup down and grabbed her things. She ran to the door, scared, dizzy, fighting desire, praying for the sound of his voice to beg, to encourage, to entreat her to stay; but he said nothing. By his silence, he had made the choice hers.

Her tongue cleaved to her palate with dryness. The muscles in her throat clenched as she tried to speak. With every bone in her body she sought the courage to leave and fought her deepest needs to stay. But in the end, her courage faltered and her needs won. She shut the door, leaned her forehead against the cool wood, listening as his footsteps came behind her, feeling his chest melt against her back like hot butter. Slowly, his fingers untied the knot of her soft headdress. Her hair billowed down, spilling to her waist for a stranger to see. As he turned her, as his mouth covered hers in a passionate kiss, she knew it was over. Her terrible war had ended in surrender.

In a single movement, he swept her from the floor and carried her to his rumpled bed, where he undressed her. With each undone button he kissed the bare pink skin until her blouse lay wide open. He hooked one arm beneath her waist and lifted her half-naked torso from the pillow, watching her breasts sway and her head

and neck fall gracefully backward as though she had no
bones. He took the blouse from her body and placed
her gently back down.

He quickly undressed, put a log on the dwindling fire,
and lay beside her. Where two shadows had been drawn
on the wall, now there was one, arms and legs entwined,
bodies united in a single flesh. He kissed her shoulders,
her throat, the soft spot near her collarbone, the nipples
of her breasts.

Shaken, with so much terrifying passion inside her,
Anya made one last effort to resist, but kiss by kiss all
barriers soon faded. She was lost to him, loving him,
following each of his moves as his fingers roamed the
soft curves and planes of her form.

His touch was light, sensitive: feathers, butterfly
wings, a caterpillar spinning a cocoon. Her heart
pounded; volcanic forces burned her groin with a white
heat. She wanted to shout her joy and found herself
swaying with each of his strokes. He massaged her back,
soothed her thighs, caressed her buttocks; when he
touched her dark and secret places, she shut her eyes.

"No, Anya!" he demanded, stopping. "There is no
shame between us."

Her eyes slowly opened to meet his, and he began
again. Then he was on her, and she heard her breath
come in short gasps as he parted her thighs and the
mass of erect flesh which before had always seared her
with pain, slipped easily inside and penetrated deeply.
She burned with exquisite pleasure as he moved, heart
pounding as she met each of his thrusts. Deep inside,
he grew—sweet, nurturing, and so generous. She
clutched at his arms, arched her hips and buttocks to
meet his rhythm. Soon her legs coiled over his, and she
heard herself moan.

". . . oh, oh, Sasha. What's happening . . . ?"

"Anyushka," he murmured. "I love you."

As he raised on his arms, as his liquid filled her, she was suddenly wrenched with shaking, with intense and unbelievable pleasure. She grasped him tightly, clinging till the last spasm racked her body and her fingers slid in deep tracks down his moist back. She collapsed on the bed soon after, with her eyes closed and her arms outstretched.

As they rested together with their arms around each other, she was satisfied as never before. She could feel his heartbeat, watch the firelight dance on his skin. She saw his collarbone rise and fall with his breathing, watched the hairless chest, the small hips and curved buttocks. The graceful line of his neck. She touched the damp, bronzed hair, felt the sweat of their passion, which clung to his skin. Somewhere in her mind was an image of him, tall and straight, standing on a bridge in St. Petersburg, demanding human rights and justice. The picture crackled with life, like the log in the fireplace. In the final moments of their lovemaking, her feelings had been a thunderstorm crashing across the sky. Now, they were as rainbows. She nestled closer to him, wishing that things were different, that they were children on a picnic in the woods near some faraway lake. Just once in her life she wanted to be his without reservation.

He opened his eyes and kissed her hand. They spoke no words, yet silent promises passed like mist between them. If it could only be this way forever, she thought.

"Hold me!" she said suddenly, as if the fire had gone out and the cold had chilled her. "Hold me tight."

"I've made a decision," he said later as she rested. "Tomorrow I go to the synagogue and take lessons. I'll change. Become a Jew. I'll go to circumcision, whatever it takes to get married, but there is no life without you, Anya."

Her eyes filled with tears as she sat beside him. "Oh, Sasha. It makes me cry to hear you say that. But Judaism isn't lessons. Or circumcision. It's a lifetime of convictions, of belief. A way to live and bring up children. You've got to love God's laws. To know and believe them with all your heart. You're all filled with new ideas and revolution, while my Judaism is abiding, constant, forever. For thousands of years we wait for Messiah, and you haven't the patience to wait for a new czar."

"But our love. It's all that matters."

"No, Sasha. There are other loves."

She left his side and lifted the window shade. There was a hint of morning in the distance. She went back and began to dress. His face was dejected, a little boy's as his eyes pleaded with her to stay. But her answer was clear. She took his hand and pressed it to her bosom when she was finished.

"I've never loved another man," she told him. "But our roads have always led to different places." She moved to the door. "I'll never be sorry for what happened tonight. For the comfort you gave and for what we shared. But I must go home now, to my children."

She opened and closed the door quickly, covering her ears as the sound of her name echoed down the street.

"Come back, Anya. Come back!"

She ran as the snow melted on her hair, realizing for the first time that she was in public without a head covering, and she was filled with regret at what this meant. How many more of God's laws would she violate? Working on the Sabbath to support herself, uncovering her hair. Worst of all, the violation of her marriage vows. God, forgive me, she thought. What have I done?

It was sunrise when Anya opened the front door. The moment she entered, Morris fell on his knees to beg forgiveness. He'd felt insecure, unloved, he said. Embarrassed at his many failures. He'd been weak, tempted by the "wicked" Sheyna, who had "twisted" him around her finger, and he made promise after promise if only Anya wouldn't leave. And when Simon and Sharon cried for Papa, she began to soften. Anya felt unworthy of many things, especially God's love and understanding. But no matter how strong her guilt or confusion, for the sake of her children she would stay with Morris.

41

PALESTINE
APRIL 1914

As more and more refugees poured in from Russian pogroms, Joshua's kibbutz expanded. The Jewish Fund purchased land from anyone who would sell, and the scorched and malaria-infested earth grew green with flowers, vegetables, and trees. Together they shared the hardships and the joys, and, with profits, they built schools and hospitals, sharing their knowledge with Arabs. Though many among their neighbors accepted those benefits, fear and mistrust prevailed. Yet, for a short time the two worked side by side, with their children playing together. And for a while it looked to Joshua as if it could work.

In the spring of 1914, European royalty enjoyed a record number of public parades and state dinners, while behind the scenes their governments formed secret alliances. The czar of Russia ordered new jewels while his country lay on a revolutionary powder keg. In Vienna, the Christian Socialist mayor preached anti-Semitic doctrines to youths like Adolf Hitler. Paris, with its inflation and rioting workers, was a gay soufflé waiting for the oven to clang shut. And in merry old England, on whose empire the sun never set, there were nervous glances at Germany's new navy and the railway she was building through the crumbling Ottoman Empire.

Still, the merry bands played on.

But beneath those happy royal façades lay violence, lay decay, anarchy, and six hundred years of regal indifference, inflating Europe into a thin-skinned balloon that needed a single pinprick. It came in Sarajevo on June 28.

Seven assassins waited along the motor route as the Archduke Franz Ferdinand, heir to the Austro-Hungarian throne, and his wife, Countess Sophie, approached in their open car. Each assassin had a bomb, a gun, and a cyanide capsule. Inside the car, the Archduke and his wife were laughing, celebrating their fourteenth wedding anniversary. Outside, the sun was brilliant and a screaming crowd lined the streets. At Cumuria Bridge, the first assassin froze, but the second threw his bomb. It exploded, wounding many. But except for a small splinter which hit Sophie's face, the royal couple were safe.

The motorcade raced to its destination, passing three other assassins. Unaware of what had happened, the mayor greeted the royal couple with a smile.

"Our hearts are filled with happiness," he began, but the livid archduke registered outrage. He wired his country, cared for his wife's wound, and together they drove to visit the injured.

On the way, the driver passed the sixth assassin. Then a wrong turn brought the royal pair beside Gavrilo Princip, the last assassin, who fired two shots. The countess died instantly, the archduke soon after.

Since the assassins were Serbians, Austria demanded an inquiry of Serbia, to be led by Austrians. The tiny Serbian state objected and turned for help to her strong ally, Russia. Hearing this, Austria looked to her strong ally, Germany. Threats were made. But it was silly. The German kaiser and Russian czar were cousins, after all, and sent personal assurances.

"Do not mobilize your army," they wrote each other, and each agreed. Secretly, they prepared. As both armies stood on both borders, the kaiser sent a last note. "Do not fire the first shot." The czar's affirmative reply was delayed in error, and the insulted kaiser declared war.

It wasn't long before the German army marched through Belgium and France. That called up England's alliances, and all her colonies joined in. The incident that had begun in Sarajevo spread across Europe and was now reaching tentacles toward the whole world. It was time for everyone to choose sides.

PALESTINE
NOVEMBER 1914

Joshua took the mail: a note from Anya with news she was expecting a child in January; a newspaper; and an official letter from the Turkish government. It sent him scrambling to the meeting hall, where he pulled the assembly bell. "The war's here now," he said. "Turkey's become an ally of Germany."

"What does that mean?" a newcomer asked.

"All Russian refugees must leave Palestine immediately or be arrested as spies. We're to be deported to camps in Alexandria. Besides that, we must close our banks, remove all Hebrew signs, and disband Ha-Shomer."

Several women began to cry.

"Don't," Joshua comforted. "There's hope, too. If the English win, ownership of all Ottoman lands will be challenged."

"I don't understand," the newcomer said.

Joshua waved the newspaper. "They're forming a Jewish Legion in Alexandria, Jewish soldiers to fight for the British. In exchange for our help, there'll be concessions. One of those concessions will be this land. If I'm going to have my nose rubbed in dirt, it will at least be Jewish dirt."

NEW YORK CITY
JANUARY 1915

The moment she gave birth, Anya knew he was Sasha's child. The eyes, nose, bone structure. The long torso and thick, bronze hair. He was placid, and because Morris wished it, she called him David, for Morris's father. In that gesture, the infant became part of Morris too. And though her days were filled with memories that faded or sharpened with her moods, the troubling questions remained. Had she made the right decision? Had the best of her life passed? Had she experienced a love that poets write about, that people live and die for, only to discard it like old shoes? Worst of all, by breaking her marriage vows had she lost God's love? Each question was torture. Each silence, even worse. To keep her sanity, she focused on the children. And since Morris was part of that, she leaned on him too. Yet, hard as she'd try, at unguarded moments, Sasha would dance in her mind like a leaf in the wind. And then she'd hold David, the fusion of her greatest joy and most profound shame.

David.

By age one he was running. By two he was speaking in sentences. At three he was following his big brother Simon's every move. Simon, lacing his shoes. Simon, brushing his teeth. Simon, eating breakfast. And David, beside him like a shadow.

David.

His rediscovery of a forgotten toy. Its abandonment for the more exciting clang of Mama's pots and pans in the dark and mysterious cupboards. Splashing with Simon in the bathtub. The power he felt when he could dig his wet fingers through the sugar bowl, then run to lick them without fear of scolding. And the softness, the clean, sweet smell of him, as he slept on his stomach with his thumb in his mouth, stroking the corner of his well-worn blanket. And his bedtime story. A tale so familiar he could fill in the missing words.

As the boys grew older, Simon took his big-brother role seriously. No one at school touched little David Barber without Simon's retribution. They played marbles and stickball. They ran races in the park. They put slugs in the penny machines to drive the candy store man crazy, and when David got the chicken pox, Simon got it too. For two whole weeks they giggled in bed, made up stories to tell each other, and drew ugly pictures of their teachers. They ate Mama's chicken soup until they thought they would bust, and when Hymie Binder came down with measles the following year, Simon got an idea.

"Wanna stay home again like last year?" Simon asked.

David laughed, and they both visited Hymie Binder.

But Simon also showed David how to use the library. How to talk dirty, and how to fight clean.

All day long they'd run up and down the stairs, driving Anya crazy. "Ice cream man is here. We need some pennies." She'd yell and throw the dish towels at them. But then she'd see them tucked in their bed, asleep, with their feet jutting out, dirty elbows, and rumpled hair. And they'd have such angelic faces it would make her smile. She'd cover them and close the door, feeling a happiness deep inside that nothing in the world could replace.

Morris turned his attention to vaudeville. In vaudeville, he could address the audience and make them laugh. At first he copied routines from others. Eventually he wound up with a character he called The Schlemiel. The Schlemiel did things which led directly to his downfall. The Schlemiel wooed the wrong women and was drawn to games of chance. In this character, Morris began using the material of his own life. But no one wanted to hire him. He had a reputation for quarrels and backstage antics. People didn't like him, and he made many enemies. When Anya offered advice, he yelled.

"What do you know? You sit home all day like a moron."

Anya soon realized he wanted a sounding board, and she became one. And, though the names and problems changed, his story was always the same. At thirty-three years of age, Morris Barber was bitter, jealous, filled with envy at other men's talents. Worst of all, he began to realize he might never succeed.

42

MEDITERRANEAN BEACH
JUNE 1916

While the war raged on in Europe, Joshua was on a beach near Cyprus. He and his men had landed there, tired, anxious for the fighting to end, for England to win so they could go home to Palestine. They were exhausted, having come from Gallipoli, where they had delivered supplies. At midnight, Joshua spread his sleeping gear. Suddenly, he glanced toward the water, where the moon's tide had washed a small boat onshore. Fearing ambush, he and his men spread out, but they soon realized there was no danger. The boat had a single occupant, a dazed man mumbling some language no one could understand. They carried him to a fire, where they warmed him and gave him water.

When the man came to, he spoke in English. They learned that he was Vartan Sarkasian, from Van, a province in Armenia, and the story he told them was too crazy to believe. But to Joshua, it had a familiar ring.

"I must get to Alexandria," he kept repeating. "I must tell them what is happening to the Armenians."

Joshua shook him. "Tell who? What?"

For the next ten minutes the exhausted man told of the long feud the Armenians had with the Turks: How, for years, their Christian sons had been taken into Turkish armies and converted to Islam. How their women had been raped and their possessions stolen. Now, he said, the Turks wanted their land.

"They say we are disloyal in this war, that we help spy for the Russians. Now they have plans with the Germans to exterminate us."

He said that there were death camps erected near the Syrian desert. That he had escaped from one and had seen them with his own eyes: "Armenians packed by the thousands behind barbed wire, starving and waiting to die." The Turks had come to his village in the night, he said, and had burned his church while people inside were still praying.

Joshua became twelve again, hiding with Shmuel in the flames of Odessa.

"At first I thought I was dreaming," Vartan went on. "We were pushed into cattle cars with no food or water and taken away." He spoke of naked corpses lying on the desert roads while the dogs ripped their flesh.

"How did you get here?" Joshua asked.

Vartan was losing steam.

"I hid in a supply truck. When it passed the beach, I jumped and found that boat. Now you must help me . . . get to . . . Alexandria so I can . . . tell . . ." Before he could finish, he passed out in Joshua's arms. And only Joshua believed him.

NEW YORK CITY
FEBRUARY 1917

War headlines began filling the daily newspapers. Some insisted on isolation while others wanted the United States to respond to certain provocations. The war became the topic of discussion, even argument, at every gathering. It even found its way into the conversation at Anya Barber's table, where Morris and four of his cronies played their usual Sunday poker game.

"Raise you," Morton Hirsch said.

Morris peered over his glasses and above the smoke. "And call." He tossed his cards on the table. "Ah, who the hell cares anyway; we'll soon be in war."

"You think so?" Jacob Kravitz asked.

Morris raked in the money. "Don't you read?" he said.

"What makes you so sure?" Morton asked. He peeked at his hole card. "President Wilson says no."

"Just read the headlines. First the Germans invade Belgium. Then they sink the *Lusitania*. Now comes the Zimmermann note."

"The what?" Morton asked.

"Listen to the *schmigeggy*. Don't you know Germany sent a secret note to Mexico, that if Mexico gives the U.S. border problems, Germany will help them take back New Mexico, Texas, and Arizona?"

"No kiddin'? Raise you five," Morton said.

Within weeks, after more attacks on U.S. ships, President Wilson broke diplomatic relations with Germany and war was declared.

The United States threw itself into World War I with a passionate fervor: Patriotic songs. Posters of Uncle Sam plastered everywhere. Rallies to support liberty loans, and Boy Scouts with American flags marching down Fifth Avenue. Though America's army was ill prepared to fight, it mobilized, culling troops from recent Mexican border skirmishes with Pancho Villa and Emiliano Zapata. Then the draft began. There were meatless days, lightless days, gasless days, and whiskeyless days. But there were violent outbreaks of anti-German sentiment too, and a ban on speaking the German language.

Because Cohen & Son was a reliable company, it received a contract from the government to manufacture uniforms for the United States Army. With airplanes able to scout from above, uniforms of pageantry, blazing reds and blues, had to give way to the inconspicuous colors of khaki and brown. Charles offered Morris a job and gave Anya more piecework than she could handle. Soon the whole family was at work, and the steady checks gave them an opportunity to save, to think seriously that Simon might really make it to medical school. Best of all, they could move from crowded Hester Street to a nicer place.

As Charles spent more time in New York, Sonia began handling the Chicago factory, and, though her ulcer grew worse, she became proficient at business affairs. Her ability did not surprise Charles. What did, however, was her insistence on receiving a salary and profit participation. She began to make important choices without his help, investing her money in real estate, for which he chided her. He accused her of being a "suffragette," which amused but also angered her. When he had stock-market tips to share, she declined, preferring to buy land.

The war in Palestine was winding down. For Joshua, entering Jerusalem with General Allenby was a dream come true. His return, the return of his people to this ancient and promised land—a lonely journey begun by Dr. Leon Pinsker, Theodore Herzl, and so many others—was now in view. Five minutes in, he fell to his knees and wept for those who had died, those who'd been wounded, who had sacrificed, dreamed, prayed, and would never see this place. He was proud of the victory and hoped it would not be in vain. Hundreds of years of Ottoman rule were over. And it was now possible for Jews, scattered the world over, to come home.

The Balfour Declaration, written on November 2, 1917, was finally made public.

> *His Majesty's government view with favour the establishment in Palestine of a national home for the Jewish people, and will use their best endeavours to facilitate the achievement of this objective. . . .*
>
> *Signed: Arthur James Balfour*
> *Foreign Secretary*

But the Sharif of Mecca, Hussein, produced his own surprise, another letter, signed by Sir Henry McMahon, British High Commissioner of Egypt. It was dated October 24, 1915, and promised to him all Arab-populated areas of the Turkish Empire, excepting portions of Syria that lay west of Damascus, Homs, Hama, and Aleppo. It had been for this, as well as money, that some Arabs had supported the British cause.

Neither Jews nor Arabs were happy. Both sides felt betrayed. Now, it became the job of the conquerors to carve up the old Turkish Empire into new countries. There was anger, despair, but there was hope, too, as Chaim Weizmann and Emir Faisal began talks to agree to live together.

EUROPE
NOVEMBER 11, 1918

In Europe, the firing ceased. The war was over, and on the eleventh day of the eleventh month at 11:00 A.M., the armistice, agreed upon in a railway car in the Compiègne Forest, went into effect. In April the Germans came to Versailles to sign the treaty. They were to admit full responsibility for the war and turn over the kaiser and "significant others" as war criminals. Germany's rivers were to be internationalized and her military force decimated. Many said there was the stench of retribution. Others said the treaty hadn't gone far enough. Financial reparations would begin with a five-billion-dollar down payment, and Germany would lose her colonies, coal mines, and huge chunks of disputed land. From these lands, new nations and borders were carved: Finland, Estonia, Latvia, Lithuania, Poland, Austria, Hungary, Czechoslovakia, and Yugoslavia. But from these ashes, new despots would arise. In a hospital dormitory, Corporal Adolf Hitler wept in humiliation. Begging for a Bill of Rights was a young leader of Vietnam. President Wilson had no time for Ho Chi Minh. The Japanese asked for a clause on racial equality. But President Wilson and others refused that too. The war no one had wanted to fight was over. Millions were dead, millions wounded. Millions of dollars had been wasted. Worst of all, the seeds of future world destruction had been planted.

NEW YORK CITY
OCTOBER 1919

On Friday afternoon, Anya found two letters in the mailbox. One held a note and family photographs from Joshua; the other bore a Swiss postmark. She opened the Swiss one last and found two empty pages inside. Puzzled, she crumpled the papers and threw them away.

She shared Joshua's note with her family and forgot about the other until the flames of the Sabbath candles jolted her memory. On Saturday night, she combed the garbage can, found the crumpled pages, and took them to the stove. There, she held the pages to the heat. Just as she had assumed, a message began to appear.

Dearest Anya,

A friend has smuggled this letter and I pray God it reaches you. I pray also it finds you and your family well. I'm in Siberia, jailed for opposing the czar's murder. The war was a nightmare, and when the end came all of Russia rejoiced. I had so much hope as we crossed Alexander Bridge and marched toward a royal regiment. Where blood might have flowed, we came together like a gaping wound. It should have stayed that way, but Lenin returned and we were soon at each other's throats.

I'm tired and I miss you. The moment you left I knew your decision, but I still cling to hope. Forgive my audacity, Anyushka. And pray for me.

S.

43

The family moved to Rivington Street. Morris's investment in Sheyna's business was successful, and they received profits through a lawyer. There was also steady work from Charles. Anya was happy that Sharon had her own room and that her boys shared another. She liked having a real kitchen with a porcelain-covered bathtub, a small closet toilet, and an icebox inside. No more frozen butter and milk on the window ledge in winter. No more spoiled food in summer.

Simon, now a bar mitzvah, worked two jobs to save for medical school. Anya could no longer count the sick dogs and cats he'd bandaged in her hallway. And David; they called him the Defender because he stood up to bullies. Sharon grew tall, with round, slim hips, a woman's bosom, and a tiny waistline. She had long black curls, dark blue, almost purple eyes, and white teeth against dark olive skin. At fourteen, she was a beauty and could hardly walk down the street without boys gaping or girls whispering. Even grown men would glance and their wives eye her with envy.

It was two hours before *Shabbos*, and a weary Anya had been cooking all day. It was time to set the table and prepare the candles. Though she had abandoned some ways, keeping a kosher home, observing the Sabbath and some holidays were all she had left of her religion, and she kept them for her sanity and for her children to know something of their roots. In America there were powerful influences, wrong choices her children could make: cars, movies, gangsters, skirts up to the knees. And that crazy dance—what was it?—the Charleston. Already, she'd caught Simon smoking under the staircase.

Sharon opened the door. She held her nose against the smell of chicken fat and frying onions. "I'm home, Ma," she said. "Can I roller-skate?"

"A kiss first," Anya said. "And be home before *Shabbos.*"

Sharon pecked her mother's cheek, then threw her books on the bed. She changed her clothes, thinking how sick she was of all those silly customs, that candle mumbo jumbo. She was an American. Tired of chicken every Friday. Chicken! Chicken! Chicken! Worst of all, she knew her mother would not let her go to the roller rink the next day. She'd have to sit in a chair like a lump. Not even listen to the new radio Papa had bought. But she couldn't understand why. Sometimes, her mother worked on *Shabbos.* And her father, too. If only she were older. She'd quit school, get her working papers, and leave.

She heard David and Simon slam the front door, heard them wrestling and giggling on the bed in the room next to hers.

"Ma! He's hurting," David screamed.

"He started!" Simon called out.

"In a minute you'll both cry," Anya yelled.

A second later, Sharon and her roller skates were gone.

On Sunday, Sharon paid her nickel and walked into the red-carpeted lobby. She bought a box of candy-coated licorice and sat in the front row waiting for the show to begin. The lights dimmed, the movie screen lit up, and the moment she saw Rudolph Valentino, she was dizzy. She saw herself in his arms, carried to his desert lair, smothered by his lips and caressed by his dark eyes and strong hands. She stayed in the magical darkness until late, then went reluctantly home.

In bed, she thought of him, dreamed of him, couldn't wait to go to the movies again. One thing she knew for sure. She could never share her secret longings with her mother. How could *she* possibly understand the yearnings of a young girl?

Two weeks later, Sharon became a woman. As she lay with a hot-water bottle warming her belly, she wondered how she could get away from her dreary life. Get married, perhaps. But to whom?

On her fifteenth birthday, Sharon received an invitation to tea at the Palm Court with Sonia, and she could hardly wait. Anya made her a dress. White organdy with a blue ribbon belt and long sleeves. Sharon hung it on the door, where she could see it at night. When the day finally arrived, Sharon put on her shoes and gloves while Simon and David sat teasing her at the kitchen table. They were dressed in underwear, wearing two of Anya's cast-off hats, drinking make-believe tea in teacups and speaking with English accents.

"Some tea, my de-ahhh?" David started.

"Awfully good of you, dahlink," Simon replied.

"You see the queen?"

"Ra-ther. Just yesterday, she borrowed two bits."

Sharon put on her white picture hat, said good-bye, and playfully yanked Simon's hair before racing downstairs. Behind the street door, she composed herself, then opened it and walked gracefully past the old stoop yentas.

"Tante Sonia," Sharon said, entering the limousine.

"No *Tante*," Sonia said. "*Aunt* will do nicely."

As they drove to the Palm Court, Sharon peeked at Sonia. Her aunt was much older than her mother but looked so much younger. She was tall and slim, with mysterious slanted eyes. Her salt-and-pepper hair was finger-waved, pinned at her neck in a bun, and covered with a beige cloche hat. Stone marten tails lay across her shoulders, complementing a champagne beige lace top and accordion-pleated skirt. She wore handmade lace gloves and a strand of opera-length pearls, fastened at her neck with a cluster of diamonds.

When they were seated at the Palm Court, the crystal chandeliers sparkled above Sharon's head. Bright marble gleamed beside polished mahogany and gorgeous antique Chinese urns. A trio of violinists strolled by as Sharon opened her menu.

"Am I doing something wrong? Everyone's staring," Sharon said.

"You're not and they are. You're the most beautiful girl here." Sonia flourished her linen napkin onto her lap as tea was set, and Sharon followed.

"So, how are your brothers?" Sonia asked.

"Fine."

"And your mother?"

"Don't get me started." Sharon regretted her words instantly and covered her mouth.

"It's all right," Sonia said. "I understand. All girls reach an age where they feel that way."

"They do?"

"Of course! It's perfectly natural. Want to talk about it?"

Sharon hesitated a moment, then began. "Well, to be honest, Mama's so old-fashioned; not like you. I mean, look how you dress, and your English is so perfect. Then she drives me crazy with the religious stuff. I don't mean to talk bad, but what's so terrible about wearing a pretty hat in the Easter Parade?"

"Religion and tradition mean a great deal to your mother, Sharon. Except for you, that's all she has."

Sharon laughed. "Me? I mean nothing to her. It's the boys that count. You should hear her. Simon's education. David's future. I have no choice but to get married."

The familiar chords made Sonia smile. "I once felt that way about Uncle Joshua when we were little. Seems so silly now." She took command of Sharon's eyes. "Listen to me, Sharon. Life is short. We're here one minute and gone the next. You must learn a very important lesson. This is a man's world, and the power to make choices comes only through money. And a woman's money comes only through men. Find a rich man, Sharon, and marry him. Then you'll be free to choose."

As Sonia continued, Sharon hung on her every word.

"And here's a promise," Sonia added. "When you find that man, call me. I'll give you a wedding the world will never forget." She pulled a package from her purse. "Now let's have some French pastry while you open your present."

When Anya saw what Sonia had given Sharon, her heart sank. She was happy for her daughter, but her own present paled by comparison. No matter how beautifully stitched, no homemade linen suit could compare with a strand of real pearls. "How beautiful, Sharon," Anya said. "How lucky you are to have such a generous aunt."

At their weekly poker game, Morris watched the well-to-do Morton Hirsch stare at his beautiful daughter. It made his head pregnant with notions. Sharon was almost sixteen, ready for marriage, and Morton seemed very intrigued. They continued the game for two more hours, until Morris owed Morton Hirsch another hundred dollars.

The following week, Morris and Anya sat on the stoop. It was a sultry summer evening, and Simon and David were playing stickball. Not far away, they could hear the jingle of an ice-cream cart. Three floors above, someone practiced piano scales. Simon hit a sudden pop fly, and when Morris didn't cheer, Anya asked what he was thinking.

"I'm thinking of Morton Hirsch as a husband for Sharon."

Anya looked at him as if he was crazy. "He's too old for her. And the gossip about him is not good."

Morris kept watching the game. "He's rich, Anya. He'll give Sharon a good life."

"Rich isn't everything," Anya said and went inside.

The day Rudolph Valentino died, Sharon was beside herself. She wept openly in the rain with fifty thousand mourners. Day and night she stayed in her room, staring at the dead actor's photograph, wondering how someone so young and handsome could die. It made her think about Aunt Sonia's words at lunch the year before, about how short life was.

"Do something, Morris," Anya begged. "She's been in that room for weeks since he died."

That was when Morris began the first part of his plan. In spite of Anya's well-voiced objections, Sharon was introduced to Morton Hirsch at the next poker game. Morris invited his daughter to help serve sandwiches and soda. He made her dress up and fix her hair, then he watched Morton drink in Sharon's beauty. Morton was mature, good looking. He dressed well and wore expensive jewelry. He was a self-made man who owned

his own window-cleaning and floor-waxing establish-
ment. What could be bad?

From her bedroom, Sharon heard her parents argue
that night.

"I'm still against it, Morris. Sharon doesn't need Morton Hirsch."

"But he's rich, Anya. And Sharon's growing up too
fast."

So, Sharon thought. Her mother was against Morton
Hirsch. Naturally. Why should Anya's daughter do bet-
ter than Anya had? And if her mother was against it,
Sharon liked the idea even better.

Sharon began serving at the poker games wearing long
stockings and short dresses. She bobbed her hair in the
latest fashion and wore makeup, lip rouge and a dot of
clear Vaseline on each eyelid. She tweezed her eyebrows like Gloria Swanson's and penciled in faint black
lines that made her large, dark blue eyes even more
beautiful. Morton's tongue was hanging out when he
asked for Sharon's hand in marriage, and the wily Morris played the last of his cards.

"To tell the truth, Morton, Anya's against it. She
thinks you're too old for Sharon."

As Morris had hoped, Morton began to "sweeten"
the deal. "I'll cancel your debt, Morris. As for Anya,
tell her if anything happens, I'll take care of her and
the boys."

Hearing those words, Morris gave his blessing,
against Anya's wishes. Sharon sent a letter to Sonia and
waited for a reply. It came with a check for a down
payment on a luxurious hall. A few weeks later Sonia
came to New York City, where she checked into the
Waldorf-Astoria and the two began planning the wedding.

Anya was happy for Sharon but felt pushed aside.

Once again, Sonia's money had triumphed. Yet she couldn't put her foot down without seeming petty. Sharon had the chance every girl dreams of. A custom-made gown and beaded headdress. Exquisite French cuisine and wedding cake. Waterfalls of champagne and an orchestra. No matter what Anya said, she'd look jealous. So she smiled and accepted. But inside, resentment was building. For the first time in her life she was jealous of Sonia.

On the morning of the wedding, Anya lovingly wrapped Sarah's comb in tissue and presented it for Sharon to wear. Her daughter thanked her but explained that it would not fit beneath her beaded headdress. That Aunt Sonia had loaned her a pair of real diamond and pearl earrings, and a mother-of-pearl comb would look silly with those. A heartbroken Anya hid her tears. Time would pass, she kept telling herself, and this would be forgotten. She did not want to recall Sharon's wedding day as a battle. Still, it cut like a knife. Then the last straw came when she was relegated to the catering room to be sure the canapés were properly arranged. Though she maintained the façade, inside she was burning. If the right person said the wrong thing, she'd burst into flames.

The prior morning, Sharon had refused to visit the *mikvah* with Anya. She made it perfectly clear that the bathtub would do nicely, and that she did not plan to follow any other old traditions, either. It hurt Anya to think she had not passed a love for Judaism on to her daughter.

The ceremony, with Morton's rabbi officiating, was beautiful. But at the last moment, Sharon invited Sonia to stand beneath the *chuppah*, and as Anya moved sideways to make room, it rankled her to the bone.

Then the music played. They ate, they drank, they danced. "An easy ten thousand not counting the dress,"

Anya heard someone whisper. And when the gifts were displayed, the set of dishes she and Morris had purchased for the newlyweds seemed puny beside the others. But Sharon looked so beautiful, seemed so happy, and that was what mattered, Anya kept telling herself.

After the photographs, after Sharon and Morton had headed for the train station, after the guests had gone and the wine-stained tablecloths were cleared of flower arrangements, Anya took her tears to the deserted ladies' room. For fifteen minutes she cried silently, nonstop, thinking nothing had come out right. All she'd ever wanted from life was a home, a husband who cared, the love of her children, that magic which links one generation to another. Fancy cars? Jewelry? Things like that meant nothing. Just Sharon, David, Simon. Helping her children achieve their dreams.

She opened the door and walked down the hall. Here and there an inebriated straggler offered slurred compliments and words of congratulation. Then she entered the cloakroom, where two coats remained. Side by side, her cloth coat and Sonia's sable. The sight of them touching brought the anger again. *I gave your daughter what you never could*, they seemed to shout, and her fingers blindly grabbed the fur to reply. The door suddenly opened, bringing the silence of an empty wedding hall, and the sound of Sonia's voice as she spoke in Russian.

"Would you like to try it on?"

The smugness of her question was all too obvious—poor sister touching the rich one's fur—when it hadn't been like that at all. "Thank you, no."

Anya felt her emotions coming to a head as Sonia stood beside her—all the frustration, the knowledge that her sister had enjoyed great sport at her expense, spoiling what should have been the happiest day of her life. And by the look on Sonia's face, she had loved every moment.

"What a beautiful wedding," Sonia sighed.

"I know *you* enjoyed yourself."

"Anya, you sound angry. Today you should be proud."

"I've always been proud of Sharon," Anya said. "I didn't need a rich wedding for that."

"Then why are you so upset? With Sharon gone, you'll have time for your sons."

"My sons!"

"There's that tone again." Sonia looked at Anya with a tight-lipped grin. "Why don't you get what's bothering you off your chest?"

So, the challenge was on, and Anya faced her sister. "Why have you always tried to hurt me?"

"What nonsense, Anya. You're just jealous that I gave Sharon what you couldn't."

"That's not true, Sonia, and you know it."

"How stupid of me. How could dear Anya be so petty as to feel the same dirty emotions we common people do?"

"Why do you hate me, Sonia? What have I done to hurt you?"

An agitated Sonia moved about the room. "Because," she said, turning. Each word flew like poison darts. "Because of the pain you caused Mother the day you were born, how her hands and feet were tied to a filthy whore's bed."

Anya was startled. "Marishka was no whore. She was a friend."

"Fairy tales," Sonia shouted. "A lie from your own mother's lips. I was there!" she continued, snarling. "And there's more, dear sister. Because of you, I married someone I never loved. I gave up my dreams so

Mama and Papa could come to America. But you got sick and they had to wait. By the time they came, Mama was so weak she died." Sonia's long, accusing finger became a dagger. "It was *your* fault I never saw Mama again. And for *that*, I'll never forgive you. As for Saul? His death is on your head."

Each new revelation made Anya dizzy, as if she were on a high mountain with no air to breathe, with the wind blowing through her ears, hanging by her finger-nails. Her heart thumped like a rock. She could feel it banging her ribs like a drum as Sonia went on.

"And the ultimate insult. In my own home. The night I found you and Charles—"

Instantly, Anya was on her, eyes wild and blazing white, curved fingers sunk deep in the well-coiffed hair, dropping to the shoulders of silk and shaking them as she vaulted her sister against the wall. The old secret boiled in her throat like hot oil. She had to get even.

"You're the liar," Anya shouted. "Your whole life has been a lie. Look at your face, the shape of your eyes. Like a Tartar, a Mongol. You're not even Papa's child. Mama was raped by Cossacks at Grandma's. She told me on her deathbed."

As her own words echoed in her ears, Anya realized what she had done and wished God would strike her dead. To reveal her mother's deathbed confession was a terrible sin. Quickly, she tried to repair things, to ask forgiveness, as tears filled Sonia's eyes.

"No," Sonia kept mumbling in a disembodied voice. Her eyes wouldn't focus. "You made it up to hurt me."

Anya let Sonia go, apologized, grabbed her coat, and ran sobbing from the room.

44

Sharon's wedding-night expectations had come from watching Valentino's performance in the movies. She knew, without question, Morton's passion for her would unfold like a flower on soft bed sheets and satin pillows. But what happened that night was a nightmare. There was no kindness, no passionate kiss. No emotion or sweetness. Later, she would learn that Morton suffered some sexual problems, problems he'd hoped her youthful beauty would be able to cure. And when that didn't occur, when he couldn't sustain his erections for more than a few moments, he became a disappointed and angry tyrant. Emotionally abused and deprived as a child, he began to abuse and deprive her. Someone would pay for his sexual frustration and unhappiness. And that someone would be his wife.

He began by berating her looks, her cooking. Then he doled out money like a miser and remained silent for weeks on end. He forbade her to leave the house without his permission, and she realized that by marrying him she had gone from the frying pan into the fire. To make matters worse, he demanded she keep a kosher kitchen. Soon her life with Morton became an exercise in avoidance and a dance on hot coals.

Their daily life became routine. After a fitful night, he'd rise at 5:00 A.M. and leave. She'd lie quietly in bed, feigning sleep to avoid a confrontation. He'd make his own breakfast, a single egg cooked for two minutes and swallowed warm, cracked into a whiskey glass. He'd dress in layer upon layer of shirts with gloves and a fur cap over his thinning brown hair, which he parted in the middle. He'd pack his things—a squeegee, a chamois cloth, some strong soapy solution, wax, his pail and ladder—and take them to a small truck where his "helper" waited. They'd follow a route, cleaning storefront windows and waxing floors. He'd have lunch at a local luncheonette—the same thing every day for his nervous stomach, cottage cheese and sour cream with tea and toast. Then it was back to work until dark.

He'd arrive home with a splitting headache, take two aspirins, and bathe until his skin wrinkled and flaked. He'd have a silent dinner, then leave to play poker, and she'd be alone. When he came home, he'd take her to bed, and two minutes later, he was through. She was afraid of him, though he never struck her. She had this feeling that she'd done something wrong and found herself placating him, running after him like a servant, picking up his things, cooking his favorite foods, keeping the house as spotless as he wanted, and creating the idle chatter she thought would please him.

"Mrs. Goodman stopped by today."

Silence as he undressed and took a bath.

"The union called. I told them to call you back. Why should you be charged?"

Silence as she waltzed on eggshells.

"I saved a nickel today going to the market on Fourth Street. The nerve of Finklestein to charge extra." She heard herself and hated the whine. The more she chattered, the more moody and sullen he became. And, worse, she was ashamed to tell anyone she had married a madman.

For days, weeks, months, Anya pondered her fight with Sonia in the cloakroom, hating herself. All along she'd sensed the anger and unfinished business coming to a head. She could have avoided it, but the mean-spirited way she had acted frightened her. She had violated a most sacred trust and couldn't change a thing. A dozen times she'd sent Sonia apologies. But it was fruitless. Not even time would heal this breach.

Once again Morris was late for the theater. He had an argument with someone in the dressing room and complained to the manager. Ten minutes later he was dressed and waiting in the wings for the preceding act to finish. The offstage applause came, and the stripper passed him by, throwing her boa across his head. He flipped it back in annoyance as someone announced his name. His welcoming applause was light, and he came onstage wearing a huge smile. The spotlight warmed him as he took his place center stage and began his routine. Two minutes into "The Schlemiel," the crowd was yelling.

"Throw the bum off!" "We want our money back!"

From the wings the manager coaxed him off with a beckoning finger, but Morris made believe he didn't see. How dare he do that? Morris thought. No one could treat him this way. He continued singing—higher, louder—falling down harder, climbing the curtain, stumbling, bashing his head against the floor until he was bloody. He used every trick in the book, but no one laughed. Not even a titter. His heart was a shambles as the bright spotlight was extinguished, and the warmth it gave went as well. As he left the stage, a chill pierced his clothes and lodged in his bones. He was nothing. Absolutely nothing. And this moment of awareness gave him dangerous options.

Once again Simon walked his brother David to Hebrew School. In a little while David would be a bar mitzvah. On the way home, David kicked a can in the gutter while Simon's ruler snapped against the iron slats of an arrow-topped wrought-iron fence. Suddenly

Simon grabbed David's arm and dragged him behind a car.

"Damn! There's Papa."

"Where?" David peeked out to see.

Simon pointed. "Oh, God. He's kissing her. Mama would die."

"You know her?" David asked.

"It's the lady Mama lived with on Hester Street."

"Holy cow!" David said.

"Don't tell," Simon said.

"You think I'm nuts?"

At dinner that evening, everyone was quiet.

"So," Morris began, "how was your day, Simon?"

"Fine."

"Fine? What's fine?" Morris asked.

"He was a good boy," David said. "Like you."

Charles Cohen had been in New York City for two weeks. He had orders to place, new fabrics to find for the coming season. There was a note from his stockbroker telling him that the market was going up again and that he should buy. RCA. Sears. Everything was on the rise. He placed a telephone call and gave his broker the word. If there was a good game going on, he wanted to be a player.

At the beginning of November, Simon sat on the stoop near Anya watching David roller-skate down Rivington Street. The day was sunny and crisp, and Anya felt a special joy. Simon had grown taller in the last year. He was handsome, sixteen, a dead ringer for Morris, with his broad shoulders and soulful brown eyes. He had Morris's broad, aquiline nose, which began at the forehead and led to a soft mouth that except for its fullness would have been called serious. His lower lip lay above a strong chin with a cleft, and his voice had become a deep alto.

David was the opposite. He was mischievous, with lots of girlfriends who came to the door each morning to walk him to school. He was not handsome the way Simon was but cute, with charm and personality. His perpetual smile yielded dimples. A thick mop of light brown hair covered his square-shaped head. Huge blue eyes, as clear as glass marbles, were bookends to a nose that tilted at the tip. His skin was naturally tan, and a small beauty mark lodged itself near the corner of his left eyelid.

David suddenly roller-skated to the stoop. He grasped the iron banister and called, "Hey, Simon! I see that guy again."

"Where?"

"By the corner newsstand."

Simon peered over his brother's shoulder. Anya did too, and couldn't believe her eyes.

In the next days Anya couldn't think straight. She was frightened she would see him. Afraid she would not. She cut her finger chopping onions, forgot to add salt to her soup, wore her good coat when she went out, and saw his face on every street corner. She found him the moment she least expected, on Canal Street, on a Wednesday afternoon as she shopped for Chanukah presents.

"Anyushka," the voice called in Russian. His breath was so close it raised the hairs on her neck.

Turning, smiling, she felt her knees become jelly. In the midst of the crowded street, his lips drifted down like a snowflake and melted on hers. Without a word he took her arm, her packages, and they hurried to a diner, where they sat in a booth holding hands. He had changed so much, she thought. Older, more self-assured, so handsome, with the sea still guiding the color of his eyes. His thick, white hair was topped by a navy blue stocking cap, and his skin was as dark as a Tartar's. He unbuttoned a navy blue jacket, revealing a dark sweater with a bit of white shirt, frayed at his leathery throat.

"How did you find me?" she asked. Her voice was low, solemn as he rubbed her cold hands.

"Your neighbor, Mrs. Silverstein."

She became self-conscious. "I must look a mess," she said, more aware of her graying temples and crow's-feet.

"No," he replied. "You look more beautiful than ever."

He ordered tea for both of them and told her how he had escaped from prison and that one day he would write a book. They caught up on lost years, and her mind reeled as she silently repeated to herself, No, God. No. This time I must resist. His next words terrified her.

"He's mine, isn't he?"

She said nothing.

"You don't have to answer. I see myself in every bone of his body. How perfect he is, half you, half me. You'll never know how happy I feel. God, Anya. I love you both."

She trembled. Every part of her feared his hunger.

"You won't hurt him, will you?"

"Don't torture yourself, Anya. It's enough for me just to see him. To hold him in my heart. The revolution of my youth is over, and I have nothing left. The Bolsheviks have destroyed a million dreams. One of those was mine. At least I can think of you and the boy."

"Oh, Sasha! I'm so sorry."

After the waitress poured their tea, Sasha asked a million questions.

"Tell me about him. His name. His favorite food. Tell me everything."

"His name is David."

"David." He said it like a poem.

"He'll be bar mitzvah soon. A ceremony at the synagogue where he becomes a man."

"A man," he repeated.

"His grades are good. And he sticks up for people."

"Yes. I like that."

"But sometimes they send him home from school for being funny."

He smiled. "A sense of humor is important."

"And he has girlfriends. Too many."

On and on she went: David's chicken pox, his jokes, how he hated string beans and loved baseball. His love for lollipops and potato knishes with extra onions. Sasha's face changed expression with each revelation. Suddenly, he excused himself, returning a few moments later from the men's room with bloodshot eyes. Then he sat down again and tried to say more. But Anya insisted it was late. She had to leave. From outside, she looked at him through the frosted glass window and noticed him drawing a heart in the condensation. S. loves A., he wrote. Then his fingers spread like a fan and pressed against the windowpane. She put her hand to his, matching him finger for finger. It wasn't long before the heat of his palm met hers. She felt her whole being dragged back down into that abyss, and she ran this time, swearing she would never see him again.

On the day of David's bar mitzvah, Simon guided the guests to their seats. He took his own as the candles in the small shul flickered a warm welcome. As the rabbi called David to read the Torah portion, a side door slowly opened, and an unnoticed stranger slipped in. He put on a skullcap and sat quietly on the last bench.

David, dressed in a navy blue suit, white skullcap, and tallis, began to pray, to dedicate the rest of his life to God and his family and to take his place proudly as a member of the Jewish community. His speech pleased Morris and made Anya cry; Simon and a pregnant Sharon shared their parents' pride. Tonight, David had filled their hearts with joy. But the unseen stranger at the back of the shul thought his heart would burst with pain. Seeing David, Anya's family, the ceremony, Sasha removed his skullcap and ran weeping from the temple.

45

PALESTINE
1928

At breakfast Yael stood with her heart-shaped buttocks squeezed into a tight pair of shorts, the sleeves of her khaki blouse rolled up and her breasts straining at the buttons. The Englishman couldn't take his eyes away. Along with the other women, Joshua disliked the way she dressed. He cornered her later to "discuss" it. But she kissed his nose. "Be reasonable, Joshua. Not jealous."

Then she turned and wriggled away.

* * *

When the war had ended, England was in a position of strength. She controlled Egypt, the Suez Canal. She held the oil fields and the Palestine Mandate. She put Faisal in to govern Iraq and his brother Abdullah to govern Transjordan. This made the French feel cheated. Syria and Lebanon seemed such a little prize compared with all that. They felt the lands of the Upper Galilee had been unfairly divided and considered all the new boundaries open to question. The French set Arab against Arab to try to change those borders. The Jews, however, were in the line of fire. Fired upon, they fired back. And the border feuds began.

Before the Passover of 1920, the Arabs had come for the Nebi Mussa festival. "Slaughter the Jews!" the sheik had cried at the end of a long tirade, and a frenzied mob had rushed headlong through the narrow lanes of the Old City to loot, maim, and destroy. Three days later, without government help, six Jews were dead, two hundred wounded, women raped, property stolen, and synagogues burned. Yet some Arabs had shielded and helped their Jewish neighbors. Vladimir Jabotinsky, leader of the Jewish Legion, a man who had helped the British fight the war, had been arrested and jailed for possession of firearms. It was clear now, the Jews needed more than Ha-Shomer, more than the so-called British government to protect them. They needed something stronger, independent of foreign control, and they needed to keep its dimensions secret. So began Haganah.

Hajj Amin al Husseini was sentenced in absentia to ten years' imprisonment for his part in the 1920 riots, but he was soon given amnesty and made mufti of Jerusalem. The British hoped this act would help to tame him and make him a responsible part of government.

They were wrong. The mufti now had more authority and power, more access to influential people and monies with which to foment more strife.

At nightfall the men met secretly on Haganah while some women talked of home defense matters. There was a grievance about sentry duty they wished to take to the general membership. Then Ruth attacked Yael for wearing shorts and a blouse that day. Yael was annoyed that such a petty matter would even be discussed.

"It's hot, and I'm sick of wearing the scratchy Arab smock we all use," Yael said. "I'm even sicker of the smelly petroleum jelly I have to smear all over my irritated skin. And I can't believe with all the problems we're having, with murder and rioting now in Hebron, with Joseph Trumpeldor killed just trying to close a gate to his compound, that you're bringing up my clothes."

Suddenly the lights went out, bombs burst, and ear-shattering sirens wailed. Women rushed the children into cellars. Teenagers freed the livestock from a burning barn. The dining room exploded, and flames shot upward. The women at Yael's meeting dropped to the ground as the doors burst open and bullets sprayed every corner of the room. Yael lay shivering, nose to nose with Ruth, whose dead eyes were still open and whose warm blood dripped slowly onto Yael's cheeks.

Footsteps approached. Yael heard the chink and scrape of a blade against a sheath. Soon a foot was beside her, and her hand felt a strange, quick sting. Then someone shouted, and a moment later the intruders were gone. When Yael opened her eyes she saw blood spurting everywhere. Then she looked at her hand and fainted.

When the attack was over, there were four dead and seven wounded, with Yael in shock. They had just fought a war. They had the Balfour Declaration. This was to be the Promised Land, Joshua thought as he held his wife, who had just lost a hand. Promised to whom? And for what?

The following day they rebuilt and fortified their defenses. No one was to move without a gun. They ordered more drills, more walls, more bullets. Worst of all, their hearts hardened.

NEW YORK CITY
SUMMER 1929

Joshua came to America to raise money. With the war over, they needed funds to support Haganah. Anya was so happy, she planned a special Sabbath dinner. She had not laid eyes on her brother since Russia, and she was anxious to see him again. On the morning of his arrival, she waited at the noisy pier with Simon and David. As the ship docked, the crushing crowd rushed the pier. Then Joshua appeared on the gangplank, and Anya knew him from the photos he'd sent over the years. His muscular body was straight like an oak, skin a brownish red from the sun, with thick salt-and-pepper curls covering his forehead. He had a mustache and short beard neatly sculpted to his cheekbones. With a Star of David hanging proudly from his neck, he looked like a biblical patriarch.

"Joshua! Over here."

Joshua turned toward the sound of her voice, and their eyes met. He quickly pushed his way through the crowd and wrapped his arms around her. When he pulled away, they were both crying. "Look at you," he said. "Pretty as ever."

"Go on," she said. "Sharon made me a grand-mother."

Simon extended his hand to shake, but Joshua hugged him instead. Then it was David's turn.

On the way home, Anya held her brother as if he might disappear. Then Morris came home, and Sharon and Morton arrived with their little girl, Patricia, who was chattering gibberish. Together they dined and sat listening to the Jewish soldier speak of the Holy Land. Sharon held her daughter and gazed proudly at her uncle, while Simon asked about the New Hebrew University they were building. David wanted more war stories. Joshua talked about Jerusalem, the war. He spoke of Yael and his two grown sons.

"Do you think it will happen?" Anya asked. "A homeland?"

"I'm here to raise money for it," Joshua said.

"But we hear so much about the riots in Jerusalem and Hebron. Why stay and fight when you can come here?" Morris asked.

By that question, Joshua knew Morris's character. He was disappointed and couldn't understand why Anya had married such a selfish man. He had to confront him.

"Morris," Joshua replied. "Sometime in his life, every Jew must stop running. He must stand still and ask himself two questions. Who am I? Where do I belong?" He picked up David's play gun. "The guns my sons use are real. Real, because they've asked and answered those questions. With no homeland, a Jew must depend on the goodwill of others. I've seen that goodwill. It pours in daily—Jews from Africa, Asia, Europe. All colors, sizes, with only two things in common. They're Jews, and no country wants them. So they come home to Palestine." He looked at Simon and David. "Your life here is good, now. But will the misdeeds of a single Jew inflame the nation tomorrow? We Jews are blamed for a bad economy, for revolution and plague. We're called Capitalist! Socialist! Anarchist! Communist! And all at the same time." He laughed. "Of course, when times are good, we don't get credit." He grew serious again. "But if I die tomorrow, I die in Palestine. At home." He raised his wineglass and shouted before he drank. "*L'chaim!* To life!"

In the following days Joshua went from Jewish Agency to Jewish Agency seeking financial help. He visited businessmen and financiers, spoke at numerous luncheons, anywhere in the country. He visited with Sonia in Chicago and gave speeches wherever he could. The response was more than generous. Most Jews who contributed had at one time been victims of the czar's pogroms. They were eager to share their new prosperity, to help those now coming to Palestine. And Joshua, in God's wisdom, perhaps, had come just in time. He had no way of knowing what was about to happen in America.

NEW YORK CITY
SEPTEMBER 1, 1929

Monday was a holiday. Tuesday, the stock market opened. It was the hottest day of the year. The market had been a bull one, and the bull trend continued. Even the *Wall Street Journal* commented on the favorable conditions. Then prices slipped. On September 5 an economist told a business convention he thought a crash was coming. When his words reached the stock exchange, a series of wild fluctuations began. Responsible people begged investors not to panic. On October 22 the market rallied. Then came Black Thursday, and prices hit rock bottom. Sell, sell, sell, was the word. Everyone prayed it would end. On Monday, the market fell again. Tuesday, October 29, it was all over. The depression had begun.

The day the stock numbers fell, Charles Cohen came in early to be sure he understood what was happening. He tried to call his broker several times but was unable to get through. Still, he stayed calm. There had been times like this before. Then his broker reached him with the news, and he made a decision. He set his books and desk in order. He washed his face and combed his hair. He put on a new jacket and tie, shined his shoes, and brushed his teeth. He called his secretary and told her he didn't wish to be disturbed. Then he opened the window of his fifteenth-story office and climbed onto the ledge, where the pigeons roosted. He leaned his back against the wall, feeling the wind coax him outward. And when a strong gust came, one he knew he could depend on, he closed his eyes and leaped.

Anya came home from the doctor's office to find Simon and David in the kitchen whispering. They looked nervous, and she knew instantly something terrible had happened.

"Simon. What is it?"

"Sit down first," Simon said.

"You're making me nervous, already. Tell me!"

"It's Papa," David said.

Her head began to spin with terrible possibilities. Simon looked at David. "Give her the letter."

David handed an envelope to her. She looked at her sons as she removed the contents. Inside, she found a note written in Morris's childish scrawl, and as the first line hit her, her feelings collided and her head exploded in pain.

Dear Anya,

I'm leaving for California. I have no choice. I gambled on bad investments in the stock market and the shylocks are after me. I didn't mean to hurt you, but it came out that way. I'm ashamed, Anya. You're a good wife and mother, but believe you me, it's better I should leave. In the meantime, go to Morton for the help he promised. Don't hate me, and please don't talk against me to the children.

Love, Morris

BOOK III

1929~1947

46

All night long Anya was like a sleepwalker, afraid to stop moving, afraid her heart would stop beating and she'd die. She was scared to tell her sons the rest—happy news under other circumstances. Now it just made things worse. While the boys forced her to drink tea with schnapps, a notice was shoved under the door. Morris had not paid the rent for the last two months, and they had two days to "settle up" or leave without their belongings. She went immediately to Charles's office, hoping he'd give her a loan.

A policeman in the lobby explained in unemotional tones. "Jumped from the window." "Splattered across the pavement." Anya was already overwhelmed, so nothing registered. There was no time to judge or be sorry, and she left feeling numb, with a familiar wind in her ears, howling, *"Survival!"*

At midnight, she and the boys crept away with the radio, the candlesticks, the sewing machine, the family Bible, and Anya's jewelry. They left behind their furniture, a rug she had crafted, a bedspread made from scraps, each circle laboriously cut, hemmed, and stitched together—it had taken two years to make and two minutes to discard. They took the cold subway to Sharon's, where they would ask to stay until her sons could find work.

*   *   *

"My God, Mama! What's wrong?" Sharon closed the door.

"Papa's gone," Simon said, helping Anya to a chair.

"Yeah," David added. "With two months rent due." He gave Sharon Morris's letter. Sharon read it near the Tiffany lamp, then gestured for Morton to come to their bedroom. Anya and the boys could hear them arguing.

"They can stay the night, but that's all," Morton snarled. "I'm not a charity ward. The boys are strong; they can work."

"They will. But they can't sleep in the streets. And you promised Papa you'd take care of her, remember?"

"I also remember she didn't think I was good enough for you, so she can starve for all I care."

Listening, Anya felt her heart sink. If it hadn't been for the boys, she'd have been gone already. Instead, she slept on the couch while David and Simon shared the floor.

In the morning, after Morton went to work, Anya played with Patricia. As they ate, Sharon came up with a daring plan.

"You can all sleep in the basement. Morton won't know. It's cold, but better than the streets. On Thursday nights, Morton plays poker there with his friends, so you'll take a room. It'll only be for a few weeks, after all. How long can the depression last?"

For several months her plan worked perfectly. They slept in the basement, then ate upstairs when Morton left. And while Anya, Sharon, and Patricia stayed home, David and Simon looked for work. Before Morton came back, all traces of them were gone. On poker nights, Anya and the boys rode the cold subways from end to end, or slept in rat-infested hallways or a Bowery mission. Then it all fell apart. Morton realized the food budget was out of line, and little Patricia began to talk.

Sharon denied everything at first, but Morton soon discovered them below and ordered them out.

"Look how fat your mother's getting on my money!" he yelled.

It was then that a tearful Anya revealed what she had been trying to hide. She was pregnant, nearly in her fifth month. Months ago, when Sharon had heard about Uncle Charles's death, she'd sent Aunt Sonia condolences. Now, she wrote begging for a fifty-dollar loan. Until the money arrived, Anya and the boys, dressed in rags and misery, stood on street corners near fire-filled barrels, listening to people sing "Brother Can You Spare a Dime?"—not a song but a request—or "One Meatball"—not a ditty but a hunger declaration. Back and forth they walked with stoop-shouldered people who carried signs on their broken bodies saying, "WILL DO ANYTHING, ANYWHERE, ANYTIME." Apathy spread its infected tentacles and squeezed the wretched, the tired, the farmer, the city slicker, the hillbilly, the Okie, the southerner, northerner, easterner, westerner—all of whom stood in lines coiled like snakes around city corners, waiting for a bowl of soup. And in those lines, while her feet and back hurt, Anya would think of Morris, who'd left them, think of Morton and his selfishness, think of how she hated her pregnancy, hated being dependent, hated her shame, and, in her weakest moment, even hated God.

Then Sonia's money arrived, and they went to Brooklyn and rented a three-room flat in Brownsville. A week later, Simon found a job in a junkyard for thirty cents a day. When he wasn't working, he and David combed the garbage for old clothes, junk, old furniture to sell. But pickings were slim. On weekends they chased vegetable trucks hoping food would fall. And sometimes they stole. The Jazz Age was over, replaced by the Age of Lines: soup lines, unemployment lines, bread lines, and the lines that crisscrossed the frightened faces of simple Americans who did not understand what was happening. But they took it day by day, and, in late May, Anya gave birth to a boy she named Sheldon, in honor of her father, Shmuel. And life went on.

The Brownsville apartment was in a five-story tenement on the corner of East New York Avenue and Stone. Three and a half gray rooms of roaches and bedbugs, of rusty pipes, with a cracked toilet seat and noisy plumbing that leaked. Anya's front window looked beyond that barren misery to tree-lined Eastern Parkway, where the spires of a Catholic church pierced the blue sky and billy goats grazed in grassy fields. Across the street were small homes, an Italian grocer, and some gypsy fortune-telling parlors. Several blocks behind was Pitkin Avenue, Brownsville's Broadway, a street of bright lights, theaters, restaurants, and stores where people loved to walk, flirt, and dream. And on the corner was Manny's candy store, a hangout for girls and boys.

In March of 1933, the Barber family gathered around the Crosley radio waiting for the new president's speech. David kept spinning the dial, cursing as the radio sputtered and cackled. Then President Roosevelt's voice suddenly came in loud and clear.

"We have nothing to fear but fear itself," he said. He told people to banish fear from their conversations. He begged them not to hoard food or money but to share, have faith, barter with one another for services instead of cash. He asked them to stop spreading defeatist rumors and to shun those who did. Americans were in this together, and together they could turn it around. He broke a long-standing precedent that night by not attending the inaugural ball and spent the time with his advisers, examining new ideas, creating legislation to regulate wages, hours, and employment, to repeal prohibition, and to help the farmer breathe again. He closed banks to stabilize the economy. He insured deposits and loosened credit. And he made plans to send America's youth from the severely depressed cities to improve roads, parks, sanctuaries, and forests in Montana, Idaho, Oregon, Washington, and Tennessee. After a while things settled down. David got a job laying linoleum, and the boys made friends.

It was mostly a good crowd of kids, some guys a little too coarse, but this was Brownsville, one of Brooklyn's toughest sections. Some guys smoked, even reefer. They drank homemade hootch and carried "zip guns"—small homemade pistols, or "shivs"—switchblade knives. Most nights they hung out at Manny's candy store, swapping comic books, drinking egg creams, sharing a black-and-white ice cream soda if they were flush: Willie Ryan, Joey Milano, Bobbie Glickman, and the Barber boys. Saturday nights they'd go to the movies and throw things at the girls up front. The girls would giggle and call the manager, a pimply-faced kid in a red-and-gold uniform with frayed cuffs and too-short trousers, who'd march down the aisle with his flashlight and say in a quivering voice, "Please stop or I'll have you removed." The boys would mutter a promise, and when the manager disappeared they'd begin again. After the movie, the girls and guys would walk down Pitkin Avenue and flirt.

Anya wished Sharon were happier. Her once feisty daughter had disappeared, replaced by a frightened woman who could not even decide if she preferred an egg cream to a cherry Coke. At first Anya said nothing. Then Sharon's pregnancy brought it all to the surface. She may not have known if she wanted an egg cream or a cherry Coke, but she knew that by staying with

Morton she'd plunge deeper into despair. And a few weeks into January, 1935, Sharon packed Patricia and, without a single protest from Morton, moved into Anya's apartment.

When Morris had deserted her, Anya had been angry at God for her own pregnancy. Later, she realized what a blessing Shelly had been. His care, his needs, had kept her sane. Now Anya had to make Sharon see *her* pregnancy as a blessing also. In those next months, as Sharon leaned on her mother, a deep love grew where there had been contempt. Bonding was taking place, and instead of the things Sharon had always wanted came the things she had always needed. After a dinner that left them still hungry, they would look across the table and smile, knowing they were poor, but also very rich.

When they first moved to the apartment, Anya made the kitchen pretty by pasting cockamamies on the closets and icebox. She fixed the peeling paint, nailed the cracked linoleum, and stuffed the broken window corners with rags to keep out the winter cold and summer flies. With little or no income, she found creative ways to feed her family, even if it was only mayonnaise on white bread.

On her trips to the grocery store, she'd walk in with her head held high, authoritatively squeezing the bread, smelling its freshness while her mouth watered, then hearing the grocer call, "Next?" And she'd wonder, as she sang her order in mixed Yiddish and English, in that carefree tone she'd cultivated, if he could tell she had no money that day.

"I'd like a nice pumpernickel, Mr. Stockman, and a quarter pound of sweet butter, and, let's see, a *bissel* pot cheese, so big." She'd measure a space with her fingers, then feign surprise. "Goodness, I forgot my purse. Please put it on my bill." Then she'd walk quickly away. It took skill, guts, courage, the will to tell a lie in front of a host of knowing people. And she'd feel so small and trapped, like a fly on flypaper with its little legs squirming. And God forbid if Stockman said no. God forbid if she'd have to walk out humiliated, or worse, knowing her kids wouldn't eat that night.

President Roosevelt announced he'd be forming the Civilian Conservation Corps. It would pay thirty dollars a month, twenty-five of which would be sent home to the family. This money would do three things: feed people, get the economy rolling, and restore the American spirit. Along with thousands, David and Simon applied at the army recruiting office, passed the physical, and received their orders. Simon would go to Elkmont, Tennessee, on road construction. David, to Priest River, Idaho, and forestry.

A week before he left, David heard her laughter. It rang from across the alley and bounced into his bedroom. He'd slept in that room since the start of the depression and the desertion by his father. He could have used her joyful sound then. But it came in 1935, the year Sharon moved in and he would leave for the CCC. The laugh belonged to a girl on the brink of womanhood, and it gave him gooseflesh. When he finally caught her eye from his window, it was just like in the movies. Cupid shot an arrow through his heart.

From the neighbors he learned her family was Italian: Mama, Papa, their seventeen-year-old son, Tony, and Constance, the laughing girl. Constance. Slim, beautiful, without an angle on her body, and with long shapely legs. She had large eyes, the color of brandy, and light brown, shiny hair cut in a page boy. It dripped like honey onto her shoulders and dipped over one eye. The dip was a killer, a lighter shade than the rest, as though God had painted it with a single brushstroke.

At night, David secretly watched her from his room. He hated admitting it, but he was unraveling like one of Mama's badly sewn seams. Her window was wide open, and she was combing her hair, dancing to the radio in a pink nightie. What a dirty deal, he thought. In a few days he'd be in Idaho—wherever the hell that was—and she'd be flirting with some other guy. That was when he decided to make a move.

The very next day she passed him and dropped her book. He tried to keep cool as he picked it up and gave it to her.

"Hi! I'm David Barber, next door."

"Thanks. I'm Constance Romano."

"I know," he said with a goofy smile.

"Really! How?"

"Little birdie," he told her, walking away.

"Hey!" she called. "What else he tell you?"

He came back and pinched her cheek. "That I got dibs on you." Then he turned and quickly left.

Constance Loretta Romano was in shock. The nerve of that jerk. Who did he think he was? She was fifteen, had just broken up with her boyfriend. Now, he comes along and says "dibs." What was he, nuts? Sure, she'd dropped the book on purpose. She was new here and wanted to make friends, not get engaged. Later, the incident made her smile. There was a sweetness about him, like how shaky his hands were when he gave her the book. That night she dreamed about him. And just when she asked about him, her brother Tony said he'd left for the CCC. It surprised her how upset she was. Then she decided there were other fish in the sea. Better to forget him. But she couldn't.

47

David arrived by train dressed in army issue, in the midst of an Idaho forest of tall pine and spruce.

"Hey, Sarge! Where's the hotel?" someone called out.

"You're gonna build it, buddy," the sergeant called back. "The Waldorf-Idaho. Now, get to work."

For the next two weeks they built cabins, slept in tents, and ate from stewpots. If Ma saw me eating this, she'd scream, David thought. But like his father once said, "God overlooks."

Settled in, they repaired trails, created access roads, cleared firebreaks, thinned forests, fought pine blister, gypsy moth, and bark beetle. They ran telephone lines, built ranger stations, and improved public campgrounds. "City boys raking leaves," the locals snickered. And though they began by putting up with one another, before long, there was genuine respect.

Anya's nightmare had her lost in some foreign land, walking through great columns of stone. Where the columns converged, the stone crumbled and a child stood in the path of danger. Anya started running, but her legs were like rocks in mud. Then the mud turned sandy, and the child was soon buried. She tumbled down a long hill, wakening to find Sharon groaning beside her. "Sharon. What's wrong?"

"It's my time, Ma," Sharon said. She was doubled over. "Go to the candy store. Call a taxi, and hurry."

Anya jumped out of bed and dressed while that dream haunted her. "The pains are fast?" she asked.

"Five minutes, and one's . . . coming—" Sharon sucked in sharply and screamed. *"Now!"* She fell on the bed, one hand clutching her belly, the other shoved in her mouth. Anya comforted her until the pain passed. Then she dressed five-year-old Shelly and three-year-old Patricia and ran for help.

The labor was hard, but at 9:30 A.M. Sharon delivered a healthy baby girl she named Candace, a pretty child with thick, dark curls and eyes as huge and shiny as black olives. Resting afterward, Sharon felt lonely and depressed. All around her were women with loving husbands, picture postcards. Why had she mucked up her life like this?

"I should call Morton, maybe?" Anya asked her.

Sharon shrugged. "He won't care."

That night, Anya arrived home from the hospital, took care of Shelly and Patricia, and found a letter from Simon.

Dear Mom,

It doesn't seem like it but four months have passed and I miss you. It's hot as heck grading roads in Tennessee, but knowing you, Shelly, and Sharon, and the kids are getting three squares a day makes it all worthwhile. Not much to do here but read a little, go to classes; now there's talk of a transfer to Montana. And the food's either getting better or I've lost my taste. I'd really love some of

your chicken soup, Ma. Guys here think a matzoh
ball's something you hit with a bat.

Love, Simon

PRIEST RIVER, IDAHO

A seething spring and early summer had drained every
stream till the forests were dry as tinder. Somehow, a
blaze had begun, and David's group had been fighting
the raging fire for twenty-six hours. It was almost under
control when wind reversals barreled in from the plains,
raining fiery cinders on Bitterroot and Cabinet. As the
blaze flared again, David's group mobilized at the fire
circle. Thunder rumbled. Lightning lit up the smoky
yellow sky. Sparks fell like rain, setting David's shirt
on fire. As he ripped it from his back, a bolt of lightning
snapped a treetop and someone screamed, *"Hey, Bar-*
ber! Look out!"

MISSOULA, MONTANA

On the train ride to Missoula, Simon thought about
Morris. About what he'd known but not shared with
the others. Only time would tell if he'd been right or
wrong. When the train stopped, his thoughts did too.
At sunrise, he laced up his boots, packed rations, and
explored the back trails. There were towering mountain
ranges, granite peaks, and wild rivers everywhere. He
learned that *montaña* was a Spanish word which means
mountain country. He learned about the Indians who'd
once lived here—Crow, Sioux, Nez Percé, Shoshone,
Arapaho, Blackfoot, Cheyenne, Flathead, Kootenai—
most gone now in the flesh but not the spirit, and Simon

believed in the spirit. He could feel their presence at the Clark Fork of the Columbia River, imagine the great herds of buffalo that had once roamed the Great Plains. He returned that evening feeling deeply moved. In his mailbox was an official notice from Washington, D.C. He shook like a leaf as he slit the flap open but was relieved as he read the words: THOSE WHO WISH TO ATTEND HIGH HOLY DAY SERVICES IN SPOKANE, WASHINGTON, SEE YOUR SUPERVISOR.

                                   SPOKANE, WASHINGTON

Simon entered the lobby of the Hotel Davenport, clean shaven and wearing the gray suit, white shirt, and dark tie he had taken from home. He was greeted by a short, bearded man in a blue suit and yarmulke, who shook his hand vigorously.

"Hello, Barber. I'm Rabbi Goldman. The Jewish community of Spokane welcomes you. We've reserved a room for you here, with tickets for services." He handed Simon some papers. "These will pay for your other meals. Dinners are at my house."

"This is great, Rabbi!" Simon said.

Rabbi Goldman chortled. "Hey, *boychik*. We're all Americans." Then he whispered. "Personally, I'd thank me *after* you taste my wife's cooking." He laughed and left.

On Rosh Hashanah morning Simon walked into shul wearing his yarmulke. He said the prayer, kissed his tallis, then placed it on his shoulders, flapping an edge over each arm. Now he was ready to acknowledge God's presence in his life, to pray, to appeal for a year of blessing and peace for all mankind. He took a seat up front near several youths who stood as he passed and shook his hand in welcome. Seconds later, he was staring into the eyes of his brother, and they fell into each other's arms moments before services began. People turned to see the boys, who were praying harder and with more joy and devotion than all the rest.

Walking to dinner after services, Simon had a thousand questions. David explained the fire, the lightning, the tree.

"They sent me to Missoula for treatment," he said. "When the notice came for services, I stayed. I had no idea you'd be here."

"God's hand," Simon said, and David agreed.

At dinner they prayed and dipped apple slices in honey to symbolize a sweet year. They ate roast chicken and *tsimmes*, the first kosher food they'd tasted since leaving home. Most of all there were blessings, the closeness they felt to the Goldmans, knowing that the bloodline that flowed through them all flowed also through Abraham, Isaac, and Jacob.

With dinner over, they thanked the rabbi and his wife and returned to the hotel to share news of Shelly and of Sharon's new baby, Candace. Eventually the talk came naturally to Morton.

"Guy's a bastard," David said. "I could never treat my kids that way."

"Hey, dummy. You need a wife before you have kids."

David's smile gave him away.

"Sonofagun! I know her, maybe?"

David's silence brought Simon upon him in some brotherly wrestling. After a few Indian burns, Simon had David in a choke hold.

"Name's Constance," David coughed. "Romano."

Simon let him go. "The shiksa? Catholic?"

"Bingo!" David said. He rubbed his aching neck.

"Yeah, bingo. That's what they play in church on Wednesdays. Only you'll do it from jail. Besides being a Gentile, Davie, she's also jailbait. Ma would have a fit."

"No," David said. "Connie's father would kill me first."

They prepared for bed, then, seconds before lights out, Simon decided it was time to share his secret. It was the new year, time to wipe slates clean. He shook David's shoulder. "I have something to confess."

David stuffed his head under his pillow and yawned. "God forgives, Sy. Remembers stuff even you've forgotten."

"It's not God I'm worried about."

David sat up.

"It's Papa." Simon looked away. "He's not in California. He's living in New York on Fourth Street."

David mimed clearing his ears. "Come again?"

Simon repeated his words.

"So. The old guy's come back," David said.

"No, David. He never left New York. He's been hiding from the shylocks all along."

David's glare nailed Simon to the wall. "How long have you known?"

"I ran into him by accident six months after Rivington."

David left the bed, paced tracks in the carpet. His fist smashed the hollow bathroom door.

"That's why I didn't tell, David. I thought you'd kill him."

"So why tell me now?" David rubbed his hand.

"Because he wants to come home. Because I won't tell Ma till we settle it."

"He know about Shelly?"

"Yes. He made a mistake. Now he wants to change it."

"No mistake, Simon. That's when you give the wrong

change. Papa left a pregnant wife with two kids, the rent due, and no place to live. That's criminal."

"It's the new year, David. He's asking for forgiveness. He was running for his life, then."

"And what the hell were we doing? Living with the queen? You forget about eating garbage or sleeping in hallways? You forget how we watched at night so nobody raped Ma?"

"I guess I'm willing to overlook."

"God overlooks, Sy. I'm not such a good guy."

"Ah, David. I'm all mixed up. I don't want to do the wrong thing. Suppose Ma wants him back?"

David's finger aimed at Simon. "She won't. And you tell Pa if I ever catch him near her, I'll kick his ass all over Brooklyn."

CHICAGO, ILLINOIS

Charles's death had been a shock to Sonia, and she found to her surprise she missed him. If only he'd confided his financial troubles, she could have helped him. Her land purchases and investments had paid off, and she was richer than ever. But a week after his suicide, she was in the hospital with a perforated ulcer. When she was better, she sold the lakefront home and bought a small brick house on Clyde Avenue, where she built a magnificent aviary, keeping thirty of her best rollers, some finches, and a single cockatiel named Piper. Soon, the new house made her forget the violence in which she had been conceived, the violence and humiliation of her early life, the violence of her husband's death, and now, as the papers reported daily, the violence in Adolf Hitler's Germany. She spent her time in the aviary, where the temperature never varied a degree, where there were no drafts, where the lighting was regulated, where only beautiful singing filled her ears. She did not want to think about or be touched in any way by the human race and their bag of dirty tricks. Then letters arrived from Joshua and Sharon.

Dear Aunt Sonia,

Just a note to say I miss you and to see how you're feeling. Also, there's a new arrival I've named Candace, after Uncle Charles, because I thought he was a special person. Candy has thick black curls and big eyes that are starting to turn hazel. I'll send pictures when I can.

I don't know if you're aware, but Morton and I are separated and I'm staying with Mom for a while. David and Simon are away at CCC and will be home for Chanukah. I have a new job as a bookkeeper's assistant, and as soon as I can I'll pay back the loan. Aunt Sonia, you'll never know how that money literally saved my life.

Love, Sharon

Sonia's eyes filled with tears as she closed Sharon's letter. Inside was a five-dollar bill, Sharon's first installment on her loan. For the first time in her life, Sonia felt that someone really cared. A week before, she'd had a visit from her attorney, who'd begun to badger her about the disposition of her huge estate.

"There's so much good you can do with your money, Sonia," he'd said. "Scholarships, endowments, hospitals, orphanages, research. The list is endless."

Now, Sonia held the five-dollar bill in her hand, and rereading Sharon's last words she realized what her money could and should be doing. She placed an immediate call to her attorney and began to set things up.

48

The first night David was home, he hid behind his shade, peering into Constance's window. She was there, prettier if that was possible, visiting with some girl-friends, and he lay down on his bed as her laughter rose above that of the others to throttle him. It was as if she knew he was home and was deliberately torturing him. He stayed awake that whole night thinking of her.

With all her children together, Anya planned a Chanukah feast. She grated pounds of potatoes for pancakes. She bought candles for her menorah, *draydels*, and chocolate Chanukah gelt for the children. She put the menorah in the front window, not like in Russia, where they'd had to hide it. In America they could worship God as they chose. And when they were all gathered and the blessings said, Shelly begged Simon to tell his version of the Chanukah story.

"Long ago," he told the children, "a wicked king ruled Jerusalem. He lost a war and, in his anger, attacked the Jews. Because it was the Sabbath, the Jews were not prepared, and the battle was lost. The king built idols to worship. He sacrificed pigs on God's holy altar. When he forbade the study of Torah and the observance of the Sabbath, a wise man named Mattathias refused to obey. He declared his rebellion and fled to the hills with his five sons, where his bravery attracted others. When Mattathias died, his eldest son, Judah, took over. Inspired by a scripture in the Book of Ex-

odus, Judah called his group the Maccabees. And they
continued to fight.

"Now, the wicked king had to do something about
these Maccabees, so he planned another attack on the
Sabbath. But Judah had warned his men. 'If we don't
fight, there will be no more Sabbaths. Without Sabbaths, there will be no more Jews.' This time they were
ready. They fought for three long years, smashed the
king's idols, and took back the Temple. On the day of
rededication—*Chanukah* means 'rededication'—they
found a single vial of kosher oil—good for only one
day. They lit it anyway and, lo and behold, it burned
for eight days. That was God's miracle and the reason
we light eight candles. But we celebrate Chanukah to
remind ourselves how precious religious freedom is, and
that, no matter what others believe, we must keep to
the light of our own faith."

"That was a great story, Uncle Simon," Patricia said.
"But why do we spin the *draydel* tops?"

"When the study of Torah was forbidden, Jewish
children kept *draydels* handy. If a soldier came, they
hid their books and spun a game with the tops. They
weren't going to let the soldiers keep them from studying Torah!"

While the children laughed, Anya brought a platter
of crispy potato pancakes with bowls of thick sour cream
and applesauce. Then they sang and danced together.

Carmine Romano had a beerbelly, though he did not
drink beer. He loved red wine with his pasta, and he
loved pasta. He was strong, with thick black hair
combed straight back from a wide forehead, bushy eyebrows, a broad nose, and a widow's peak. His wife,
Angelina, was small and sweet, with a head of salt-and-
pepper hair she pulled back and wound in a single braid
at the nape of her neck. She had round black eyes, with

dark circles beneath them, and, except for small gold loops in her long earlobes, she dressed simply and in black.

Angelina Romano's spaghetti sauce was the best in Brooklyn. She made it from scratch, and Carmine would boast about his wife's cooking to anyone who would listen. Angelina would begin Wednesday's sauce on Monday, starting with fresh tomatoes, the best olive oil, garlic, fresh basil, green peppers, onions, and oregano. On Wednesday nights Carmine would go to Angelina's pot, rip off some fresh Italian bread, and dip it in her bubbling sauce. While Angelina waited, he'd smack his lips. Then he'd smile, say "*delizioso*," and throw in a pinch of sugar to show he was boss.

Carmine would sit at the table with a cloth napkin tucked inside his T-shirt, a fork in one hand and a spoon in the other, while Angelina grated fresh Parmesan cheese. Their dog, Skippy, a small Pomeranian-Pekingese, would lie at Carmine's feet. But Carmine's true joy came when his family was seated with him. *La famiglia*. The family! He loved it. Here in America, Carmine was happy and safe, a long way from the northerners who'd tried to control his life in Collesano, Sicily. In America, his children would never grow up like he and his ancestors had, just peasants scratching a life from dust.

A week before Christmas, the front door opened. Carmine and Tony carried in the biggest tree Constance had ever seen. "There's more stuff downstairs," Carmine said to Tony. "Be a good boy and get it."

The dark-haired Tony—"handsomest guy in Brooklyn," the girls would whisper—ran to oblige.

"Quick!" Carmine said to Connie. "Give Papa a hug." After squeezing her, he pulled a bag from his jacket. "Only for you," he said. "Don't let Tony see."

Constance opened the package and found the chocolate marshmallow cookies she loved, the broken ones the foreman let Carmine take from the Brooklyn Biscuit Company, where he worked. She threw her arms around him, then sailed to her room.

Christmas was the Romano family's favorite holiday. The scent of fresh pine from the tree filled the apartment, and they decorated it with sparkling ornaments, silver tinsel, lights, cellophane-wrapped candy canes, rotating garlands of popcorn, and strings of cranberries, all enhanced by spidery angel hair. Below the tree were Connie's treasured crystal animals placed on tiny mirrors, set in snowy, absorbent cotton, circled by Tony's windup train set from his sixth birthday. And around the train lay piles of beautifully wrapped presents. Hanging from a fake fireplace Carmine loved were Tony's and Connie's stockings. Angelina placed baskets of apples, oranges, and hard-shelled nuts on every table and pinned a holly wreath with a big red bow to the front door. Red poinsettias stood in every corner of the room, and Carmine hung bits of mistletoe so he could kiss the ladies. And the mailbox was crammed with Christmas cards. For weeks, Angelina baked and cooked: fruitcakes, puddings, apple jelly, panettone, Hussar's Kisses stuffed with fudge and coated with crushed almonds. She built sugar churches, made candy snowmen, and planned a huge Christmas dinner.

Four days before this Christmas Eve, Carmine decided the linoleum in Constance's room looked shabby. He chose the flooring, called the union hall, and the job went to Simon Barber. When Simon saw the Romano name, he scratched his own out and passed the job on to David. He thought it was time his brother met and forgot his shiksa dream girl. But Simon's plan backfired. The sight of Constance as she opened the door shocked David so, he could only hand her his union card and mutter the word "Linoleum."

Constance smiled. "Well, well. Lookie who's here. Mr. Dibs."

David's face turned red as he remembered that moment.

"So, what can I do you for?"

David pulled out the order slip and handed it to her. "From your father. I'm supposed to do the floor."

"Oh," she murmured, reading it. "Follow me, then." She smiled wickedly as she turned and led him to her bedroom.

While David worked, Constance peeked. She watched his muscles flex, watched his hands and arms. Arms were important to her. Arms told of a man's strength and masculinity. She liked smooth arms with broad wrists, sensitive fingers, and clean fingernails. And David's arms were perfect.

David worked hard for the next two days, but he couldn't keep his mind on his work. He was inside *her* room, around *her* things. He touched her chenille bedspread, brushed against a robe that hung on a hook behind her door. He saw her diary lying on the dresser, and a devilish voice prodded him to open it. He looked at a single page and noted the dedication to Humphrey Bogart. He felt guilty, and when he returned to work, he cut his hand, nicked the floor, stumbled into a closet, and burned his elbow on the steam pipe.

When Carmine Romano came home the second evening, the floor was finished. "Good job," he told his family at dinner. "Nice boy, that David. Too bad he's not Catholic."

"What do you mean, Papa?" Constance asked.

Carmine looked at Tony, then at his wife, who passed him a steaming bowl of meatballs. "He don't mean nothing," Angelina said. "We're all God's children."

"The hell I don't!" Carmine corrected her. "There'll be no mixed marriages in *my* house."

The big night arrived, and everyone met at Lady of Loretta Church on Sackman and Pacific Street. Midnight mass always sent chills down Constance's spine. It wasn't so much the religious part she loved but the beauty and fellowship, being with her two grandmothers, the singing, candlelight, the priests and altar boys dressed in their robes. The following day they met at Carmine's house to exchange presents, to sing, dance, and eat—roast turkey and baked ham with mashed potatoes, candied sweet potatoes, pumpkin pie with whipped cream. Dressed in her red-and-green-plaid taffeta dress Mama had bought at Boxer's on Pitkin Avenue, Constance wore her first pair of hose and patent-leather high heels. After dinner, Angelina brought out a bowl of eggnog, and they drank and sang carols while Cousin Frankie played the concertina.

David saw the first Bogart movie he could find. He studied the actor, imitating him in every way until Shelly caught him and threatened to tell unless David paid him off. It was ridiculous, he thought to himself, as he handed Shelly a dime. David Barber, a lovesick sap.

A week after St. Patrick's Day, David walked up to the roof. There was something about looking down and across the city's landscape that made him feel good. He opened the door with a hard push and walked outside, surprised to find Constance pulling clothespins off some dry sheets flapping in the wind.

"Hi," she called.

"I didn't know you were up here," he answered.

"I thought you knew everything."

He folded his arms and tapped a foot. "You starting up again?"

"My, my. Can dish it out but can't take it."

"Says who?"

"Says me. Now grab that corner and help me."

David obeyed like a puppy. "You always this pushy?"

The sheet almost flew away. "Hey!" she screamed. "Watch out!" She grabbed it, and they continued folding.

"Tony said you were in the CCC. Where'd you go?"

"Priest River, Idaho," he said, smirking. "In China."

She peered at him above the sheet, with arched eyebrows. He gave her the best version of his latest Bogart smile, one that made his mouth drift to the side, but she didn't say a word.

"Was it nice there?" she asked.

He became David again. "If you like trees."

He looked into her eyes. They made him dizzy, the way the sun got behind them and they glowed. But it wasn't just that. It was *how* she looked at him. Like she could see inside and know what he was feeling.

When the sheets were folded and put in a basket, they sat down near the roof's edge. Slow music drifted up from a radio, and they were quiet for a while.

"Quit it!" she said.

"What?"

"You're staring."

"Can't help it. You're cute."

"David!" She punched his arm and giggled. "Anyone ever tell you you look like Humphrey Bogart?"

His heart pounded, but he made believe he didn't know. "Humphrey who?"

"The actor, stupid. Jeez!"

"He good lookin'?"

"No," she said. She grabbed the basket and ran for the roof door. "Got a monkey face and a monkey brain."

David chased and caught her, and their hands touched on the doorknob. It was like an electric shock.

The basket fell, the clothes tumbled out, and the door jammed his toe. He felt like a jerk as he stood there. Then they started laughing.

Together, they spoke a million things with their eyes. Something powerful was happening, something powerful and terrifying and wonderful, and they both knew it. And though everything was against it—age, religion, family, poverty—none of it mattered. It came down to something stronger than all that combined.

"Wanna go to the show Sunday?" he asked.

"Sure," she answered, and they made plans.

When David got to the movies, Connie was standing by the poster showcase. She looked like a princess in a pink angora sweater with a brown skirt and a pink beret over her page boy. She took his arm while he bought the tickets and chose popcorn at the candy counter. Inside, the Movietone News cut the darkness, and it took awhile for their eyes to adjust. They waited, then found two seats in the middle. For a while all he heard was his own heartbeat, then the problems began. Two arms, one armrest. Real stupid. Then his knee accidentally touched hers, and he wondered how one little pink knee could cause such a reaction. And just when his feelings were under control, he sniffed her cologne and it sent him reeling. He did the stretch and yawn bit Simon had taught him, until his arm rested on her shoulder. In his whole life he had never been happier, and he knew if the world came to an end right now, he just wouldn't care.

Tony Romano walked into the movies with his friends and sat in back waiting for the feature to begin. There had been a cartoon festival that morning, and the spillover of kids annoyed him. He ignored them as best he

could and watched the screen. The Marx Brothers were
a riot, pushing fifty people into one small room, and
that made him laugh. It made everyone laugh. But one
familiar laugh caught his ear. It belonged to his sister,
Connie, who was supposed to be with her friend Gracie
today. He searched the darkness, the halos on backs of
heads. Then he saw her. She was sitting with some guy
he couldn't make out. Then the guy turned his face
toward Connie's ear and the screen lit up real bright.

At 6:30 P.M., Tony Romano closed the door to his
sister's room and hugged her. She was really puzzled.
"What's wrong, Tony?"

He pulled her to the bed and sat next to her, with
his fingers laced together and his head bowed. "I gotta
say something, Connie, but I don't want you mad, understand?"

"Will you stop acting crazy, please?"

He looked into her eyes. "I saw you today. With
Barber."

She stared back without wavering but said nothing.

"It's not so much you goin' against Papa, I've done
it too. But you're a nice Italian girl, too young to sneak
around with a guy David's . . . age."

"Or religion, right, Tony? I mean, let's be honest
here."

"Hey, I've got nothin' personal against this guy. I
even like him. But you heard Papa."

Connie sighed. "You gonna tell?"

"No. But someone else will. I just want you ready
when it hits the fan."

That spring, Connie became David's girl, and everyone knew it but Carmine. They'd meet on the roof,
hold hands, share dreams, make plans. He practiced
for weeks how their first kiss would be, using a pillow,
watching in the mirror how to part his lips and squint

his eyes. How to reach and pull her to him while looking cool. He developed this Bogart nostril flare, but it looked too much like he was about to sneeze, so he dumped it for a Bogart glower he prayed didn't make him look like Dracula. Then it happened one night on the roof while a big yellow moon balanced on some bridge. She had on a three-piece playsuit, some contraption with shorts, a skirt open to her thighs, and a top that let part of her tummy show. Soft skin, skin he could touch, warm skin that turned his arms to jelly and made his stomach knot.

He kissed her lips, and they were moist and willing. The touch was so soft it felt like cream. When he pulled away, he wondered how the moon had slipped under her skin and shimmered there. He felt his own eyes unable to do anything but float in their sockets like in some Saturday cartoon. Then a deeper, more powerful hunger unfurled, and he kissed her again. And when his hand moved so naturally to the gentle curve of her breast, and when she didn't stop him, he pleaded, "Oh, Connie, please tell me no." And she did.

They met every chance they could. On the roof, at the movies, on Pitkin Avenue. Then the guys in his gang—Willie Ryan, Joey Milano, Bobbie Glickman—found girls, and Simon began seeing Elaine Markowitz, and they soon became a happy gang of Saturday-night bums eating chow mein, pizza, or hot dogs from Kishke King. On every street corner of the neighborhood, Shelly and Patricia drew chalk hearts with David's and Constance's initials inside. Then David bought a Brownie camera, and they posed for photos. Photos on fenders, running boards of cars, on stoops and street corners. Photos at the beach, Betsy Head Swimming Pool, and Kitsle Park. They played stickball, stoopball, potsy, marbles, jacks, kick the can, ring-a-lievo, opened fire hydrants, and threw dice when they could find a vacant hallway. They went to Ebbets Field, or took a train to Coney Island, passing stop after stop as the cement ugliness of East New York turned to green trees and pretty houses on places called Cortelyou Road, and David dreamed that one day he and Constance would have a home there.

At Coney Island they'd remove their shoes under the boardwalk and tramp through the cool, moist sand. Moments later, their feet would burn in the hot, dry sand as they headed for the ocean. They'd fight about where to put the blanket: "Near the ladies' room," the girls would cry. "Near the soda bar," the boys would insist. Then they'd agree on a place in the middle, peel their clothes down to their bathing suits, and lie side by side. Constance wore this royal blue thing that fit her like snakeskin, and David would try to keep his mind out of the gutter, where it had been spending a lot of time lately.

They'd dance in juke joints to their favorite songs, or go to Prospect Park, lie on the grass, and hold hands near the lake. Being together was all they needed. No words. Words told them they were different. Words divided them. Italian/Russian. Sixteen/Twenty-one. Catholic/Jewish. Easter/Passover. Christmas/Chanukah. Priest/ Rabbi. On and on. But quiet, shared moments like these would be for all time, for when they would grow old together and remember it had once been like this. It wasn't long, though, before Carmine Romano put one and one together, and the two he came up with was Constance and David, and that match would take place over his dead body.

49

Simon Barber had been keeping company with Elaine Markowitz, and it was time to make some decisions. He loved her. She was intelligent, cute, a young girl from a large, close-knit family, with three brothers she adored. Simon sometimes felt a competitive edge, but he respected and admired each of them. Then, the unexpected passing of her mother, followed shortly by her father, drew Elaine closer to him.

They took long walks down Pitkin Avenue, saw good movies, and read books together. It satisfied him to sit in a quiet room with her and read aloud something he'd found exciting, some passage of poetry, philosophy, art, sociology, books with ideas to share. They rarely disagreed. But when they did, Simon gave in. It was hard to argue with Elaine's translucent skin, or her midnight black hair and dark eyes, or that teeny-tiny space he loved so much, which separated her two front teeth. And she was vain about wearing her eyeglasses, especially to dinner at some nice restaurant. When they dined, she'd pass her menu to Simon and say sweetly, without her glasses, "You choose." And some old-fashioned waiter would smile as if thinking, All's right with the world, and wait for Simon to make the selections.

And Elaine was artistic, too. She wore pretty clothes, "sophisticated," Sharon called them, little black crepe dresses with peplums, trimmed with fuchsia or chartreuse. She'd pin a platinum lavaliere on her shoulder and buckle elegant wedgies on her ankles. But the day she really won Simon's heart was when he told her he'd dreamed of becoming a doctor and she offered to work two jobs to put him through medical school. Her gesture touched him so deeply he almost cried, and he knew then he'd never find another like her. And at midnight on New Year's Eve, dancing beneath a spinning mirrored mosaic ball that flashed bits of silver on her bare shoulders, Simon asked Elaine to be his wife, and she accepted.

When Carmine Romano discovered that David was seeing his Constance, he was wild with fury. The guy was too old for his little girl; he was poor, uneducated, Jewish. Not that he had anything personal against *them*, like some of his friends, who called them misers and said they were Christ killers. But he had plans for Connie. A big wedding in a Catholic church. A fancy white gown with a long train. Lots of bridesmaids and flower girls, everything he and Angelina had never had. He'd even saved for a honeymoon. He'd help the newlyweds buy a new home, then look forward to lots of grandchildren to spoil in his old age. He'd planned it for years. But it wouldn't happen that way if the groom was David Barber. So he had to nip it in the bud. And when Constance came home that day, he hugged her, gave her the bag of cookies she loved, and sat beside her.

After a long silence, Constance stopped nibbling. "Okay, Pa. What'd I do now?" She waited for the roof to fall.

"Nothing, baby." He paused. "You're my little girl, right?"

"Papa. I *knooow* you," she sang.

Carmine took her hand. "Can't fool you, hah? Smart like your papa. So, okay. I'll be straight." He kissed her. "From now on, don't see the Barber boy."

She didn't act surprised. "And why not?"

Carmine's eyes swept the floor. "He's . . . too old."

"Like you and Mama?"

"And he's poor. Got no future."

"Oh, say it, Papa. It's because he's Jewish, right?"

"I only want your happiness, Connie. That's all."

"Be honest, Papa. We're talking about *your* happiness, not mine."

Carmine dropped her hand and glowered at her. "I asked you nice, Connie. Now, I'll tell you. You can't see the Barber boy again." Then he stood up and left the room.

All night long, Connie tossed and turned. In the morning she called her friend Gracie, and they met for lunch at Manny's. They'd been friends since kindergarten, and it was good to have someone to talk to. She felt comfortable as the plump Gracie sat twirling her red finger curls, blinking her friendly brown eyes while the two devoured grilled-cheese sandwiches and Connie explained. "Papa hates my boyfriend."

"Hey! Italians never give their daughters up without a fight. It's a rite of passage." Gracie pounded her chest like a gorilla and laughed. "Just give him time, honey."

"I wish it was that easy," Constance said.

"Nothing can be that bad." Gracie bit into her crisp sour pickle. "Mmmm, good," she said. "One thing these kikes know how to make is pickles. I'll say that for them. Now, tell me who your Prince Charming is."

At Gracie's anti-Semitic remark, Connie's stomach tightened. She didn't even know her best friend. "David Barber," she said.

Gracie stopped in midchew and crossed herself. "Holy Mary, Mother of God. No wonder your father's nuts. Mine would've killed me." Gracie leaned across the table and whispered. "A Jew, for God's sake! You crazy? Goin' with someone who killed God."

"I don't believe this," Constance said. She stood and gathered her things. "If God is dead, Gracie, it's people like *you* who killed Him, not David." Then she took the check and left.

*   *   *

A week later, Carmine headed home early from work. He took a shortcut on Thatford Avenue and saw Constance with David. The bastard's arm was around Connie's waist, and they were laughing. His heart was heavy. Rage burned inside him. Constance had disobeyed him completely. Jesus! Whatever happened to Honor thy father and mother? Incensed, he walked home, thinking of solutions. He'd asked her nicely. He'd made demands. And her answer was to stand on a street corner and make a fool of him. Okay. Okay. It was time now to make his point another way.

Dinner that evening began in silence—Carmine's anger building as he played with his lentil soup; Tony nervously cleaning his plate with bread; Connie passing bits of food to Skippy beneath the table. And Angelina, moving ghostlike from stove to sink to stove to table. Suddenly, Carmine folded his arms across his chest and spoke Italian. "So, Connie." He leaned over and pinched her cheek, hard. "What'd you do today?"

Constance stared at her plate. "I went to the library," she answered in English. The pinch burned.

"That so?" he said. His eyes narrowed. "Three o'clock, I left work early and went down Thatford . . ."

Before he finished, Constance knew. She looked with pleading eyes at Angelina, who glanced at Carmine, whose eyes never strayed from his daughter's face. Tony suddenly dropped his spoon. It clattered to the floor and made Constance jump.

"Okay, Papa. No games," she said with a touch of defiance. "If you were on Thatford at three, you know darn well I was with David." She threw her fork down. "And I might as well say the rest. David and I are in love."

Carmine's eyes launched daggers. *"Basta!"* he yelled.

He stood up and grabbed Connie's elbow. "So, you lied to me. What am I? Garbage?"

Before she could say anything, his hand slammed across her face. She felt his fingers burn right through her skin. When his hand raised to strike again, Tony leaped between them.

"No, Pa! Don't! She won't do it again. Say it, Connie!" he begged.

Carmine shoved Tony against the wall. "Don't interfere!" he shouted. Then he dragged the frightened Constance down the narrow hallway and threw her onto her bed.

Constance cowered as Carmine unfurled his belt from his trousers. She pleaded for him to stop as he doubled the belt over and struck her again and again.

"Ouch, Pa. No!" she cried. "You're hurting me."

Above her screams and tears, Carmine beat her arms and legs, slammed her back and chest, following as she scrambled across the bed, bounced against the walls, crawled along the linoleum, David's linoleum. As her hands flew to protect her bare skin, she searched the cool floor for safety and solace but found only her father's fury.

David heard Constance's screams ricochet across the alley, and all he could do was pray. *Make him stop, God. Please make him stop!* Sometime later, the screaming ceased, and he stood by his window waiting for a sign. Fifteen minutes passed before her shade went up, and he grabbed his jacket and raced to the roof, where he opened the door.

In the last daylight moments, he looked past the steam vents, beyond the pigeon coops, until he saw her. She was huddled near a brick chimney, shuddering so hard he thought his heart would break. He raced there, dropped beside her, and held her tightly.

"Sh, baby. Sh. Don't cry," he begged.

He rocked her till she calmed, till she'd cried her whole story, and each word cut him like a knife. Before the light faded, he saw her swollen eyes, the red welts, the black and blue bruises on her legs and arms, and he wrapped his jacket around her as the evening cooled and kissed her cheeks, her eyes, and her forehead.

"Don't worry, Connie. I'll fix it so he'll never hurt you again. We'll get married soon, and I'll take care of you." He searched her eyes for signs of indecision but saw none. "Besides, he's your father. He doesn't mean it. He's just trying to scare you."

"No, David. You got it backwards. He's the one who's scared, and I know now he'll go a long way to keep me from seeing you."

The hair on David's neck went up. "Well, I've got friends too if—"

She pushed him away. "Great! He bashes me, you bash him. He's my father, damnit. Not some street hoodlum."

David stood up. "I'm only human, Connie. I won't crawl like a worm for permission to love you. I want marriage, kids, a house with a white picket fence. I have a right to that." He sat beside her again. "I also have a right to wake up each morning and see your face."

Their lips met in a long and passionate kiss. His whole body was a mass of rhythms, converging in a symphony of skipping heartbeats, erratic pulses, and blood pounding through his veins. As they settled against the chimney back, a star flashed across the midnight blue sky, and he made a wish. They were so close their hearts were a single beat, their shadows, one black outline. As the sky grew darker, it scared him to think how much they loved and needed each other. It scared him equally to think how much she loved and needed her father, too.

When Connie went home, she found Angelina waiting with clean towels and boric acid solution.

"Come in. Don't be scared. Papa's gone."

Connie sat down while Angelina sponged the bruises. She sensed a lecture coming and didn't want to hear it. "Whatever it is, save it, Ma. I'm old enough to make my own decisions."

Angelina wrung out the wet rag and patted the scratches. "You smart, Connie. Why can't you see how you hurt him?"

Connie pulled away. "Why can't he see how he hurts *me*?"

Tears filled Angelina's eyes.

"Oh, Mama, please don't cry." She hugged her mother. "I can't help it if I love David. It doesn't mean I care less for Papa. But he's wrong about David, and you know it. The only reason he's against him is 'cause he's Jewish."

Angelina's black eyes glared. "No, Connie," she said. "It's 'cause he's not Catholic. It's a big difference."

Carmine hated himself. He'd never hit Connie before, and he felt guilty and ashamed. He sat in a bar trying to understand, but there were no easy answers. Yet one thing kept bothering him. He hadn't raised his children as strict Catholics, and *that* had been the mistake. He wished now he could go back and change it.

Though he loved the church's traditions, he'd taken his children only on holidays and special occasions. He'd kept them away because he never liked to see Christ on the cross. As a child in Sicily it had frightened him. Jesus, in pain, hanging there with the nails in his palms, with the blood on his body, and the crown of thorns. It scared him so much then, he swore he'd spare his own children. And he didn't believe in confession either. No man could speak to God for another, he believed. A man did that himself. After all, as his father used to say, "Priests are still men and nuns are still women." For him, religion lay in the family. Family gave a man true strength and pleasure. Without a close family, a man was nothing. And David Barber was a threat to all that. If Barber took Connie away, Carmine's world would disappear. With Barber there'd be no big church wedding, no baptisms, no Easter Sundays, no midnight mass, no Christmas dinners. Hell, he knew how *they* felt about Jesus. Oh, God. It scared him. If they ran off and got married outside the church, his grandchildren would be illegitimate, and the two of them, living in sin. No. It couldn't happen. Whatever it took, he had to keep them apart. And that was when he decided to call David at the union hall and set up a meeting at Manny's. It was time for them to reason.

At Manny's, Carmine sat with David in a booth in the back. He ordered two coffees and some pastries, and spoke his piece in English. "I'll be honest, kid," Carmine said. "It's a papa's duty. Someday you'll have your own kids, and you'll understand. The truth is, you're a nice boy, but not right for Connie. So, don't see her again. Okay?"

"Excuse me, Mr. Romano. But I'm confused. You say I'm nice. I have a steady job, and I love Connie deeply. So what have you got against me?"

"Please, David. Don't make me say."

"You have to, sir. Give me a good reason to cut off my right arm, 'cause that's what you're asking."

"Look, David. Your people—they're good."

David smiled knowingly. He wouldn't play the silly game. "I like my family, too."

Coffee sputtered from Carmine's mouth. "Hey! You

show respect!" He looked David in the eye. "I come in peace, but you want trouble. So, now I warn you. Stay away, Barber. You see Connie again—I'll break your legs."

50

Anya wakened at two in the morning. She found David at the kitchen table with his head in his arms and a look of confusion and worry on his face. She tied her tattered robe around her thickened waist, and, with her long silver braid hanging to one side, she put the teakettle on.

"So, *tateleh*, what's wrong?" She sat beside him at the table and brushed the curls from his eye.

David looked up, startled. "Ma. I didn't hear you. Anything wrong?"

"With you, maybe. Not me."

He took a fork and scraped an old nick in the red-checkered tablecloth. She gently slapped his wrist, and her action made him smile. "I'm in love, Ma. Or I think I am. I mean, how do you know?"

Anya's mind flashed a million miles away. She was young, running in the rain with Sasha, and they were laughing. "You know," she answered simply. "It's a special feeling . . ." The teakettle sang the rest for her, and she prepared tea and sat down, listening as David continued.

"You feel that way about Pa?"

She hesitated. One answer or the other would damn her. "I tried. But it never happened."

David didn't seem surprised or even upset. "If you

didn't love him, how come you lived with him all those years?"

"There are all kinds of love, David."

"Give me a for instance."

"Love of children. Love of God."

He shook his head. "Children maybe. But I can't believe God wants my misery."

"Of course He doesn't. What are you talking about?"

"Before I say, I want to know if you've ever been in love, and I don't mean with God."

The irony of that question coming from him made her think. Dearest God, sometimes You do the most peculiar things. "Yes," she replied. "Once upon a time I was deeply in love."

He perked up. "With who?"

"So long ago. Why bring it up?"

"Ma?"

She hesitated. "A Gentile."

Speechless, David knelt beside her and kissed the back of her wrinkled hand. The gesture was so dear she felt like crying. "What is it, David? Tell me."

"First, I have to know why you didn't marry him."

"We were different."

"What's more alike than two people in love?"

"David, you're making me crazy. Isn't it enough he was Gentile, and as a Jew I couldn't marry him?"

"No, Ma. It's not. Because I'm in love with a Gentile, too. And *nothing* would make me give her up."

When he'd said that, David told his mother about Constance, and Anya realized it was Sasha all over again. But this was a new world, and her David might not resist temptation as she had. As she sat listening to him, she wondered what she would say when he'd finished. How could she tell him that what he was doing was wrong, that if he married out of his faith, his children would not be Jews, that every intermarriage meant the death of their people? That if he did it anyway, she was supposed to cut him out of her life forever, to mourn him as if he were dead. She shivered. That would be impossible. David was her son, her flesh and blood, and she loved him. All she had were her children, and she couldn't imagine life without every one of them.

When David had finished, they stared silently at each other, David, waiting for more wisdom, Anya waiting for David to see the light himself.

"I could tell you that by marrying her you'd be dead to me," she said.

"I know," he said. "But you won't."

Anya was silent.

"Ma? Will you?"

She sighed a no and went to her bed.

With her head on the pillow, Anya blamed herself for this. If only Morris had been different. If only she had raised her children in a proper Jewish home, this would never have happened. Now she had to find a way to make them see that what they were doing would hurt not only them but their families and the children they would have. And that was when she decided to invite Constance to their next Sabbath dinner. Perhaps tradition would make them realize how different their lives really were.

Across the Sabbath candles, they had that look in their eyes, a glow Anya recognized. None of them knew how well. And how crazy it all was. How God must be looking down and wondering, Kinderlach, why do you keep doing this to Me?

Though by Jewish law David was a Jew, his father was still a Christian. Now David was in love with a Christian whose father didn't want him as a suitor because he was a Jew. If it wasn't so sad, it would be funny. And when Anya realized that her little plan hadn't worked, that Constance had enjoyed the Sabbath, Anya asked David and Connie to stop seeing each other for a few months. "To see if you really care." When they agreed, she prayed to God for resolution.

For Constance and David, the next months were heaven and hell. They tried staying apart but soon found themselves making phone calls to each other at Manny's. For a long time, they met on the sly, at the movies in Williamsburg instead of Pitkin Avenue. After David and Simon bought a rumble-seat jalopy together, David's weekends were spent on picnics with Connie in the country. They went to Times Square on New Year's Eve. They danced in Manhattan nightclubs instead of Brooklyn, swam at Jones Beach instead of Coney Island. And sometimes they'd tempt Fate and meet on the roof.

They shared spaghetti dinners, hot dogs, knishes in out-of-the-way places. They smoked the same cigarette because it was sexy, even though he complained she wet the tip too much. Then, as the year-end holidays came and went, it began to bother him, and he told her.

"I hate to say it, but our parents are right. Kids and the religious stuff has to fit, or the marriage won't work."

"David! What are you saying? I love you. You love me. That's all we need."

"That's all *we* need. But not our kids."

"We've talked about this. We'll celebrate both holidays and give them a choice."

"I thought about it, Connie. But it's not that simple. It isn't fair to ask a child to choose between Mommy's way and Daddy's way. It's a crazy idea. Grown men are still killing each other over the answers."

"You've got a point," Constance agreed.

"More like a knife in the ribs," he said. "I only know my children can't be strangers to me."

"Look at me, David. I'm no stranger."

"That's because you won't come to me at five years old and ask, 'Who's the Son of God, Daddy?' or 'Has Messiah come?' They'll want honest answers, and I can't give them yours."

"So, what's the solution?"

"We have no kids . . ."

"Never!"

". . . or, for obvious reasons, bring them up in my faith. If we do that, we have to agree never to disagree about it as long as they're young." He kissed her cheek. "When they're older, wiser, wiser than we, they can make up their own minds, and I won't stand in their way. Think about it, Connie. Think if you can live with it."

It didn't take her long to reach the same conclusion. Two religions for small children would be confusing. Deciding that, the choice of which one became automatic. Marrying David, she'd be cut off from her family, torn from her aunts and uncles, cousins, brother, parents, ripped from all that support. Their children would only know David's ways. David's family. They'd grow up in a Jewish house with Jewish Sabbaths, food, holidays. Their love and nourishment would come from Judaism. Realizing and acknowledging that, the next day she told David she'd agree.

When David told his mother the news, he found her sitting at the table, looking like a ghost. "What's wrong, Ma?"

"Papa just left. You didn't see him on the steps?"

David felt an instant anger. "What'd he want?"

She lowered her head in shame. "To come back."

"What'd you tell him?"

"That I'd ask Shelly, Simon, and you."

He waited a moment. "You want him?"

"*Ver vaist*. My heart in its old age says maybe, but my remembering head says no. So, what do you think?"

He knew perfectly well what *he* thought, but he didn't have the heart to say it. "Let me roll it around for a while." Seconds later, he was out the door, running until he found him standing on the corner waiting for a streetcar.

Morris.

The same, except thinner. Shabby clothes, face unshaven, hair a matted mess of greasy gray and black waves. He had finally become the Schlemiel.

"Hey, Pop!"

Morris turned, squinted. "David?"

The question amused David. "Yeah, Pop. It's me."

Morris hugged him. It was a one-sided exercise as David felt his anger swell, felt the pain of abandonment, the gut-wrenching hunger. Memories of combing through garbage cans, sleeping in subways, and his mother's degradation and humiliation flashed through his mind.

"Ma says you want to come home."

"What can I do, David? I still love her."

"You had a funny way of showing it, Pop."

Morris backed away. "Believe you me, it wasn't on purpose, David. I was up to my neck in hock to the shylocks. I still owe. To tell the truth, I'm lucky to be alive." Morris paused. "So. What's your answer? Mama said she'd ask."

David didn't even take a breath. "The answer's no, Pop."

"What do you mean?"

He said the letters. "*N O* spells *No*."

Morris began to cry. "David. I'm an old man. Alone. I've lived a life of hell."

"Hell!" David shouted. He was shaking. "Mama.

Me. Simon. Shelly, who worked on a pushcart at seven years old. Even Sharon and the kids. Since the crash *we've* lived in hell. Never once did I see you there."

"So what do I do?" Morris wiped his eyes with a filthy handkerchief. "Where do I go?"

Great actor, David thought. Hasn't lost a beat.

"Go back to her. To that liar Morton. Go back to where you lived all these years. We don't need you, Pa. And if I ever catch you near Ma again, I'll call the shylocks and turn you in."

Constance was supposed to meet David at Stone and Pitkin at 8:00 P.M. It was after nine when he realized she wasn't coming. He stopped at a small corner stand to buy a charlotte russe for Candy. He would hide it in the icebox tonight and surprise her tomorrow. Five-year-old Candy loved charlotte russe, and David loved Candy. He loved her giggle and, because she had no father, he liked giving her surprises. He pleaded with the salesman to put two extra cherries on top of the whipped cream, had the box carefully wrapped, and headed home.

Walking toward East New York Avenue, David kicked the broken glass that littered the sidewalk. Almost every streetlamp lay broken and scattered across the pavement. Damn kids, he thought. Destroy everything. He couldn't wait to get away, bring his kids up in a decent place, with friends like Andy Hardy, maybe. Brownsville was no place to raise children.

Behind him, he heard a sudden shuffle of feet. Instinctively, he turned. An alley cat leaped from the garbage can and vaulted in front of screeching brakes. He watched the cat disappear, then continued on. The shuffling noise came again. This time his muscles clenched and, without looking back, he ran. As he passed the alley, a set of hands snatched and thrust him against a brick wall. The first blow hit his jaw, and, though the pain shot through, all he could think about as he fell was Candy's splattered charlotte russe.

"See the whipped cream, Barber?"

David knew the sound of Carmine Romano's voice.

"That's your brains when I'm finished."

David raised himself on his elbows and dropped again. His body was weak, but his mind was clear. "Don't do what you'll regret, Mr. Romano. You can stop me from seeing her. But not from loving her."

A second pair of hands grabbed David's collar, lifted him from the ground. David looked at Carmine Romano and some other goon, but he wasn't afraid. They could break his bones but not his spirit. Then Carmine taunted him. "Take a shot, Barber," he said, jutting out his own jaw.

David smiled. "So that's it. You want me to hit you. You want to show Connie what a louse I am. Well, no dice. You won't get me to play your game."

At Carmine's nod, the big guy grabbed David and kneed his groin. He finally lost his footing and slumped to the ground.

"You're a shit, Barber," Carmine Romano shouted. "But I've got a surprise for you. Next time I raise my fist, I won't hit you, I'll hit Connie. Every time you see her, I'll beat hell from her." Then he spit on the pavement and left.

David got up feeling mad as hell. All the way home, he was terrified for Connie but more determined than ever. No one was going to push them around. No one was going to hurt his girl. Then he started to think straight. And every thought he had was worse than the one before. Then he remembered Connie's words: *He's my father, damnit. Not some street hoodlum.* And the more he wanted to hurt Carmine Romano the more he knew he couldn't. Carmine was Connie's father, and he had to bring peace. That was when the idea hit him, and he made up his mind.

"What the hell are you talking about?" Constance cried. She followed David as he packed a suitcase.

"I'm talking about our future, Connie. We have to find solutions."

"But how dare you make a decision like that without asking me?" She touched his face. "What the hell happened to your jaw?"

"I ran into something."

"Don't change the subject, David!"

"You'll just have to trust me, Connie."

"But why a whole year?"

David stopped. "Because it's the only way to win. Your father doesn't care how we feel about each other. I'm not Catholic, and that's that. So the only way to reach him is to prove we're willing to sacrifice. Carmine's a father first. If we can prove that our feelings are genuine, we'll have a chance to be a family, and I want it."

He threw the last things in his bag—toothbrush, shaving gear. "I want him to be my friend, Connie. I really want him to like me. If I can't have that, maybe I'll gain his respect."

She clung to him frantically, tears in her eyes. "But a *year*, David. I couldn't last six weeks before."

He pulled her close and hugged her. "It's gonna kill me to be away from you, too. But if it means his blessing, it'll be worth it. Now, quit blubbering. Barber women don't cry. Besides, you know the saying, Absence makes the heart grow bolder."

"Fonder," she corrected, still sniffling.

"That too. Now, here. Give this letter to your dad, after I go."

She opened and read it.

Dear Mr. Romano,

Connie and I have tried respecting your wishes. We didn't see each other for a while, but it was impossible. So, we went on the sly, and I apologize. Now, I've made a final decision. I'm heading back to the CCC for a year. During that time, Connie and I will not write or telephone. If we still feel the same when I return, we intend to marry and expect your blessing.

Respectfully, David Barber

David stood on the last step of the silver train in Grand Central Station as the family said good-bye. It was cold, mid-December 1940, and Simon, Elaine, Shelly, Sharon, Patricia, and little Candy all huddled together for warmth. Anya was crying and laughing as they teased her for buttoning David's coat. And, while David loved them for caring, his mind was on Connie, on the distance that would soon be between them, on what they were having to go through to prove they belonged together.

"Keep warm," Anya said. "The mountains are cold."

"Who says?" David asked.

The train started; white smoke curled out from the wheels.

"You did."

"I lied," David told her.

The whistle cried; the conductor called, *"All aboard!"*

"You never lied in your whole life," Anya shouted.

The train surged. Everyone kept pace.

"I love you," David called as the noise and distance grew. .

"Write!" Anya yelled. She had tears in her eyes.

David noticed Elaine hugging Simon. "Hey, you two. Don't get married till I get home."

Elaine laughed and waved. She hooked her arm through Simon's and threw David a kiss. So much had changed in these last years, David thought. And as the train moved from the station and his family became specks in the distance, he wondered what the future had in store.

51

PALESTINE
1939

For Joshua, these last years in Palestine had been heaven and hell. Watching his children grow, get married, have children of their own. Celebrating birthdays, weddings, anniversaries, holidays, fighting for their rights, planting, reaping, winning, losing, giving, taking. And his sons: The eldest, Avidan, thirty, husband to Ilana and father to four-year-old Nomi. Yonatin, twenty-eight, husband to Sharai, father of two-year-old Adena. So much history. So much happening—joy, sorrow, sadness, madness, and the greatest pleasures he had ever known. Now, as they checked and fortified the compound with more barbed wire, Joshua reflected on the things that had brought them here.

In 1929 he and his family had changed their names. Now, he was Joshua Ben Abraham, son of the great patriarch. Off and on the fighting with the Mufti had continued, first around the Wailing Wall, then anywhere the Mufti chose. Attacks continued in Jerusalem,

Hebron, Tel Aviv, Haifa, Safed, until blood mixed with sand, until the Jews fought back and the British decided to restore order. Then the white papers began. One by one the British whittled away the meaning of the Balfour Declaration until the arrival of General Sir Arthur Albon-White, who brought a little peace and quiet.

Arabs and Jews worked together peacefully for the first time. Because of new Jewish industry, Arabs had jobs. They had medical benefits, schools to educate their children. Palestinian Arabs became the envy of others. Then Emir Abdullah and the Transjordanian tribal chiefs entered into secret negotiations with the Jewish Agency to explore new ways to help Arabs living in Transjordan. But the sovereign British objected because they weren't calling the shots. And the Mufti called his own Moslem conference, continued to harass Jews, and published daily anti-Jewish diatribes.

In 1936 the Great Arab Revolt began. A year later England presented a plan for partition. There would be two states, Arab and Jewish, with a British mandate between them. The Jewish land was to be a bare corner of northwestern Palestine, which some would have accepted because of the German dictator Hitler and his Nuremberg Laws. Other Jews hated the land sales restrictions and the immigration restrictions that went with them. But before it could be explored, the partition plan was sabotaged by the Mufti, who would not cede a single grain of sand.

"Abah!" Avidan called. "Be careful of the barbs. Your mind is a million miles away."

Avidan, the elder son, was a dark, brooding, introspective man with a diplomatic flair, while Yonatin, the younger, was a daredevil, blessed with Yael's thick red hair, a curly beard and mustache, and a warm smile with teeth like ivory. Both sons called Joshua *Abah*,

the Hebrew word for "Father," and both were active
in the Jewish Settlement Police, formed to protect the
settlements because the British would not. In reality
the JSP was a de facto legalization of the Haganah.

After nailing the barbed wire, they secured the lookout posts, checked searchlights, and determined who
would do crop watch or armed escort that evening. Even
planting was dangerous as more and more Arab ter-
rorists burned their fields.

"Watch your step, Abah," Yoni called.

Joshua gave his younger son a dirty look. "I see. I
see. I'm not blind." Their comments annoyed him. He
had come here a fighter with Theodore Herzl, and they
were treating him like some old *zeyde* instead of the
proud pioneer he was. After all, he had made history.
He'd given them a legacy.

Some legacy.

Perhaps Morris had been right. Perhaps America
would have been easier. Instead of farmers, soldiers,
marksmen, watchdogs checking for bombs or combing
beaches for lost souls, his sons could be doctors and
lawyers. Then he'd recall the faces of those they had
rescued from the water—refugees from Hitler's Europe, unwanted Jews set adrift, old grandmothers hanging from ships, terrified babies thrashing for survival—
and he'd regret nothing. Yes. America would have been
easier. But at fourteen life had sent him on another
journey.

Palestine.

He'd given it everything, his love, energy, strength,
two sons—may they live and be well—two grandchildren. Here, he had found old loving roots and put down
strong new ones that said, "*Finally, I am home.*"

"Lines are secure, Abah," Avi called. "I'm going
up." While Avi climbed the lookout ladder to see if the
searchlight beams would reach the farthest outposts,

Joshua and Yoni searched for snipers. With inspection finished, they drove back to rest before dinner and the general membership meeting.

On their way home, they passed vineyards Joshua had planted forty years before, which now yielded wine, grapes, raisins. They drove by tall, graceful pepper trees and olive groves. As they entered the compound gates, a brisk wind rustled the banana trees and brought the scent of carnations and roses.

Avidan parked the jeep near Dvorah, a nineteen-year-old girl teaching blindfolded teenagers how to assemble and mount a machine gun in three minutes. She should have been teaching them the tango, Joshua thought. But everyone had to fight. They waved to her, and when the jeep stopped Joshua got out. He said good-bye to his sons, picked a few red poppies for Yael, then went to his small apartment.

"Shalom," Yael called from the kitchen. She took the poppies and kissed her husband when he entered.

Yael was still slim and pretty, her once red hair a yellowing gray, and her body all muscles from working the fields. Despite her missing hand, she still taught young women how to protect themselves.

Joshua uncovered a pot of stew on the stove, unaware as water dripped from the cover to the floor.

"What are you doing?" she scolded. "Go! A nap before dinner," she insisted.

Joshua was disgusted. "First my sons and now you. What am I? A baby?"

"No. You're an old war-horse who thinks he's twenty-one and who can't uncover a pot without spoiling my floor. Now get some rest before the meeting."

Joshua lay in bed thinking. He could smell the fear and danger around him. His family was right. Once again they were small and powerless in an unsympathetic world. With the news coming in, with the refugees' own testimony, what could he do but hope and pray? But how long could they go on? How long could they keep this small piece of earth from being wrenched apart so nothing would be left for the refugees or the new generations?

He punched his pillow. He couldn't sleep. His mind burned with the images coming out of Europe. He could see the German pageantry, the sensationalism, the press pandering to Hitler as he stood before the Reichstag with his back to the big red flag and its black swastika, proclaiming the Nuremberg Laws.

Jews, including those with a single great-grandparent and those who are baptized, are no longer citizens of the Reich. They shall not work in public service, journalism, civil service, radio, teaching, films, theater, farming, stock market, law, medicine, pharmacy. They shall not own or carry weapons, go to Gentile establishments except at specified hours. They must carry identification papers and wear armbands with yellow Stars of David. They are forbidden to go to beaches or sit in dining cars of trains. All social contact with Gentiles is forbidden. They may not drive. All evictions by German landlords are legal, and every Jew must raise his hat when passing a German. All new marriages between Jews and Aryans are forbidden. Old marriages are dissolved. All sexual relations between Jews and Aryans are a crime, and German women may no longer be servants in Jewish households.

With these laws, the anti-Semitism of feelings became the anti-Semitism of law, supported by judges, lawyers, physicians, policemen, and government officials.

Joshua had seen it coming when Hitler had proclaimed those laws and repudiated the Treaty of Versailles. All over Germany, there were signs—JEWS FORBIDDEN HERE. JEWS ENTER AT OWN RISK—as the people supported him too. Then had come the book burnings: Helen Keller, Mark Twain, Jack London, Émile Zola, Sigmund Freud, Albert Einstein. Ideas and intellectuals terrified Hitler. Then the *Anschluss*, Germans marching into Austria with crowds cheering while 180,000 Jews became instantly stateless, forced on their hands and knees to scrub the sidewalks of Austria as their homes and shops were looted. Then came the *Kristallnacht*, the night of broken glass. Brownshirts hurled missiles through the windows of Jewish homes and shops as all across Germany and Austria Jews were forced naked from their beds, beaten and robbed while people laughed. Two hundred synagogues were burned to the ground, 850 shops demolished, 8,000 looted, and 25,000 Jews were arrested and taken to camps. Throughout the night the pitiful screams of those dying could be heard in the streets.

At the kibbutz meeting, they talked about the rescue of refugees, a meeting in England, and the problem of self-protection. From their original needs had come Ha-Shomer, then Haganah, then the Jewish Settlement Police and Maccabees. Now there was Irgun, ready to fight fire with fire. Many protested.

"We must study the new white paper," Avidan began.

"Let the British choke on it," Yonatin shouted. "Our job is to get guns and save Jewish lives."

"Think! Yoni," Joshua said. "Illegal boats are being towed back to sea, and our people are drowning. We cannot rescue them with guns. There is need for diplomacy."

"What about the needs of Arabs?" Avidan added.

"They have the Mufti," someone shouted.

"Please!" Joshua called out, restoring order. "Your question is fair, Avi. And under fair circumstances, it must be asked. But right now it will be seen by our enemies as doubt, and doubt is a luxury we cannot afford. Because of Hitler we are at the crossroads of extinction. And there is only one basic question to answer. Do *we* decide if we live? Or do *they?*"

The room grew silent as everyone realized Avidan's four-year-old daughter Nomi had been sitting in a corner listening. She ran to her father and hugged his legs.

"*Abah?*" she asked. "Does it hurt to die?"

Avidan picked her up. "No, little one," he answered, carrying her into the cool night air. "You just close your eyes and sleep. Soon you'll waken to Messiah's silver trumpets."

LONDON

On the subject of a new white paper, they met in separate groups because the Arabs would not sit at the same table with the Jews. Joshua was outraged.

"You want to give us a strip of coastline and take away what the Balfour Declaration gave us, what the world ratified, what we've been cultivating with bare hands from rock and sand," he said. "It's unfair, and you know it."

"There's a war on, old chap," the Englishman said.

"We know. We've been picking up Hitler's outcasts for months now," Joshua told him.

"And that's stopping, as well. We can't allow any more refugees to enter Palestine, legally or illegally."

"No!" Joshua cried. "If you close off immigration now, it's a death sentence for every European Jew.

You're trading people for oil, and you damn well know it!"

"Look here," the man said. "You're overstepping your bounds." And Joshua was dismissed.

The war reached Africa in June 1940, and the bloodshed continued. Arab landowners who sold land to Jews were murdered. Arabs who were friends with Jews were murdered. Arab policemen who worked with the government were tried in kangaroo Arab courts, found guilty, and murdered. Pipeline after pipeline was set afire. The Mufti extorted money from rich Arabs who wanted peace and used it to fund more warfare. His men descended on Jewish settlements and British outposts, while he went to the German consul in Jerusalem, then to Germany, where he met with Hitler, who agreed to put an even tighter net around European Jewry in exchange for oil. In Baghdad, where the Mufti had his headquarters, the English asked the French to restrain him, but their requests went unanswered. With no alternative, the Jews allied with the British, knowing that if the British lost to Germany, they would lose too.

In November 1941 Joshua went to mail call. He was surprised to find a letter with a name from the past. He slit the envelope open with great joy. After reading the shaky, Yiddish scrawl, he was crestfallen.

Dear Joshua Kaminsky,

I pray this letter somehow reaches you or we are doomed. I pray also that you remember us, your old neighbors from Kashkoi. My wife, Rachel, and I, our children and grandchildren were smuggled into France. Now, in Romania, we have booked passage on a ship bound for Haifa, called the Struma. *It is our only chance to escape the horror*

*that is happening here. I know I ask a great deal,
but there is no dignity in the face of death. With
God's help, we sail from Costanja, December 16,
and will be in Haifa within a few weeks. If you
could meet us and help in any way, I would be
forever in your debt. I pray to God you and your
family are well.*

Your friend, Maurice Bierkoff

When Joshua told Yael he was going to Haifa to meet
the *Struma*, she was visibly upset and begged him to
stay home. The roads had become more dangerous than
ever. But Joshua's will prevailed. So she asked her sons
to go with him.

Their journey to Haifa was without incident, and
after a three-day wait, news came that the *Struma* had
been detained by Turkish authorities in Istanbul and
would not be released without British authorization.

"We must go there," Joshua told his sons. "We
must!"

The day they arrived in Istanbul, they found the
Struma still in quarantine, 769 stateless Jews, hanging
on to the rafters of an unseaworthy boat built to hold
one hundred. As he watched it sway in the water,
Joshua had an ache in the pit of his stomach; it was as
if he were once again staring into the jaws of Hell. Many
ships like this had met watery ends. Though a few had
been rescued, with survivors sent to detention camps,
most ships had been sunk or bombed.

After questioning the authorities, Joshua learned that
the *Struma* was in a legal bind. Because it was over-
crowded, with a leaking hull and defective engines, the
authorities refused it passage through Turkish waters
unless the British granted it special certificates to enter
Palestine. The British were debating. Messages flew
from Turkey to England to Romania, but each country

refused responsibility. Though the passengers had paid one thousand dollars per ticket, though the Romanian authorities had boarded the *Struma* and stripped all passengers of their valuables, they claimed the ship had left port illegally. And when the English refused to grant it permission to land in Palestine, the Turks hitched tugboats to the ship and pulled it out to international waters.

Joshua's eyes clouded with tears as the ship receded from view and a whole generation of Jews, who would never grow up, marry, or bear children, sailed away to die. He thought of the old, the young, the unborn. He thought of the pasts, presents, and futures to be obliterated in a single moment of indifference. And he thought of the Armenian, Vartan Sarkasian, of their meeting long ago on the beach, of the warning then and the indifferent world from which Hitler had learned his lessons. No one really cared.

Joshua shaded his eyes against the sun and watched the spectacle. The wind blew softly; the water splashed against the dock. The onlookers stood silent and curious, waiting to see what would happen, but Joshua already knew. He was grateful to be far from shore, not like the week before, when the very air in Haifa had vibrated with horrible screams.

Suddenly, in the distance, a huge banner went up across the ship. SAVE US, it said. Then a small explosion on board made the *Struma* list portside, and it slowly bubbled down. For the next hours Joshua watched bodies float to shore. One by one, they appeared, like strange fish of the deep, one by one until the death toll reached 767. There were only two survivors, neither of them Bierkoffs.

The following week Yonatin joined a special British fighting unit. His last words before leaving were "I'm ready to die."

52

The world had gone mad with dictators, Anya thought, Hitler in Europe, Hirohito in Asia, Mussolini in Africa. But some called Roosevelt a dictator, too. He was now in his third term, the first president to break a long American tradition of two terms. But these were perilous times, and the country needed someone experienced. In January, Roosevelt had sent the Lend-Lease Act to Congress, arms for Britain. If Britain lost, America would be next, he said. With America helping Britain, Germany began bombing U.S. ships on the high seas. Then Japan attacked Asia, destroying American hospitals and civilian missions in Indochina. When she bombed a U.S. ship, America boycotted Japanese goods and froze Japanese assets in retaliation. The twenties had ended with a crash, Anya thought. But the forties were beginning with explosions.

Anya still counted every penny. Though Roosevelt had saved the depressed nation from starving, they were not home free. Each day was a struggle. But with her piecework, with Simon and David working, with Sharon's part-time bookkeeping, and Shelly on the pushcart, they managed. Soon, David would be home.

Anya heard Shelly's harmonica. For a kid with no lessons, he played well. No doubt the talent was inherited from her father. But the sound made their new dog, Blackie, howl. "Shelly," she called. "Play something the dog likes, already. You're giving me a headache. Why not take him for a walk?"

Shelly, now eleven, thin and wiry, with dark hair and brown eyes, tapped his harmonica on his palm to empty it of saliva. He put the instrument in his pocket and hitched Blackie to a leash. Outside, Candy was playing ball. "A my name is Anna, and my husband's name is Abe, and we come from Alabama, and we sell apples." He gave her a playful smack on the head and kept going. His roving eye caught Patricia standing near the red fire-alarm box. She was talking to one of his buddies, and he decided to assert himself. "Hey, Paulie!" he yelled, pulling his body to full height and making a fist. "That's my niece. Talk dirty to her and I'll break your face."

Turning down Pitkin Avenue, Shelly saw a young man get off the bus. The face was familiar, and, after a better look, he screamed David's name, and the two were hugging.

"Hey. Who's this?" David leaned over and scratched Blackie's head. The mongrel jumped up and licked David's face.

"I found him in the rain a few months ago," Shelly said. The two talked as they headed home. "Ma know you comin'?"

"No," David said. "It's a surprise."

Anya heard the door click. The silence was unnerving. Shelly always entered like a hurricane, and her heart skipped a beat. She lifted her foot from the sewing machine treadle and walked down the hall. She saw David, and tears of joy ran down her cheeks. Soon David's arms were curled around her back.

"Let me look at you," she said. He stepped back, turned. Anya was disgusted. "Sure, I send them a man, they send back a rail." Five seconds later, she made a grocery list.

*   *   *

David hated how his mother had aged. She was bent and overweight, with her legs swollen like tree stumps. She had difficulty walking—from her years at that damn sewing machine, he knew—and he blamed his father.

"You feel okay, Ma?"

"Fit like a violin," she said in English.

He laughed. "You mean 'fiddle.' "

"Violin, fiddle. Who cares? My English was never so good." She handed Shelly the grocery list with some money. "Go to Stockman's. Get fresh lox and cream cheese. And squeeze the bagels," she yelled before the door closed.

David sat down with her. "And how's my other girl?"

"Fine," Anya said. "Comes every day to say hello." She smiled. "If you ask me, she comes just to hear your letters. *Nu?* What can I do? I let her."

"Hear any yelling over there, at her house?"

"I never thought I'd say this, David, but she's good as gold. I only hope you two know what you're doing. If her father throws her out, it will be a terrible thing."

"We all have to grow up sometime, Ma."

Shelly returned, and David stuffed himself with lox, bagels, and cream cheese. Then he went to his room to wait. Finally, he heard Connie's voice and gave their secret whistle from the window. Seconds later they were on the roof, lost in each other's arms.

"I missed you more," she said between kisses.

"Bet?"

"Bet!"

They laughed, cried, kissed, then the roof door opened. It was Candy. The butterball of ruffles was gone. She was now a hank of hair, a rag, and some bones. "Your papa's looking for you, Connie," she said. Her two front teeth were missing. She had dirty knees, and the hem of her dress was torn and hanging.

"Uncle David!" she cried. She ran to him and threw her arms around his neck. Then she turned to Connie again. "*Bubbie* said to hurry. She sounded afraid."

"She'll be right down, honey," David said. He flipped her a quarter. "Here. Buy yourself a treat."

"Poor kid," Constance said when the door closed. "She and Patricia need a father so bad."

"Doesn't Morton ever see them?"

"Once a month he comes in a brand-new car, honks his horn, and they both run down. He gives Candy a half a buck and sometimes takes Patricia for a bite to eat."

"How's Sharon holding up?"

"She's so pretty, she can't walk down the street. But no man in the picture. Afraid to make another mistake, I guess."

He laughed. "Who could be worse than Morton?"

"You never know," she said, settling back in his arms.

"How're Simon and Elaine?"

"Getting married in April."

David kissed her. "We'll beat 'em by four months. How's that?" When Constance said nothing, David went nervously on. "Hey! You know something I don't?" Constance looked away, and David's stomach did somersaults. "Spit it out, Connie! We promised each other a year, and time is up. I still want you. Do you feel the same?"

Constance still didn't answer, and David's whole life flashed before his eyes. Maybe he could become Catholic, deny his family, heritage, his grandparents, his mother. Maybe he could forget his past, his bar mitzvah, the holidays and their meaning. Maybe he could erase Abraham, Isaac, Jacob, Jerusalem, pain, suffering, joy, warmth, lox, bagels, the Sabbath. Maybe, in a single day, in a church somewhere, he could denounce all this and believe that Messiah had already come. He could do that, but it would only be lip service. It would just put a hole in his heart. "Connie?"

She looked at him, then the words left her lips. "Can we wait a little longer?"

David breathed a sigh but girded up again. "No. No more waiting. I won't sneak around to see you. I told your father that in the letter, and there's no going back. We go for blood tests next week, for a license. Then we tie the knot."

Her eyes pleaded for understanding. "I'm trying to be fair to my father, David."

David smiled. "No, you're not, Connie. You're trying not to choose."

A few moments of silence, then her answer. "You're right. Okay. I'll tell him tonight. Just have your mom make up a bed."

At dinner that night David told the family his plans. Everyone congratulated him except his mother. He expected her reaction and caught her when she was alone, asking her to share her feelings.

She hesitated.

She'd hoped the year apart would have changed things, helped them see that what they wanted was impossible. It wasn't prejudice, she kept telling herself, just survival. A Jew was a Jew by virtue of his birth mother. If he married Constance, David's children would not be Jewish. It was difficult to explain, but it was decreed that way for many reasons. So the People of the Book would not die out. So they would know Messiah when he came. And, as she understood it, he had to come from the line of King David. She felt guilty and ashamed telling him these things in light of her own indiscretions, but it was her duty. She explained all that, then said the rest. "You'll be married at City Hall. I always saw you beneath a *chuppah*. You have no job, so you'll come to live with me. Well, you're my son and she'll be my daughter and I'll love her. But how do I teach a young Catholic girl to live as a Jew? How do I explain that a dish used for meat can't also be used for butter or milk? That they can't even stay in the same sink. That in my house, she can't even eat those foods together. And what about the Sabbath? The holidays? They're all I have left of who and what I am, and I won't give them up. You know the laws, David. After living here one week, she'll hate me."

David kissed his mother's head. "I know you're disappointed, Ma, and I understand. As for the other stuff, I'll have a talk with her."

"Some talk. She'll run away before the ceremony."

Constance walked up the stairs to her front door. She knew what was coming. She hadn't told David that when he'd gone to Idaho she'd been dancing on eggshells, with every member of her family bringing suitors. There was this nightly parade: fat, skinny, homely, attractive, rich, some who couldn't speak English. It hadn't changed her feelings for him, but it proved that her family was not willing to accept David. Well, she and David had passed the test of time, and that should have shown how much they cared. But as she opened her apartment door, she remembered that old eggshell dance and felt a new one about to begin. She only wished this time she knew the music and the steps.

"David's home," she yelled, slamming the door.

Angelina and Tony remained silent.

"We're making plans."

"For what?" Carmine asked.

"C'mon, Pa. Stop. David and I want to get married."

Carmine stood up. "Over my dead body," he threatened.

Constance looked at Angelina, who huddled near her

stove, at Tony, whose hands went flat against the table.
"Okay," Constance said. "I don't need you—"

"Don't talk to you Papa like that!" Angelina shouted.

"Let her!" Carmine yelled. Anger flashed in his eyes.
His mouth tightened. "I'll take care of her." His belt
flew off his trousers, but Tony jumped up.

"Pa. Calm down. Let's talk like normal people," he
said.

"Normal people stay with their own," Carmine
snarled. "They don't stand on street corners like *bu-
tans*."

Tony faced him. "Nobody calls my sister a whore!"

Carmine's hand slammed across Tony's face. For a
second, Tony was stunned, then he went wild. He
leaped for his father's throat, choking until Carmine's
face was red. Angelina jumped between them and beat
Tony's fingers until the men were separated. Then
Tony grabbed his coat and left. Angelina tended her
husband as Constance ran to her bedroom. She
snatched a purse and a small valise stashed beneath her
bed. When she reached the front door, Carmine pushed
his wife aside.

"Hey! Where do you think you're going?"

"As far away as I can get," Constance sobbed.

"You leave now, you *never* come back!" He shook
his fist.

Constance turned the knob. She looked back at them
both, then slammed the door.

A hysterical Constance banged on Anya's door.
David opened it, took the valise, and comforted her
while Shelly opened his folding cot for her to sleep on.
Candy piled the kitchen floor with old rags and thick
coats for Shelly's new bed.

"I feel awful," Constance cried. "I hate putting you
out."

"Beans!" Shelly said. "I sleep good on the floor."

He flexed his scrawny arms to nonexistent muscles. "Look!" he said. And Constance smiled.

In the next days, David and Constance went for blood tests, a marriage license, a ring. They made an appointment with a judge and set the date for December 5; then Constance went shopping for clothes. On Pitkin Avenue she found a china blue faille suit with a peplum and a matching blue hat with a dotted-swiss veil. She bought black pumps, white gloves, and a beaded clutch purse, in which she kept her rosary beads. David wore his only suit, dark blue, with a new white shirt and a navy print tie. On their wedding day, he bought white orchids for Constance, gardenias for the ladies, and carnations for everyone else. Simon borrowed Willie Ryan's car, and they drove to City Hall, a double convoy with Simon honking his horn behind.

They stood side by side in the judge's chambers. Simon was best man; Sharon, maid of honor. They held hands through the sweet, short ceremony, listening to the judge's solemn words. As questions of love and honor were asked, David looked at Constance and thought how lucky he was. She was so beautiful, with her honey hair curling across her eyes, with that cute round hat sitting like a blue candy mint on top of her head. And when it was time to say "I do," he stumbled.

"David?" the judge called. "You can kiss the bride."

David lifted the veil and saw Constance's amber eyes. They were glistening. He took a deep breath and kissed her.

Outside, Candy and Patricia threw rice while Shelly tied cans to the car bumper. Then Sharon snapped pictures. At a kosher restaurant on Pitkin Avenue, they had a wedding lunch. Finally, Constance and David headed off alone for their hotel.

"Any regrets, Mrs. Barber?" he asked her, in the car.

"Just one," she replied. "Shoulda done it sooner."

They entered their room at the Saint George Hotel in Brooklyn and talked about everything but making love. They agreed the mattress was soft and there were lots of towels and free soap. And it was so clean. Then David had had enough; he grabbed her and kissed her until they were lying on the bed in each other's arms, unable to breathe. They were two virgins who loved each other deeply but didn't know how to begin. He fumbled with her buttons, her bra, clumsy, embarrassed. They knew no pretty words to call places of desire, just felt desire itself. Then the clumsiness faded. All thumbs became ten deft fingers, then two sets of knowing hands. Their embarrassment changed to teasing and certainty. Hesitation and fluster became enchantment and bliss. He soon claimed the luminous skin, the silky hair, the soft down on her upper thighs. And as her crazy laughter filled his ears, he knew she was finally his. Not his in the way one owns something but like the rays of the sun as they tan the skin, or like a paper napkin absorbing spilled milk. Soon, it all came easily.

They made love on the bed, on the carpet, in the shower, on a chair. They sat naked, facing each other without shame. He brushed the velvet petals of her orchid down along her forehead, nose, past her lips till it rested between her breasts. Soon, their arms and legs entwined and they made love again. He let himself go to the rhythms of his wildly beating heart, flew on a cloud where the sun's rays slanted toward an ocean. He rode those rays like a child's slide and let the waters cool him. In all his life he had never been more satisfied.

They slept naked that night, with her rump tucked into his groin, his arms around her waist, his hands cupping her breasts, and his nose buried in her hair. He fit her body like a glove. And when he wakened in the morning, he thanked God it hadn't been a dream. He watched her face as the day charged through the venetian blinds and the sun painted stripes across her body. Naked from the waist up, she lay on her right side, with the white sheet rumpled across her legs and rear, her lips parted, chin raised, hair mussed and fanned out across the white pillow. He was content to watch her. Her usually animated hands, always caressing, expressing, were quiet, one arm curled above her head, the other modestly covering her breasts. It made him warm all over. Then her eyes slowly opened, and she smiled. But she quickly rolled over. "Don't look!" she yelled, hiding her face. "I'm Gravel Gertie in the morning."

"Yeah!" he agreed.

She jumped up and socked his arm, but he grabbed her, and they made love again and again.

Later, they showered and dressed. Over scrambled eggs and toast, they talked about the future, swearing never to beat their kids or make them eat broccoli. Neither spoke of important issues. Those would come soon enough.

In the evening, they dressed for dinner and had champagne cocktails in the lounge. The romantic atmosphere set the mood as they danced for hours, letting the lyrics of songs say what they were both feeling, letting their heat and emotions pass from arm to arm, cheek to cheek. It was foreplay: their moist kisses and sexy whisperings, thighs rubbing, warm fingers on cool necks. The sweet, sweet scent of silky hair and cologne. Aroused, they raced upstairs and made love again until they were exhausted.

Packing in the morning Constance cried. When David asked why, she said, "Because I know now, how wrong they were."

He didn't know how to tell her, she had made him

happy beyond his wildest dreams. But the fairy-tale part
was over. Now, they were going home to reality. And
it terrified him.

The door to the Romano residence opened. Angelina
looked frightened when she saw them.

"Who's there, Angelina?" Carmine called from the
back.

Angelina didn't answer.

"I'm talking, Angelina," Carmine called again. A few
moments later, Carmine, Tony, everyone was face-to-
face.

"We got married," Constance said. "We wanted you
to know."

Carmine Romano looked at his daughter as if she
had just said she'd committed murder. Contempt mixed
with anger as he turned and left the room. Soon, her
mother followed, and her brother too, until she and
David stood alone in the kitchen. And, with Constance
in tears, they left.

53

On December 7, Sunday, moments after David carried
Constance across the Barber threshold, the Japanese
bombed Pearl Harbor without a declaration of war.
Americans were stunned. The family sat by the radio
listening as news trickled in. It was grim. Great American battleships—the *Tennessee*, *Arizona*, *Utah*, *Ne-
vada*, *West Virginia*, *Oklahoma*, *California*—were sunk
or crippled. Thousands of servicemen killed, hundreds
wounded, with many missing and unaccounted for. The

U.S. Navy had been decimated, and Hickam Field was a shambles. The following day, after President Roosevelt declared war on Japan, American boys went to their recruiting stations. Simon and David passed their physicals and in a few weeks were in the navy. Then, on December 11, Germany and Italy declared war on the United States. There was no time to think about danger. Everyone knew it meant long separations, maybe death, and the night before they were to leave, the family came together for a farewell dinner.

"It'll be over soon, and we'll all be together again," Anya told her family. "When God closes one door, he opens another."

"And don't worry!" Shelly chimed in. "I'll take care of everything."

Candy cuddled on Simon's lap while they tried to joke. Then Anya gave each son a gift. For Simon, a small Bible engraved with his name, a fitting present for someone who loved reading. For David, a chain with a *chai* on it. "From a dear friend," she said. As the chain slipped around David's neck, Anya felt destiny come full circle. The *chai* had gone from Sasha to her and now to his son. After dinner, Elaine and Simon took a walk while Constance and David went to their room. It was difficult to say good-bye. They held each other, crying, touching, talking, making promises. Then, early in the morning, Elaine and Constance went to the train station to say good-bye. When Constance came home, she cried like a baby in Anya's arms.

Constance Barber was forced to grow up quickly. In one week she'd lost both her family and her husband. She was living in a strange house with rules that made no sense. But out of respect for their religion she would follow them. Soon she found those same rules keeping her grounded and her mind off sadness. She had to refer to the Bible so much she was contemplating God instead of feeling sorry for herself. But those first weeks were difficult.

"Sweetheart, don't mix the meat and milk dishes together, even in the sink."

"Why, Ma?"

"Because God commands it," Anya said. She showed her the passages in Exodus and Deuteronomy. "You shall not boil the kid in the milk of its mother."

"But what does it mean?"

Anya thought. She wasn't a scholar, but she recalled her father and mother talking one night. "To eat meat, we must shed blood; while milk is the giver of life. To mix life and death so thoughtlessly makes us hard to the suffering of all God's creatures."

When Constance slipped, Anya reassured her. "It's all right, darling. You can't fit a lifetime of learning into one month. Go slow, it will come." When Constance wasn't looking, Anya threw the *traife* dishes out.

On a Thursday in February, Anya got sick. With Sharon working, it was left to Constance to make the Sabbath. Anya lay in bed with a hacking cough and chest pains, explaining things to her daughter-in-law. And some of it was funny, she thought.

"When you buy the chicken tomorrow morning, cover your head in a *bindle*, like this." She wrapped Constance's head with a scarf and waited for the question to come. And it did.

"Why, Ma?"

"For respect. And so the ladies won't think you're a goy." Anya smiled at the remark. "Well, you are a goy, sweetheart. A Gentile. But to some Jews, I'm a goy too. It's when you don't follow all the commandments. But never mind. Hold your head high. You're doing a mitzvah."

"A mizvat?"

Anya smiled as she corrected her pronunciation. "A mitzvah, doing good. Following God's commandment.

"Now listen," Anya went on. "You watch the hens closely and find one with spirit. Before you buy, you feel for eggs in her belly. If there's money left, pay a chicken *flicker*, a lady who plucks the feathers. Then buy five cents' worth of soup greens with lots of dill. Come right home, because dinner must be cooked and ready to eat before sundown, when we light the Sabbath candles."

At 5:00 the next morning Constance covered her head and went to the Belmont Avenue chicken yard. She caught a live hen, squeezed the belly like Anya said, and found the eggs. "Here," she told the chicken boy. He grabbed its wings and carried the squawking bird to the *shochet*, who would humanely slaughter it. Anya had explained it to her yesterday. How his knife had to be razor sharp without a single nick, twice as long as the animal's throat, and how he was permitted just a single cut to sever the jugular while reciting a prayer so the animal's death would be swift and painless.

After the *flicker* had cleaned the feathers, Constance bought soup greens. At home, Anya was starting the *challeh*. Constance knew she'd have to learn that too, one day. But for now she had to *kasher* the chicken and make it fit to eat. Following Anya's instructions, she cut the chicken open and cleaned out the intestines, being careful not to break the bile. Then she rinsed the bird under cold water, pulled the remaining pinfeathers, dried and held the skin over a lit stove burner to singe microscopic hairs. It soaked in more cold water, then lay on a slant board covered with coarse salt until all the blood was drained. Half an hour later, she rinsed away the salt and began the chicken soup. By dinnertime the house smelled of dill and fresh bread, and eighteen minutes before the sun set, Anya called the family to the table. She sat at one end, with Shelly at the other. Everyone was neat as a pin, and though Anya noticed that Candy's otherwise clean arms had long streaks of dirt riding up her elbows, she said nothing. God sees the heart, she reminded herself.

Anya set out her candlesticks and placed two extra candles on a dish for Constance. "Here, darling. You've done the work, now share the joy. Come welcome the Sabbath with me." Constance covered her head as Anya did, with a towel. She lit the candles and repeated the Hebrew words Anya recited. She didn't understand them like the Latin in church, but the ritual made her feel good. When Anya covered her eyes, Constance covered hers too, and when she opened them, the candles gleamed brightly.

"Good *Shabbos*," Anya said to her family.

"Good *Shabbos*," they all replied and kissed each other.

The following day, Constance asked about the Sabbath, and Anya explained as Shmuel had taught her. "It's God's commandment that we rest on the seventh day. We're not to work but to be with our families, to study Torah and celebrate His Creation. But more important, if we don't keep the Sabbath, our children won't remember who they are and the Jewish People will cease to be."

And one explanation led to more questions, and soon more difficult inquiries came, and Anya had to weigh her answers carefully. What did she know? Pious men dedicated their lives to learning these things. But she still had to try.

"Do Jews believe in sin?" Constance asked.

Anya thought. "A sin is when you don't live up to God's expectations. Like not keeping the Sabbath, or breaking the commandments."

"If you sin, how do you ask God's forgiveness?"

"Well, you talk to Him. Apologize and say you'll do better. Then keep your promise."

Day after day, Anya listened to herself talk. She was saying the words to Constance, needing to hear them herself. Then she realized her Catholic daughter-in-law was bringing her back to Jewish awareness and a return to faith. She began her daily prayers, covered her head again, and found the peace and comfort that had been missing from her life starting to return.

Soon letters arrived from David and Simon. Though times were perilous, they found things to laugh about.

Dear Ma,
You sure spoiled me. I spent my first day trying to make my bed so a quarter would bounce off. It took twenty-four hours. Thanks a lot!
Love, Simon

Dear Ma,
Where are you when I need you? My pants are baggy and the top's too tight. Help!
Love, David

While American servicemen trained for battle, the home-front war began. Children were taught to identify enemy aircraft. Every area had air-raid and fire wardens in case of bombings. There had been sightings of German U-boats on the East Coast and Japanese submarines on the west. All windows, especially skylights, were painted black or covered with blackout shades so light would not be visible at night. Some nights, air-raid sirens screamed and great searchlight beams crisscrossed the skies. Defense plants opened, and women went to work. White banners proclaiming, A BELOVED SON, HUSBAND, FATHER, SERVES OUR COUNTRY hung from windows. Things were rationed: cigarettes, tires, food, clothing, shoes, gasoline. And with his finger pointing, Uncle Sam appeared on signs everywhere. Citizens saved grease drippings, which provided glycerin for explosives. Old tires, even girdles were melted down for rubber. And foil chewing-gum wrappers and tin cans were salvaged for metal. People planted victory gardens and bought war bonds. Women in churches and synagogues rolled bandages. President Roosevelt proclaimed the four freedoms on radio: freedom to worship and speak out, freedom from want or fear. Everyone was entitled to these, he said, and Americans united. But fear still prevailed. Alien Germans, Italians, and Japanese had to register in their hometowns. And American citizens of Japanese descent were sent to detention camps while some of their sons fought bravely in Europe.

At the end of May, a letter came from David. He had a twenty-four-hour pass—not enough time to make it to New York and back without going AWOL—and just enough dough for a hotel. Could Constance borrow a few bucks and meet him in Virginia Beach?

Constance was frantic. She had to find a way. But three days later it still looked hopeless. She needed train fare, money for food, and nobody had a dime to lend her. She called everyone she knew, but money was tight. Anya watched worry blossom on Constance's face and didn't know how to help. Money. It always came down to money. Then it hit her.

"Pack. Get ready," she told Constance. "I'll have the money this afternoon." When Anya came home, she handed Constance an envelope with enough money for everything.

"Where'd you get this, Ma?"

"Never mind," Anya said. "Go buy what you need. And, Constance. Kiss him for me."

The next day, Constance went to iron her wedding suit and realized the silver candlesticks were gone. She knew then what Anya had done to get the money and swore she'd find a way to redeem them.

54

It was a perfect June day when Constance boarded the train for Virginia Beach. As the wheels turned she thought of Anya, thought of seeing David, realized how lucky she was to have such a good and caring mother-in-law. She closed her eyes as the train's rhythm spun its melody. Before long, she was asleep; then the conductor nudged her.

"Virginia Beach," he said. "Ten minutes."

Constance walked on wobbly legs to the ladies' room and washed her hands. She combed her hair and fixed her makeup, and as the train began to slow she took her seat. Faces passed by her window. Sailors were crowded onto the busy platform, craning their necks, waiting for loved ones to arrive. Then she saw him, wearing his sailor suit, and she fell in love all over again. White bell-bottoms with gold buttons on his tummy. A white middy blouse and a long blue tie. On the crown of his adorable head was this cute white hat, and her heart began pounding. Seconds before the train stopped, he was on board in her arms, kissing her. "My luggage," she said, breathlessly.

She was embarrassed by his public display and turned away, but he grabbed her wrist and pulled her with him into the ladies' room. She was startled; her wide eyes never left his as he snapped the latch closed, pulled down the window shade, and pinned her against the wall. Scattered light from a small flowered lamp that hung above the mirror glittered like stars and made her dizzy. His silence soon became hers as he pulled her to him by her collar and passionately kissed her. Time stood still until the conductor yelled "*Boo-aard!*" And she came to her senses.

"David. My things!" she sputtered.

As the train lurched forward and moved from the station, he whispered in her ear. "Not a room in the city, babe. It's this or the streets. You pick."

Her eyes smiled her answer, and, as the train gathered speed, their mouths met. Soon, Constance was aware only of his strong arms around her; of their love; of his deft fingers as he undid her jacket, button by button, and slid it from her shoulders; of her unhooked bra and his soft mouth on her raised pink nipples. With the train at high speed, his hand flashed to her thigh and snapped her garters. Pushing aside the panties, he raised her knee, and as he moved up and into her moistness, they were together, and she knew ecstasy for the first time. Their sex life had begun in innocence, but time, absence, war, and the fear of dying had brought them to this place.

For twenty-four hours they rode that train together. Destinations were meaningless, time forgotten, only need wrapped them in a magic cocoon. They found a loving rhythm that suited them, and, passing towns, villages, stations, rolling through tunnels and over mountainsides, they made love. For twenty-four hours they dined, dozed, shared their thoughts. It was their own special joyride, a temporary home that was a symbol of their journey through life. And it suited them both. When they returned on the northbound train, he left her at Virginia Beach, but she took his heart back to Brooklyn.

* * *

On her first day home, Constance took the money they'd saved on a hotel room and redeemed Anya's candlesticks. They made the next Sabbath sweeter than the rest. Then came the happiest news of all. By the second month Constance knew she was pregnant. When she became nauseated in the mornings, Anya and Shelly brought her crackers and seltzer. But all she needed to feel better was to recall that train ride. A few months later she wrote,

> *Darling,*
>   She *kicked: Strong like an ox. In four more months, she'll give this world one hell of a fight.*
> > *Love, Connie*

To which he replied,

> *Dearest,*
>   *I'm so happy I could bust.* He *sounds like a baseball player ready to crack the Babe's record.*
> > *Love, David*

David's letters came regularly at first. Then sporadically. Sometimes three or four at a time. Inside, certain words were blacked out or cut out with scissors by the government censor, who read each letter to be sure no secrets were accidentally given to the enemy. The family would sit at the table, and Constance would read the letters aloud until she came to the special parts. Then she'd slip into her room, lie on her bed, and read slowly and alone. When Simon's letters came, it was Anya who read.

By October, Anya could no longer climb the five flights of stairs. The circumstances were difficult for Constance too. It was very upsetting to be pregnant and always bumping into her parents. And, as the war continued, Shelly, Patricia, and Candy were growing into young people. They needed privacy. They needed a bigger apartment. Constance searched every day until she found a place on East New York Avenue between Bristol and Hopkinson, close to a synagogue for Anya. At first Anya was hesitant because there were saloons on both corners. But there was only one flight of stairs, and that mattered a lot. Her blood pressure had climbed perilously, and with only one flight of stairs she could at least go down and sun when the baby came. Besides that, the apartment had a large kitchen, two and a half bedrooms, a living room, and a bathroom with its own tub—the height of luxury. She would no longer have to clear the kitchen for baths. A week later they were in their new home.

Immediately, Constance found problems with the new apartment. Problems she had overlooked. Every mattress was infested with bloodsucking bedbugs, and the weekend they moved in Sharon and Constance put each mattress on its side and sprayed it with Flit. To destroy the nests, they took flaming candles to the coils of each box spring. For the mice, they set traps using slices of potato bait; then made plans for the roaches. While David and Simon were killing vermin on the high seas, roaches as big as fists were marching in armies up and down their family's kitchen. Constance organized the family into battalions, and, using Flit guns, they fired away. Roaches died valiantly on ceilings, on walls, beneath tables, in cupboards. When they were through, Constance felt victorious. Then she saw a roach creeping inside the radio and was sick at heart.

"I hate to say this, Ma, 'cause I know you love the radio. But there's a nest of roaches inside."

Anya's only source of pleasure was that radio, and she looked bravely at Constance, aware her answer could mean the end of Charlie McCarthy. "Do what you have to," she said.

Constance put the radio on the fire escape the same night there was an air raid. It was fitting, she thought, as she fired away with the Flit gun. Two days later the radio dried and played better than ever. And the roaches were under control.

Some days were difficult. But the family continued with Anya as their strength. She was there for Patricia, whose heart was being broken not only by her father but by a boyfriend. There for Candy, who needed hugs and kisses. There for Sharon, who worked hard but still made wrong choices when it came to men. There for Shelly, who proclaimed himself man of the house and played the role to the hilt. And there for Constance as her time drew nearer. Even there for Elaine, who often came to visit.

To earn more money, Constance found work with the Red Cross, filling the bottom halves of lead pencils. She'd take them home in boxes by the gross, and, with small rubber tips on her fingers, she'd insert a thin lead strip in each small hole and push against the table edge until it clicked in. Pretty soon it became a family thing. They'd sit around after dinner, filling pencils, listening to the radio, laughing at Jack Benny, Fiber McGee and Molly, scared of the Shadow or the Whistler, Inner Sanctum, excited by the Lone Ranger and Lux Radio Theatre.

When school was out in the summer, Candy came home with a real problem. Sharon was away for a weekend, and Constance noticed the child scratching her head.

"What's wrong, honey?" she asked.

"I don't know."

Soon everyone else was scratching. Constance took Candy to the window, and her suspicions were confirmed. The child's head was crawling with lice, and so was everyone else's. Out came the kerosene, the black tar soap, the fine comb with its tiny teeth set close together to pull out not only lice but the little white nits that clung to the hair. That weekend everyone's head was doused in kerosene, wrapped in a towel turban for twenty-four hours, then washed with black tar soap. With their scalps on fire, Constance and Anya washed and fine-combed every last louse from their heads.

It was her second Christmas away from home, and a deep melancholy set in. Although Constance found Chanukah delightful, it just wasn't the same. It wasn't midnight mass and family—her family—or shopping for presents and eating Mama's turkey. It wasn't a tree, or Grandma Lena complaining about her knees and Grandma Theresa singing off-key. As the melancholy grew, Sharon noticed it, and the children noticed it, and Anya could almost hear Constance's heart break.

On Christmas Eve, Constance ate dinner and went to bed early. Everyone heard her sobbing softly. Outside, the winds howled, and a dry snow fell.

"It stinks, Ma," Shelly said. "She's crying her heart out. We gotta *do* something."

"Like what?" Sharon asked. "Get a tree?"

"Not in my house!" Anya said.

Then Sharon began reasoning. "But it'll just be once, Ma. When David comes home, it's his headache."

"No," Anya repeated. "This is a Jewish household."

"*Bubbie*," Patricia pleaded. "She's away from home, pregnant. And you always taught us to have *rachmones*."

Rachmones, empathy, understanding. To put yourself in another's shoes. It struck a chord with Anya, as they knew it would.

"Even if I allow it, which I won't," Anya said, "how can we afford it? There's no money."

"Don't need money, Ma," Shelly said. "The poor kids go just before midnight, and the man gives them trees for free."

"Stop it!" Anya insisted and went to her bedroom.

Anya sat on her bed and covered her ears to block out the sounds of Constance's weeping. But she couldn't. She finally looked up toward God and spread out her hands.

"*Nu?* I didn't need this problem," she whispered. "Usually, I don't complain. I know there's a war on, that You're busy. But this is some fix. And in case You didn't notice, except for Shelly, there's no man in the house to make decisions. So, what do I do? I can't ignore her. She's like my own, pregnant with David's child, and, like the children say, she misses her family. And, to tell You the truth, if I were her, I'd want a menorah. So. What is this tree, which is strictly for her benefit, a sin or a mitzvah? I could use a mitzvah, because to tell the truth I'm a few short this year. But You already know that."

She waited as if for some sign. Then Constance sobbed so loudly Anya thought her own heart would break.

"All right! Okay," she went on. "So she'll have it. But for one night only. And just so it's clear. It's on Your head, not mine."

Anya came out of her room and reluctantly gave her permission. She explained that it was a mitzvah for Constance, that it was for one day only and would never be given again. When they understood that, Shelly put on his coat and ran to the tree lot, where he waited in

the cold with the other poor kids, warming his hands
over a fire barrel. When he returned with the tree, they
all went to work, and, ten minutes before midnight, it
was done.

"It ain't Macy's," Patricia said, standing back. "But
I think she'll be happy. Who's gonna wake her?"

"Me," Shelly insisted.

Constance heard the knock. It was dark as she opened
her swollen eyes and saw Shelly holding a flashlight.

"What's wrong, Shelly? Is Ma okay?"

"The light's broken. Ma needs you."

Constance put on her robe and followed him down
the dark hallway, with Blackie tapping his toenails on
the linoleum behind her. Just as she entered the living
room, someone threw the light switch and she saw it.
A moth-eaten, tilted Christmas tree, trimmed to the
hilt.

At the base lay white absorbent cotton. All the spiky
green branches sparkled with Lux Flakes. Silver bits
from Sharon's aluminum ball, saved for the war effort,
shimmered in the light and sparkled near spools of
brightly colored thread. Anya's gleaming gold and silver
buttons dangled from every branch. Chanukah cookies
sat near long strips of white newspaper cut thin as tinsel.
At the tip was a star made from a wire hanger and
covered in silver paper. And beneath the tree were little
presents they'd made for her. When Constance saw it—
the love and affection, but most of all the sacrifice it
meant—she cried. It was a Christmas she would never
forget.

55

With so many people crammed into such close quarters, there were constant problems. Fights for the right to radio programs. Or poor Anya, complaining that her home wasn't a restaurant and that dinner would be served at 6:00 P.M. except on *Shabbos*. But it was the bathroom where the most patient of family members lost their reasoning.

Mornings were the worst time, with the kids getting ready for school and the adults rushing to work. Faces had to be washed, hair combed, teeth brushed, makeup applied. And the bathtub at night, with hot water at a premium, was also a source of friction. The scenarios invented to get to the tub before the hot water was gone were ingenious. Only Candy didn't mind; the fewer baths, the fewer bathtub rings to wash.

Possessions had to be labeled. Someone was always "borrowing" someone else's deodorant, lipstick, bobby pins, or toothpaste. And no one dared make Sharon laugh if the toilet was occupied, because she had a weak bladder and always peed her bloomers while banging on the door.

As for sleeping arrangements, poor Candy had the worst. She, Patricia, and Sharon shared a double bed, with Candy sleeping in the middle. *Tse-feesons*, they called it in Yiddish, "feet to head." While Patricia and Sharon slept with their heads at the headboard, Candy slept with hers at the foot of the bed, between their bunioned feet. But she never complained.

And the fights over whose turn it was to walk Blackie, or buy the newspaper, or go to Stockman's grocery to do the "Goodness! I forgot my money," bit. Candy begged not to go to Stockman's. She hated shopping there because Mr. Stockman had a finger missing on his right hand, and she feared finding it in a salami package one day.

But the time they remembered best was the night the electric company shut off their lights because they couldn't pay the bill. That same night, they had nothing to eat but oatmeal, and Anya cooked a huge vat to feed everyone. Twenty minutes later they were lined up at the toilet, doubled over with cramps and diarrhea. In the morning, Anya understood why. Unable to see in the darkened, candlelit kitchen, she had mistaken Epsom salts for kitchen salt and dosed everyone with laxative.

There were daily cries of "Who took the last cherries?" or "Who ate my dessert?" Everything in the icebox was sacred, some things privately owned. Yet nothing was safe. More than anything, they laughed, told jokes, listened to the radio, played cards, or predicted fortunes with the Ouija board when Anya wasn't around. Then a letter would come from David or Simon, and they'd sit and listen and decide again that it was all worthwhile.

Elaine Markowitz spent her days working at the five-and-dime on Pitkin Avenue. She was saving every penny for when Simon would come home and they would marry. Her days and nights were generally the same, and the only social life she permitted herself— besides visiting Simon's family—was her weekly game of Mah-Jongg. Most of the time she read books, or wrote letters to Simon. And he wrote frequently as well.

It was an exquisite pleasure to come home from work, where she would nurse a scissors bump from cutting ribbon all day in the ribbon department, to find his letter waiting in the mailbox. She'd set it down on the kitchen table, where she could see his handwriting, teasing herself as she prepared and ate dinner. She'd wash her face, brush her dark hair, cream her skin with Pond's, rinse out her panties, then slip into a lace nightgown. She'd turn on some romantic Frank Sinatra music, curl up in an easy chair, and read.

> *Dear Elaine,*
> *Miss you a lot and think of all the good times we used to have. And just so you won't fall for some Bristol Street zoot suitor, or send me a "Dear John" letter, I'm forwarding some photos so you won't forget how cute I am. Yuk! Yuk!*

She looked at the photographs and laughed. Simon, with his head shaved, deeply tanned and wrapped in a sheet, sitting cross-legged like Mahatma Gandhi. Simon, with five of his buddies, dressed in boxer shorts, holding shoulders, their legs stuck out like chorus girls kicking. And Simon, with his big brown eyes, his sensuous lips, and his white sailor cap at a jaunty angle.

> *Can't say anything about my work, or destination. Just want to wish you Happy Birthday this month.*

It wasn't really her birthday, but from this prearranged code, she knew he'd be sailing near the Panama Canal, and realizing he was so close to home made her happy.

Her days continued like that: working, writing Simon about home and old times. Sending photographs and packages of salami from Katz's Delicatessen. Describing the house they would buy and the kids they would have. And one week followed the next as she marked days off the calendar, waiting for his return.

*   *   *

In her eighth month, Constance began to stain. She was sent to bed and waited on hand and foot. By the end of February 1943, she was ready to deliver. In the middle of a Monday night her water broke, and Sharon called a taxi. In the hospital, Constance hollered for hours. She yelled in a sterile white room, while the others waited outside. Later, a bone-chilling scream filled the halls. By noon Tuesday a baby girl was born: five pounds, thirteen ounces; they called her a screaming meemie until Constance named her Tracey Louise, after both her parents' mothers.

Constance had been preparing for the baby from the beginning. She had a beautiful white crib with pink and green trim, a matching dresser and bassinet. Anya had saved pennies for a stroller so she could walk the baby to the store. Sharon bought a high chair, and Elaine, a full layette.

The infant was gorgeous. She had soft blond hair, dark blue eyes, a pink rosebud mouth, and they fought for turns to hold her. Friends stopped by with gifts, but no one from Constance's family came. David sent a large photograph with DADDY written on it, and Constance framed it and put it on Tracey's dresser. Not a single day went by that she didn't show it to Tracey and repeat the word, *Daddy*. Tracey would coo and giggle and reach for the photo with those tiny fingers. She brought new life to the house, especially to Anya, who loved watching her change. The blue eyes turned to pale brown. The blond hair to light brown. And by the time she was six months old, she was sitting up in a high chair, laughing out loud, cutting two front teeth, and throwing cereal at Blackie.

It was cold and still dark outside when Tracey's cry wakened Constance from a deep sleep. She comforted the child, banged on the steam pipe for some heat, and carried the colicky baby in her arms. Halfway to the kitchen, Constance realized that Anya's bed was empty, and she hurried down the hallway. She found her mother-in-law seated at the kitchen table with her head bowed between her hands. As Constance entered, Anya looked up. There was fear in her eyes; her skin was chalk white. Constance placed Tracey in the high chair and went to Anya.

"Ma? You look awful. What's wrong?"

"I had a bad dream."

Constance sat beside her. "Tell me, you'll feel better."

Anya needed little coaxing. "It was so dark . . . ," she began. "Simon, David . . . I couldn't see. Climbing till his foot got stuck. Bombs. People running everywhere; such a commotion."

Constance felt her heart start to flutter; her stomach tied itself into knots. She could see it, see him; it was David's face. As Anya talked, Constance put Tracey's bottle in a pan of water, her heart accelerating with each of Anya's words. Nothing made any sense. David. David. No. Please, God. Not David. In a little while, the baby's bottle rattled in the boiling water, and Constance shook some formula onto the inside of her forearm. The temperature was perfect, and she gave Tracey the bottle while listening to Anya.

"I heard a voice screaming, 'Mama! Mama!' " Anya went on. Constance could hear it too, right now, right here in this room. It was David's voice echoing in her ears. It was David. She swallowed the tears burning behind her eyes and tried to stop her hands from shaking.

"It's all right, Ma," Constance said, though she was filled with terror. "It's just a dream."

But Anya never forgot it. And neither did Constance.

*   *   *

The last Mother's Day had hurt Angelina deeply. Now, when she saw Anya and the baby in the grocery, she'd hide in another aisle and wait for them to leave. It was like a knife in her heart. Her daughter had a baby girl, and it was killing her not to see. Though Carmine had warned her to keep away, more and more she felt pulled to what was natural. Yet she couldn't disobey her husband. In all the years they'd been together, she'd never once gone against him. So, to lessen the anguish, she began shopping at a different time.

Anya pushed Tracey's stroller through the streets, feeling Angelina's eyes following. How she wanted to fix things between them. As a mother, she could not understand how Angelina could stay away from her first grandchild. But Angelina had a husband to answer to. And that made the difference. She only knew that if things were reversed she could never stay away. Then an idea came to her. She could fix things between them if she planned carefully. How could Carmine be angry if it was Anya's fault! Her idea seemed good, and she began to scheme. Finally the day came.

Constance left for work, and Anya waited for the new time Angelina went grocery shopping. She dressed Tracey in her cutest outfit, carried her into the store, and headed straight for Angelina. The poor woman looked horrified at the two of them and backed away. "Please, Anya," she begged. "Don't do this. I can't—"

Before Angelina could finish, Anya thrust Tracey at Angelina. "I'm dizzy," she said. "Don't let her fall."

Angelina's heart pounded so hard it drowned out the echo of her husband's voice. "You don't understand," Angelina said, following Anya to a milk crate. Then her granddaughter giggled, and a tiny hand touched her cheek. And as Anya "rested," Angelina began falling in love. She looked down and saw a duplicate Constance. The eyes, the thick Romano hair, and a tiny button nose.

"What's her name?" Angelina asked. She had a smile on her face and tears in her eyes.

"Tracey Louise," Anya said. "For your mama and Carmine's."

After dinner that evening Carmine cornered Angelina. "What's wrong with you?" he asked. "You look at me strange tonight."

Without a word, Angelina did her dance from stove to table, clinking glasses and drying plates.

"I'm talking, Angelina. Answer me!"

His voice was so harsh it startled her. The plate she was holding slipped from her hands and crashed to the floor. She looked at the pieces, then at him, and felt a surge of strength. "I saw Connie's baby today." There was fire in her black eyes. "And I'm gonna see her again."

Carmine launched into a tirade, but Angelina stood her ground. "You can holler at me all night, Carmine. It won't matter." She slapped her chest. "She's my flesh and blood. Yours too! Stay away if you like. But not me. I won't die bitter and old with no grandbabies."

Carmine looked at her as if she were a stranger. Then he left the room. From that moment on they rarely spoke. But every chance she got, Angelina saw Anya and the child. They met in the store, the park, and, when Anya had difficulty walking downstairs, they met in Anya's apartment while Constance was away. They soon realized they had a great deal in common.

On a Thursday, Constance cleaned Tracey's crib. She lifted the mattress and found two red ribbons lying beneath it. One was coiled at the crib's head, the other

at the foot. Puzzled, she walked to the kitchen, where
Anya was drinking tea. "What's with the red ribbons,
Ma?" she asked.

"Nothing," Anya said. "From the old country, to
ward off the evil eye."

Constance laughed. "Okay. But why two?"

"What two? I put one by the headboard."

"But there's another under the feet."

Anya gasped. The color drained from her face. "Your
mother," she said in a low voice.

"My mother?"

"Don't be mad, Connie," she pleaded. "She's come
every day for the last three months." Then Anya told
her the story.

Constance dropped into a chair. "I don't believe it,"
she kept saying. "She went against Papa."

"Please, Connie. Please don't be mad."

Constance put her arm across Anya's shoulder.
"Mad? At you? Not in a million years."

And the next time Angelina came, Constance was
waiting.

It was a crisp fall morning, and Constance heard the
dog scratch at the door. "Blackie's gotta go," she called.
"Whose turn?"

Candy, eight and a half, and Shelly, a week from his
bar mitzvah, called out each other's name.

"Kiss my *tuchas*," Shelly said to Candy.

Candy stuck out her skinny little rear. "Kiss mine."

Shelly chased her over the couch and chairs while
Blackie pawed the door. Then came a stern call from
Constance, and Shelly hitched up Blackie's leash and
skipped downstairs two steps at a time. On the way, he
passed two naval officers, checking mailboxes.

"Who you lookin' for?" Shelly asked.

"Barber," the officer replied.

"That's me. First floor."

As they passed, Shelly yelled, "Got two brothers in the navy." Then he pulled Blackie's leash and left.

A loud rap at the front door gave Anya chills. No one knocked in Brownsville unless it was trouble or the insurance man, and she'd just paid her fifty-cent premium. She called Constance, and they went to the door together. When they saw the officers, their fingers and arms wound tightly together.

"Mrs. Barber?"

Both women answered.

"United States Navy. May we please come in?"

GERMANY
1942

Hitler's decision was that Europe had to be totally free of *Untermenschen* or "subhumans"—anyone non-Aryan, but especially Jews. In the beginning, the SS Einsatzgruppen, his chosen "killing machine," carried out these death orders, combining diesel exhaust and skull bashing, which made burials easier. But his soldiers complained. The method was too dirty and time consuming, and they wanted to use bullets. After shooting 1,500,000 Jews, they realized that bullets, though quick and easy, were not cost efficient. So the best and most scientific minds of all Germany conceived a brilliant plan: a combination of lethal gas and baking ovens in which to burn dead bodies. Thus, the bidding wars commenced, with eager German businessmen competing. When it was over, I.G. Farben, which owned the patent on the inexpensive Zyklon B gas, and I. A. Topf & Sons, which presented the lowest bid on crematoriums, won. This solved the economic problems. Now, the way was clear for the end.

* * *

In Wannsee, a suburb of Berlin, at a meeting of the Gestapo with nine ministries represented, including Adolf Eichmann, there were lunch, drinks, and laughter as thirty copies of a Goering directive were passed around. Reinhard Heydrich presented plans for "The Final Solution to the Jewish Problem."

The strongest male Jews would be used for hard labor. Most would die of starvation, but the Jews who survived would be shot the moment their work was done. "By natural selection, they will be the most dangerous Jews alive," Heydrich told the representatives.

The other Jews would be told of "work" in the country. They'd pay their own train fares and ride with their families in boxcars. Fake train platforms would be built, with names of familiar cities posted on them. Riots were to be avoided and people kept calm. Soldiers would pass out picture postcards for Jews to mail to loved ones.

" 'Awaiting your arrival,' they'll say," Heydrich told the gathering.

Everyone laughed. Heydrich was funny.

"Lawns and gardens will be planted. Chamber music will greet them at some places."

"Chamber music for the gas chambers," someone shouted. And they all laughed again.

SS doctors were to carry out the "selection process" when the Jews arrived. Healthy, young ones would work for the Reich. The sick, elderly, babies, and deformed would go right to the chambers to save on food and lodging. Arrows would point the way; signs saying BATHS would be posted, and towels distributed. They would undress before entering; then the doors would be locked and the deadly gas crystals dropped in the vents. Those outside who wished to watch would find glass portholes. Within fifteen minutes, it would be over.

The gas would be pumped out. The hair on heads shaved for sale. Eyeglasses and clothes, salvaged. Gold would be extracted from teeth, melted down for the Reichsbank. Vaginas and rectums would be slit open and searched for jewels, then the bodies would be carted to the furnaces and burned for salable fertilizer.

"Nothing will be wasted," Heydrich assured his listeners.

"A brilliant plan," a general said to applause. "But what of an outcry from the rest of the world?"

Heydrich laughed heartily. "The world will do nothing. They won't know, and they won't care. Remember the *Struma* in Turkey? The *St. Louis*, recently forbidden entry at Miami, even Cuba? There were many like that, and no one said a word. And think of our Fuehrer's words last week"—and he quoted Hitler—"Who now remembers the Armenians?" And, with no further questions, the men smiled, and the meeting concluded.

BROWNSVILLE
FEBRUARY 1943

Anya had been home from the hospital for three weeks. A mild stroke they'd called it. But it was a broken heart.
Simon.

His death was a deep wound from which no blood flowed, yet her life was ebbing away. Lying in bed, she recalled when the officers had come to her door, the words they'd spoken. Over and over it played in her mind.

They had been gentle, comforting her as she sobbed. Their voices were soft as they expressed regret and encouraged her to share her sorrow. They explained

Simon's bravery in the face of sabotage, how he'd grabbed a live grenade which had fallen on deck near a gunnery station. He'd used his body as a shield, grabbing the grenade and intending to hurl it to sea, but it burst seconds after it left his hand, throwing him against a rope ladder, where his foot got tangled. He'd been flown to a nearby hospital, then transferred to a supply ship en route to the United States. An hour from New York City, he'd died of complications.

"Your son was a valiant man," the officer had explained. "He died bravely and with honor."

Now, when Anya thought about it, she remembered passing the Statue of Liberty the day her ship had come into New York Harbor. She remembered her feelings as she'd looked into the eyes of the great lady with her liberty torch and how grateful she'd been to be here. America. It had given so much to her and her family, she thought. Safety, dignity, freedom to worship. Most of all, a home. Now, with Simon's passing, she felt a debt had been repaid.

Though Anya could get out of bed, she continued to grieve. Death had knocked at her door so many times, and she had answered, giving up those she had loved. From her mother to Saul to her father—all gone, all missed. But this surrender was different. This was her child. And nowhere was it written that a child should die before its mother. A mother grows old with her children, in the company of *their* children. Now she would simply grow old.

She lost weight. She hardly ate or slept. She lost interest in everything except the grandchildren. And even *that* was forced. There seemed to be no meaning to anything. Life was simply not the same. The rabbi came frequently to offer comfort, but even he couldn't help. Her heart had been ripped from her chest and chopped into pieces. Night and day, day and night, she felt the pain of Simon's absence. It would begin in the morning with a heartache, the awareness that he would never kiss her again, never touch her hand or give her his children. It would end at night with a terrible emptiness. Finally, she began to rail at God. Shaking her fist at the sky with her mouth in an angry line and her eyes black with fury. Some days she'd sit at the window, just staring into space. Finally she found the strength to take the Bible and write the date of Simon's death, and soon after a healing began.

In between air raids and scrap drives, the children grew. Patricia was now a pretty girl, slender, with black hair and huge dark eyes against white skin. Every morning before school, Candy would peek out over the bedcovers, fascinated by her big sister's primping before the mirror. Patricia would tease her hair into a mess, then brush it into two side pompadours. Watching her fix the back was even more fascinating. She'd take this thing called a rat—a strip of brown wadding sewn into a hairnet—pin it above the back of her neck, and wind her long hair around it into one fat, U-shaped curl. She'd fasten it, ear to ear, with hairpins, then poke a fishtail comb inside to make it look thicker.

Her lipstick took thirty minutes to apply. On and off it went half a dozen times, until it was just right. Then she'd blot it with toilet paper, back away from the mirror, and squint her eyes as if she was looking at a stranger.

Shelly hung out with a rowdy gang on Bristol Street. With Simon dead and David gone, he took charge of everything, including changing light bulbs, banging on the steam pipes, Blackie, and the radio. He'd play his harmonica and get into general mischief.

Candy went to P.S. 175 near Betsy Head Park. It

was a long walk, especially in the winter, when it was freezing. But she made friends with the girls on Amboy Street and traded comic books. In the summer she'd take the train to Coney Island, eat Nathan's hot dogs, and go to Steeplechase. Sometimes she'd roller-skate at the Eastern Parkway Roller Rink. But every Sunday, she'd pack a salami sandwich in a brown paper bag and take four milk bottles from the top steps to redeem at the grocer's for twelve cents. She'd buy one cent's worth of licorice at the candy store, save a penny, and go to the Stadium Theater, where for ten cents she'd see two movies, a dozen cartoons, a serial, previews of coming attractions, and the Movietone News. On certain days they'd stop the show and the lights would go on. The ushers would pass containers to collect money for the March of Dimes or for the Red Cross, and Candy would put her penny inside and proudly pass the carton along. Then the show would begin again. When the movie was over, she'd walk sadly into the glare of daylight and wonder what life would be like if she had parents like Andy Hardy.

56

PALESTINE
1943

Early in the year, news arrived that Yonatin was missing. His RAF plane had been shot down behind enemy lines. Yael was devastated. Joshua took a harder line.

"He's too tough," Joshua told his wife. "Whatever

happens, he'll survive." He demanded they go on as strong as ever. "There'll be no handwringing in this compound," the patriarch concluded. "I forbid it!"

At first Yael thought Joshua heartless, and Yonatin's wife didn't speak to him for weeks. But they gradually came around to his way of thinking. For Joshua, it was the only way to survive. Long ago, escaping from czarist Russia, he had realized he could change only what lay within his sphere of influence, as he called it. What lay outside, he would leave to God. Yet every day he'd climb the watchtower, wait for the sun to break the darkness, and pray that Yonatin would come walking through those olive groves.

In the fall, horrifying news leaked out. Joshua called a meeting of the compound to explain. "We've had reports from the underground. A Polish courier traveling inside Russia has seen Nazi atrocities. A place called Babi Yar, near Kiev. People were rounded up at night, ordered to dig their own graves, then shot. Thousands of bodies were found in a gulley: men, women, children. There were eyewitnesses." He bowed his head. "And there is news that the Warsaw ghetto is gone."

Everyone gasped. "What do you mean, 'gone'? There are four hundred thousand Jews in there."

"Of the four hundred thousand, only fifty-five thousand survived. They fought to the end, with a few pistols, some homemade bombs, and bare hands. But it's over," Joshua told them.

"We must pressure the British to ease restrictions on immigration," someone shouted, after a long silence. "Or we are lost."

"Pressure. Yes!" Joshua agreed. "But *never* say we're lost!"

That night, Yael pressed her body against Joshua's back. Gently, she stroked the grizzled old beard. White hair curled at the nape of his neck and gleamed in the dark. "What if it's all true?" she asked in a small voice. "What will we do?"

He rolled over and held her. A lifetime of loving, living, sharing lay between them. "Prepare yourself, Yael," he said. "Terrible times are coming. I feel it in my bones. But to those who wish us ill, who want to destroy us, I say this: *We are still here!* And when the time comes, we will do what is necessary."

CHICAGO, ILLINOIS
DECEMBER 1943

Sonia had been ill for months. Now she had chosen to die, not in a hospital, but in her own bed, in her own home, near her beloved birds and their melodies. She wanted her soft, familiar pillows, her faithful servants, her own doctors, her lawyers, the best care her money could buy. All her affairs had been settled, and it was just a matter of time. Her plans were simple. A burial near Charles, without fanfare. No service—who would come? All her life she'd been alone. In death, she'd be alone too.

She looked at the tubes dripping liquids into her veins. A sudden pain grabbed her insides. It felt like a corkscrew twisting, gathering bits of flesh as it bore deeper.

The nurse lifted her wrist and took her pulse. A spasm in Sonia's belly pushed her diaphragm into her stomach; she couldn't breathe. A shot of painkillers relieved nothing, just clouded her vision and brought a terrifying silence. As the room grew darker, she tried to remember her birds, their songs, the color and softness of their feathers. But the silence persisted. She hated it. Silence allowed terrible memories to invade her thoughts, to parade boldly their blackness. Mama. Odessa. Anya's ugly revelation. The knowledge that God was—a joke.

"Ooohhhh!"

She felt the doctor's hand on hers.

"Sonia? Does it still hurt?"

"Yes," she groaned. "You think you're a miracle worker?"

"No," he said softly. "Though I wish I were." He turned to the nurse and whispered something. In a few minutes Sonia felt warm, heard her birds, thought she felt Piper walking on her hand. She smiled as she said his name, and the pain slowly left her body as she gently floated away.

BROWNSVILLE

Tracey Louise was every mother's dream child. Rosy face, bright eyes, a sense of wonder at the world. Every morning Constance would play with her on the bed. They'd roll and hide beneath the covers, then Constance would take David's picture from the shelf and show it to the child. So began a daily ritual they had followed for nearly two years.

"Who's this?" Constance would say.

Tracey would point. "Dad-dee?"

"And what will you do when you see him?"

Tracey would take the photograph and kiss it.

"What else?" Constance would coax.

Tracey would think until her face beamed with a smile and she'd shout the answer. "Huggie!" she'd cry and clap her hands. So their day would begin.

Only this was different.

In one more week David would be home, and Constance worried. A photograph of Dad-dee was one thing. The reality of him, quite another.

That whole week Constance stewed. She hardly ate or slept, and Anya scolded. "Eat, already! You'll be a toothpick when he comes."

Constance couldn't admit that she was nervous, that David's homecoming seemed a double-edged sword. So she began to comfort herself with random thoughts. It would all be fine. Tracey was lovable. Tracey loved people. She had never been afraid of strangers.

Strangers.

The word frightened her. David wasn't a stranger. He was Tracey's father, damnit! Then she thought of Carmine and herself. And she thought of David and Morris. All strangers.

The big day arrived, and Constance was a bundle of nerves. When she wasn't in the toilet peeing, she was changing her clothes. The yellow dress and black coat with a chenille snood. The three-piece light brown gabardine and pumpkin-colored blouse. She finally wore a dark green cape suit with a white top. She fixed her lipstick, straightened the seams of her stockings. She dressed Tracey in pink and combed a fat finger curl in the middle of the child's head. Finally, she was ready to go.

"You'll come right home?" Anya asked.

"Of course, Ma."

One flight down, and Constance was back up again. She gave the baby to Anya and went to the bathroom. Finished, she was halfway down to the landing when Anya's voice boomed. "And don't keep the baby too warm. She'll get heated up and catch cold."

At the noisy train station, Constance stood on the platform. She lifted Tracey in her arms as a great silver locomotive whooshed by. "That scare you?" she asked.

The child giggled as white steam filled the air. Everywhere there were people, sounds, voices. Servicemen scurried by with duffel bags: sailors, soldiers, marines, rushing to the arms of loved ones. Here and there were bits of conversation, but her ears were tuned to the loudspeaker.

She walked to the platform's edge and peered down the tracks. David's train was ten minutes late. She tapped her foot on the pavement, wandered back and forth. Waiting. It was the story of their lives. Two years, she thought. Two whole years without him. Now, ten minutes seemed an eternity.

She hugged Tracey. "Now, don't forget," she said. "When Dad-dee comes, you give him a big kiss and hug, okay?"

"Okay," Tracey repeated.

Constance felt nervous down to her toes. She put Tracey down, fluffed the child's pink dress with its big petticoats, fixed the lace socks, spit on a hankie and brushed dust from the white leather shoes. Then she heard it. *"Track 22."* It was finally here.

She hoisted the child as the train rushed by. It blew her hair as window by window she searched for a glimpse of David's face. First car, second car, third, fourth, fifth—her head was spinning. Then she saw him. Tears of joy filled her eyes as the train screeched to a halt. Then he was on the steps. Her heart beat a mile a minute as he leaped from the train and pushed through the crowd. She felt her legs sway as they reached each other.

"David! David!"

"Constance."

As they locked themselves in each other's arms, the world went totally silent. For a long time, they were a tangle of tears, kisses, hugs, until Constance pulled away. She offered him Tracey and, though he was all thumbs, David took her. For the first time in his life, David Barber held his little daughter, touched the skin, the hair that belonged to Constance, the lips that were his, a perfect blend of their love in a single beautiful child. Then Constance began.

"Tracey? Who is this?"

The child, twisting a lock of her own hair, arched away to see his face more clearly. She looked from David to her mother, but it was not as Constance had prayed. So Constance coaxed.

"Don't you remember, Tracey? Don't you remember?"

David smiled. Constance watched Tracey struggle to make the leap from photograph to person, and it hurt to watch. And just as she was about to give up, Tracey shouted.

"Dad-dee!"

Constance almost fainted. David laughed out loud.

"Dad-dee!" Tracey said again. Then she puckered up like a guppy and kissed him.

At home, big signs greeted him. WELCOME HOME, DAVID. There were balloons, cake, wine, and tears. Anya put her hands around her son's neck and held him for a long time. His return brought back memories of Simon, and her joy mixed with sorrow. They were all over him—Shelly, Patricia, Sharon, Candy—hanging on his thighs, fighting for his lap, with Blackie pulling at his trousers. David, the hub of the wheel, was home. At dinner, they talked about everything. His life at war. Their lives at home. And Simon.

The following day David went alone to Simon's grave to pay his respects.

David scanned the sea of tombstones, loved ones resting beneath the earth. Grief mixed with rancor, then a terrible loneliness, as he removed his cap. Simon had meant so much to him. How does a person walk when a leg is severed? How does one see without eyes? He'd have to learn.

He put down the flowers he'd brought, pushed the staff of a small American flag into the earth, and looked at the grave. He swallowed, trying not to cry. His brother was inches from his grasp, and he couldn't touch a hair. Simon.

He studied the headstone. A small Star of David. Unpretentious. Like his brother. The grave was overgrown with neglect, and he cursed the caretakers as he pulled at the weeds. This is it, he thought. All that's left of a warmhearted guy who fixed puppies and kittens and who gave the shirt off his back. Suddenly, a sharp pain lodged between his eyes. Then tears gushed like water from an open spigot as he fell on his knees.

"God!" he cried. "Why the hell did you have to be so brave?" He heard the moan of a wounded animal and turned. He soon realized the sound was his own. Shaking, he looked up at the sky and began to shout.

"Why? Why'd You take him? He was the one who did things right." He wiped his nose with his sleeve. "There are killers in the streets. Guys who'd sell their mothers for a dime. I don't get it. *Who the hell are You?*"

His tears were like acid on raw skin as he stood up and placed a rock on the headstone in the age-old way of respect. Then he put on his cap, stood at attention, and saluted.

57

The war in Africa had finally wound down. In January, the Eighth Army entered Tripoli. In February, General Rommel attacked Port Said and stormed the Kasserine Pass to threaten Allied airfields. But when the German general met the Eighth Army, he was finally defeated. By the thirteenth of May the Desert War was over.

Joshua received the news of Sonia's death. He grieved deeply, feeling the separation of his family with each passing day. He sat *shivah* and a week later planted a tree in Sonia's name. When he discovered she had left her estate for him "to build a home for Jewish war refugees," he cried. Sonia had spent a lifetime denying her Judaism. Now, in death, she had affirmed it.

When the money arrived, refugees were still coming illegally. Though there were many dead and much to grieve about, it was the living who needed him more. *"Here I am!"* had come Abraham's response when God had summoned. *"Here I am!"* had come Isaac's answer when God had called. *"Here I am!"* had come Jacob's reply when God had beckoned. And Joshua's reply would be the same. He would roll up his sleeves and do the work. He would build a home for the homeless. And though others would cry out for a miracle, Joshua knew he was standing on one. *Eretz Yisroel*. The land of his fathers.

BROWNSVILLE

At Sonia's death, Anya searched her heart for the sadness that should have been there, for the sense of loss. She found it, but it wasn't for Sonia's passing. They had parted long ago. It was for what should have been but never was. Two sisters, torn by circumstances, by misunderstandings, alienated further by silly human pride, anger, a useless envy that should have been conquered. In the end, only Sharon truly grieved. But to acknowledge her sister's passing, Anya sat *shivah*, lit a memorial candle, and had someone say kaddish at the synagogue.

EUROPE
JUNE 1944

On June 4, Rome fell to the allies. June 6 brought the D day invasion of the Normandy beaches. One by one, European cities were captured or liberated: Cherbourg, Brussels, Bucharest, Antwerp, Athens. There was light at the end of the tunnel.

In February of the following year, President Roosevelt met with Stalin and Churchill at Yalta to work out peace plans. Then, on April 12, President Roosevelt died. The man who had led a nation through a terrible depression, the man who had guided America through a world war, was gone, and the country was plunged into deep mourning. But the new president, Harry S Truman, rolled up his sleeves and went on.

By mid-April, Russian and American soldiers met seventy-five miles south of Berlin, dancing and singing at the Elbe River. Then the Allies saw their first concentration camps. No one could believe their eyes. Buchenwald, with its skeletons piled high in uncovered graves, with its lampshades made from tattooed human skin. Dachau, Treblinka, Bergen-Belsen, with its odor of still cooking flesh. Auschwitz, where 3,000,000 had died, where several thousand still living creatures lay down in the dirt and wept, kissing their liberators' shoes. They didn't look like people anymore, just walking sticks with haunting, vacant eyes and tattooed numbers on their arms. Nearby, piles of scattered bones, the remains of an orgy by crazed beasts.

Soldiers found baskets of human hair waiting for export, thousands of pairs of eyeglasses, dentures, clothing bins stuffed with countless baby shoes. The horror stories were finally confirmed. But they were worse than anyone had imagined. In 1939, 9,000,000 Jews were living in Hitler's occupied territories. By the war's end, only 3,000,000 remained.

BERLIN
APRIL 29, 1945

The statistics were coming in as Hitler paced in his bunker beneath the Reichschancellery. He was incensed. His army of "warriors" had been reduced to twelve- and fourteen-year-olds. News of treason by his closest friends and advisers obsessed and angered him. Then the execution of Mussolini and Mussolini's mistress, told over and over on the wireless, frightened him: how they had been murdered, hung by their heels, dragged through the streets like garbage, urinated and spat upon. He did not want to be treated that way. He did not want to die humiliated, then be buried in a pauper's grave. He wanted a Viking funeral, with flames and ceremony. So he began making plans.

He poisoned his dog, Blondi. He dictated farewell messages and instructions. After putting his affairs in order, he summoned his new bride, Eva Braun, and said good-bye to his staff. The couple retired, and on April 30, at 3:30 P.M., the guards opened his bedroom door. Eva Braun had been poisoned, and Adolf Hitler had shot himself.

The soldiers wrapped the bodies in blankets, which, according to Hitler's instructions, were carried to the Reichschancellery garden, where they were doused with fuel and ignited. There the flames consumed him as he had consumed life.

"Give me ten years and you will not recognize the Fatherland," Adolf Hitler had told a cheering crowd in 1933. "The world will tremble at our youth. I want an untamed animal, cruel, with one mind and no pity. I will restore you to a warrior nation and make you hold your heads up high for a thousand years."

At his death, 3,500,000 Germans were dead. Over 1,000,000 were missing, and Germany was a shambles.

BROWNSVILLE
MAY 7, 1945

In America the headlines screamed: GERMANY SURRENDERS. They danced in the streets. And though the moments they shared were happy, there were those for whom the war would never end: Those who had lost loved ones. Those who had survived the death camps. Those who would spend their lives with horrible images burned behind their eyes. For them, for people like Anya, life would never be the same. And while the others danced and cheered, those like Anya silently wept.

In Japanese, the word *kamikaze* means "divine wind."
And as the war in Japan was being lost, more and more
kamikaze pilots were sacrificing themselves by crashing
their planes onto the decks of U.S. ships. President
Truman ordered B-29 bombers to pound Japanese factories and docks, hoping for an end to hostilities, but
the Japanese would not give unconditional surrender.
With more air raids, their cities fell like dominoes—
Tokyo, Nagoya, Kobe, Osaka—but still no surrender.
On July 26, Japan was warned of America's new atomic
bomb, but the Japanese government ignored the warning. President Truman felt his back against the wall.
Too many American servicemen would die in battle if
he didn't use it. On August 6, the first atomic bomb
fell on Hiroshima. When no surrender came, the great
atomic cloud mushroomed over Nagasaki. On August
26, the Pacific war was over.

Six men waited in the dark, waited for the sound that
would come like an owl's wings—swiftly and in silence.
Joshua had insisted on going; Avidan and Yael had
argued against it, but he wouldn't listen. No one could
look in the eyes of a frightened child and see what *he*
saw. Yael, Avidan, they had grown up differently. Only
he had run from pogroms at the age of thirteen. Only
he knew what it was like to be cut off from family, alone
and frightened. So when the others left, he joined them.

He checked his watch; the plane was late. He

wouldn't contemplate the awful possibilities, so he thought of the reasons he had come. The night before he had seen films taken by the Allies who had liberated the death camps of Europe, and he still couldn't believe his eyes. Six million Jews—most of Europe's Jewry—had been butchered like dogs, and no one had cried out. As he sat on the ground waiting, those screen images whirled in his brain, and he recalled the exact moment his pity had turned to violent anger. How dare they? How dare they destroy and degrade a whole people? Even in death a man deserves dignity. His past should be carried off gently on the wings of birds, not dragged through the earth's bowels and disposed of like garbage.

And what of the pitiful living? Naked ribs, pelvises, shoulder blades—stick figures that were once human. All of them marching, most of them Jews—devoid of armpits, groins, pubic hair and navels—like Sunday cartoons. And he knew, as surely as he waited for the plane, that while diplomats would smile and politely debate, he, Joshua Ben Abraham, would have to dip his hands in blood.

The signal finally came. Dozens of flashlight beams cut the darkness to create a human runway. Then it quietly descended, a great iron bird landing on a hidden, illegal airstrip near Yavreel. He waited for it to halt, then waited some more. If the British caught them, they'd be jailed and the children shipped to Cyprus to rot with the others in refugee camps. But tonight they were lucky. No moon, and the Haganah's Palmach squads were waiting in their trucks. The Jews of Palestine would no longer sit by and let the British white papers determine their fate. They would do what they could to help their people.

The all-clear sign was given. Six men, including

Joshua, ran to unload the passengers. One by one, terrified, orphaned children were carried aboard trucks without a single sound. Then they all pulled out.

"Your parents may be lost," Joshua told them when they reached the kibbutz. "But the family of Abraham, Isaac, and Jacob will never die." Then he thought, How ironic. What had been the reason for their pain would become the source of their healing.

As the sun rose, Joshua climbed the watchtower. With each rung, he knew it was time to step down and let the younger ones take charge. He was tired and knew Yael was right. He was an old war-horse who couldn't lay down his guns. He'd finish today, have breakfast and a nap, then go back to the children. He noticed a trail of dust and followed it to the outer limit of the compound. Friend or enemy, he wondered. He raised his field glasses and watched more closely. A jeep with two men. It stopped near the outer gate, which divided the dun-covered ground from the green oasis they had worked so hard to cultivate, then blasted its horn. Two years before they had been fooled this way by Arab attackers, and his muscles tightened. He alerted the inner compound and prepared for emergency.

He adjusted his field glasses as they approached. A British soldier and a steady blur. If only his glasses weren't so dirty, or his eyes so old. He kept focusing as the jeep drove past the orange trees, the fig orchards, and finally through the olive groves. That's when he saw him.

"Yael!" he screamed, skipping down the ladder two rungs at a time. "Our son's come home."

58

Anya spent time gazing at old photographs or braiding Candy's long black hair. She'd sing Russian and Yiddish lullabies to Tracey, and, though her grandchildren fought for her attention, for her stories of the old country and the time when there were no automobiles or airplanes or radios, they shared equally in her affection. But her health was deteriorating.

"Patricia, come thread the needle for me. And, Candy. Do that dance like Fred Astaire and Ginger Rogers in the movies."

While Anya hummed and mended clothes with her gnarled fingers, Candy dressed in old chiffon curtains, painted red lipstick on her mouth, and stuck a flower in her hair. She put on wobbly high heels, and, with the radio playing, opened the door of the closet and jumped out. Her bare, toothpick legs tapped out the rhythms on the linoleum, while her eyes flashed and her skinny arms swayed or perched on her bony hips. Anya loved to watch her leap from chair to floor.

"She's going to be something one day," Anya would tell the others. "Mark my words."

When Candy finished, the family applauded, and Anya hugged the child. Then she went back to her sewing.

"Ouch!" she cried. She sucked her finger where the needle had pricked her while Constance ran for cotton and iodine.

"Turn the light on, Shelly," Anya said.

Everyone looked at one another. The light was already on.

After she went to sleep that night, Constance and David changed all the bulbs to a higher wattage.

The women planned Thanksgiving dinner: turkey, stuffing, sweet potatoes in brown sugar, and fresh peas. For dessert, stewed fruit with cherries. David went into the living room to read the newspaper. He sat in the tattered easy chair, put his feet on the peeling green hassock, and scanned the pages. Then an article caught his eye. He couldn't believe what he was seeing and read it again.

America had issued a carefully worded statement in favor of the principle of partition for Palestine. It was the first time the country had done that, and it pleased him. He felt sorry for all those homeless Jewish refugees from the war still rotting in refugee camps in Cyprus. No country in the world wanted them. What were they supposed to do? Die? The statement surprised him, because the United States usually voted with her ally England, and England's views on Palestine were well-known. He thought it was glorious. America was finding her own voice.

Then again, it wouldn't matter, he thought with despair. Real partition had little chance. They needed a two-thirds vote in the United Nations, and it wasn't there. The Moslem and Arab countries would vote as a bloc. The Catholic countries would support the Vatican, and that meant against. The pope wanted Jerusalem to be an international city, but the Jews refused. Without Jerusalem, their land would have no heart. But with this new statement from America, there were possibilities.

The following night he was shocked again. More

statements in the news. This time from Russia. He went to the kitchen and told everyone.

"It could come true," he said. "Israel."

Anya smiled. "From your mouth to God's ears."

On Thanksgiving Day, Constance opened her eyes at 6:00 A.M. Tracey had scrambled from bed and was prodding her mother to make breakfast. Constance rose, and as the two tiptoed to the kitchen Constance put a finger to her lips, reminding Tracey to be silent. But they found Anya silently choking, clutching the sheets to her throat. Constance's scream wakened everyone, and, while she held her mother-in-law, David called an ambulance. Fifteen minutes later, Anya was at Kings County Hospital. She'd had another stroke.

Anya had a slight fever, and Constance put cool compresses on her brow. Her eyes were closed, the gnarled fingers rested at her sides, and a small mound of belly rose and fell with each breath. After two days of testing, there were bruises along her arms where needles had intruded. It made Constance angry. How many times had they stuck her? How many times had they hurt her without knowing how precious she was? Constance watched Anya's lids suddenly flick open at the noise of a nearby radio. With her mouth half open, she'd try to focus, then wrinkle her brow as if she was in pain. "An automatic reflex," the doctor told Constance. "Don't worry."

With every passing hour, Constance felt her heart break. She couldn't look at Anya without crying. Couldn't look at the woman who had taught her how to face life and not be afraid. This grand lady, once so vital and vibrant, lay meek and humble, eyes crusted, lips and cheeks sunken, teeth yellow with age. Her long white hair lay uncovered, lost against the white of the pillowcase. Long ago, Constance's father had told her blood was thicker than water. He was wrong, and Anya was the proof.

The radio played gently as Anya thought of home. She was a young girl, running in the fields of Kashkoi, gathering flowers. She saw her parents, saw Saul, Sasha, and her beloved Simon. Sometimes, she heard the United Nations on the radio calling for the partition vote on the state of Israel and saw her brother Joshua, tall, strong and handsome. Drifting in and out of consciousness, she tried rolling over, but her body wouldn't move. She tried reaching for some water, but her arm flailed.

"Her glasses. She wants her glasses."

"No. She wants some water."

"Over here, Ma. Can you see me?"

Anya saw them all: David, Sharon, Shelly, Constance, Candy, Patricia. Then she saw Simon. He was standing behind David, and he was waving to her. *Simon, oh, Simon.*

"Why does she keep calling him?" Sharon asked.

"Hallucinations, the medicine," David said.

Anya heard him. Hallucinations, her eye. Look! Sarah, Saul, Shmuel, Simon. Even Sonia. Couldn't they see? *Hello, Mama and Papa. Look at them. Look at my children, my grandchildren. What a moment. Together at last.*

As she closed her eyes, she heard the radio again.

"Belgium?" *"Yes."*

"Canada?" *"Yes."*

"Czechoslovakia?" *"Yes."*

"China?" *"Abstain."*

Moving in and out of awareness, Anya wanted to tell David about his real father. She beckoned him to her bedside with her eyes, and he came to her, bent his ear to her lips as the radio intoned.

"Egypt?" *"Against."*
"Greece?" *"Against."*
"India?" *"Against."*
"Iran?" *"Against."*
"Iraq?" *"Against."*
"Mexico?" *"Abstain."*

David left Anya's bedside. Constance followed him, weeping quietly.

"What'd she say to you?" Constance asked.

David lifted the *chai* from his neck and shook his head. "I'm not sure. She kept touching the chain and saying it was my father's. Then she kept saying some name, like Sasha."

In her dream, Anya heard Sasha's voice so clearly. She looked up and saw his beautiful eyes above her.

Oh, Sasha. Why didn't you come for me?
Sh, Anyushka. I'm here now.
But I look a mess.
No, my darling. You look beautiful.

"Norway?" *"Yes."*
"Union of South Africa?" *"Yes."*
"United Kingdom?" *"Abstain."*
"United States?" *"Yes."*

Anya smiled. She could hear the commotion on the radio as country after country cast its vote and the resolution passed. *Oh, Joshua. Dearest brother. At last! We are home. Israel.*

Suddenly, she felt exhausted. Then Sarah's voice called to her from across a pond. *Come, darling. Come.*

Constance returned to the bed where Anya rested. There was a peaceful look on her face as her lips moved in prayer. Then Anya smiled, and her eyes drifted closed.

* * *

They stood at the gravesite dressed in black, in skull-caps, in armbands, in silence, in pain and loss, bearing that moment when life and death become absolute truth. In the weeping void, as the sun's rays beat on their heads, the family held hands and prayed together. Each was aware that what had once held them together was now gone. The linchpin had been removed forever. They were an open wound. Constance, with her heart in her mouth. Sharon, feeling the loss of her mother as she'd never felt her presence. The children not truly understanding but aware in their own way. And David, peering at the graves of those who had preceded his mother. Now Anya would join Saul, Shmuel, Simon, three generations sharing death as they had never shared life. Constance, strong yet fragile, rocked back and forth, comforting herself to the rabbi's song. She felt the pain deeply. But she had a secret.

As she stood to leave, she saw her mother, her father, her brother, Tony, walking toward her with open arms. And she thought instantly of Anya's words, "When God closes one door, He opens another." She walked quickly toward them with her arms and heart open to receive. Then Carmine vigorously shook David's hand and lifted his granddaughter into his arms.

At home, they washed their hands at the door. Immediately, they felt the loneliness. With Anya's passing they would scatter to the winds, and they all knew it. Pictures without frames. Chairs without a table. Pieces. Pieces that would never fit again.

Constance lit the memorial candle, covered the mirrors, and turned the calendars to the walls. She walked into Anya's bedroom, took the family Bible, and kissed it. She opened the pages to the back, where her fingers caressed the names, beginning with the grandparents and parents of Sarah and Shmuel, passing Sonia and

Saul and Simon, to the place where she wrote, as tears burned her eyes:

Anya Barber. Beloved mother, grandmother.
November 29, 1947

Then she joined David and the family to sit *shivah*, thinking of names for the new life within her.

Those who do not remember the past
are condemned to relive it.

GEORGE SANTAYANA